THE MYSTERIOUS DEATH OF MISS AUSTEN

Also by Lindsay Ashford and available from Honno

The Megan Rhys Series

FROZEN

STRANGE BLOOD

DEATH STUDIES

THE KILLER INSIDE

THE MYSTERIOUS
DEATH OF
MISS AUSTEN

by
Lindsay Ashford

HONNO MODERN FICTION

First published by Honno
'Ailsa Craig', Heol y Cawl, Dinas Powys,
Wales, CF64 4AH

1 2 3 4 5 6 7 8 9 10

ISBN 978-1-906784-26-3

Published with the financial support of the Welsh Books Council.
Cover design: Sue Race, ShedMedia
Printed in Wales by Gomer

To my children,

Isabella, Ruth, Deri and Ciaran,

and to Steve

'There are secrets in all families, you know…'

Emma, Jane Austen

6 July 1843

I have sent him her hair. When I took it from its hiding place and held it to my face I caught the faintest trace of her; a ghost scent of lavender and sun-warmed skin. It carried me back to the horse-drawn hut with its wheels in the sea where I saw her without cap or bonnet for the first time. She shook out her curls and twisted round. *My buttons*, she said, *will you help me?* The hut shuddered with the waves as I fumbled. She would have fallen if I hadn't held her. I breathed her in, my face buried in it; *her hair.*

To the ancients it was a potent, magical thing. The Bible calls it the source of a man's strength and a woman's allure. How strange that it should have this new power; this ability to bear witness after death. Science tells us it is dead matter, stripped of life long before the body it adorns.

I suppose he has had to destroy it to reveal its secret; he can have no idea what it cost me to part with it. All that remains are the few strands the jeweller took for the ring upon my finger: a tiny braid, wound into the shape of a tree. When I touch the glass that holds it I remember how it used to spill over the pillow in that great sailboat of a bed. If hair can hold secrets this ring must surely hold mine.

Now that the deed is done I fear what I have unleashed. This is what he wrote to me yesterday:

Thank you for entrusting the letter from the late Miss J.A. to my keeping, along with the lock of her hair bequeathed to you. You are quite correct in your belief that medical science now enables the examination of such as has not perished of a corpse with regard to the possibility of foul play.

Having applied the test recently devised by Mister James Marsh, I have been able to subject the aforementioned sample to analysis at this hospital. The result obtained is both unequivocal and disturbing: the lady, at the time of her demise, had quantities of arsenic in her person more than fifteen times that observed in the body's natural state.

You have told me that the persons with whom she dwelt, namely her sister, her mother, a family friend and two servants, all survived her by a decade or more. I must conclude, therefore, that the source of the poison was not any thing common to the household, such as corruption of the water supply. Nor could any remedy the lady received – if indeed arsenic was administered – account for the great quantity present in her hair. It may be conjectured, then, that Miss J. A. was intentionally poisoned.

This being the case, I need hardly tell you that bringing the perpetrator of such calumny to justice, after a lapse of some six-and-twenty years, would be next to impossible. If, however, you are willing to explain the exact nature of your suspicions to me, I will gladly offer what assistance I can.

I remain your humble servant, Doctor Zechariah Sillar

It is a source of some relief to me to know that the disquiet I have felt these many years is not without foundation, though I burn with rage to see it written there as scientific fact. To him her death is nothing more than a curiosity; his interest is

2

piqued and he offers his assistance. I have not even hinted that the guilt lies with someone still living.

Where would I begin to explain it all? Elizabeth, surely, is the first link in the chain. But how would he see the connection unless he acquainted himself with the family and the secrets at its heart? How could he understand my misgivings without knowing her as I knew her? To weigh it up he would have to see it all.

But it was not meant for other eyes. I am well aware of the danger of opening this Pandora's Box. People have called me fanciful. Indeed, I have questioned my own judgment. But the possibility that I might be right makes me more inclined to take this man into my confidence. He has the twin virtues of learning and discretion, and knows nothing of the family. If it *is* to be seen, there is no one I know who is more suitable than him. The question remains, is it the *right* thing to do?

3 January 1827

Jane's nephew wrote to me yesterday. He asks me to contribute to a memoir he wishes to compile. I will have to tell him that I cannot – and furnish him with some plausible excuse.

His letter has unsettled me. Quite apart from the scandal a truthful account would create, the way the request was framed infuriates me. I have thrown the thing away now but the words he used still parrot away inside my head: 'Although my aunt's life was completely uneventful, I feel that those who admire her books will be interested in any little details of her tastes, her hobbies, etcetera, that you might care to pass on.'

Completely uneventful. How can anybody's life be described as *completely uneventful?* He wishes, I think, to enfeeble her; to present her to the world as a docile creature whose teeth and claws have been pulled. The respectable Miss Austen; the quiet, pious Miss Austen; the spinster aunt whose only pleasures apart from her writing were needlework and the pianoforte. Meek, ladylike and bloodless. How she would have hated such an epitaph.

I suppose he believes that I would relish the task of serving her up to the public like a plate of sweetmeats. I hope he lives long enough to understand that one does not have to be young or married to be racked by love and guilt and envy. How affronted he would be if I revealed exactly how I felt about his aunt.

His letter has had quite a different result from that which he intended. I have decided to make my own record of all that passed between us; a memoir that will never be seen by him or any other member of the family. I will write it for myself, to keep her close, and as a way of releasing what eats away at me. When I am dead Rebecca will find it amongst my papers and she can decide whether to read it or toss it on the fire. My feelings, then, will no longer matter.

Chapter One

1805

When I first met Jane her life, like mine, was an indecipherable work in progress. I had no notion, then, of what she was to become. But in the space of a few weeks she rubbed away the words other hands had scrawled beneath my name and inked me in; made me bitter, passionate, elated, frightened...all the things that make a person jump off the page.

Godmersham was where I lived in those days, although I never would have called it home, for I belonged neither above stairs nor below. I was one of that strange tribe of half-breeds, a governess. Educated but impoverished. Well-born but bereft of family. To the servants my speech and manners made me a spy who was not to be trusted. To Edward and Elizabeth Austen I was just another household expense. My only true companions were books. Like friends and relatives, they fell into two categories: there were the ones I'd hidden in my bed when the bailiffs came – old familiar volumes that smelled of our house in Maiden Lane – and there were the ones I was permitted to borrow from the Austens' library. This held many favourites, expensively bound in calf or green morocco, with gilt edging and endpapers of crimson silk. Their pages brought back the voices of all those I had lost.

Jane arrived at Godmersham on a wet and windy day in the middle of June. I remember the first sight of her, still clad in mourning for her father, her eyes bright with tears as she greeted her brother. The hall was bustling with servants, eager to organise the newcomers, and I could tell from the way she held her head that she found it all rather strange and discomfiting. I saw, too, the way Elizabeth looked her up and down like a housewife buying a goose. *Feathers rather too sparse and shabby-looking*, I caught her thinking; *not really fit for our table.*

Elizabeth Austen had given me a similar look when I first came to Kent. She was heavily pregnant and surveyed me from her armchair, peering over the rim of a teacup that rested on her belly. Her face reminded me of a doll I had when I was a child, a doll with blue glass eyes and real hair whose cold, stiff hands used to poke my flesh when I hugged her.

'Well, Sharp,' she said, 'I hope that you will live up to your name. Fanny is a good girl but she's easily distracted. She needs to be watched not indulged. The boys have no need of you: they are being schooled at Winchester. You may be required to teach Lizzy and Marianne when they are older – *if* you last.'

By the summer of 1805 I had lasted a year and a half, during which time Elizabeth had given birth to a boy, fallen pregnant again and been brought to bed with her ninth child, a girl this time. I wondered if I would still be at Godmersham when this little creature was old enough to take lessons, and how many more babies would arrive in the meantime.

The day Jane came I was standing at the top of the stairs, high above the gilded columns and marble friezes, holding the older children at bay until the formalities were over. But Fanny, who was twelve and the leader of the pack, broke free and hurled herself at her aunt, knocking Jane's black straw bonnet backwards. I remember fragments of laughter drifting up to me with the smell of wet grass and horses that had followed her in. She wrapped her arms around the child and hugged her like a saviour. I felt a stab of jealousy, for Fanny was more than just a pupil. She was the reason for my existence.

Fanny had become the closest thing to a daughter I could ever have imagined. I used to think about it often in those days, what it would be like to have a child of my own. Just one. Not a great brood, like Elizabeth's, for I saw how it was for her, a clever woman turned idle by her own body. No wonder she was irritable with those who served her; no wonder she sometimes looked at me with spiteful eyes. Perhaps she wished that she had been born plain, like me. Perhaps she wished she had not married a devil-dodger's son who loved ladies as long as they knew their place.

'Who taught you to think, Miss Sharp?' Those were the first words her husband spoke to me when I entered his house. I had been there a week without our paths crossing, which not unusual in a house of such grand proportions. I was coming into the hall by the door opposite the frieze of Artemis and the huntsmen; he was standing on the second tread of the staircase, which made him almost my height but not quite.

'My father, sir,' I replied, smiling at the courtesy he showed in addressing me. I thought he called me 'Miss' because he had known of me before I became his employee. But I was wrong about that. The prefix was used only to convey his displeasure.

'Indeed? I cannot believe that your father was a follower of that Wollstonecraft woman, so I can only assume *you* are the disciple. I will not have you filling my daughter's head with such errant nonsense!' He was not looking at me as he said this. His eyes were on the window, through which Elizabeth could be seen walking with a gentleman whose identity was not yet known to me.

'I am sorry if anything Fanny has repeated has caused offence to you,' I began. He made no reply, still looking away from me. His face looked very red against the white wig. A little of the powder had fallen from it, riming one eyebrow like frost on grass. I *was* very afraid of offending him. His silence made me panic. What I said next was ill-judged; it came from my heart, not my head: 'Am I wrong in trying to give her thinking powers, sir? I'm sure you would not wish her go out into the world as a tulip in a garden, to make a fine show but be good for nothing.'

'Better a tulip than a trollop!' He muttered it under his breath but loud enough for me to hear. I thought I was about to be sent packing.

He was halfway to the door when he turned and said: 'All that I wish for Fanny is that she should have a sound head and a warm heart. Shakespeare, Fénelon and Fordyce's Sermons: that is all she needs in the way of improving literature. They were good enough for my wife and they are good enough for my daughter.'

I was very careful after that, but I wanted more for Fanny than her father had in mind. While she was debarred from all the possibilities open to her brothers, I was determined she should be every bit as well-educated. If marriage and motherhood were the only parts she was to be allowed to play she must develop abilities that would exact respect. Ignorant as I was of the married state, I believed that although Edward loved his wife, he did not respect her. How could he, when she was reduced to a role that differed little from that of his cattle and pigs? I vowed that Fanny would grow up to be a very different sort of woman.

The fault in all of this was my own pride. I saw myself as Fanny's champion and closest ally. I feared any challenger and that made me resentful of Jane when she first arrived at Godmersham. Fanny was impossible to teach in the days that followed her arrival. All her talk was of Aunt Jane. Clearly she worshipped this woman and I wanted to know why. I found myself watching Jane at every available opportunity.

I remember one afternoon, that first week of her stay, when I got a glimpse of what the child found so beguiling. I had taken Fanny and the older boys – who were home for the holidays – to spend their allotted hour in the company of their mother, who was entertaining Jane and the other Austen ladies in the salon. They made a strange group, Elizabeth so elegant and expensively dressed; Jane and Cassandra in the garb of a pair of old maids, even though they were no older than she; and their mother, Mrs Austen, who looked perfectly neat until she opened her mouth, from which several of her front teeth were missing.

Cassandra suggested they should play riddles. I was at the other end of the salon, trying to amuse the children with a game of spillikins. Forced inside early that day by the weather, they sat fidgeting, smelling of dogs and damp wool. When they got wind of what the grown-ups were doing they all wanted to join in.

Elizabeth raised a languid, jewelled hand to ruffle the head of George, her second boy, who had seized a pencil and paper. 'This is much too hard for little heads! Go back to your game!' With grumpy faces they did as they were bid, but listened all the same as the verses were read aloud.

Elizabeth was quite put out when George called the answer to her riddle while everyone else was still writing it down. Mrs Austen's was more obscure but Jane managed to guess it after a few minutes' thought. When it came to her turn she spoke the lines in a clear, strong voice:

'Three letters form me while I've breath,
 Though, newborn, I had four;
 But if you e'er put me to death,
 You must give me three more.'

After ten minutes of frowns and scribbling, no one could furnish an answer. Five minutes more and the children were tugging at her sleeves, begging her to reveal it. She beckoned Fanny to her and whispered in her ear. 'Now,' she said to the others, 'go back over there and you will have a charade.'

A few seconds of Fanny crawling about on all fours crying *Baa!* brought them close to the answer. 'No, not *sheep*, you simpletons!' the child cried, 'It's ewe! E-w-e! A *ewe* is born a *lamb* and if you kill her she becomes *mutton*!' Jumping to her feet, she said: 'What a brain you have, Aunt Jane! I wish I could be like you!'

From where I sat I had a good view of Elizabeth's face. Her eyes narrowed and she drew in her lips. Jealousy, I guessed. In that respect Elizabeth and I were very much alike. She did not like being outshone by her husband's sister, while I wanted Fanny to admire *my* brain, not her aunt's.

There was something else about Jane that drew my attention in those first few days. There was something very familiar in her appearance. I felt I had seen her somewhere before, even though I knew this was most unlikely, for I had never visited Bath, where she lived. It came to me all of a sudden in the salon as I watched her reading out her riddle. She was a female version of Henry Austen, the man I had seen walking in the garden with Elizabeth a few days after my arrival in Kent.

Henry always caused a flurry of excitement when he came to stay, since half the servants seemed to be in love with him. I overheard the scullery maid telling one of the scrubs that he was the handsomest of the Austen tribe. This I could not vouch for, as he was the only one of my employer's brothers I had so far encountered. But I could see that he drew people, as the earth draws the moon.

He was only three years younger than Edward but he had the look of a man still in his twenties. Perhaps it was because he never sat still. He flitted between London and Godmersham like a butterfly, arriving at any hour of the day or night, staying for a week here, a fortnight there. It came as some surprise when Fanny told me that Uncle Henry had a wife.

He dealt with me in a very different manner from Edward and Elizabeth, beaming at me every time he poked his head into the schoolroom. I tried not to return his smiles, for he distracted Fanny from her lessons and she was never the easiest pupil to engage in study. But he was hard to resist.

'What are we reading today, Miss Sharp?' he would say, slipping behind me and leaning over my shoulder to peer at the text. I would feel the stout wooden chair back shudder slightly as his hands grasped it; a mingled scent of something – like an orange spiked with cloves – would drift from his clothes to my nose. He would read a passage aloud, his breath ruffling the lace on my cap. And then, swooping across the room to plant a kiss on Fanny's head, he would disappear.

I liked Henry. Apart from anything else, he was the only adult in that great house who ever asked me how I did. What really won me over, though, was his affection for the children. Sometimes, in school holidays, when I had charge of all the older ones, he would ask if he could take them off to play. 'It's no trouble at all, Miss Sharp,' he would say, holding my gaze with big, round eyes. 'You would be doing me a great service, believe me. I get so tired of London life and all the false ways one encounters there. I find the company of children so refreshing, for they always say exactly what they mean.'

I had never seen a man so eager for the company of children. So intrigued was I that I asked Fanny if her uncle had any himself. 'Oh, no,' she replied. 'Mama says Aunt Eliza is far too old for that.'

Now the curiosity Henry had aroused in me transferred itself to the willowy creature who might have been his twin. She shared not just his tall, slender figure but dark-lashed, intelligent eyes of the same hazel hue. Both had olive skin and curly chestnut hair that framed their faces. They looked so very different from Edward, who clung to the fading fashion for powdered wigs and had the ruddy complexion of a man who was happiest outdoors with a gun across his arm. I soon noticed, though, that while Jane looked like one brother, she had the air of neither. There was no trace of Henry's ebullience about her and none of Edward's easy confidence. From the snippets of family background Fanny came out with, I formed the impression that, like me, Jane found it difficult to be herself in a place where she was neither fish nor fowl.

'Grandpapa Austen was a parson with grey whiskers that tickled,' Fanny told me one day in an attempt to forestall a test on Latin verbs. 'But he's dead now, so Aunt Jane and Aunt Cass live with Grandmama to keep her company. Mama says they must because they don't have husbands.'

I wanted to ask why they didn't have husbands. I guessed that Jane was in her late twenties, like me, and her sister a little older. Their spinsters' caps suggested that they had given up looking. And yet I would see Jane each morning, creeping away from the house, as if for an assignation. I could never sleep beyond sunrise and as I sat reading at my window I would catch sight of her heading for the little Greek temple that sat on a hill high above the river that snaked through the parkland. She would be there for an hour or two each morning, rising long before her mother and sister were up and about. I never saw anyone else take that path at that time, but there were ways through the woods for those familiar with the

12

estate. As one who missed the solace of family, it never occurred to me that she might be going there to escape that grand house and all those within it.

Chapter Two

At the end of the first week of her holiday I was sent to seek Jane out. She had promised to take Fanny on a gypsy picnic but had apparently forgotten all about it. As I searched the downstairs rooms I felt a little knot of anger tighten in my stomach. Fanny was a loving, trusting child and this was her favourite aunt. How could Jane display such casual disregard for her feelings? Did she not understand how disappointed Fanny would be?

I found her all alone in the library with a pen in her hand. Writing letters, I supposed. At the sound of my coming she seemed to jump, her ink-stained fingers flying to the paper. Seeing my face she bit her lip and glanced at the clock on the mantelpiece.

'Goodness! Is it that time already? I'm so sorry – Fanny must be wondering where on earth I've got to.' If a horse had trampled on her best hat she couldn't have looked more aggrieved. *You were quite wrong about her, weren't you?* I thought. *She loves her niece just as much as Henry does.* She shot out of her chair, her elbow catching a book that had lain open on the table beside her. It slid across the polished wood and fell to the floor with a thud at my feet. As I bent to pick it up I recognised the title on the spine. It was a volume of one of Frances Burney's novels.

'Do…do you like *Camilla*?' I think I sounded as flustered as she looked.

'Have you read it?' The shoulders lifted, the chin tilted. I saw a spark of interest in those hazel eyes.

I nodded. 'It was the first book I took from the library.'

'And have you read *Evelina*?'

'Yes,' I said. 'I have all three volumes, though they're falling apart from having been read so many times.' *Evelina* was one of the books I had concealed when everything else was seized. It was my comforter in the days after my father's death and no matter what else I happened to be reading at Godmersham, it was always on my bedside table. Like me, its heroine yearned for the family she had lost. I didn't tell Jane this, of course, but her face spoke her approval. She asked what other books I liked and we became so lost in our chatter that by the time we reached the schoolroom I had quite forgotten the reason for taking her there. Then Jane asked me if I would accompany her on the picnic. I hesitated a moment before replying, afraid of being relegated to second fiddle.

'Oh, please come!' Fanny grabbed my arm and squeezed it. The worm of jealousy went back into its hole.

The weather had turned hot and fine. Fanny's cousin Anna had come to join the family party at Godmersham and the girls had planned this outing together. We took the path that ran past the ice house and alongside the orchard, where apples hung small and green from the branches that overhung the wall. We crossed the low stone bridge over the river and skirted the Greek temple, where Fanny and Anna darted off to chase each other round the columns and shout inside the cool, dark walls to hear the echo.

'I come here in the mornings sometimes.' Jane followed the

girls with her eyes. 'It's hard to concentrate, sometimes, isn't it, in a house of that size? Always something going on; people coming in and out.'

I nodded, wondering if *Camilla* had been her companion on these early morning pilgrimages. I never imagined that someone might come to a place like this to write.

'It's strange, hearing their voices,' she went on. 'Usually I have only blackbirds and thrushes for company.'

A squeal of laughter from Fanny drowned out Jane's next few words. The girls were at that strange age when they behaved like children one minute and young women the next. Anna was just a few months younger than her cousin. She was the daughter of the eldest Austen brother, James, but had come without the rest of her family. She was a pretty little thing and had won me over the day she arrived by asking if she could borrow one of my best-loved children's books, *The Governess*. After a few minutes of running about the echoes of the girls' voices faded and died. All was silent within the temple.

'I suppose they're hiding.' Jane rolled her eyes. 'I'd better go and smoke them out.' As she disappeared into the gloom I wandered around the side of the temple where a thicket of brambles snagged the carved stones like clawed fingers.

'Do you really hate her?' It was Fanny's voice. They were hiding behind one of the columns.

'I wish she was dead!' Anna hissed back.

'Well, she might die,' Fanny whispered. 'It might kill her.'

'Oh, there you are!' Jane emerged from the shadows, her hands behind her back. 'What are you plotting?'

'Nothing, Aunt Jane!' Fanny stepped out into the sunlight, Anna behind her.

'Really?' She searched their faces. 'Do you know what the gypsies do to bad children?' They shook their heads. She whipped out two clenched fists. 'They put toads down their necks!' The girls screamed as she chased them, all three landing in a helpless heap at the bottom of the steps. They couldn't see me watching them, for the brambles were between us. Jane had not caught the sinister nature of the girls' conversation; of that I was certain. I wondered who it was that Anna hated so much.

When they had picked themselves up we headed for a wilderness on the other side of the hill. Baskets of bread and cheese and elderflower water had been packed up for the girls, who were happy to be left to set up their gypsy camp while Jane and I sat a little way off in the cool green dome of a weeping willow.

'Anna looks happier than I've seen her for a long time,' Jane said, pulling her gown out from under her knees and spreading it over the blanket. 'I think Godmersham is doing her good. But tell me, Miss Sharp, do *you* like it here?'

She must have seen the confusion her question caused me. How could I answer honestly? She was my employer's sister. I couldn't tell her how I felt, caught between the servants and the family like a sea creature stranded by the tide. I had food and a bed and the company of children and yes, of course, I was grateful: how could I forget what it felt like to stare destitution in the face? But there was a creeping sense of emptiness every night when I shut my door. I ached for something more; something I couldn't even name. To allow such a thought felt disloyal and peevish. To speak it aloud was out of the question.

'I'm sorry; it was impertinent of me to ask.' She took a bowl of strawberries from her basket and offered it to me. 'It's just that Fanny hasn't been very lucky with her governesses: the last one was dismissed after a month because she had not a word of French, and the one before that ran away with the head horseman.'

'Well, I don't think that I shall fail her for either of those reasons,' I smiled.

'She likes you very well, so I hope you'll stay.' She bit into a strawberry and scrutinised the heart-shaped half left in her grasp as if she was inspecting it for grubs. 'What are you reading at the moment?' she asked, without looking up.

'Charlotte Lennox,' I replied. '*The Female Quixote.*'

She smiled at the strawberry. 'That is one of my favourites. What do you think of Arabella?'

I hesitated for a moment. I had already formed an opinion of the heroine but I was afraid it might offend. 'I find her fascinating; complex, I suppose. Some would regard her as a silly girl who is overly influenced by French romances. But I see her as someone in search of an identity; a young woman with an artistic nature trying to express herself in a world governed by men.'

She swallowed the morsel of fruit, licking her thumb where the juice had run down it. 'What was the book you read last? Before Lennox, I mean.'

I felt my colour rising and I looked away.

'Was it Madame de Staël? Or Fielding, perhaps?'

I stared at the ground. If I told her she might think me immodest and unworthy of her company.

'I do hope that you have read *Tom Jones*,' she said, 'for I think it is absolutely necessary to read books in which the world is promiscuously described in order to appreciate what is truly better. If I were Edward, I would not wish to entrust Fanny to a governess whose knowledge of humanity was restricted to Fordyce's Sermons.'

I glanced up at arched brows and lips pressed tight with mirth. *Oh*, I thought, *he lectures his sisters as he has lectured me.* I shot her a look of happy gratitude. We were co-conspirators.

She leaned forward and pulled something out from beneath the cloth that had covered the strawberries. It was a handwritten copy of Hannah Cowley's play, *Which is the Man?* She asked me if I had ever seen it performed. I had, but some years earlier, when my parents were still living. She asked me how I had liked it. 'Oh,' I said, shaking my head, 'I liked it so well that I tried to write something of the same kind. I gave it up pretty soon, of course, as it was too terrible to merit any sort of ending.'

She looked at me then with an expression so strange I pulled back a little. It was an intense face, but smiling, like a child who has just worked out the answer to a most perplexing puzzle. 'May I read it?' she asked.

'Read it?' I laughed. 'The only thing it was fit for was lighting the fire.'

'Well, in that case, Miss Sharp,' she said, wagging her finger, 'you must help me to write another.'

In the days that followed I discovered that Jane had a mischievous spirit from which no one – be they pauper, parson or prince – was spared. She had a stock of characters in her head whose words and manners she had memorised so perfectly that she could trot them out at will. When pressed, she would admit to having met these people at a ball or some other social gathering. 'Oh, the Miss Ds?' she would nod, tapping the side of her nose, 'Yes, I was introduced to them at the Assembly Rooms in Bath.' A pause would be followed by a wink. 'I was as civil to them as their bad breath would allow.' And then: 'You wish to know about Mrs. B? Well, she appeared at a dance in November exactly as she had done the previous September, with the same broad face, diamond bandeau, white shoes, pink husband and fat neck...'

Working with her on the script it was impossible not to envy the way she conjured humour from ordinary, everyday things. It made me cringe anew at the thought of my own abandoned manuscript. I had lied about burning it. It lay in the bottom of my trunk like a broken necklace. I could not bring myself to throw it away but neither could I face trying

19

to repair it. It was different, writing with Jane: somehow lines came to me when she was there. What started out as envy turned into admiration and inspiration. I knew that my pen was guided by her brain but somehow it ceased to matter. I reveled in the pure pleasure of creating something others would admire.

Before we had even finished the writing of *Pride Punished or Innocence Rewarded*, Jane had Fanny, Anna, her mother and Cassandra learning the lines. Elizabeth declined the invitation to take part. I was not told the reason why. I wondered if she disapproved of my involvement, of this blurring of the boundaries between staff and family.

If that was her opinion, other members of the family did not appear to share it. One day, when Mrs Austen was reading a page of the script that I had given her, she looked me up and down and said: 'Well, Miss Sharp, I knew from the minute I saw you that you had a good brain, and I declare that I was not mistaken.' When I begged to know what had led her to this swift assessment of my mental powers, she replied: 'Why, your nose, of course! It is fine and large, and as I always say, "the bigger the nose the quicker the brain!"' I was not quite sure how to take this strange compliment, but I took comfort from the observation that she herself had a very prominent, rather aristocratic nose. 'Now Elizabeth, you see, has no nose at all,' she went on, 'but of course, she has many other fine qualities. She is a prodigious breeder, which is vastly pleasing for my son.' I began to see where Jane's keen eye for the character and the foibles of others came from.

'Really, Mama!' Cassandra, who was standing nearby, had overheard this last remark. 'You make her sound no better than a prize sow, when you know quite well that she is as quick and clever as anyone!'

'Who is a prize sow?' Fanny came running up to her aunt, demanding to know what they were talking about.

'Nobody, dear,' Cassandra replied, with a fierce look at her mother. 'We were just talking about one of the characters in the play, weren't we, Mama?' Unlike her mother and younger sister, Cassandra had learnt to suppress her forthright views when in company.

Sometime during those rehearsals Jane and I ceased to be guest and governess and started to become friends. She insisted that I call her by her Christian name. At the time, I had no idea why she had decided to befriend me. She and Cassandra were so close that I wondered why she took the trouble to cultivate anybody else. Looking back, I think she must have felt the need of someone outside the family to confide in, although, at first, she could not admit that need even to herself. She held her quick wit before her like a shield but I thought I sensed a sadness about her that went beyond the sorrow for her father. During the long, hot weeks of that summer she began to give me glimpses of what it was that disturbed her.

Chapter Three

It was the play that started it. One morning we were watching the girls rehearsing a scene. Looking at Anna's angelic little face it was hard to believe the words that had come out of her mouth a couple of weeks earlier in the Greek temple. How could a child apparently so sweet-natured hate anyone so much as to wish them dead? So intent was I on watching Anna that I dropped a page of the script. As I bent to retrieve it I saw that Jane's eyes were not on the actors but on the ceiling, locked in an unblinking gaze, as if her soul had taken leave of her body.

'Are you all right?' I whispered.

For a moment I thought she didn't recognise me. 'Sorry!' she gave me a puzzled smile. 'I was somewhere else.'

'Was it somewhere nice?' I asked when the girls went off for their lunch.

She gave me a blank look. 'Oh, in the rehearsal, you mean?' She closed her eyes and gave a little shake of her head. 'I was back at Steventon; at the rectory. Fanny reminds me of myself, I suppose. I was exactly her age when we put on a play in the barn one Christmas. It was the one I showed you: *Which*

Is The Man? My brother Henry was in it. And my cousin Eliza.' Jane gave an almost imperceptible nod to the chandelier above our heads. 'We hadn't met her before and she fascinated us. She had the most exquisite gowns, all made in Paris, and she used to swear at us in French. Henry was only fifteen but he—' Her eyes snapped back into focus and she bit her lip. 'Listen to me, droning on about the past! You must promise to pinch me if I drift off again.'

'Are you sure?' I turned up my palms and spread my fingers. 'Have you seen the size of my hands?'

She grasped my wrists with a peal of laughter. 'Oh, I didn't mean to find you so agreeable! It would have saved me the trouble of liking you!'

The door opened then and Mister Priddle, the butler, stepped into the room. 'Madam asks if you are coming to luncheon, Miss Jane.' His eyebrow lifted a fraction of an inch, just enough to convey the annoyance Elizabeth had no doubt expressed at Jane's absence. Turning to me he said: 'Your tray is in the morning room, Miss Sharp.'

The morning room was where I took all of my meals. I ate alone, for it was not deemed suitable for me to eat below stairs. I would not have chosen to be singled out in this way; it underlined the sense of isolation I felt. Sometimes Fanny would stray in, but I felt bound to discourage this because it got her into trouble with the children's nursemaid.

'Thank you, Priddle.' Jane stepped between me and the door. 'Could you give my sister-in-law my apologies? There's something I have to attend to. Perhaps you could bring a little extra luncheon to the morning room?'

I didn't see the butler's reaction to this, for she was standing in front of him. I could imagine it well enough, though. He was not accustomed to having the rigid order of things re-arranged. No doubt he would report Jane's instructions verbatim to his mistress. I wondered how that would go down.

'Elizabeth won't miss me,' Jane said as we sat down to eat. 'She likes my sister but she barely tolerates me. Cass is so good-hearted that no one could possibly dislike her. But I don't know what I've done to cause offence, other than reminding her of her husband's humble origins.'

I had pieced together enough of my employer's background to know what she meant. Fanny's stories about Grandpapa Austen and fragments of gossip I had picked up from the servants suggested that, by nothing other than sheer good luck, Edward had been adopted by childless relatives seeking a boy they could groom as heir to Godmersham.

Jane helped herself to a slice of the cold meat that the butler had left on the tray. 'Elizabeth likes my brother Henry very well.' She paused, a forkful of ham halfway between the plate and her lips. 'He is rich, of course, which makes all the difference.'

There was something about the way she said it, the way she emphasised the word 'all'; it brought back banished images; things I told myself I should not be thinking about. Intrigued, I prompted her: 'Fanny sometimes speaks of an Aunt Eliza. Is she the cousin you were telling me about? The one with the Parisian gowns?'

She stared at her fork as if she had suddenly discovered it was dirty. 'What does Fanny say about her?'

'Oh, nothing of any consequence.' Clearly this was dangerous ground. Her eyes moved from the fork to my face. She wouldn't be fobbed off with such an answer. 'She only mentioned something about her aunt being too old to have children.'

'She *is* older than Henry,' Jane's features seemed to relax a little then. 'She was married with a baby son when she came to us that Christmas.' She cut a piece of cheese, held it up to her nose and made a face. Reaching for a plum instead, she said: 'Her husband was a French count. He went to the

24

guillotine, poor man.' She gave a little upward roll of her eyes as she extricated the plum stone.

'I should think that Henry made a fine stepfather for her son,' I said. 'He's always so warm-hearted to the children.'

She looked directly into my eyes, slightly startled. I wondered if she knew how often Henry came to Godmersham; if she even knew that I had met him. 'Yes, he did...' she tailed off, her gaze moving away and over my shoulder. She looked as if she was remembering something that pained her to the point of tears.

'I think I heard the girls calling,' I said, afraid that I might have upset her and threatened this fragile beginning of friendship, 'Shall we go and find them?'

She nodded quickly. As we rose from the table she took my arm.

I was surprised that there were no repercussions from Jane's decision to take her lunch with me. Elizabeth came to watch the rehearsal in the afternoon but made no mention of it. I began to wonder if she might actually be pleased that Jane and I had become friends; it would, after all, save her the effort of toleration if Jane's assessment was correct.

Edward was not at home that day but he arrived in time to see the play performed. He came back quite unexpectedly, in the middle of the night, from a trip to a property he owned in Hampshire. Fanny told me about it when I caught her yawning halfway through the morning.

'It's all Papa's fault,' she said. 'He came home before dawn and turned me out of bed!'

'Turned you out of bed?' I frowned. 'Why ever would he do that?'

'I was in Mama's bed,' she sighed. 'She's been having trouble sleeping and she asked me to keep her company. She didn't know Papa would be coming back so soon.'

I said nothing in response, of course, but I thought how selfish Edward was to do such a thing – not just to Fanny but to his wife also. Was he so unable to control himself? Could he not have found a bed elsewhere in the house and waited just a few more hours?

Watching Edward that afternoon, as he sat beside Elizabeth, smiling and applauding his daughter's performance, it was hard to imagine the scene Fanny had described. He was being so affable; so attentive. Then I reminded myself of the side I had seen during the first week of my employment, when he had challenged me about the ideas Fanny should be exposed to. He had not shouted or even raised his voice but his manner had carried all the menace of a dog about to bite. Clearly he was a man who expected to have his own way in everything.

To my surprise Jane laughed when Fanny repeated the story to her. I was not sure whether it was out of spite for Elizabeth or a vicarious sense of triumph for Edward. Can a sister feel that way about her brother's conjugal behaviour? As an only child, I can never know. But I thought it a strange reaction.

A few days after the performance of the play Fanny came into the schoolroom with a tiny lace-trimmed cap in her hand. 'It's for Anna's new baby sister,' she said. 'Her name is Caroline and she was born yesterday morning at five-and-twenty to six. Mama wants me to embroider a 'C' and an 'A' on the front so it looks as if we made it especially. I don't want to do it but she says I must.'

When I asked her why not, she said: 'Because Anna must take it back with her and I don't want her to go.'

This I could understand. The girls had become very thick in the weeks since Anna's arrival and there would be no one of Fanny's own age for her to play with when her cousin left.

'She hates going home,' Fanny went on. 'She doesn't like

Aunt Mary. And I don't blame her. I feel sorry for her, not having a real mother.'

No one had mentioned the fact that Anna had a stepmother. I considered this intelligence in the light of the conversation I had overheard at the temple. I wondered if this was the person the child hated so much; it was often the way. *It might kill her*, Fanny had whispered in response to the death wish uttered by her cousin. *Yes*, I thought, *a baby might kill its mother*.

Elizabeth, I well knew, prepared herself for this eventuality every time she was confined. A few days before the birth of her youngest son, Charles, she had given me a letter, all sealed up and addressed to Fanny. 'I want you to keep this safe, Sharp', she'd said. 'I would give it to my husband but it wouldn't be fair to expect him to deliver it in the event of…' the unspoken words hung in the space between us until she glanced down at her swollen belly and I apprehended just what it was she was asking me to do. It was a death letter; a goodbye. My mother told me she had written something similar to my father the week before I was born. When I asked what had happened to it she said she threw it on the fire when I was a month old. I did not throw Elizabeth's letter on the fire. It was tucked away in the far corner of a drawer inside an odd glove whose partner was lost somewhere in the park and by the time I remembered it was there she was well into her next pregnancy. I wondered if Anna's mother had written a letter like that to her, and how old a child should be before being shown such a thing.

On the day that Anna left us Jane and I took Fanny fishing in the river. But in the absence of her cousin, the child was in a tricky mood. She tried our patience by throwing little handfuls of earth into the water when she thought we weren't looking.

'Fanny!' Jane cried, 'You are turning the river into a mud bath! It is trout, not hippopotamus that we are after!'

27

Fanny dropped her head, sullen as a horse in a heat wave. 'This is the wrong place for fish,' she muttered. 'Uncle Henry knows the best spots. He took Mama and me the day after her birthday and we caught three whoppers.'

'Oh, Uncle Henry was here for Mama's birthday, was he?' There was the slightest tremor of her eyelashes as she looked at me for confirmation.

'Yes, he was,' I replied. I remembered it clearly, for it had been a strange, unsettling sort of day. I had been left watching Fanny and the rods while Henry went with Elizabeth to inspect the walled garden. As they scrambled up the riverbank she must have dropped the key to the garden gate. I saw it glinting in the grass a few minutes afterwards and ran to catch them up. But they were nowhere to be seen. Then I saw a flash of colour; the bright yellow of Henry's coat disappearing into the little bathing house on the next bend along the river.

Of course, there could have been any number of reasons for him going in there; a call of nature perhaps, or a sudden request from Elizabeth for a parasol to shield her from the sun. But it wasn't the first time that this brother and sister-in-law had aroused my curiosity. I remember standing there, nonplussed, on the top of the bank. Fanny was calling out to me, telling me to come quick; that she had hooked a trout. My head twisted this way and that, like the hapless fish on the line, from the bathing house to the shouting child, from one river bend to the other, my mind a whirl of muddied images. I told myself that I was mistaken; that the sun had played tricks with my eyes, which have never been strong. Fanny landed her fish herself and before we knew it her uncle and mama were beside us, laughing as they slipped and slid the last few yards down the bank.

'The key, ma'am,' I said, when Fanny had dragged Henry across to the keep net to see her fish. 'You must have dropped it.'

I watched her face. The limpid blue eyes were untroubled. The tendrils of blonde hair quivered not an inch. 'Oh, thank you, Sharp.' She almost managed a smile as she took it. 'I wondered where it had gone! We had to ask old Baines to let us in, didn't we, Henry?'

I don't know if he heard what she said. His head was next to Fanny's, peering at the thrashing silver creature in the net. He simply laughed and raised his hand in a wave, as if nothing anyone could say or do could spoil the magic of the moment.

That night, as I lay in bed, I turned it over and over in my mind. I had overheard enough conversations between my father and his customers to know that stories of men desiring a brother's wife thrilled the drawing rooms of London. Could Henry really be guilty of such a thing? Was that why he came to Godmersham so often? Was his eager interest in the children just a ploy?

I thought about how he had been spending his days during this visit. When he was not with the children he was often shooting or fishing with Edward. And yes, he did spend time with Elizabeth; probably more time with her than with anybody else. Unlike Edward, she did not have an estate to run. She had all the time in the world to entertain her brother-in-law. Too much time, perhaps.

There had been one incident, a couple of months after I had taken up my post as governess, when he and Elizabeth had taken an afternoon walk. He had returned with a broken finger, saying that a buck had attacked them as they strolled towards Chilham Castle. Elizabeth was unhurt and praised Henry for his gallantry in fending off the beast. I thought at the time that it was unusual for deer to be aggressive in February; that autumn was the time for rutting.

Rutting. The word lodged itself in my brain. Were they really in Chilham Park that day? Was he really attacked as he said? Or had he come by the injury some other way? The weather had been wild and windy. Had they been in the bathing house? Had the door blown shut on his hand when they tried to leave?

Having taken this direction, my thoughts took me to an even darker place. Elizabeth had been delivered of her last-born child, Louisa, in the second week of November. I counted on my fingers. The birth had come exactly nine months after the accident in Chilham Park.

The next morning I told myself that I had no proof of anything. All I could be sure of seeing was a flash of yellow cloth at the door of the bathing house. It could have been a servant's waistcoat or a maid's petticoat; it could even have been a duster, shaken out as the place was made ready for the summer. I told myself that I must put away my suspicions as so much fancy and foolishness. For a moment I saw myself as Elizabeth no doubt saw me: a pitiable spinster with so little in her world that she must live her life through books and invent illicit encounters.

Henry left Godmersham later that same day and as May turned into June the heat of my imagination began to die down. By the time of Jane's arrival I had succeeded in putting the whole thing to the back of my mind. But something in her eyes now, as she stood there on the riverbank, looking from me to Fanny and back again, reignited that uneasy feeling. It was the same look I had seen the day she took her luncheon with me in the morning room.

Perhaps some sixth sense told her what I was thinking. She said nothing more on the subject of Henry, but I thought her rather more quiet and subdued as the afternoon wore on. There were no more hippopotamus jokes; no delicious barbs about the people she had encountered in the salons and ballrooms of Bath.

Fanny seemed to catch on to her aunt's change of mood, snapping out of her sourness into a stream of chatter. I wondered how much she was picking up from the adults around her; whether she had deliberately dropped Uncle Henry into the conversation to test her aunt's reaction. She kept a diary, which she sometimes showed me and, while the entries were mostly mundane, they revealed a keen eye for observation. A year ago, four months after the Chilham Park episode, she had shown me a whole week's worth of her jottings. Henry had been at Godmersham again and she had recorded every activity during his stay, including trips he made to Canterbury with her mother and father, places they had gone to dine, even a game of hide and seek that Henry, Elizabeth and Fanny had apparently played by themselves.

The day after his departure she had made a note of the fact that Mama had received a letter from Uncle Henry. I wondered at the time why she should record that occurrence, when her mother was sure to have received several other letters that day, as she would on most days. Now I asked myself if it could have been significant; had Elizabeth broken the news to Henry, during his stay, that she was expecting his child? Had he written to her the moment he got back to London, telling her of his delight at this news?

As Fanny chattered to Jane about dragonflies and water boatmen and all manner of innocent delights, I puzzled over Henry. He was stepfather to Eliza's child by her first marriage, but that child must be a grown man by now. According to Fanny, Eliza was too old to give Henry a child of his own. And yet he loved children: despite my misgivings, I found it hard to believe that the fondness he showed was just an act. Was it too wild an idea that he might try to father one by his own sister-in-law? A child who would provoke no whiff of scandal as long as the true identity of the father was never guessed at? A child whom Henry could see whenever he chose and could cherish as a favourite niece or nephew?

I shook my head, unwilling to own such murky thoughts.

Jane saw me and, thinking I was cold, bade Fanny pack up the rods and head for home. The girl ran on ahead of us. Weighed down with the fishing baskets, we were a good quarter of an hour after her in entering the house. As we set down the baskets she came skipping down the stairs.

'Aunt Jane, do you know what?' she said, all breathless, 'Uncle Henry is coming for the Canterbury races!'

Chapter Four

Early next morning the air was tainted with the smell of mothballs. The servants were in a whirl of activity, preparing and packing several outfits for each member of the family party. They were to stay two nights in Canterbury and apart from the races there would be balls, a tour of the cathedral and dinner at the homes of two local families of Edward and Elizabeth's acquaintance. I heard Sayce, Elizabeth's maid, reading out the list, marking each event with a tick when the requisite items of clothing were ready to stow in the carriages.

'I love dancing, but I'm in despair!' Jane led me along the landing to her room, past maids carrying armfuls of petticoats, shawls and pelisses. 'I don't know what on earth I'm going to wear!' She had put off her mourning attire a fortnight since and was now free to dress in whatever she chose. I wondered why she was so agitated. 'Look,' she said, pointing to the bed. 'It's my only good gown. But Elizabeth says there are going to be *two* balls.' She flopped down beside the pale green satin dress with its trim of white silk rosebuds. 'What am I going to do?' she groaned, 'I can't possibly wear the same dress twice!'

'Do you have a white gown?' I asked, 'Something you could trim up with a bit of lace?'

'I have one of white cambric, but no lace. Elizabeth would disown me if I stood next to her in it.'

I could just imagine it. Elizabeth had a roomful of the most exquisite gowns to choose from. I had seen Sayce take out the oyster-coloured silk, its bodice embroidered with seed pearls, and the fine India muslin with the blush satin petticoat. She would, no doubt, pack at least two more ball gowns with matching reticules, slippers, caps and fans in case the mistress changed her mind. How could Jane, the unmarried daughter of a country parson's widow, be expected to live up to that?

I wondered that Edward had not left his mother and sisters better provided for since the death of their father. He had inherited not one but two country estates and he had the command of dozens of servants, stables full of horses and the finest wine cellar in Kent. Why could he not spend a few guineas on decent dresses for Jane and Cassandra? What was the point of inviting them to stay if they could not hold their heads up in the company he kept?

Between us, Jane and I concocted a solution. I had some lace and an amber brooch left to me by my mother. She was quick with a needle and thread and by the time the maids came for her things the white dress was transformed.

'Are you sure you don't mind?' she asked, as I held out the brooch. 'It feels wrong, borrowing something so dear to you.'

'I know that you'll look after it,' I replied. 'And besides, I go to so many balls I'm quite fagged with them!' I gave a little mock shudder and she snorted with laughter.

'I wish you were coming,' she said. 'I'm bound to meet the most ghastly people.'

I wished it too. For all that I made I light of it, I would have loved to go to a ball. I had a vivid memory of the last one I had attended. It was at Ramsgate, with my parents. I had three partners, all naval cadets, none of them tall enough to look me in the eye. Afterwards, my mother and I laughed about it till we cried. It was only two years distant but it felt like two hundred.

As she put the brooch in her valise there was a knock at the door. It was a footman, wanting to know if her trunk was ready for stowing in one of the carriages. As she went across to speak to him I noticed something sticking out from under the counterpane, which had become disarranged from us sitting on the bed. It was a sheet of paper, handwritten. *The Watsons – a novel in three volumes.* That much I couldn't help reading, for it was written in a larger hand than the rest. I turned away, guilty at seeing something so private. She was writing a book. And like me, she wanted to conceal her creation, afraid, perhaps, as I was, of failing to breathe life into the people she saw in her head.

Too late. She caught the movement as she turned back from the door. Searching my face she knew at once that I had seen what it was.

'You're writing a novel.' I said it with a smile of enquiry, a clumsy attempt to mask my embarrassment. An awkward silence followed. She was bustling about with her things, not looking at me. I didn't know what to say next. Everything that sprang to mind sounded fatuous. This was a delicate subject. I knew that for myself.

'I was *trying* to write one,' she said at last. 'It's hopeless. Too depressing. I can't go on with it.'

'You shouldn't give up.'

'You have not read it.'

'But I've watched you write a play. If I thought I possessed one ounce of your talent I'd lock myself away and write day and night, even if I starved half to death in the process.'

She looked at me for a long moment. Then she said: 'Did you mean to become a governess?'

35

Now it was my turn to look away. How could I furnish an answer without appearing careless of Fanny and ungrateful to Edward? Choosing my words carefully, I said: 'It was not what my parents planned for me. My father was a dealer in rare books. He had a shop in London, just off the Strand. As I grew up I enjoyed helping in the business. I would have carried it on, I suppose, if that were possible.'

'But it was not?'

'He died and—' I shook my head like a dog shedding water. It must have made me look quite heartless. I couldn't bear to describe it, to relive those awful days. And if her brother had not told her how I came to be in his employment I was glad of it. I didn't want Jane to know of my disgrace. I was afraid that she would shun me if she did.

We were interrupted by another knock at the door: a sharp rap this time. It was Elizabeth, come to tell Jane to hurry up.

'Everyone else is downstairs.' She sounded cross. When Jane moved away from the door Elizabeth caught sight of me. 'What are *you* doing here?' Apparently I had outlived my usefulness where Jane was concerned now that they were all off to Canterbury.

'She was helping me to pack.' Jane said quickly.

Elizabeth arched her eyebrows. It was a look that said: *You? Needing help? Why, when you don't own more than half a dozen outfits?*

She stood in the doorway watching Jane gather up the last few items. I nodded a goodbye and made a hasty exit. Within half an hour the carriages had departed. A strange sort of silence settled on the house, as if the heart had gone out of it.

Lessons that morning were not a success. Fanny was cross about being left behind. She longed to be old enough for balls and parties. My own head was full of Jane and the manuscript she had dismissed so vehemently. *If only she would allow me to read it.* The thought persisted as I tried to engage Fanny in

The Tempest. Like mine, her mind was wandering. She was more interested in staring out of the window.

'Look,' she cried suddenly, 'It's Uncle Henry!'

He was in the courtyard, handing his horse to one of the grooms and she ran outside to greet him. He lifted her up and twirled her round so that she staggered like a drunkard when he set her back on her feet. Then, laughing with delight, she took his hand and dragged him up the steps to the house. I wondered why he had called at Godmersham instead of going direct to Canterbury. It seemed an odd thing to do when the rest of the family had departed.

He seemed quite unperturbed at missing them all and sat down to a hearty lunch. Fanny begged to be allowed to eat with him and she made herself quite bilious on curd pudding. She was sent off to bed for the rest of the day and when she had gone, complaining loudly that she was not really ill, Henry headed for the nursery.

I was sorting out books in the schoolroom on the floor above and through the open window his voice floated up to me. I heard him trying to charm Susannah Sackree, the children's nursemaid, into letting him take Fanny's younger brothers for a dip in the river.

'I could watch the baby for you, Caky, while you get them ready,' he said. Caky was the pet name by which Fanny called the nursemaid, having been unable to say Sackree when she was small. I thought how cunning Henry was, targeting that soft spot, for Susannah was not given to indulgence. She and I had found a way of rubbing along together by trading insults; she would throw some evil remark at me and I would try to parry it with something equally offensive, which she seemed to enjoy.

I heard her mutter a few words to Henry that I couldn't quite make out. I thought he had no chance of coaxing her, whatever charm he used. She guarded that baby as if it was her own. But to my surprise the next thing I heard was the sound of footsteps on the gravel beneath the window and a low, sweet humming, like a drowsy bee. I peered over the ledge at the strangest sight: Henry was holding baby Louisa in his arms. Rocking back and forth on his heel, he serenaded her as she gazed up at him with bright, unblinking eyes. I watched as her lids began to droop. The rhythm of his rocking never flagged and the lullaby soon worked its magic. Within a very few minutes, she was fast asleep in his arms.

I don't know how long I stood there, staring. Never before had I seen a man do such a thing. Surely, I thought to myself, no gentleman would entertain such a pastime unless the child was his own. Suddenly he turned back towards the house and I ducked away from the window, afraid that he would catch me spying on him.

The next thing I heard was the whooping of the boys as they raced towards the river, their uncle urging them on like a pack of hounds. They were gone all afternoon but by five o'clock Henry was back on his horse in a fresh set of clothes, ready to ride to Canterbury for the ball. He looked as handsome now as I had ever seen him, in a blue dress coat with velvet collar atop a waistcoat of coquelicot and a matching cravat. The clop of hooves on cobbles signalled his departure. As he passed the house he turned in the saddle and gave a little wave of his hat. This was directed at Fanny, who was standing with me at her window in her nightgown, furious at missing all the fun in the river. 'He looks like Robin Redbreast in that waistcoat,' she hissed. 'Men should only wear red if they are soldiers, shouldn't they?'

I guessed that she was thinking of her papa, who, as landowner, was also captain of the East Kent Volunteers and put on uniform whenever he inspected the troops. There was more going on inside that little head than mere disappointment at being sent to bed: I sensed that there was a battle raging, a fight between affection for her uncle and fierce loyalty to her father. She had seen Henry through a woman's eyes; as her mama would see him when he joined the family party at the ball. And if I was not mistaken, she was afraid for her papa.

The next day Fanny seemed to be over her bilious attack and we were in the schoolroom as usual, reading Mr Cowper's poems, when the clatter of wheels made us both look up.

'Who can that be?' She jumped to her feet and ran to the window before I could say a word. 'Papa!' She leaned out of the window so far I dashed across the room to catch her round the waist. 'Why are you come back?' she called to him. 'What's wrong with Aunt Cassy?' I saw Jane's sister alight from the carriage, leaning heavily on her brother as she did so. She had to be helped up the steps with Edward on one side and a footman on the other.

Fanny begged to be excused but I made her wait for half an hour until the home-comers could be attended to. She came back to the schoolroom, eager with the news. 'A man stepped on Aunt Cassy's foot at the ball and they both fell over and she landed on him and serve him right because he nearly broke it!' she gasped. 'Papa says she has to sit and rest and we mustn't disturb her.'

It seemed that Edward, who was not the greatest lover of dancing, had offered to take his injured sister back to Godmersham. He had not wanted to spoil everyone else's arrangements and so he bade Jane keep his wife company for the rest of the day's engagements, leaving Henry to escort them back from the ball that evening. I nodded silently as Fanny imparted this information. I was thinking about what I had observed the previous afternoon. What would Edward have made of his baby daughter being rocked to sleep in his brother's arms? Would Henry have done such a thing if Edward had been at home? I checked myself before my thoughts could run on any further. Surely Edward would not have left his brother in charge of his wife if there was any substance to my suspicions?

That evening Edward asked me if I would go and sit with Cassandra. She was all alone in the salon, for he was suffering an attack of gout and was bound for bed. I was a little afraid of her, thinking that she might resent my growing friendship with her sister. But she could not have been more welcoming. As the light began to fade and the candles were lit, she told me that she had been glad to come away from Canterbury because public dancing no longer held any attraction for her. I thought it impolite to inquire the reason, but she supplied it herself.

'I feel like a fraud,' she said, 'for if any man comes near me, I know it must come to nought.' I said nothing in reply, merely tilting my head a little and waiting for her to explain. 'I was engaged once.' She looked past me, her eyes fixing on the curtained window. 'His name was Tom Fowle. He was a chaplain on a ship bound for the West Indies and we were to marry on his return.'

I could keep silent no longer, though I dared not raise my voice above a whisper. 'What happened?'

'He contracted yellow fever but I knew nothing of it,' she replied. 'I had bought my wedding clothes and went to meet him at Portsmouth. Instead I got the news that he was dead.'

I murmured some inadequate condolence and a heavy silence settled upon us. The servants had all retired and the only sound to be heard was the calling of night creatures; of owls and foxes venturing forth to feast on the bounty of the darkening fields. Cassandra's face had a soft, youthful beauty, yet she made herself look older, with her spinster's cap and plain dimity gowns. She has given up, I thought. She cares nothing for herself now and her sister has taken the place of any child she might have had. I wondered what would become of Cassandra if Jane should ever leave her.

I fell asleep that night thinking about *The Watsons*. I wondered what sort of family Jane had chosen to write about and why she found what she had created so disheartening. I started thinking of the vain, silly people she so loved to mimic and the figures in my head transformed themselves into dancers at the Canterbury ball. Jane came floating by in her white dress, frowning at rows of men with fat, pink faces.

I don't know what time it was when Fanny woke me. She came knocking on my door, her teeth chattering, saying she felt sick again and had been unable to rouse Caky. I said that I would fetch something to warm her up and bade her climb into my bed while she waited.

I remember seeing a glimmer of light in the sky through the small window in the passageway outside my room, so I suppose it must have been getting towards dawn. The flame of my candle guttered and I paused to shield it with my hand. As I did so I heard the creak of the main staircase and a whispered 'Goodnight!' It was Jane's voice. I heard the sound of her footsteps on the landing then the faint thud of her bedroom door closing. I longed to go and knock; to hear all about the goings-on in Canterbury. But there was Fanny to think of. I tiptoed past her room and on towards the staircase.

As I put out my hand for the banister I saw the shape of a man on the landing below. Henry. His face was in silhouette, the aquiline nose unmistakably his. His head was turned to one side and he had his back to me. He had taken off his coat and his waistcoat shone blood red in the light from a lamp set down on the floor. As I watched, his head moved slowly from side to side, like a horse nuzzling a fence post. There was something gliding round his waist, pale and slender as a birch bough. It was a long, gloved arm. I saw the fingers separate, ripple and tense, pressing the small of his back, pulling him closer. Then he took a step back and I heard him say something, very low. It sounded like: 'Will you come?'

A second later he had disappeared into the shadows, where a door led away to the east wing and half a dozen empty guest rooms beyond. I didn't hear the door open or close, because I was suddenly aware of footsteps behind me. I turned to see Fanny coming along the landing and Jane stepping from the doorway of her bedroom. I darted towards the child and held her fast. 'Now, Fanny,' I said, trying to control my voice, 'What are you doing out of bed? I told you to wait in the warm!'

Jane put her hand on my shoulder and said: 'Are you quite well? You look as if you had seen a ghost.'

I shook my head and tried to smile, telling her that I was just a little chilled; that it was Fanny who needed attention. Jane gathered Fanny up and put her in her own bed, saying she was not in the least tired and would be happy to attend to her. As she bid me goodnight she gave me the same intense, curious look I had received that first afternoon beneath the willow. It was as if she could see her own fears reflected in my eyes.

I lay sleepless in the early morning light, the red of Henry's waistcoat burning the back of my eyelids every time I tried to close them. I felt a familiar aching of the head and a slight nausea. It usually came after reading for too long or sewing in poor light. Now I wondered if my eyes had failed me in perceiving that white, gloved hand. Was it actually a glove or just a pale arm? Could it have been a servant that I had seen caressing Henry? I wanted to believe that but I could not. I was convinced that the owner of the hand was none other than Elizabeth.

I told myself that even if it was Elizabeth, I had no real proof of any wrongdoing. Perhaps she had been overly affectionate in bidding him goodnight; perhaps he had been trying to tempt her into something more. But I had not heard her say yes and neither had I heard them open the door to the east wing. Had she gone with him to one of those empty bedrooms? Or had they heard our voices and crouched in the shadows, shamed by the thought of being discovered? Was Elizabeth lying awake now, beside her slumbering husband, fearful of what the morning would bring?

A faint knocking on my door made me stiffen. Was that Fanny again? Or had Elizabeth come to seek me out; to silence me?

'Are you awake?' It was Jane's voice. I jumped out of bed and opened the door. 'I'm sorry,' she said, 'Were you asleep?'

'Not yet,' I replied. 'What's wrong? Is it Fanny? Has she been sick?'

'No. She's sleeping now. But I was worried about you.' Her eyes searched mine. 'You looked so... anxious.' The word was a perfect description of *her* countenance. I hesitated for a moment, afraid of opening my mouth. Then she said: 'Is something troubling you?'

I didn't want to tell her a lie, but neither could I tell her the truth. I had no brother or sister but I could well imagine what it would do to her, seeing what I had seen. Bad enough, I thought, to discover that your brother is being cuckolded by his wife; how much worse, though, if her lover is another brother? It was the kind of secret that would tear any family apart.

'There's nothing you want to tell me?' There was something about the way she said it, the way she emphasised the words with a slow horizontal movement of her head. It suggested to me that she had seen something herself: not the thing that I had witnessed, of course, for she was inside her chamber then, but something very like it. If I was right in my guess she must be in agony, an agony intensified by the fear of my knowing it too. Perhaps, like me, she doubted the evidence of her own eyes; would not *allow* it to be true. Seeing the concern in her face, I formed the belief that she was really begging me *not* to tell her.

'I was just a little frightened, that's all,' I said softly. 'I heard voices on the stairs – I had quite forgotten that you were all coming back from the ball.'

'Voices?'

'Just the mistress bidding goodnight to your brother,' I said. I held her gaze, determined to make her believe me. I felt myself trembling. Whether it was with cold or with emotion I don't know. In an instant she took her own shawl and wrapped it round my shoulders.

'I'm so sorry,' she whispered. 'It wasn't fair of me to come knocking on your door.' I felt the warmth of her hand on my arm as she rubbed it through the shawl. 'I must get back to Fanny. I shouldn't have left her.' And then she was gone, leaving an invisible trail of lavender mixed with the faint, musky sweetness of a night's dancing.

Chapter Five

W hen I woke the next morning after a few fitful hours of sleep I had a pain behind my eyes. When I tried to get out of bed the room began to spin and candle flames appeared and disappeared, as if some fiendish spirit lit them, pinched them out and hexed them back to life.

Fanny, who was quite recovered from her own illness, came to find me when I failed to appear in the schoolroom. Her reaction to seeing me so indisposed was to appoint herself my nurse, solemnly rearranging my bedclothes and laying a damp flannel on my brow, which set me smiling in spite of the pain. When she could find no other means of increasing my comfort she went off in search of her aunt.

On hearing of what ailed me Jane did a strange, lovely thing. She went out into the meadows that bordered the river, spending the whole of the morning collecting wild flowers, which she brought to my room. Spreading them out on the counterpane she told me of a remedy she had got from a woman called Martha Lloyd, the sister of Anna's stepmother, who had made a careful study of the use of herbs for medicine.

'I copied this from her,' she said, pulling a folded sheet of paper from her pocket. 'My eyes sometimes give me pain and I have learned how to treat them myself.' She read the remedy aloud: '"Take of eye-bright tops two handfuls, of celandine, vervain, betony, dill, clary, pimpernel and rosemary flowers, of each a handful; infuse twenty-four hours in two quarts of white wine: then draw it off in a glass still: drop the water with a feather into the eye often."'

'Two *quarts* of white wine!'

She nodded. 'Don't worry – my brother will never miss it. He has enough wine in his cellars to float a battleship.'

'It seems a strange thing, though,' I said, 'to put wine in the eyes. Does it really work?'

'Oh yes,' she smiled, turning the paper over. 'It's Martha's best remedy for sore eyes. She has this other one, which you can try if you want to: "Take the white of hen's dung, dry it very well and beat it to a powder. Take as much of it as will sit on a sixpence and blow it into the eyes when the party goes to bed."'

She looked at me so straight-faced that I burst out laughing, my breath gusting over the flowers and scattering some on the floor. 'Hen's dung!' I grimaced as she bent to gather up the pale blue heads of eye-bright and the fragrant stems of rosemary. 'Please don't tell me you *tried* it!'

'Well, I did collect some,' she replied solemnly. 'But my mother mistook it for pepper and put it in an oyster pie.'

I almost believed her, so quick was she at mixing fact and fiction and so convincing her mask. She was such a different person from the one who had come to my room in the grey light of dawn. I think that she had set out that morning determined to dispatch whatever had robbed her of sleep the night before. I could picture her lacing up her boots and striding into the dew-soaked meadow, plucking flowers from their roots in a slow, deliberate act of extirpation.

I was glad that she asked no more questions. I shuddered to

think of the consequences of telling her what I thought I had seen; of the utter devastation it would wreak. How could she keep such a thing to herself? And how would the family survive the recriminations that would surely follow?

I thought of Fanny, already so knowing, hovering on the brink of discovery. It was one thing to suspect a favourite uncle of holding a special place in your mother's heart; quite another to find out that he had fathered your baby sister. I thought of Fanny's brothers, young Edward, George and Henry, due to return to school in a few weeks' time. A scandal of such proportions, if it got out, would put paid to any hopes for their future. And then there were the little ones, William, Lizzy, Marianne and Charles – still in the nursery and incapable of understanding why Uncle Henry would not be coming to play with them any more. And there was baby Louisa, who would never again gaze into Henry's eyes the way she had done that day of the Canterbury races. I knew what it felt like to lose the closeness and security of family. If I told Jane what I suspected, hers would never be the same again.

'This time tomorrow, when we've steeped the flowers and drawn off the liquid, your eyes will be quite better.' Jane's voice brought me up short. 'Then we shall write another play and everything will be as it was.'

'Yes,' I murmured, settling back against the pillow, 'I do hope so. And perhaps you will let me read your manuscript? I would love to know more about this family you have dreamed up.'

She plucked a sprig of celandine from the bunch in her lap and pulled off the flowers, crushing them between her finger and thumb. 'It's very kind of you, but I'd rather wait till I had something better to show you.' She opened her fingers, revealing a smear of bright yellow. If she had pressed her thumb upon a sheet of paper the swirls and creases in the flesh would have left the kind of mark an infant makes on discovering a paint box. She seemed determined to view *The*

Watsons as a waste of effort; a stillborn child that would never see the light of day. I wondered how long it would be before she trusted me enough to reveal any future creations.

Martha Lloyd's herbal remedy had a wonderfully soothing effect but we did not write another play. Elizabeth, on hearing that I had been suffering with my eyes, decreed that I should return to London with Henry to see an optometrist. I was surprised and rather taken aback by this offer. I was only the governess, not a member of the family. Why should I be singled out for such exalted treatment, I wondered?

The appointment was made for the day after Henry's planned departure. I was to stay overnight at his home in Brompton and he would escort me to and from the consultation. Mrs Austen shook her head when she heard where I was off to.

'I cannot abide London,' she said, her tongue peeping through the gap in her teeth like a mouse venturing out of a hole. 'It is a sad place. I cannot comprehend why Eliza loves it so. I would not live in it on any account: one has not time to do one's duty either to God or man.'

I was not sure what she meant by it, but her words reminded me very much of something my father had uttered as he lay dying. 'I have failed you, my love,' he said, 'I have not done my duty to God or to man; but you must promise me that you will always do yours.' I could not ask him to explain, for he lapsed into unconsciousness with the next breath. The following day, when his body was laid out in the parlour, the bailiffs came to take every mortal thing that he had owned. They would have taken the coffin itself if I had not thrown myself across it.

'Pay no heed to Mama,' Jane said, shooing me upstairs to help me pack my things. 'She loves London as much as anyone. It affords her such opportunity for her study of *noses*. There is one in particular that she always must see when she

48

goes there. It belongs to the gentleman who guides visitors around Westminster Abbey. She says he must be the cleverest man in Christendom.' I could not help but smile at the thought of Mrs Austen stalking about the Abbey in pursuit of such an unfortunate soul. 'And you should have heard her as we passed by Kensington Palace one time,' Jane went on. 'The King had employed a painter to improve the outside and my mother said: "I suppose whenever the walls want no touching up he is employed about the Queen's face!"'

How could I be gloomy with such a companion? Before I departed she asked if I would take two letters: one for her cousin and another for Madame Bigeon, Henry's housekeeper. 'You will like Madame B,' she said. 'She is the very essence of kindness. She has been with Eliza for a long time – before she married Henry. She and her daughter are from Calais – they fled France during the Terror.'

I took the letters and tucked them in my valise. 'I hope that your cousin will not think it an imposition,' I said, 'having a stranger under her roof.' I couldn't spell it out to Jane, but I was worried about how I would be received. I was the employee of Elizabeth, sent without notice to stay in the home of Eliza. If Eliza had any inkling of what I suspected her husband was up to I guessed that she would not be best pleased to see me.

'Nonsense!' Jane laughed. 'I have written three letters already, telling her all about you. But I doubt that you will see her: she is rarely at home.' This did not sit easily with the picture I had formed of Eliza; of a poor faded beauty who hid herself away while her handsome young husband did what he pleased. 'She is in great demand,' Jane went on. 'She keeps her title of Comtesse in spite of having had all her land in France stolen from her; she's always at some party or another, or going to the theatre. The only time she stays in is if she's holding a *soirée* of her own. She has the most amazing salon for entertaining: Henry says that if you sit still too long up there you get your legs painted gold.'

She was smiling but there was agitation in her voice; it had all come out in a rush, as if she was trying to bolster Eliza, to dismiss any impression that Henry had lost interest in his wife. Then she said: 'You mustn't mind him. He's a terrible flirt. He can't help it.' I tried to read her eyes. Was this a warning? Did she think *I* was about to become the object of her brother's attention?

Before either of us could say another word we were interrupted by one of the housemaids coming to tell me that the carriage was ready and Henry waiting downstairs. She stood in the doorway as I bid Jane goodbye, probably under instructions from Elizabeth to hurry me up. Jane hugged me, saying she wished she was coming too. I wondered why she could not. Surely it would have been no trouble for Henry to take his sister to London for the night? I soon discovered why Jane had not been asked; indeed, the whole purpose of my trip seemed to unfold within half an hour of our departure from Godmersham.

Henry's familiar scent filled the carriage as we climbed in, roiling my thoughts like a stick in a wine cask. All the self-doubt came floating up again. I felt an overwhelming desire to think only the best of him; to submerge the memory of a few nights before. I had to remind myself that though he smiled he was someone to be wary of.

I sat there in some trepidation, wondering what topics of conversation I might summon up to while away the hours that lay ahead. But Henry made things very smooth, talking of the games he had played with the children and repeating all the funny little things that they had said and done. It wasn't long, however, before he began to talk about Fanny. It started innocently enough, with some remark about the cow she kept as a pet, along with a collection of birds and kittens that made almost as much work as the children. 'I heard she was unwell

50

again the night I returned from Canterbury,' he said. 'And you looked after her.' He beamed at me. 'You were very kind to her, Miss Sharp: I heard you talking to her on the landing as I came up to bed.'

'I...er...I was worried about her, yes.' He was looking right into my eyes, as if he could see the images that lingered inside my head.

'I hope that everything was all right? That you were not too much...*disturbed*?' To my mind the slight pause and the emphasis conveyed his meaning exactly. I was sure that he wanted to know if I had seen him on the stairs; if I had heard what he said to Elizabeth. I felt the tips of my ears burning and was glad that they were hidden beneath my bonnet. I didn't want him to know how much those frank hazel eyes discomfited me; how trapped I felt inside that carriage with him as my escort-cum-jailer.

I could hear the bump of the wheels on ruts in the road but behind the glass a thick silence cocooned us. He never shifted his gaze from my face. He was waiting for an answer. I hesitated, still trying to weigh him up. If I let on that I had seen him, what would he do? Would he have some story ready to account for what I had witnessed? Or would he write to Elizabeth the minute we got to London, warning her of the danger I posed and advising my prompt dismissal? The thought of this made my tongue stick to the roof of my mouth.

'Did Jane come to help? I thought I heard her voice too.'

I swallowed hard. I mustn't allow Jane to be dragged into this. 'She was...in bed,' I began, my voice made gruff by the dryness of my mouth. 'She heard me talking to Fanny and popped her head round the door to see what was going on. Then she took Fanny into her bed.'

He held my gaze a moment longer before replying. 'So everything was all right?'

51

'Everything was quite all right, thank you,' I said, nodding to lend my words conviction. I had to make him believe me. It was pure self-preservation that motivated me. I was not thinking, then, of the effect this tacit agreement to turn a blind eye could have on Fanny or the other children.

'Did Jane tell you of Cassandra's little drama?' He stretched out his long legs and settled back against the padded velvet. 'Had her ankle not been sprained it would have been the most amusing thing!' I was taken aback by the sudden change of tone and subject. Henry launched into a spirited account of the ball at Canterbury, describing the man in military uniform who had been so taken with Cassandra until his foot became entangled in her gown during a cotillion and they had fallen to the floor, her foot beneath his leg and the back seam of his breeches rent asunder.

Finishing the story, he smiled at me again. It was Jane's smile. They were so much alike in their looks and their humour and yet so very different in their dealings with the opposite sex. Jane talked about men but in a sharp, funny way that shielded her from the inescapable truth that she was, just like me, a woman close to thirty years old with no husband. Henry, on the other hand, had a confident charm that made him dangerous; he had the air of a man who could have any woman that he chose. Why, I wondered had he chosen Eliza? I hoped that she would be at home when we arrived: I wanted to see this wife of his for myself.

The rest of the journey was easier. Having apparently satisfied himself that he was in the clear, Henry kept me entertained with news of London. He talked about some of the plays he had been to see and told me of a scientist called Humphry Davy, who was attracting the fashionable set to his demonstrations of a thing called laughing gas.

'It is a new pleasure that makes one so strong and happy,' Henry said, chuckling as we rumbled through the streets of

London. 'I'm sure the air in heaven must be made of this stuff, Miss Sharp.' He was eager to hear my opinion of the latest developments in the realms of science and medicine, and soon we were engaged in a most energetic debate. I was fighting myself all the way, mindful of Jane's warning; he was a man I knew I should not allow myself to admire but his eloquence and enthusiasm were hard to resist.

Before I knew it there were shops and people and houses flashing past the window. I had not been to London since my parents died and in the first few years of the new century things were changing rapidly. Everything was brighter, busier and noisier than I remembered it; some of the young women looked almost naked, with gowns cut low on their bosoms and made of a fabric so fine you could see their legs when the sun was behind them. And the men preened like peacocks in their gay coats and pantaloons, wispy curls arranged just so on their foreheads. I felt like a drowsy animal poking its head into sunlight after a long hibernation. It was an assault upon my senses; painful yet intoxicating.

I was glad when the horses headed for Westminster Bridge, for London Bridge would have taken us very close to Maiden Lane. I wondered if Edward had told his brother anything of my circumstances before I came to Godmersham. It was possible he had heard it by some other means – the men of science Henry mixed with were just the sort to frequent my father's shop.

The carriage clattered to a halt a good mile west of the river at number sixteen, Michael's Place. It was in a row of elegant, newly built houses in the village of Brompton. Steps led up to a red painted front door with a shiny lion's head knocker. The windows were veiled with fine lace panels and as I stepped on to the cobbles I saw a pair of bright black eyes peering through a gap, the lace draped like a spaniel's ears on either side of them. I wondered if this was Madame Bigeon.

The owner of the eyes turned out not to be a woman at all:

it was Monsieur Halavant, Henry's French chef, who looked me up and down in much the same way that my mistress had done with Jane when she arrived at Godmersham. He was a strange little man, not much taller than Fanny, with a thin moustache and a blue kerchief knotted round his neck. It struck me as rather an extravagance to have a chef in a place of this size. I wondered how Henry had made his money, coming, as he did, from a modest background with none of the inherited wealth his brother Edward enjoyed.

Monsieur Halavant turned his back on me while he conversed in French with his master. He seemed agitated, his hands working like pitchforks, and I couldn't catch all that he said. It seemed that Eliza had gone into town to find a man who repaired harps; hers had a broken string and needed urgent repair for a musical evening she was giving the next week. Henry looked unsurprised to hear of her absence and showed me into the parlour.

'Madame Bigeon will be with you shortly.' He stepped into the room behind me and when I glanced back at him he smiled at the expression on my face. The whole room seemed to shiver and sway. Rainbows of light slid over the fat limbs of plaster cherubs and snaked round the smooth columns of marble jardinières; mirrors caught the colours and tossed them back at the walls and the ceiling. A huge chandelier was the cause of the illusion, its cut glass prisms catching the sun's rays as they streamed through the window.

'A pretty thing, isn't it?' Henry reached up to the chandelier and tapped it, sending the rainbow rays into a frantic dance. 'It's designed to intensify the light and cut down on the cost of candles.' His arm brushed my shoulder as he lowered it. 'Sorry, Miss Sharp – how clumsy of me!' His face was so near and the light so bright that I could see spots of gold in the muddy green of his irises. Something strange happened in that moment. My mind took flight and alighted at

Godmersham; came to roost inside Elizabeth's head. I was seeing him as she would have seen him that night on the staircase – if it *was* her. I was that close; close enough to slip my arm around his waist. How would that feel, I wondered? How was it *supposed* to feel when a woman touched a man in that way?

'Will you excuse me?' Henry's voice broke the spell. 'Monsieur Halavant requires fresh fish for a dish he is preparing and as my wife has taken the carriage he must go to market in my brother's.' With a little bow he made for the door, closing it behind him. I stood there in a sort of daze for a moment. Then I moved to the window and peered through the lace panel. I thought that Henry was simply going outside to instruct the coachman but to my surprise he jumped into the carriage with the chef. As it disappeared round a corner I heard footsteps behind me and turned to see a stout, olive-skinned woman with silver hair tucked into her cap.

'Madame Bigeon?' I moved away from the window, embarrassed that she had seen me peering after Henry.

She dropped me a little curtsey. I wondered if she knew that I was merely a governess and not a proper guest. Feeling my colour rise, I bent over my valise and pulled out the letter that Jane had asked me to pass on. I thought it would be polite to address her in her native tongue and she seemed delighted by this, despite my poor accent. Seizing the letter with a warm glance she took my valise and said that I should make myself comfortable in my room while she set out some food for me.

The chamber she gave me was dominated by a huge bed with an ornate carved headboard, its coverlet of lavender silk. It was at the back of the house and its window gave a view across open fields. Over the bed was a portrait. It showed a plump baby with blond curls sitting on the lap of a beautiful, fairylike girl whose pale wig contrasted oddly with her dark brown eyes.

'Is that your mistress and her son?' I asked.

She nodded, pressing her lips together.

'It's a very fine portrait, isn't it?' I smiled but she looked away from me, out of the window to the sheep that grazed the gentle, rolling fields.

'He was such a beautiful child.' She said it in a voice so low that I could barely make out the words. I hesitated before replying, working out from what Jane had told me that Eliza's child must now be around twenty years old. I wondered where he was now.

'We all miss him terribly.' Madame Bigeon turned her face back to me and I saw that there were tears in her eyes. 'He suffered more than any child should. The doctor said it was a mercy when God took him. But my poor mistress...' she tailed off, wringing her hands, 'She cannot bear to have this painting hanging in a place where she would see it.'

'I am so sorry,' I said, fumbling for the right words. 'I didn't know...'

She shook her head and put out her hands, sweeping the air. 'My mistress doesn't talk about it,' she said, 'and nor does Monsieur Henry. He was a wonderful father to the boy – and there are not many men who would take on a child with such afflictions. It is such a tragedy that she could not have another child.' She blinked and drew in her breath. 'Please come downstairs when you are ready,' she said. 'Do you like buttered shrimps?'

I stared at her stupidly for a moment, still taking it all in.

'They are small shellfish,' she went on. 'Have you tried them? They are very good to eat with new bread.'

'Oh...yes,' I mumbled, nodding vigorously for fear she would think me ungrateful. I had not tasted shrimp since I was a child. The memory of it conjured up picnics with my parents on Hampstead Heath.

She smiled at my eager face. 'I will have it ready for you in five minutes.' I listened to her footsteps fade away to nothing as she went down the stairs. I found myself unable to move, transfixed by the eyes of Eliza. She looked so delicate, almost transparent, next to the pink-cheeked baby on her knee; I thought it sad and strange that this healthy-looking little boy had passed away while she still lived. I wondered what lay behind Madame Bigeon's words: had there been a miscarriage or a stillbirth? Was there a second, failed pregnancy with her first husband, the Comte, before he went to the guillotine? Had Henry married her knowing that there would be no children? It seemed unlikely, given his undisguised affection for his nephews and nieces. More probable, I thought, that he had given up hope as the years rolled by.

I stepped closer to the painting to read what was written on the small gold-coloured plaque mounted on the frame: *Eliza, Comtesse de Feuillide and her son, Hastings. Painted for Warren Hastings, Governor General of India, by John Hoppner.*

I ran my finger under the name of the patron, whispering it to myself. I knew of Warren Hastings, as every person in England capable of reading a newspaper knew of him: he had made a vast fortune in India from timber and carpets and opium and had very nearly lost it all when he was accused of a multitude of crimes against the people he had governed. His trial had provided more of a spectacle than anything on offer in the theatres, with crowds gathering before the sun was up to queue for it. His accusers had been some of the most eminent parliamentarians in England. Against the likes of Edmund Burke, John Sheridan and Charles Fox he seemed to stand no chance. But to the amazement of everyone the case had, eventually, been thrown out of court. According to the papers, he now lived in somewhat reduced circumstances in a country residence in Gloucestershire.

I wondered why Warren Hastings had commissioned a painting of Henry's wife and stepson. Apparently the child had been named for him, which suggested that he was a relative. Jane had told me that Eliza's mother was the sister of her late father, Reverend Austen, so the connection must be on the other side. To have such a wealthy and influential man in the family must surely have enhanced Eliza's prospects. Had his influence helped bring about the match with the French Count? If so, I wondered if he had played any part in Eliza's choice of a second husband.

A distant voice from down below made me jump back from the portrait. Madame Bigeon was calling me. I hurried downstairs, my head bursting with questions.

Chapter Six

The housekeeper was chuckling to herself as she set down the plate of buttered shrimps. She begged my pardon, saying that Jane's letter had caused her such amusement that she could not think of it without wanting to laugh. 'What a wonderful time she has been having with you in Kent,' she said, 'It will do her good – she has been so unhappy since her father died. And she tells me that you have been looking after little Anna as well as Fanny.'

'Yes,' I began, 'Anna was with us for a…' Before I could finish the sentence she was off again.

'Ah, poor Anna,' she sighed. 'Her new mother is very mean to her, I think. Have you met her?' I shook my head, thinking that she was very free with her opinions. There had been several Frenchmen amongst my father's clients, but none as bold as this lady. 'Mary Austen is a very jealous woman,' she went on. 'Do you know, she will not allow my mistress to accompany Monsieur Henry when he visits them in Steventon? And do you know the reason why?'

I shook my head but I doubt if she noticed, so intent was she on telling me.

'It is because she is the second choice. When Anna's mother died her father wanted to marry my mistress but she turned him down. She said she could not imagine herself as the wife of a country parson!' She rolled her eyes, as if the very thought was quite insane. 'So now James Austen has a scold for a wife. Not only is my mistress banned from their house, her name must never be mentioned, Monsieur Henry says. Imagine how difficult that must be for him, when he goes to visit!'

'Does he go there often?' I asked, with a sudden presentiment of dread.

'Quite often,' she replied. 'He has plans to open a branch of his bank nearby.'

Seeing my blank look she chuckled again. 'Did you not know? That is where he is now: not in Hampshire – at the bank he has in town.'

I nodded silently. So that was where Henry's money came from. As I tucked into my buttered shrimps I wondered how he had come by the means to start such a business. Had Edward helped him out? This seemed unlikely, given his apparent reluctance to spend even trifling amounts on clothes for Jane and Cassandra. I decided that the money must have come from Eliza's side of the family. That would explain why two Austen brothers had vied for her hand in marriage.

'It is an amazingly clever thing, to run a bank,' I ventured. 'Your mistress must be very happy to have made such a match – her parents, too, I should think.'

Madame Bigeon gave a little sigh and rubbed her hands on her apron. 'I wish that poor Madame Hancock had lived to see the day,' she said. 'She was the very best of mothers – and it was not easy for her, being left a widow so early.'

'Oh?' I said, 'Eliza's father is dead, too?'

'Yes,' she replied, 'it is a great pity. She hardly knew him at all because his business kept him far away. But she is lucky to have a godfather, a very kind and generous man, Monsieur Hastings. He was a great friend of her parents when they lived in India. She named the child after him, you know, because he has none of his own.'

I turned my face to the shrimps to consider this. The Governor General was Eliza's godfather, then, not a relative, and India was the connection. By 'generous', I assumed that Madame Bigeon was alluding to money. Henry's wife was becoming more intriguing than ever. I wondered when she would return from her errand and whether I would have the chance to meet her. *Goodness, what a busybody you are turning into!* I heard my mother's voice, as clear as if she had been sitting at the table beside me. I suppose I was poking my nose in further than I should, taking advantage of the garrulousness of Henry's housekeeper. The fact was that I couldn't help myself. Two years at Godmersham, almost starved of adult society, had turned me into a glutton for every morsel I could gather from the lives of others. I felt like Arabella in the *The Female Quixote*, locked in a castle with only books to give colour to her life.

Before I could probe any further, though, a face appeared round the door. It was a woman of about my own age, very similar in features to Madame Bigeon.

'This is my daughter, Marie Marguerite.' The housekeeper beckoned her into the room. Marie Marguerite had the same warm smile as her mother. I thought how very different these women were from the servants at Godmersham. It was as if Henry's affability had rubbed off on them, in the same way that Elizabeth's discontentedness seemed to settle on those who served her.

When the daughter discovered that I had spent the past few weeks with Jane she sat down next to me, eager for news of her. 'You must tell her that we miss her very much. She has not come to London this year. Will she visit on her way back to Bath, do you think?' Before I could reply there was a faint rumble from the street outside. 'Is that Madame?' Marie Marguerite and her mother were on their feet in an instant.

I stayed where I was, listening to the conversation, all spoken in French, that drifted to me from the hall. From her voice I would have supposed Eliza to be much younger than she was. She was in good humour, pleased at having found someone to repair her harp quickly and delighted with a new Mameluk cap she had purchased from a milliner in the Strand. I heard Madame Bigeon tell her that Henry was back from Godmersham. Then she was informed of my presence in the house and the reason for my visit to London. There was a moment of silence.

'You say she is here to see a doctor? About her eyes?' There was no mistaking the note of suspicion in Eliza's voice. I shrank back in my chair, apprehensive of what might be going through her head.

'Yes, Madame. She is a great friend of Miss Jane's, you know: they have been writing a play together.'

'A friend of Jane's?' I heard the brightness return. 'She must take tea with me. And will you tell Monsieur Halavant that I will not be dining at home this evening – I ran into the Comtesse d'Antraigues in town and she begged me to accompany her to the Albany. Did Henry say whether he would be here this evening?' This question was put in an even manner, with no hint of emotion, as if it was a matter of no great importance to her if her husband came home or not. I didn't hear Madame Bigeon's reply; nor could I see if she had nodded or shaken her head. I wondered whether *I* would be Henry's dinner partner that night. For all his good humour and lively talk the thought of it made me uneasy. I felt as a goldfish must feel, swimming in a bowl as a cat approaches. I hoped that he would stay away and leave me to dine alone.

Eliza took tea in the upstairs drawing room, a place of breathtaking elegance that ran the whole length of the first floor. Its overall effect was of unbounded treasure: there were gold clocks and candelabra; glittering chandeliers and gleaming statuary. Rich tapestries and huge gilded mirrors hung from the walls, while the ceiling was painted with scenes of clouds and cherubs. There were ottomans piled with richly embroidered cushions and oyster-coloured lambrequins hung at the windows. The arms and legs of chairs glinted with more gold leaf, reminding me of the joke of Henry's that Jane had repeated.

Eliza looked perfectly at home in these dazzling surroundings. She rose to greet me as Marie Marguerite ushered me in, holding out her hands to clasp mine. She was easily recognisable as the girl in the portrait despite the twenty years that had elapsed since it was painted. Her eyes, though darker than Jane's, gave away the Austen connection: they had that same lively, mischievous look I had seen so many times in the past few weeks. But her frame was very different: standing side by side I guessed that Jane would be head and shoulders taller than her cousin. Eliza's hands in mine were like rabbit paws in cabbage leaves.

My apprehension at meeting her was quickly dispelled by her easy manner. She plied me with questions about myself, but did it in such a way as not to appear intrusive, only interested and concerned. When I told her that I had obtained work as a governess after the death of both my parents, she shook her head sympathetically. She said that never a day passed when she did not mourn her own mother, who had been her wisest counsellor, best helpmate and dearest friend.

She didn't mention her father, but went straight into talk of Jane's papa, the Reverend Austen, who, she said, had so resembled her own mother in features that it had given her much comfort to look upon him after her passing. 'Is Jane very much distressed, still?' she asked. 'She covers it well in her letters but I fear the loss of him has cut very deep with her. Henry seems much less affected; he has a bright spirit that cannot be dimmed for long.' She smiled as she said it, but I thought it a weary smile.

'I think that she was quite afflicted when she arrived at Godmersham,' I replied, remembering her brimming eyes when she greeted her brother, 'But I hope that the country air and the change of scene have had a good effect on her state of mind.' As the words came out of my mouth I thought that this remark was not quite true; for the benefits of the visit to Godmersham had surely been eclipsed by what I suspected Jane had seen on the night of the ball. Perhaps Eliza saw something of this in my face, for her next question was about Henry.

'Has my husband been enjoying himself in Kent?' she asked. 'I believe he was attending the Canterbury races?'

I reached for my teacup, mumbling a reply into it, so concerned was I that my expression would give me away.

'What was that?' she went on, 'A ball, you said?'

'Er…there were…two, actually…' I faltered, waiting for her countenance to change.

To my surprise she let out a peal of laughter. 'Two balls! Trust Henry to make the most of an opportunity! He would have been in good company, I suppose, with all the military men stationed thereabouts. He was a soldier, once you know.'

I said that I did not know and she told me how he had confounded his family by running off to join the militia when he was still at Oxford, studying to be a clergyman. 'It *is* amusing, isn't it?' she said, noticing the upward movement of my eyebrows. 'The idea of Henry standing up in a pulpit giving sermons! He is much better, I think, at talking people into parting with their money…' She tailed off with a mischievous look that creased the corners of her eyes.

I remembered Madame Bigeon's scornful dismissal of the marriage proposal by the older brother, James. I wondered if Henry had given up the Church in his quest to win Eliza.

'Tell me,' she went on, 'How is the new baby? Henry says she has the Austen mouth, so perhaps she is talking already?' That impish smile again. If she had any inkling of the thing I had lain awake fretting about, she was very adept at hiding it.

'She is a little young for that, yet,' I replied, returning her smile, 'although her brothers and sisters never cease coaxing her.'

'What a busy household it must be! I must confess I sometimes lose count of them. What is it now – four daughters and five sons? Am I right?'

I nodded and she shook her head, as if the thought of so many children made her dizzy. 'I suppose there will be another on the way before long,' she went on, 'and that will make ten – a good, round number, don't you think?' She said it with a wry glance that could have meant something or nothing.

'A good, round number, yes,' I agreed. I had very nearly said something about the family's luck in not having lost a single child thus far but, remembering Eliza's loss, I held my tongue.

'I have never known the joy of a brother or a sister,' she said. 'Henry is very fortunate in that regard. He loves to visit Edward at Godmersham. Do you know, he has even written a poem about it?'

'A poem?' I said brightly, 'Well, it is a very beautiful place.'

'Yes,' she nodded slowly. 'He calls it "The Temple of Delights."'

I swallowed a mouthful of tea so quickly that it went down the wrong way. When I looked up she was staring at me with what looked like a mixture of concern and amusement. 'Are you all right, Miss Sharp?' she asked. 'Is the tea a little too hot for you?'

She had set the trap and I had fallen right into it. Now I struggled to get myself out. Jane, or rather the memory of her, came to my rescue.

'I beg your pardon, Madame,' I said, 'but your mention of the poem brought to mind something I had quite forgotten.' Slipping my hand into my pocket I brought forth Jane's letter to her cousin. 'It was most remiss of me,' I went on, handing it to her, 'I should have delivered it earlier.' At that moment Marie Marguerite appeared to clear the tea things and my audience was over.

'I hope you will not mind eating with *Maman* and me tonight,' she said as she led me downstairs, 'Monsieur Henry has brought two gentlemen home to dine with him.' I did not mind. After the encounter with Eliza I felt like a bone unearthed by a couple of dogs, gnawed on by each in turn for the marrow it might yield. I wondered how Jane felt when she came here. A brother married to a cousin could be quite delightful, I imagined, with all the easy familiarity of a close family circle. But this did not appear to be a conventional marriage. Eliza was clearly no biddable wife. She seemed to be the mistress of herself, free from the burden of childbearing and wealthy enough to do as she pleased, with a husband whose presence or absence did not greatly disturb the rhythm of her life. What did Jane make of this partnership? What would a writer make of it? Were the characters in *The Watsons* based on members of her own family? Was that why she had become despondent about the book and decided to give it up?

That evening I spent a comfortable few hours with Madame Bigeon and her daughter, talking mostly of Jane and the things she liked to do when she visited London.

'Have you heard her play the pianoforte?' the housekeeper asked.

'Oh yes,' I replied 'She is much in demand in the evenings at Godmersham.'

'Last time she was here Madame held a soirée – and what an evening it was!' She threw up her hands, turning to her daughter. 'How many musicians did we have, Marie Marguerite? Was it five singers and three harpists or the other way about?'

No *Maman*, it was three singers, a pianist and a harpist. You should have seen the drawing room that night, Miss Sharp. The chimney piece was lit with a hundred tiny lanterns and there were flowers everywhere. We had so many guests – sixty-six of them, I counted – that they spilled out onto the landing and into the rooms upstairs. Monsieur Hastings came, of course, and when he heard how much Jane had enjoyed it he invited her to accompany him and his wife to the opera the next night.' She arched her eyebrows. 'He has his own box, you know.'

So Warren Hastings was not living in such reduced circumstances as the papers had suggested, I thought to myself. I tried to picture Jane sitting between the great man and his wife and wondered what she would have made of them. No doubt any peculiarities of speech, dress or manner had been squirreled away with the bad breath, fat necks and pink husbands of the good ladies of Bath.

Eliza was not yet up next morning when the carriage arrived to convey me to the optometrist. I took my leave of Madame Bigeon and her daughter, as we were to go directly to Godmersham after the appointment, stopping only to pick up Elizabeth's younger sister, Harriot Bridges, who was to travel with us.

Monsieur Halavant accompanied us for part of the way, off on another quest for some new ingredient that could not be dispensed with, and I was happy to sit in silence while the chef prattled away to his master, complaining about the rising price of Darjeeling tea.

The optometrist occupied rooms above a gun shop in Pall Mall. This was familiar territory to me. I used to walk this way with my cousins on summer evenings *en route* for the Green Park. We would compete with each other for the stupidest hat, the craziest wig, the most buffed-up dog and puffed-up person we could spy as we wound our way along from The Strand.

The optometrist could have amused himself in much the same way if he'd had a mind to, as his window looked out over the grand sweep of the avenue at its junction with St James' Square. He was an elderly Italian gentleman called Francesco Molteni and his gentle manners put me quite at ease.

'No, Miss Sharp, you are not going blind,' he smiled as he peered into my eyes through a glass that made his own eye the size of a saucer, 'but you need spectacles. And until they are ready you must rest: no reading or sewing for six weeks, do you hear me?'

'She should go to the seaside!' Henry spread his palms in a gesture of largesse. 'You must stay on at Worthing, Miss Sharp, after the family have taken their holiday. Don't worry, you won't be alone – my sisters are planning to be there until November.'

I had the distinct impression that Signor Molteni had prescribed just what Henry had been hoping for. I couldn't help thinking that he had cooked up this scheme to get me out of the way well in advance of our arrival, and that if the optometrist had not recommended rest Henry would have prompted him on the subject. But far from despising him for such a trick I felt indebted to the man. Nothing could have delighted me more than the prospect of a holiday by the sea with Jane for company.

Chapter Seven

From Pall Mall we did not go directly to collect Elizabeth's younger sister, as I had expected. Instead Henry took me down to the Thames, to a warehouse owned by a cloth merchant. We stepped out of the carriage into a swirling mist laden with familiar London smells. Wood smoke, rotting fish and river slime mingled with traces of tobacco and exotic spices. I was suddenly a child again, playing on the muddy foreshore with my cousins, throwing stones at floating bottles or leap-frogging the fishing boats while their captains lay snoring down below. I wondered what Catherine and Constance would think if they could see me now, driving about London with the sort of man who, in better times, might have visited the shop to take my counsel on some venerable gold-blocked volume of poetry or classical literature. I thought also of how my father would have disliked Henry, for he despised any man who thought more about money than books; this prejudice, no doubt, was part of the reason he sank so low.

'I want muslin for my sisters,' Henry's voice brought me back once again to the here and now. 'I hear this place has rolls of cambric from Flanders. It's quite a new design, with a pattern that does not run or fade when washed. I would be glad of your opinion of it, Miss Sharp.'

I was immensely surprised, not only by his generosity to his sisters – which was apparently sadly lacking in his older, wealthier brother – but by his very extensive knowledge of muslin. Never before had I encountered a man who knew his muslin from his bombazine, let alone one who appreciated the subtleties of texture, colour and pattern.

'What do you think of this for Jane?' He was rubbing the end of a roll of fine cream fabric between his finger and thumb. 'Do you think the green sprig would complement her eyes?'

I had to say that it would. I doubted I could have found anything so agreeable if I had searched the place myself.

'And what about this for Cass?' He took a few steps to the left, pointing to a roll on the shelf above. It was a white muslin with a delicate tracery of pink rosebuds printed upon it.

I nodded. 'That will suit her very well, I'm sure.' It looked expensive. He did not ask the price, though: simply ordered a dress length from each roll and escorted me back to the carriage while they were wrapped.

The drive back to Godmersham was easier for me than the outward journey had been. Henry oozed charm towards Harriot Bridges, who was as pretty as her sister and eight years younger. Her conversation was as lightweight and inconsequential as ostrich feathers but Henry seemed perfectly happy to indulge her. By the time we reached the gates of the park he had promised to give her drawing lessons and a time had been arranged for their first session.

I began to wonder whether Henry was nothing more than the incorrigible flirt Jane had warned me about. Had I misunderstood what I had seen on the stairs the morning after the ball? Surely he would not be so attentive to Harriot if he was engaged in a clandestine affair with her sister? Then it occurred to me that this behaviour might be a deliberate attempt to put me off the scent.

Jane was nowhere to be found when we entered the house. I sought out Sackree, who greeted me in her usual acerbic manner: 'Good afternoon, Lady Muck,' she muttered, 'Did you enjoy swanning around London while the rest of us were slumming it?'

'Yes, thank you, Sackree,' I replied, 'One finds such a superior class of servant in London. None of your Kentish country bumpkins up there, you know: Mrs Henry Austen will only employ fluent French speakers.'

'Is that so? Well, she'd better not send any of them down here, is all I can say: show a Kent man a Frenchy and he'll string him up from the nearest tree!' She gave me a broad grin and went to swipe me round the head with the napkin she was folding. 'I suppose you want to know where Miss Jane has disappeared to? Well, she's tired of you: she and her sister have gone to spend a few days with Lady Bridges, so hard cheese!'

I tried not to show my disappointment at this news and disappeared myself before Sackree had a chance to rub it in. Fanny, who had gone along with her father to deliver her aunts to Ashford, filled in the details. She said Aunt Jane would not return from her visit to Grandmama Bridges until the day before the trip to Worthing. Then she quizzed me about my trip to London, making me describe all the clothes, the hairstyles, the jewellery, even the ornaments on the hats that I had seen in the few short hours I was abroad in the city. I said: 'Fanny, I know that you long to be a lady, but there is more to life than fashion, you know,'

'But Miss Sharp,' she frowned, 'I must know about such things: what will become of me if I don't learn how to make myself beautiful? I might end up like Aunt Jane and Aunt Cass, mightn't I?'

'Would that be so very terrible?' I felt my lip quiver as I said it, caught between exasperation at her vanity and the sober realisation that she counted me among the sad failures peopling her world.

'Would you not like a husband – if I was grown up and didn't need you any more, I mean?' She was looking at me with such solemn eyes I felt compelled to answer honestly.

'No Fanny, I would not.'

'But why? Don't you like men? What about Priddle? I know he has no hair and his skin shines like goose fat, but he's nearly as tall as you, isn't he? Taller than all the other servants.'

We both laughed then and she seemed to forget what she had asked me, chattering instead about a gown she had seen in one of her mother's fashion papers. I was glad that she had dropped the subject, for it was something I tried very hard not to think about.

That evening Edward and Elizabeth held a dinner party for some of their Canterbury friends. Afterwards Henry entertained everyone with a reading of Shakespeare. Fanny was allowed to stay up for this, so I was admitted to the proceedings as well. I have to own that he was one of the best amateur performers I have ever seen: the way that he altered his voice to suit every different character was most accomplished. It was clear that he had many of the passages off by heart and was able to imbue them with such feeling that he held his audience spellbound.

Edward was the first to applaud when the reading was over, jumping to his feet and shouting 'Bravo! Encore!' I stole a look at Elizabeth, seated beside him. She was clapping along with everyone else but her lips were forming words that were inaudible above the sound of the applause. Henry's eyes held hers for a split second as he took his bow. The air between them seemed to sizzle, as if a bolt of lightning had shot across the room. I looked at Edward then, wondering if he had noticed it, but he was leaning over his wife's head to speak to someone in the row behind. This was Louisa Bridges, one of Elizabeth's other sisters, for whom the latest baby had been named. I had seen her only once before, when she came to stand godmother to the child at the christening. I thought then how very like Elizabeth she was: the difference in their ages was four years but they might have been twins. Their manner was markedly different though; she was a watcher, not a doer, and seemed content to hide in Elizabeth's shadow.

It occurred to me then that Edward was looking at Louisa the way I had often seem him look at his wife. One side of his mouth curved up in an appraising sort of smile; the kind of look my father would give when he ran his hands over a particularly handsome book. I wondered if Edward failed to notice what was going on under his nose because he was too preoccupied with illicit conquests of his own. What *was* this fascination the upper classes seemed to harbour for the sisters of their wives and the wives of their brothers? Was it the tablet they saw each Sunday hanging from the church wall, listing every forbidden union, which fuelled such fantasies? And was the phenomenon really as rife in the quiet country seats of Kent as in the jaded salons of London? I reminded myself of the story Fanny had told me, about her father turning her out of her mother's bed in the middle of the night. Could a man who so desired his wife really be taking his pleasures anywhere else, let alone with her own sister?

That night I sat a long time in my room, staring out of the window at the moonlit garden and, in the far distance, the columns of the Greek temple silhouetted against the purple sky. Being forbidden to read I was at a loss for some occupation to fill the hours before sleep.

Though the house was full of people I felt dreadfully lonely. There was an expectation that, having being allowed to attend the play reading, I would make myself scarce once it was over. I had been used to this, before Jane came; of sometimes being treated as a member of the family and sometimes not. But Jane had changed everything. She treated me as her equal; as her friend. Her taste in books and plays and poetry mirrored my own and she made me laugh in a way I hadn't done for years. And now she was gone away I felt what had been lacking in my life more keenly than ever before.

The thought of the coming six weeks in Worthing to be spent at leisure with Jane and her sister acted like a balm on my troubled mind. I determined that nothing must be allowed to spoil this time; nothing must be said or done by me to upset our friendship. I was thinking, of course, of Henry and that gloved hand. I vowed to myself that whatever I saw or heard at Godmersham in the next few days I would not voice a single word of it while at Worthing. I would do nothing to make Jane anxious, nothing that might turn her against me.

As I gazed out of the window I caught sight of a figure moving across the grass. From the shape and the gait I guessed that it was a man. He paused by the lime walk, glancing this way and that as if he was waiting for someone. After a little time I saw another figure draw near – a person of smaller stature whose silhouette showed a skirt and a shawl. I do not know what happened next. Tempted as I was to watch, I turned my head away and pulled down the blind. Unless they were both servants, it was better I didn't know.

To while away the evening I decided to begin packing for the trip for Worthing. The weather was still warm but if I was to stay until October, as Henry had suggested, I would need winter clothes as well as summer ones. I was rooting about for a pair of thick gloves when I came across the odd one I had tucked away eighteen months since; the one I had used as a hiding place for Elizabeth's death letter. The folded paper slid out as I rummaged clumsily about. I had forgotten its existence and held it up to the candle to see what it was. The seal had broken and the letter fell open. There was Fanny's name in Elizabeth's writing. I was not supposed to be reading anything – least of all a final farewell from a mother to her daughter – but my eyes had already caught the first lines:

'My darling daughter, if only this was not to say goodbye; if only we could be together again, you and me and your Papa, as we were in the days when you were born: so happy, so carefree and so full of love…' I swallowed hard and laid the letter face down on the chest of drawers, bringing the flat of my hand down upon it. This was not meant for me to see. Now that it was no longer intact I should burn it. But my eye was caught by a postscript written on the bottom of the paper – part of it that would have been concealed when the letter was folded: 'Kiss Uncle Henry for me and tell him it is his job to make you laugh, as he made me laugh. Remind him to read his Bible every day.'

If my sins had been read aloud from the pulpit I could not have felt more chastened. Screwing the paper into a ball, I tossed it onto the fire. I watched the embers flame green as it ignited and heard the hiss of the wax melting onto the coals. A mocking sound, it seemed to me; a warning to keep my nose out of the affairs of this family.

Chapter Eight

We arrived in Worthing on a warm September afternoon, having travelled for two days. I had not seen Jane to speak to, for she had come back from her visit to Lady Bridges very late the night before our departure. The next morning we had been put in separate conveyances, she in a barouche with her sister and mother and I in a carriage with Fanny and her parents. We had spent the night at Horsebridge near Battle and while Jane and her family went to see the Abbey I stayed with Fanny, supervising her meal and putting her to bed because Sackree was left behind at Godmersham with the younger children.

By the time we reached the seaside Fanny could barely contain herself, begging to be released from the carriage to go onto the beach. Her father seemed inclined to indulge her and said that we could all take a walk while the servants were making our rooms ready.

We came to a halt beside a white stucco house about the size of Henry's home in Brompton. As I stepped down from the carriage and breathed in the salty air I saw my parents, as clear as if they were standing before me. I reached out for the blue-painted railings that ran along the front of the house, for the ground beneath my feet seemed to buckle. I remember tensing the muscles of my eyelids in a vain attempt to keep the image from fading away. I saw them walking across the sand, Mama in what she called her seaside bonnet – the straw dyed blue and trimmed with white ribbon – and the cashmere shawl with the pine cone weave about her neck. The wind was taking the tails of the shawl and whipping them across Papa's face, knocking off his hat, which he chased across the beach, both of them laughing as he raced it to the water's edge.

My fondest memories of my parents were of such days by the sea. Ramsgate was the favourite haunt of my father's, the place where we had spent our last carefree week together along with my cousins Catherine and Constance and my Aunt Edith. A fortnight after our return my mother was dead of the typhus fever that swept through London in the autumn of 1803. Catherine, Constance and their mother died a week later. My father, who had never been the cleverest of men with his money, sank even further without Mama's guiding hand. Within six months he had gone to join her and his creditors made sure that I was the only tangible reminder that he had ever walked this earth. It was his wine merchant – the one to whom he owed more than all the rest – who took pity on me. One of his other clients was Edward Austen, who happened to be in urgent need of a governess at the time. Some sort of bargain was made between them, the details of which I was never privy to. But it was a full year before I received anything for my labours beyond my bed and board.

Fanny was pulling at my skirts, chiding me for being so slow. 'Come on,' she said, 'I want to go collecting shells! Aunt Jane will help us, won't she?' The others followed us across the road to the steps that led to the beach. The tang of the sea was mixed with other scents now; of oysters, whelks and vinegar on the carts along the promenade; of rotting seaweed washed

77

up by the tide; of donkeys, dogs and people gently baking in the heat.

Seagulls tumbled above us as our feet became acquainted with the strange sensation of walking upon shingle. Fanny raced along, stopping every few seconds to crouch over some treasure that was scooped up into a little tin bucket she had carried with her all the way from home. Edward and Elizabeth walked behind her, with Cassandra and her mother following at a little distance. Jane and I fell into step behind them.

'Your company was sorely missed at Ashford.' Jane slipped her arm through mine. Her words set off a ripple of pleasure which I struggled to conceal.

'Oh?' I said, trying to sound nonchalant, 'Was Lady Bridges out of sorts?' I had observed Elizabeth's mother many times and found her a most unpleasant, meddling sort of woman who used her title to intimidate all around her.

'Where should I begin?' she grimaced. 'First of all she was cross with the Duke of Gloucester for dropping dead last Friday, which meant the ball at Deal was cancelled. Then she was hatching a scheme to marry poor Harriot off to a grumpy old parson with hairy ears. When Harriot returned from London to find him waiting in the parlour she turned and ran from the house. They say he is so much hated by his flock that when he married his first wife they sang the funeral hymn instead of the nuptial psalm.'

'Seriously?' I saw her lips were twitching mischievously. I wondered if this was another one of her tall stories.

'Absolutely true,' she grinned, crossing her finger over her heart. 'And now I want to hear all about your trip to London. I hope you were not too fagged by the journey? Henry will talk people half to death when he has a captive audience.' She was smiling still but there was an edge to her voice. If she was fishing I was not going to take the bait.

'The journey passed quite quickly,' I replied, 'and Henry had business to attend to so I saw little of him after we arrived.' I launched into a description of my visit to Signor Molteni, telling Jane of the spectacles and the enforced idleness I must now endure.

'Oh! I am sorry for your eyes,' she said, 'but I will read to you every night, if you will let me!'

I replied that she was very kind but I must not interfere with the entertainment of the family on their holiday. 'Nonsense!' she cried. 'I don't expect we shall see much of Edward and Elizabeth in the evenings – they will be dining out with their friends – and by the end of the week they will be gone back to Godmersham, my mother with them. We shall be left a very snug three, and we will spend our days exactly as we please. Now,' she went on, hardly pausing for breath, 'tell me more about London. It seems an age since I was there. How was Madame Bigeon? Did you meet Marie Marguerite?'

I began to describe the glimpse I had had of the life of the household in Brompton. I had not intended to mention Warren Hastings, but I found myself recounting the conversation about Eliza's musical evening, at which point Jane interrupted me.

'Oh yes, I well remember it! I was seized upon by an insufferable woman – the wife of Eliza's godfather, Mr Hastings. She spent the whole evening criticising the pianists with her mouth full of sweetmeats and macaroons – she left the servants black and blue, pinching them by the arm every time they strayed near her with a tray – and then she had the nerve to suggest that she could offer me something far superior by way of entertainment.' Here she paused and rolled her eyes. 'Had she been anything *resembling* a civilised human being I would have been thrilled by her invitation to the opera; I had to accept, of course, for fear of offending Mr Hastings. How a woman like that ensnared such a man as he I cannot fathom; he is as refined as she is coarse; as courteous as she is rude. I suppose I should not blame her: after all, nobody minds having what is too good for them.'

I laughed heartily at that, picturing a grizzled old dame with bulging cheeks hanging on to the arm of a silver-haired gentleman with fine bearing and a benevolent smile. 'Madame Bigeon told me that Eliza's parents met Mr Hastings in India.' I could not resist the urge to probe deeper, now that she had provided the opportunity.

She nodded, kicking up a little shower of broken shells as her foot slid sideways on the lumpy surface of the beach. 'My Aunt Philadelphia decided there were no good husbands to be found in England so she set out for India to find one. Mr Hastings was on the same boat but they did not meet properly until some time after they arrived in Calcutta. She was married within weeks to a man called Mr Hancock, who then, a few years later, went into business with Mr Hastings.'

'And the horrible wife? Was she in Calcutta too?'

'Not at that time,' she replied, 'She was married to someone else then; a German, I think. Mr Hastings had been married too, but he was a widower when he got to know my aunt and uncle. He had a little girl who died and Eliza was named after her. My aunt was lucky to have a child herself: she was married for eight years before Eliza came along.'

A flock of tiny birds alighted suddenly on the stretch of wet sand between the shingle bank and the sea. Fanny ran at them, calling out, and they scattered like a shower of stones flung across the waves. As I watched them disappear I said: 'I suppose Mr Hastings treasures Eliza, having no living child of his own?'

'Yes, he does, and he has been her salvation. He put ten thousand pounds in trust for her when she was still a child – little did she know how much she would need it.'

Somewhere behind us a donkey began to bray and Fanny

ran between us, catching our hands and pulling us round to see the beast, which had plucked off an elderly woman's bonnet and was trying to eat the artificial strawberries that adorned it. I stared but did not take it in. I was thinking of the ten thousand pounds; calculating that if I worked for fifty years and saved every penny of my salary, it would not make a quarter of that sum.

'You cannot blame the donkey, can you?' Jane was saying. 'The old dame should have chosen paper violets or silk roses: I cannot help thinking it is more natural to have flowers grow out of the head than fruit.'

The others had turned back at the sound of the hubbub on the beach. By the time the fuss was over we were half way up the steps to the road. Edward waved us onward, standing guard as his gaggle of females made their way across to the house. Once inside, the business of allocating rooms got underway. Edward and Elizabeth were to have the largest one at the front of the house, which had French windows and a little balcony overlooking the sea. Mrs Austen was given the chamber next door to them. At the back of the house were two more bedrooms, one of which Jane and her sister were to share and the other to be tenanted by Fanny and myself.

'It is a shame that Henry isn't with us,' Mrs Austen declared as we sat down to tea, 'but where he would have slept, I do not know. I suppose the servants have taken all the attic rooms?'

'Yes, Mama,' Edward's eyes darted to his wife as he turned his head towards his mother. I saw Jane shift slightly in her seat. 'There are three rooms in the attic,' he went on, 'Sayce has one, Roberts and the footman another and the cook shares the third with the housemaids.'

'Didn't Henry say that he might come later in the week, though?' Mrs Austen persisted.

'I think not,' her son replied, 'his business calls him back to Hampshire.'

'Oh?' his mother said. 'He will be staying with James and Mary, then, I suppose. Will you see him there, when you visit your estate at Chawton?'

'I don't know, Mama.' Edward drew in a breath, lips pursed, as if he was tired of her questions. 'You know as well as I do that Henry is a law unto himself. How long he will stay and whither he will fetch up next are a mystery to us all, I'm sure.' I could not see Elizabeth's face at this point, for she had raised her tea cup to her lips. 'Now, Fanny,' Edward turned to his daughter, wishing, so it seemed, to change the subject, 'What do you say to a dip in the sea before dinner?' This produced predictable squeals of delight. 'Will you escort her, Sharp? He put his hand in his pocket and pushed a sixpence across the table. 'You must go directly, before the sun loses its strength.'

As I rose to my feet I saw that Jane had risen too. 'I'll come with you,' she said. 'I do love to bathe in the sea.'

'Oh, no, Jane!' her mother cut in. 'You and Cassandra must help me to unpack! You can't imagine how fagged I am with all this travelling! There will be plenty of time for bathing later on!'

I caught Jane's eye across the table. I could guess just what she was thinking: *I am nine-and-twenty and still she tells me what I may and may not do! Would you be me?* What I would have said, could I have answered, I am not certain. I saw that, like me, she was a species of prisoner. Although she did not have to work for a living and had no husband to answer to, there were other constraints on the manner in which her life was conducted. Was it better to be told what to do by a domineering mother or an employer? In the latter case there was some financial reward, however small.

My mother had never tried to control me, despite the disappointment I caused her by refusing to enter the marriage market. I wondered if Jane had chosen spinsterhood or merely settled for it, as Cassandra had; and if it *was* her choice, was there a chance she had made it for the same reason I had?

The next few days passed in a whirl of activity and my time was governed by Fanny, who woke up early every morning and threw open the curtains, eager to know what the weather would be. Mrs Austen, who was herself an early riser, would usually take her down to the beach to buy fish, giving me a little peace before the merry-go-round began in earnest.

When they had gone I would get back into my bed, listening to the squawking of the gulls outside the window. In the lulls in their banter I sometimes caught Jane's voice through the wall, chatting away to Cassandra. How I envied them, those sisters. How I longed for that closeness, that intimacy, with a creature such as Jane. I was well aware that my time with her was limited; that once this holiday was over I knew not when I might see her again; and I found myself fighting a battle inside. I was wishing the days away, wishing Fanny and her parents to be gone so that I could make the most of those few precious weeks of Jane's friendship, and yet I knew I would miss Fanny terribly: much more, I suspected, than she was likely to miss me.

On the Saturday evening Edward and Elizabeth went to dine with the Johnsons, a Kent couple who, like them, had rented a house in Worthing for the summer. Mrs Austen was feeling unwell and had taken herself off to bed with a cup of tea. Cassandra had gone to visit a Miss Fielding, another native of Kent whom she had got to know on a previous visit to Godmersham. That left Jane and me to entertain Fanny until her bedtime.

It had begun to rain for the first time since we arrived, so a walk on the sands was not possible. Jane suggested charades but Fanny said it would not be any fun with only three players and begged for a game of cards instead.

'I will fetch Mama's pack,' she said, leaping out of her chair with her usual boundless energy, 'I know where she keeps it.'

She returned in less than a minute, clutching an exquisite little card case of tortoiseshell inlaid with mother-of-pearl. 'Look,' she said, turning it over and bringing it near to my eyes, 'it has Mama's name engraved on the back. It was her present when Louisa was born.'

I nodded my approval, unable to decipher the letters at such close range. Jane took the box from her and bade her go to the kitchen and ask for wine and cheese to sustain us while we played.

'What shall we play?' she asked. 'Will it be loo or vingt-et-un?' She pressed the garnet clasp that held the case shut. As she drew out the cards I saw something flutter onto the table. She picked it up and stared at it. I saw the colour drain from her face.

'Cook says what kind of cheese?' Fanny marched into the room, hands on hips. 'What's the matter, Aunt Jane? You look all funny.'

'Nothing, Fanny dear,' Jane replied, stuffing the paper into her pocket. 'Tell cook that any kind will do. Now run along!'

I turned to her as Fanny left the room but her face was set like a mask. 'Well,' she said briskly, 'I think loo would be the easiest for Fanny to play, don't you? Will you shuffle the pack for me? I've never been very good at it, I'm afraid.'

As she passed the cards across the table I saw that her hands were shaking. She would not meet my eye, but chattered on about the merits and demerits of loo and picquet and whist, as if she was afraid of leaving any gap for me to fill with a question. Before long Fanny was back and the card game began.

Jane seemed unnaturally bright throughout and the colour that had left her cheeks returned in abundance, giving her a rosy glow that fooled Fanny into thinking all was as it should be. I saw, however, that she had drained her glass of wine before the first game was finished and was well into her second as I shuffled the pack once again.

By the fourth game Fanny's eyelids were beginning to droop. I told her it was time for bed, ignoring her pleas to be allowed to play another round. She kissed her aunt goodnight and Jane gave her a brittle-looking smile, as if the effort of containing her feelings was becoming too much to bear.

I sat beside Fanny as she settled down on the pillows, bidding her to cease her chatter and try to go to sleep. In the quiet moments that followed I listened to the rain beating on the window and the growl of the waves as they surged against the shingle. I wondered what Jane was doing, all alone downstairs. I stroked Fanny's head, willing her to close her eyes so I could go to Jane. At length I saw the regular rise and fall of the bedclothes and, moving the candle closer to her shadowed face, saw that the child was indeed asleep.

I tiptoed out of the room and onto the landing. I could hear a low rumble, something quite like the sound of the tide. It was Mrs Austen, I think, snoring in her sleep. I heard the creak of the back stairs, which I took to be one of the servants on their way to bed, but otherwise all was silent. I hurried down, afraid that Jane, too, might be bound for her chamber to guard herself from my inquiring eye. But no, there she was, sitting just where I had left her, an empty glass in one hand and the tortoiseshell card case in the other.

'Is she asleep?' I heard the jewelled clasp of the case snap shut.

'I think so,' I replied. Her eyes were downcast. I could not catch them.

'Shall I read to you now, before they all come back?' It was not so much a question as a command. Without looking up she rose from the table and crossed to the bookcase, selecting a large, black-bound volume from the bottom shelf. 'I think you should rest your eyes,' she went on. 'Sit in that chair by the fire and close them tight.'

I faltered for a moment, uncertain of her motive. Was she

secretly hoping I would seize the book, cast it aside and ask what was in her heart? The set of her chin as she placed the volume on the table did not seem to invite opposition. So I did as she bid me, sinking stiffly into the armchair and tilting my head back until all that I could see was a smoky corner of the ceiling.

'Now close your eyes.'

I did as she asked. I heard the gentle thud of leather on wood as she opened the book. The fire answered with a sudden crackle. Instinctively I moved my legs away from the heat. I wanted to open my eyes but I dared not.

'Thou hast ravished my heart, my sister,' she began. Her voice, usually so clear and strong, sounded strained. She paused and coughed a little. 'Thou hast ravished my heart with one of thine eyes, with one chain of thy neck. How fair is thy love, my sister! How much better is thy love than wine!' She paused again. I waited for her to continue, wondering what text this could be. I heard a little rush of air in the chimney as the wind sighed into it. The coals shivered and settled themselves.

'Well?' she said at last. 'Do you recognise it?'

'No,' I admitted, 'I do not. Is it John Donne? Or Milton?'

'Neither of those,' she replied, 'although I can see why you mistook it for Donne. Have another try.'

I trawled my mind for other likely candidates. It was not Shakespeare, of that I was certain. Who would write of love in such a style? It must be some new poet, I decided; someone that Jane had discovered before me.

'Well?' she repeated.

'I have no clue,' I replied. 'You will have to tell me.'

'I shall, by and by. One more question first: if a man were to copy such lines and send them to you, how would you feel?'

My eyes snapped open and I raised my head from the chair. 'To me?' I turned towards her with a little snort.

'No looking!' she cried, covering the book with her hands and throwing me a stern glance. 'Close your eyes and answer the question!'

'Hmmph. Very well – if you insist: I would suppose him to be in love with me, of course. More than that, actually: I would believe that I had bewitched him.'

'But would you not be offended? Do the lines not suggest that the writer and his subject are lovers already? Listen to the last line again: "How fair is thy love, my sister! How much better is thy love than wine!"'

'Well…' I hesitated, thinking it through. 'I suppose it *does* convey that meaning, yes. As to whether I would be offended, that would depend, wouldn't it?'

'On what?'

'On what the man was to me. If he was my husband or my fiancé, I suppose it would be a sweet thing to receive. But if he was a…or I was…' I tailed off, letting my upturned hands convey my meaning. 'But do tell, now, Jane! Who is the poet?'

'It is the Bible,' she said. 'The Song of Solomon.'

'Really?' I turned to her in blank astonishment. I thought I knew the Good Book as well as most but I had not realised it contained such lines as these. 'Did you choose the passage or did it just fall open at that place?'

'*I* did not choose it,' she replied, 'but someone else did: I found it in the card case.' Her face began to swim before me, as if the sea had burst through the door and turned the air to liquid. But I could clearly hear the next words that she said: 'I recognise the hand that copied it: it is Henry's.'

Chapter Nine

I stared dumbly at her stricken face, the words of the passage echoing through my head. *Thou hast ravished my heart, my sister…How fair is thy love, my sister…* Now it had a horribly sinister ring. Henry had used words from the Bible to charm a forbidden woman who was, indeed, his sister by marriage. And she had left it in a place where her own daughter might have discovered it. A spasm of recall brought back the postscript of Elizabeth's letter to Fanny: *Remind him to read his Bible every day.* Was that some sort of coded message to Henry? Could she really have thought of using her child in that way?

The chinking of glass pierced the black silence. Jane's hand was on the decanter, shaking violently as she pulled out the stopper. No sooner had she got it out than she thrust it back in and slumped forward onto the open book, cradling her head in the crook of her elbow. Instinctively I ran to her but my hands froze in mid-air. I stood there like a thing made of stone, afraid to touch her; at a loss for what to say. I gave up a terse, voiceless prayer for the right words to come.

'Jane, please,' I began, 'it might not be what you think.' I hesitated, unable to think of any innocent explanation for what she had found in the card case. Jane let out a low moan, like an animal in pain. I cursed Henry, cursed Elizabeth, for bringing her so low, for ruining everything. And then I cursed myself for my selfishness, for thinking even fleetingly of my own happiness when she was wretched.

'It could be nothing,' I tried. 'You know what Henry is like; how he loves to perform. Why, only last week he was reading Shakespeare to us all in the library. I expect he copies all manner of texts for evenings of that sort: what if this was something he left lying about the place? Perhaps she found it one evening when she was playing cards and tucked it away without a second thought. Have you considered that?'

I didn't think I could believe this but I hoped it might convince her. She raised her head an inch or two from the table and I dropped down beside her so that my eyes were level with hers. I could see that she wanted to grasp this straw that I had cast upon the water; that she was desperate to restore Henry to the cherished place he held in her heart.

'Do you...' she faltered, her lower lip trembling. She bit down on it then tried again: 'Do you really think that is possible?' I could not look into her eyes as I replied that yes, it was entirely possible. 'But there have been other things; other times when I have thought that all was not...as it *should* be. You have been living in that house for more than a twelvemonth: have you never seen anything that made you...wonder?' She sucked in her breath and I wondered what was coming. 'That night of the ball, when I saw you near the stairs...you saw something then, didn't you?'

The ghost had chased me all the way from Godmersham; it was hovering between us, demanding recognition. I rose to my feet, avoiding Jane's gaze, for I couldn't, *wouldn't*, tell an outright lie. The fire spat out a glowing cinder as a cold draught blew across the room.

'Where is everybody? Have I missed dinner?'

I turned to see Mrs Austen, her cap slightly awry and a shawl draped over her nightclothes, standing in the doorway with a puzzled look on her face.

The next day was Sunday. Fanny and I awoke to the sound of pealing bells competing with the cries of the seagulls. Jane did not come down to breakfast and the first sight I had of her was when the whole household assembled for church.

She looked a little paler than usual but otherwise there was nothing amiss with her face. I had heard no sound from her room during the night save the soft tread of Cassandra, back very late from her visit to Miss Fielding. There was no knowing whether Jane had disclosed anything to her sister but I suspected that she had not: judging by the way she had rallied when her mother appeared at the door, I felt that her relatives were the last people she would wish to know of her discovery.

Elizabeth did not accompany the rest of the family and the servants to church. She kept to her bed, complaining of sickness. Edward said that the fish served at the Johnsons' dinner table had disagreed with her but I couldn't help wondering if she was in the early stages of another pregnancy.

The rain had cleared up, leaving Worthing basking in sunshine once again, and Fanny was cross about having to sit through a service when she might have been on the beach. As soon as it was over she ran to her father, tugging at his arm as we walked through the churchyard. She was clamouring for a final dip in the sea.

'But it's our last day, Papa!' she grumbled when Edward suggested a walk to Herstmonceaux Castle instead. 'I don't want to go for a boring old walk! I can do that at home – but I can't go in the sea at home, can I?'

'What?' Edward turned to his sisters with a grin. 'She has a private stretch of river to swim in any day of the week and yet she pleads to splash about with hordes of unwashed strangers! What an odd little creature she is!'

I watched Jane's face as she listened to her brother baiting Fanny. He was talking about turning the bathing house into an extra potting shed for the gardeners because it was so little used. Jane stooped to examine a gravestone, letting Edward and Fanny walk on. I wondered if she, too, had her suspicions about what had been going on in the bathing house of late.

'Uncle Henry will be very cross if you give it to the gardeners, Papa!' Fanny stuck out her bottom lip, determined not to be beaten. My heart missed a beat. Edward's teasing smile had been replaced by a beady frown.

'Oh! Uncle Henry will be cross, will he?' he said, mocking his daughter's childish lisp. 'Pray, tell us, Fanny, why would that be?'

I glanced at Jane, wondering if she could hear the conversation from where she was standing. Cassandra and Mrs Austen were smiling at Fanny, waiting for her answer, clearly oblivious of the imminent danger.

'Because he likes to go swimming in the river, of course!' Fanny gave a theatrical sigh. 'He took the boys in while you were at the Canterbury races and he goes in on his own nearly every day when he stays with us; I've seen him.'

'Seen him?' Edward's eyebrows shot upwards. 'I sincerely hope that you have not!'

'Not seen him bathing, silly Papa! I've seen him going down the path: the one that leads to the river. And when he comes back his hair's all wet, so I know that's where he's been. Anyway, he told me himself: he says he loves swimming more than anything.'

'Does he indeed?'

I was relieved to see that Edward was smiling again. 'More than fishing and shooting? I can't believe it!'

'It's true, Papa!' Fanny jabbed her father in the ribs. 'Now can I go in the sea? Please!'

Edward grunted his assent with a playful swipe at Fanny's head. Jane came noiselessly up the path behind us, casting me a brief smile as she caught up with her mother and sister. There was no chance to ask her how she did, for Fanny was in a state of high excitement, tripping over my skirts in her rush to get us all home and off to the beach.

The house was very quiet when we returned. A dread feeling overtook me as we entered it, for such was my state of mind after the events of the previous night that I imagined Elizabeth's sickness was just a pretence; that Henry had ridden to Worthing and slipped into the house while we were all at church.

There was no sign of Elizabeth, or Henry, of course. She appeared a few minutes before we set off for the beach, saying that her sickness had passed and the fresh air would do her good. Edward fussed round her, organising all manner of comforts, and she spent the day stretched out on a deck chair, shaded by a huge parasol, while he sat at her feet like a slave.

Mrs Austen fell asleep in the sun with her bonnet over her face and Cassandra took her sketch-pad to the water's edge to capture a pretty sailboat anchored a little way off. Fanny was asking her father for money for a bathing machine and once he had obliged, she skipped across to where Jane was unfolding a blanket, begging her to go in the sea. Jane looked across at me.

'Oh, yes! You'll come too!' Fanny danced across the sand, seizing my arm and pulling me over to where Jane stood.

'Fanny, you cannot *order* Miss Sharp to go in the sea!'

'It's all right,' I laughed, 'I watched Fanny swimming the other day and I thought I might like to try it.'

'Very well,' Jane smiled. 'I hope you will not regret it. They say that the sea is warmer now than in summer but that is rather like saying Greenland is warmer than the North Pole.' She glanced at her mother, who was snoring open-mouthed beneath her bonnet, revealing the cavernous gaps in her teeth. 'I don't think that Grandmama will mind not being invited: perhaps she will have caught a fish or two by the time we return.'

Female bathers were confined to a small stretch of the water at the westerly end of the beach. The bathing machines were clustered around a little hut behind the ropes that kept curious male eyes at a safe distance. Fanny raced ahead, eager to make the transaction with the attendant without any assistance from me or her aunt.

I glanced at Jane. This was my first opportunity to speak to her without being overheard. But she kept her head down, as if her mind was on nothing more than dodging the tangled heaps of seaweed that lay across our path.

'I'm sorry I could not be of more use to you last night,' I began. 'It grieved me to see you go off to bed like that.'

'No,' she said, without looking up, 'you helped enormously: you were the voice of sense, the voice of reason.'

This brought me up short. It seemed that she had decided to accept the flimsy explanation I had dreamed up. Her pace quickened as mine slowed. Her very gait conveyed an unwillingness to discuss the matter any further. I stumbled after her, catching up as we reached the bathing machines.

'This is ours!' Fanny cried, stretching out her arm to pat the nose of a chestnut mare with three white socks. 'Her name is Clover and she likes sugar lumps, don't you, Clover?'

Jane and I clambered into the bathing machine while Fanny bribed the horse. Soon we were bumping our way across the beach. Fanny would not sit down. As the wagon lurched into the water she started pulling off her clothes.

'Come on, Aunt Jane! Come on, Miss Sharp! I'll be in the sea *hours* before you if you don't hurry up!'

'The sea is not going anywhere,' Jane replied, 'and if you insist on stripping off while we're still moving you are likely to acquire a most inelegant splinter.'

'No, I won't, for I shan't sit down,' Fanny grinned, casting off her petticoat with a flourish, 'I shall ride into battle standing up, like Boadicea in her chariot!' A moment later she had shed the last stitch of clothing, for those were the days when people still bathed naked in the sea.

'Anna has a black feather down here.' Fanny swept her hand across her thighs. 'Aunt Mary forbade her from swimming in our river – that was mean, was it not?'

'I am sure Aunt Mary had her reasons,' I said, glancing at Jane.

'Anna says the baby made her fat and grumpy and jealous.' Fanny grabbed the side of the wagon as the horse came to a sudden halt.

'Fanny! You really should not repeat such disrespectful...' Before I could get the sentence out she leapt onto the ledge, lifted the canvas and jumped into the water.

Jane shrugged at me and kicked off her shoes. 'It is a pity about Anna,' she said. 'Cass and I had the care of her when her mother died. We adored her, of course, but then James married Mary.' These few words made her feelings quite plain. Jane was on Anna's side: she did not like this new sister-in-law. I was anxious to know how she now felt about her other sister-in-law; whether she had decided to treat last night's discovery as a mere misunderstanding. But I dared not ask.

'Will you help me?' She was on her feet, reaching for the buttons of her dress. As I fumbled with the tiny, muslin-covered things I felt ham-fisted. I could hear Fanny calling, urging us to hurry up, but she sounded very far away. A wave came and the wagon shuddered. For a second I clutched Jane to me, fearing we would both lose our balance. My face brushed her neck and I breathed in the scent of her skin and hair. Then the strangest sensation overtook me. Something slid through my belly like warm treacle down a spoon. I had never felt such a thing before. It was dizzying, bewildering and thrilling and I sensed that it was wrong; that it was not how I was *supposed* to feel. All I knew in that moment was that I felt connected to Jane in a way that I had never felt connected to anyone before.

Another wave rocked the little wagon. The horse gave a snort and pulled at its harness. I heard the woman talking to it, soft and low, as she might coax a sweetheart. The horse settled itself and the sea became calm. Jane smiled as she unpeeled my hands from her arms. The movement sent her dress slipping to the floor. I found myself staring at the white curves of her shoulders. She bid me turn around and I stood, still as a statue, feeling her breath on the back of my neck as her fingers undid my gown.

'I know that you have something you want to tell me,' she whispered. My skin tingled where she touched it. For a brief moment I thought she had read my mind. 'If I seemed ungracious on the beach it was only because there was no time to talk properly. You mustn't hold anything back out of loyalty to Elizabeth.' She brushed aside a lock of my hair that had fallen in her way and I shivered as if someone had stepped upon my grave. 'You are cold,' she said. 'Are you sure you want to go in the sea?'

'I'm not cold – honestly,' I replied, pulling my arms out of my sleeves.

She murmured something inaudible and I turned to see that she was pulling her shift over her head. She stood before me, quite unabashed. I suppose she was used to taking off her clothes in front of her sister but it was the first time that I had seen a woman naked and I fear it must have shown in my eyes.

'Don't be afraid,' she said, mistaking the source of my unease. 'There is nothing you can tell me that can make the misery any worse. Remember – you are not the one who has caused it.'

She stepped forward to help me out of my under clothes. Her face was very close to mine. For a second it was Henry that I saw. Jane must have felt me flinch. She said nothing but took my arm, leading me to the wagon's edge. 'Hold your breath,' she said, 'We'll jump in together.'

Chapter Ten

I still see her as she was that day, her hair glittering with sea spray. She dived beneath the waves, as lithe and sleek as a fish, while I flailed about, not brave enough to follow. I waited agonising minutes then saw her body, pale and green, floating slowly to the surface. She burst from the water with a peal of laughter, beckoning me to swim with her to Fanny, who had already reached the rope at the boundary of the beach.

It was as if Jane had left her cares along with her clothes in the bathing machine. She seemed to have a knack of living in the moment, of shutting out the darkness. I was reminded of what Eliza had said about Henry: about his spirit being too bright to be dimmed for very long. Jane was different, though: she could flame like an ember in the bellows but could not sustain it. The darkness was never far away.

As for me, it was a day of pure joy. I suppose that I, too, was living in the moment, trying not to think of what must follow; for despite Jane's reassuring words I feared that things would be very different when I opened my heart to her. While the water held my body I was free. I was not a skinny beanpole with hands like a man: I was a sea spirit. I was the companion of a mermaid.

By ten o'clock the next morning Fanny and her parents had gone, taking Jane's mother with them.

'What a relief it will be to get back to Bath,' Mrs Austen said as she bid us goodbye, 'This sea air is the ruin of my face! Now, girls, you must all take care to stay indoors when the wind blows. Do you hear?'

We disobeyed her instructions at the first opportunity. After lunch Cassandra went to meet Miss Fielding at the warm baths and Jane and I set off for a walk across the sands.

The weather had turned much colder and the sea spat gobbets of foam at our feet as we made our way along the shoreline. Jane was laughing about her mother, telling me how she refused to go outdoors whenever there was frost on the ground because she believed cold air was what had made her front teeth fall out.

'I did ask how she thought the Eskimos survived. "They must all starve to death," I said, "trying to eat reindeer meat without teeth." But she paid me no heed.'

I laughed with her but I couldn't help feeling that the shield was going up again; that despite what she had said in the bathing machine she was dreading what I might have to tell her.

The wind was blowing so strongly now we had to hold on to our bonnets with both hands. The sea was the colour of slate and the sun sent spears of light through the gathering clouds, turning the air a menacing yellow.

'It's going to rain!' As the wind whipped my words away I felt the first stinging darts upon my face. I glanced back the way we had come but the houses were a distant blur of colours. I looked the other way and spotted a clutch of upturned fishing boats. I pointed and began to run.

I could see a blue-painted hull sticking up at a different angle from the rest. It was propped up on two wooden crates, leaving a small gap for us to scramble under. The shingle beneath it was warm and dry. We crouched for a moment, panting like wet dogs. Then Jane said: 'We really are alone now, aren't we?'

'No one can hear us, at any rate,' I replied, echoing the nervous lightness of her voice, 'and no one can see us, either.'

'I can hardly see *you* in this gloom,' she whispered. 'What are you thinking?'

It was a long moment before I answered. The wind blew blackened fragments of seaweed into our shelter and the rain beat hard over our heads. 'I am thinking of what you want me to say and how loathe I am to tell it,' I said. 'I am thinking of your face as it was two nights ago and how I should feel if I caused that look to return...' I waited but she did not speak. I could not see her eyes, for they were cast in the deepest shadow. 'Do you really want me to go on?'

'Yes, I do.' I felt her fingers on my arm. 'Daylight makes me a coward, you see. Yesterday, in that dark little cocoon above the water, I felt safe. I could allow myself to think of it. And I feel safe here, like a snail coiled up in its shell. Do you think me strange?'

'No,' I said, 'not strange. Just afraid, as anyone would be.'

'But I must know the truth. Please, tell me what you have seen.'

'Well, if you are sure...' I pulled my knees up tight to my chest. 'Before I begin, I must say this: I have seen or heard nothing that would stand up in a court of law as irrefutable proof of wrongdoing. I do not doubt that my testimony would be demolished by any lawyer worth his salt.'

She listened without interruption while I related it all, beginning with the scene on the stairs, then describing the fishing trip and Henry's account of the incident with the buck in Chilham Park.

'I think you underestimate your evidence.' Her voice was unnervingly calm. 'It was a gloved hand you saw round Henry's waist? You are sure of that?'

'Yes,' I said. 'I went over and over it in my mind that night: my eyes might be weak but I am certain they did not deceive me.'

'And the fishing trip: that was around the time of Elizabeth's birthday, wasn't it?'

'It was,' I answered, wondering what direction her thoughts were taking.

'What about the walk to Chilham? Do you remember the date upon which that took place?' Now I guessed where she was going: I didn't want her to make the connection I had made – but how could I withhold the truth when she had expressly asked for it?

'It was some time in February, I think.' This attempt at being vague did me no good.

'Do you mean this year or last?' she said.

'Last year,' I replied.

'Early or late in the month?'

'Around the middle, I think.'

'Louisa.' The name rang out like a shot in our wooden cell. My ribs and stomach contracted. I held my breath, wary of what I had unleashed. 'I wonder how many of the others?' She said it softly, as if she was holding a conversation with herself. 'It could be as many as six out of the nine.'

Although I could not see her face I felt her eyes boring into me, as if the answer to this terrible conundrum could be found inside my head. The boat creaked as the wind changed direction. The rain hammered louder still on its barnacled hull. This was worse, far worse than I had imagined.

'I never could understand why Miss Pearson jilted him; I thought she was jealous of Eliza. But now…' she tailed off with a faint hiss.

I opened my mouth. My tongue was as dry as the shingle beneath me. 'What are you saying?'

'I think that this has been going on for years.' She scooped up a handful of shingle. Broken shells came trickling through her fingers. 'I didn't tell you, did I, that Henry was engaged to someone else before he married Eliza? She was an admiral's daughter. We had seen her miniature and she looked very beautiful. But when I met her I saw that the artist had taken a great many liberties in its execution.' She twisted her knees round to the other side. I could see a little more of her face now. Her eyes were darting over the planks of the boat, as if a scene was painted upon them. 'Henry was with the militia and we hadn't seen much of him for a while. But that summer he was granted leave. He said he wanted the family to meet his new fiancée and of course, we were all dying of curiosity.

'Cass and I were going to stay with Edward and Elizabeth. It was before they had Godmersham – they lived at a place called Rowling – and we thought we could call on Miss Pearson on the way. Edward came to Steventon to collect us but while he was there Henry sent him a letter. It said that we would find him at Rowling when we arrived. We naturally assumed that he had taken Miss Pearson to stay, so that we should not have to go via London to meet her. But he had not.'

'He was there alone? With your sister-in-law?'

'Well, when we arrived, other members of her family were dining at the house. I don't know how long they had been there. Henry seemed as attentive to these relatives as he was to Elizabeth. But on the second day of our visit he took to his bed. He said he felt too unwell to go shooting with Edward and the other men. Elizabeth would often leave us all sewing while she went to see how he did, which was no more than any hostess would do and I thought nothing of it. After a week Henry went off to Great Yarmouth to see the army doctor and we went to London to meet Miss Pearson. Then, two months later, we heard that she had broken the engagement off.'

101

'You think she knew? How could she have found it out?'

'I don't know. What I do know is that nine months after our visit young Henry was born.'

Henry. If she was right about this it was an audacity that beggared belief.

Jane must have known what I was thinking, for she said: 'Of course, Elizabeth has a brother of the same name, so no one thought anything of it.'

'But can it really be true?'

She dropped her head and gave a deep sigh. 'You said that nothing you had seen amounted to proof of wrongdoing: that is exactly what I told myself. As I said to you, Henry has always been a horrible flirt; he can't seem to help it. And I convinced myself that it was *only* flirting; that it didn't mean anything.'

'What makes you so certain that you were wrong? The verses in the card case?'

'If I am honest, I knew before that,' she replied. 'I saw something the same night that you did, on the way back from Canterbury.'

'What did you see?'

'It was just a look, nothing more. He was helping her into the carriage and I was standing nearby, saying goodnight to some friends of Edward's. I turned round and saw them both in profile. There was a lamp directly overhead. I could see their faces quite clearly. There was such ardour in their eyes: it was a look that only lovers would give.'

'But do you really believe that he is capable of...' I quailed at putting it into words. She had conjured up a terrible spectre: a man for whom adultery was a way of life; a man who had betrayed his own brother while making free with his hospitality; a man who was founding a dynasty of bastards with his own sister-in-law.

'I have watched him,' she whispered, 'since I was no older

than Fanny is now. And while I love him best of all my brothers, I have to own that he has always overstepped the boundaries. It is as if he breathes different air from the rest of us and sees the world in different colours.' She closed her eyes and shook her head. 'I am beginning to believe that he is capable of almost anything.'

Chapter Eleven

Jane's ability to live in the moment, to snap out of the blackest of moods in the blink of an eye, was never more apparent than on that bleak September morning. She stuck her hand out from under the boat and announced that the rain had turned to drizzle. Then she stretched out her legs, rubbed them up and down and said:

'Do you like lobster?'

'I have only had it pickled' I said, 'and I could hardly distinguish it from crab.'

'Oh, you have not lived until you have tasted fresh lobster! We had some last year at Lyme and the fisherman who caught them told us the very best way they should be cooked: you tie them to the spit alive, baste them with water and salt, till they look very red then baste them with butter and more salt. Then you put out little dishes of oyster sauce and melted butter, crack open the shells and dip the meat in.'

'That sounds rather cruel,' I said, 'Like burning heretics at the stake.'

'I thought so, too, but the fisherman said that shellfish feel no pain. I asked him in what language they had conveyed this intelligence to him, and for an answer he pinched one on its claw. "There!" he said. "Do you hear him complain?" I'm afraid to say that I allowed my palate to get the better of my brain that day and now the mere memory of the taste deadens all reason. So, come on!' She rolled sideways and squeezed out between the wooden crates. I followed, and emerged with a twig of seaweed sticking out of my bonnet.

She said that we could buy lobster at the other end of the beach but the heavens opened within minutes of leaving the safety of the boat. We raced up the steps to the road and dived under the striped awning of a butcher's shop. We were still far from the promenade with its grand tearooms but we discovered that there was a place above the butcher's where cakes and hot drinks could be bought. Cold and wet as we were we decided this was too tempting a prospect to resist.

The wallpaper was flecked with mildew and the windows were so steamed that we couldn't see the sea. However, the smell of gingerbread and plum cake made up for the dismal surroundings. The girl who served us commented on the rain having driven all the trade away and indeed, we were the only customers she had. When she had gone I took a bite of cake. Jane picked off a corner of hers but did not put it in her mouth. Her eyes were moving restlessly around the room. She picked up her teacup then put it down again.

'Do you think Fanny knows?'

My mouth was full of cake, which prevented an immediate reply. I was glad of it, for it gave me a few seconds to choose my words. 'I'm sure that she does not,' I said, watching her face, 'but sometimes she says things that make me wonder what she's thinking: it's as if she's feeling around in the dark, trying to make sense of her surroundings.'

'I've thought that, too,' she said. 'What sort of things has she said to you?'

'Oh, nothing of any real consequence.' I told her about the

entries in the diary and the comments she had made about Henry's clothes on the day of the ball. 'She's not a child any more, Jane: she's beginning to notice things. She loves her uncle and she loves her papa; she loves her mother above everyone and wishes to be like her in every way. I think that it perplexes her.'

'And the older she becomes the more she will understand.' Jane raised her cup to her lips and stared into it before drinking. 'She reminds me so much of myself, you know. I can remember exactly how I felt, watching Henry and Eliza that first Christmas at Steventon. It was like stealing sweetmeats: I knew I was in on something wrong but I found it absolutely compelling. Sometimes I would be in a room where they were rehearsing a scene from a play. The directions would require him to strike some pose or place his hand upon his heart and she would come behind him, wrapping her arms around him as she corrected his posture or clasping her hand over his to emphasise the move. I would watch his face, see the flash of desire in his eyes and the colour rising from his neck to his cheeks. I saw the power she had over him and the thrill it gave her to enslave him…' she trailed off with a small, hopeless shake of her head.

'Do you think that Henry and she were…' I glanced at the steamed-up window. 'You said he was only fifteen…and she was still married to the Comte…'

'I don't know.' She gave a small sigh and sipped her tea. 'Eliza has always been wild. She never allows anything or anybody to control her. Her cardinal rule is that a woman may do as she pleases as long as she is discreet. She told me this herself when I was sixteen years old.'

I thought of the woman who had received me in the gilded salon; of her undimmed beauty and her apparent disinterest in the comings and goings of her husband. Yes, I could easily imagine this woman seducing a handsome boy. Had she made

Henry into the kind of man he now was? Had he learned from her example?

'There's something I don't understand,' I said. 'If, as you say you now believe, Henry fell in love with your sister-in-law before he married your cousin, why did he marry her? Why would he marry anyone?'

'For her money, of course.' Jane put down her cup and looked directly at me. 'He wanted the means to go into business and she offered it. It wasn't only that, I admit: there always was passion between them. But it wasn't the incandescent passion of that earlier time.'

'So why did she agree to it? Surely not just for the sake of providing a father for her son?'

She shook her head. 'She could have managed without Henry: she had Madame Bigeon, who was absolutely devoted to the boy. The fact is that she, too, was in need of money. When Henry came to see her to tell her about his broken engagement to Miss Pearson she'd been trying to get at the ten thousand pounds her godfather had put in trust for her. But there was an obstacle in her way.'

'What obstacle?'

'My father, to put it bluntly. He was one of two trustees Warren Hastings had appointed to manage the fund. When Eliza wrote to ask for it to be made over to her, she got a letter back saying that it couldn't be done.' She broke off a piece of plum cake and popped it in her mouth. 'He pointed out that there was no absolute proof that her husband had met his death at the guillotine; that it had only been reported by the despots who ruled France at the time. "What if her husband should turn up one day and demand the money himself?" my father wanted to know. "We would be bound by law to pay it out again and where would that leave us?"'

'Yes, I see,' I said. 'So what did Eliza do?'

'She went to see my father and told him she only wanted

the money for Henry's sake. She said that they wished to marry and she wanted to set him up in business. Of course, it worked like a charm. My father forgot his objections and once he had signed the paper, the other trustee fell in line. Within a fortnight the money was hers. She and Henry were married a few weeks later by special license.'

'And Henry told you all this?' I was torn between admiration for the boldness of this scheme and distaste for the cool, calculated bargaining it had required.

'No he did not,' she said. 'My father told me. I was at home when Eliza came to see him. I was the only one there because Mama and Cass were visiting James and Mary. Eliza was so unlike her usual self that I knew something was up. When she'd gone I wheedled it out of him. He made me swear not to say a word until the marriage had taken place.

'Why not?'

'Because my mother didn't approve. She knew Eliza could never give Henry a child and she thought it a sad thing; a waste, she called it.'

'Knew?' I said, reaching for my tea, which was by now lukewarm. 'How?'

Jane hesitated a moment before replying in a whisper: 'Eliza had a miscarriage. It happened just after her mother died, when her husband came over from France for the funeral. He took her to Bath for a holiday which, according to her, was a disaster because they hardly knew one another after all that time. Then he had to return very suddenly because his lands were under threat. She found out she was pregnant but within three months she lost the child. She was staying with us at Steventon when it happened. The doctor said she must never try to have another because the consequences would probably be fatal.'

'Oh!' The implications of this were horribly clear. Henry had entered into the bargain in the full knowledge that no children could result from his union with Eliza. The world of marriage was a foreign country to me, but the scanty knowledge I possessed was enough to grasp the fact that Eliza's condition was unlikely to bring about conjugal felicity. 'How long after the...' I broke off, trying to find a polite way to put it. 'That business with Miss Pearson,' I said, 'how long afterward did the marriage take place?'

'I know what you are thinking.' She closed her eyes with a small shudder. 'Elizabeth gave birth to little Henry in May 1797: Eliza came to see my father in the middle of August that year.'

So if Jane's suspicions were correct, Henry had already known that he was a father when Eliza came up with her proposal. 'Much easier, then, for Henry to agree to it...' I said.

The creaking of the treads on the staircase prevented any further speculation. The girl who had served us appeared round the door, wanting to know if we required more tea. When we said that we did not, she gave us a look that said: *Well, hurry up and go, then.* She stood in a corner after that, folding napkins and sorting cutlery with an accompaniment of loud sighs, which soon brought about the desired result.

We stepped outside into weak, watery sunlight. The quest for a lobster was resumed and before long we found a fisherman who sold them. I tried not to look at the squirming creatures in the weed-strewn crate as Jane stood bartering over the price. I heard the snap of rubber as the bargain was made. Wrapped in newspaper, the lobster continued to wriggle all the way back to the house. Jane talked to it from time to time. She urged it to stop struggling and enjoy the last few minutes of its life in peaceful repose; when it refused she peeled back the newspaper, held the creature out before her and began to recite Gray's *Elegy*. By the end of the second verse it had entered a state of relative torpor. 'There,' she whispered, tucking it back under her arm, 'I knew it would work: I use it on my mother when she's irksome – it always sends her to sleep.'

I had a vision of the two of them sitting by the fire on a cold winter's night in their lodgings in Bath. Mrs Austen would be stitching patchwork while holding forth on some well-worn topic, such as the dearth of eligible young men at last season's balls, or the shocking display of naked bosoms occasioned by the latest London fashion. Jane would slyly reach for the poetry book and ask her mother if she cared to be read to while she sewed. Gray's wheeling beetles and drowsy tinklings would act upon Mrs A. like a dose of laudanum, sending the patchwork slipping from her lap as she drifted into sonorous slumber.

'Come on,' Jane said, hooking her free arm through mine, 'let's get him home before he wakes.'

I took to my room while she cooked the lobster – something she insisted on doing herself, despite protests from the cook – and though I cringed at the idea of eating the trembling, whiskery thing, the smell came wafting up the stairs to tempt me. It was every bit as delicious as she had predicted.

'Now,' she said, as we wiped our fingers, 'you are my partner in crime. I have committed murder and you have helped me eat the evidence. How do you plead?'

'Guilty,' I said, returning her wry smile.

'For which the appropriate sentence must be imposed.' She reached for a clean napkin and set it upon her head. 'It must be death, of course. Though there are some would say that hanging is too good for you; that you should be dispatched in the same manner as the hapless victim. What say you to that?'

I thought for a moment. 'I would do as you do – that is, I would resort to poetry in my hour of need. Not Mr Gray's verses, I think, but Mr Donne's:

"Death be not proud, tho' some have called thee
 Mighty and dreadful, for thou art not so,
 For those whom thou think'st thou dost overthrow,
 Die not, poor death, nor yet canst thou kill me.'"

'Bravo!' Jane cast off her judge's cap with a flourish, catching sight as she did so of a familiar face through the window. 'My sister returns.' Her face clouded. 'You won't repeat any of the conversation we had this morning, will you? Please, promise me that you will not speak of it.' She took my hand in both of hers and clasped it to her. I felt that strange, warm liquefying of my insides again. It startled me. I withdrew my hand, nodding as I did so.

'It would destroy Cass if she knew,' Jane hissed. 'She has attended the birth of seven of those—' she broke off at the clanging of the doorbell.

'Of course I won't speak of it,' I whispered back. 'She will never hear it from me.'

Cassandra stepped into the room, her face rosy from the steaming heat of the warm baths. Jane's mask was on in a trice. She demanded a description of the bodies on display at the baths and Cassandra laughingly obliged with details of the fattest and the ugliest.

As I watched them I wondered how long the awful secret could be kept from the rest of the family. I was thinking of Fanny, growing older and more knowing with every passing day. By this time tomorrow, I thought, she will be back at Godmersham; she will wave her father goodbye and see her mother's smiles as Henry rides into the courtyard a few hours later. How long will it be before she works out what is really going on? That it is not just her father's guns he is keeping warm when he comes for a week's shooting?

A few days later a letter came for me from Fanny. It was mostly about her pets and the fact that baby Louisa had just

111

taken her first steps. But a couple of paragraphs gave me cause for concern:

The weather was vile yesterday and I was so very dull without you. Uncle Henry came today, though, and he cheered me up by sending me off to Canterbury with money for a new dress. Sayce was going anyway to collect a length of jaconet for Mama, so I went with her in the carriage. The shops were very gay and it took me a long time to decide what to buy. In the end I chose a figured dimity cloth in a shade called wild rose.

It was nearly dark when we got back and it took me ages to find Uncle Henry to show him what I'd bought. It turned out he was fast asleep in his chamber. My knocking woke him up and when he opened the door his face was all sweaty, like someone with a fever. I asked him if he was ill and he replied that he had taken to his bed feeling rather unwell. Mama was looking after him, though. She brought a jug of water and some towels from his dressing room and bathed his forehead. He was quite all right by dinnertime.

I didn't show the letter to Jane. Fanny wrote a joint letter to her aunts a few days later but there was no reference to the visit from Henry. This I knew because Cass read the letter aloud to Jane at breakfast. Why had Fanny told me about her uncle's visit but kept her aunts in ignorance about it? Was this a veiled appeal for help? Had she already guessed what was going on? It dawned on me that to her, I was the only person who *could* help; the only person she trusted who was not a member of the family. Of course, she couldn't know what the consequences of my intervention were likely to be.

I wrestled with my conscience for a long time. What was more important: to lose my post or protect Fanny? Either way the child was likely to suffer. And what of my own sufferings if I was cast out of Godmersham? I had nowhere to go and no more than a few shillings to my name.

After a few days something like a plan began to form in my mind. I reasoned that Henry loved his niece and would be horrified by any suggestion that he was hurting her. If I could somehow get him alone, appeal to that kinder, softer side I knew he possessed, perhaps I could make him see what damage he was doing. I would be taking a huge risk in confronting him with what I suspected but I clung to the belief that he was, at heart, an honourable man who, if he could not stop what he was doing, would at least see the wisdom in behaving more discreetly.

Jane never knew of this plan. I decided I had more chance of success with Henry if I could assure him that no one else was party to it. Perhaps that was naive; perhaps I should have realised that secrets of such magnitude cannot be boxed up and forgotten. Perhaps we should have gone together to confront him. Would it have made a difference to the awful events that followed? That is something I try not to contemplate, for I can never know the answer.

Chapter Twelve

Those next few weeks passed too quickly for me. Jane never once alluded to what we had discussed beneath the boat. What I had failed to grasp thus far was that a person whose tongue could be so sharp could inhabit a skin so thin. I didn't fully understand this until she sent me, some nine years later, the first edition of *Mansfield Park*. 'Let other pens dwell on guilt and misery,' she wrote in the final chapter, 'I quit such odious subjects as soon as I can…' It was the chapter that reported the adultery of a married woman with a man named Henry. What her family made of that I cannot know, but I believe the book was a way of releasing the pent up rage she felt at what she believed her brother had done. I do not think that rage is too strong a word, although no one would have guessed it that autumn at Worthing.

In the middle of October, when the mornings misted up my bedroom window, Martha Lloyd, maker of potions, came to join us for the last fortnight of our holiday. Jane told me that Martha's mother had died earlier in the year, an event which had left her homeless as well as bereaved. It had been decided that Martha would join Jane, Cassandra and their mother as a fourth member of their household in Bath, bringing a small income which would help pay the rent.

In looks and character Martha reminded me very much of Madame Bigeon. She was small and round and very solicitous; a person whose sole concern seemed to be the comfort of others. She was ten years older than Jane but this made no difference to their affinity for one another. I might have been jealous but it was impossible to bear such a woman any malice.

'Her sister is closer to me in age,' Jane told me while Martha was unpacking her trunk, 'But I like Martha much better. She is like us: she loves books. Mary thinks reading is a waste of time: she would far rather count James' money than look at his sermons.'

Although I was a stranger, Martha treated me with as much regard as her two friends. When I told her that Jane had made me a wash for my eyes from her book of remedies, she took my face in her hands and studied it closely. 'Your eyes look much recovered but your lips are a little cracked. Are they sore?'

'Yes,' I said, 'the sea air has not been kind to them.'

'I will make you a salve, if you like,' she said. 'Is there an apothecary in Worthing? I need alkanet root; the other ingredients I think I will find in the kitchen.'

I watched her later as she busied herself in the kitchen, gathering butter, beeswax and claret to boil over the fire. As she reached for the pestle and mortar she turned to me and said: 'Is Jane happy, do you think?'

'Well, I think so...' I hesitated, wondering what had prompted this. 'Certainly she has been enjoying the holiday in Worthing.' I paused for a moment, watching her deft movements as she peeled the alkanet root. 'Do you have reason to think she may be unhappy?' I ventured. 'Apart from the loss of her father, I mean?'

'I know that she hates living in Bath,' Martha replied

115

without looking up, 'and that she dreads returning. She has never really settled since she left Steventon, you know, and that was five years ago.'

'Oh?' I said, 'She never told me that she hated it; I would have thought it a most enlivening place to live, judging from the tales she tells about the balls and the card parties and the gatherings in the Pump Room.'

'I think that is her way of making it bearable.' Martha sliced up the root and dropped the pieces into the mortar. 'She despises most of the people she meets there. She would go back to Hampshire in a moment if she was able.'

'She always talks of her old home with great affection,' I said. 'Why did they leave it?'

'Her father decided it was time that he retired. Her mother has relatives in Bath and it is thought to be a good place for husband-hunting.' She glanced at me, eyebrows raised. I wondered if this was the real reason for Jane's dislike of the place. Perhaps she had fallen in with her parents' plans only to be disappointed in her expectation of a marriage proposal. 'I was with her when her parents gave her the news,' Martha went on. 'She had been staying with me and we returned to the rectory just before Christmas. No sooner had we crossed the threshold than her mother said: "Well, girls, it is all settled: we have decided to leave Steventon and go to Bath." Jane was so shocked she actually fainted on the spot.'

I would never have imagined Jane to be a person prone to fainting fits; she seemed far too robust a character for that. But, as I have said, I was still getting to know her. There was no doubt that I underestimated her sensibility.

Martha pounded the alkanet until it bled white juice. 'What made it all much worse was that my sister and her husband moved into the rectory,' she said. 'James was the curate at Deane but as soon as his father retired he was entitled to the living at Steventon. Jane's parents insisted on selling nearly

116

everything in the house and what didn't sell was given to James and Mary.' She shook the contents of the mortar into the pan. 'Jane thought this terribly unfair,' she went on, spooning in the beeswax and the butter. 'Although Mary is my own sister I couldn't help but agree. I remember the week we spent sorting through all the books in her father's library: there were close on five hundred volumes and James got most of them for a pittance. Jane was absolutely furious.' She poured a pint of claret into the pan and stirred it over the heat. 'That same month was James and Mary's wedding anniversary. They invited Jane to join the celebration but she refused to go.'

A bittersweet aroma wafted from the pan. I pictured Jane, seething at the injustice of leaving her childhood home and all the old familiar things that were so dear to her. It reminded me of my own anguish when the bailiffs had arrived on the doorstep. I wondered how she had managed to remain on civil terms with her eldest brother and his wife. For the sake of her niece, perhaps, I thought. To Martha I said: 'Little Anna is a lovely child; her aunt is very fond of her, I think.'

'Oh, yes,' she replied. 'She and Cassandra were like mothers to her when she was small. It has been difficult for her, learning to love a new mama and sharing her father with a new brother and sister.'

'And how does your sister and her baby? Both are well, I hope?' I found it hard to visualise this sister of Martha's: her disdain for books, her love of money, her bitter jealousy of Eliza and her coldness to Anna – these traits all warred with the sunny image of a new mother nursing her baby.

'Very well, thank you.' She took the pot off the stove and poured the steaming contents into a muslin bag set over a bowl. 'She won't be having any more children, though: she managed a space of seven years between James-Edward and Caroline and she says that two is quite enough.'

I wondered how she could prevent it, short of turning her

117

husband out of the marriage bed for good, for how else could she be so sure of avoiding the pains and perils of childbirth a third time? As I watched Martha squeezing the muslin bag to extract the last precious drops of her concoction another possibility occurred to me. I had heard of women taking all manner of things to prevent or terminate a pregnancy: was Martha the source of her sister's confidence?

'What's this witches' brew, Martha?' It was Jane, peering round the door with her nose in the air, sniffing loudly. 'Are you teaching Miss Sharp the black arts?'

'Not exactly,' Martha smiled, setting the bowl to the window sill and lifting the latch. 'I am making her a salve for her lips. Would you like some?'

'Not if it contains hen's dung or boar's grease: I shouldn't like either of those on my lips, thank you.' Jane tugged at her friend's apron strings as she turned round. Martha was transformed into a ship in full sail as the calico billowed out in the draught from the window. She took a swipe at Jane, who ducked away, grinning. 'Gracious, what a colour!' Jane was now bending over the dark, congealing liquid in the bowl. 'I declare that you mean to turn my friend into a ruby-lipped temptress!'

Martha gave a small sigh and smoothed down her apron. 'It is not so red when it is rubbed in,' she said. 'If you don't want any I shall pack up two pots for Miss Sharp to take back for Elizabeth and Fanny.'

With a heavy heart I remembered that it was less than a week before I was due to return to Godmersham. The happy anticipation I would naturally have felt at being reunited with Fanny was muted by apprehension at the thought of confronting Henry. I wondered if he would be there when I returned. I hoped that he would not. I found myself willing something to happen, some event of such moment that it would end the affair without my intervention.

I must have shuddered at the thought of what lay ahead, for Jane reached across to close the window. 'I think it will set all right now,' she said to Martha. 'And I *will* have some, if you please. I'm sure Cass has need of a pot, too, so there won't be any left to send to Godmersham, will there?'

On the day that Jane and I were to part I woke up with a start. I'd been dreaming of the time we sat on the riverbank at Godmersham, cocooned in the branches of the weeping willow. She had the bowl of strawberries in her lap. I watched as she bit into one, swallowing half then reaching towards me, smearing my lips with what was left. Suddenly the willow leaves parted and Henry materialised, a knowing smile on his face. *This is the ruby-lipped temptress*, he hissed, stepping aside to let Elizabeth see my stained mouth.

My eyes snapped open and I threw off the covers, my skin hot and sticky. I stared at the familiar objects on the dressing table. Everything looked grey. I suppose it was the wintry dawn light filtering through the blind that made them so. But it looked as though my body had put out tongues of flame as I slept, turning everything to ashes.

I was ashamed of the dream, I suppose. It stirred up the same feelings of guilt and confusion I had experienced in the bathing machine. Jane and I had known each other only four months; less than half a year; and yet I dreaded the thought of being without her. I tried to pick my feelings apart. Was it the shared secret of Henry and Elizabeth that had brought us so close? *No*, my heart answered, *you know it's more than that*. But I struggled to name what lay at the root of the strange kind of longing she provoked in me.

Later that morning, when our trunks were packed in separate coaches, I hovered on the steps like an awkward child. 'You will come and visit us in Bath, won't you?' She went to kiss me goodbye and I tensed as her lips brushed my cheek, half afraid to kiss her back. 'I'm going to write to you as soon as I get home.' This last was said with a determined nod and an inflection of the eyebrows. What was I to read into it? Was she trying to convey feelings similar to my own; feelings she couldn't express in front of Martha and Cassandra? Or was it something more prosaic: that she was relying on me to act as her spy in the coming months?

Martha was my travelling companion on the journey home. She was to accompany me as far as Rye, where she had arranged to stay for a few days with an old friend of her mother's before travelling home to Bath. I was glad of her presence, for my heart felt like a lead weight as I clambered into the carriage.

She did not mention Jane at all in the first hour or so of the journey and I wondered if she had guessed how downcast I felt and was trying to distract me from the cause of it. But suddenly she leaned across the space between us and touched my hand with hers.

'You are like me, my dear, aren't you?' Her eyes, small and brown, darted over my face. She had the penetrating look of a bird searching for a worm. I felt a ripple of fear. What did she mean? Had she read my mind and recognised herself on its pages? Did she harbour the same guilty longing for Jane that I did?

Seeing my consternation she gave a small sigh. 'I thought as much. You have lost your parents and your home, haven't you? Just as I have. I know how wretched that feels.'

My shoulders and my spine sank into the velvet back of the seat. I nodded in dumb relief, which she mistook for suppressed anguish and clasped my hand tighter, telling me to cry if I felt like it, for there was no one but herself to hear. This made me feel doubly guilty. I said that it was all right; I had cried enough tears to flood the Thames when my parents died.

'Can you talk about it?' she asked.

I shook my head and told her it still pained me to recall it. I asked what it had been like for her and after a slight hesitation she said that if it had not been for Jane and Cass she would certainly have killed herself.

'I had the means to do it,' she whispered, looking not at me now but out of the window at Pevensey Bay, where the wind whipped white horses across a charcoal sea. 'I walked out into the woods the morning my mother died and I picked enough Friar's Cap to send a whole village to sleep.'

I watched her face. Her eyes no longer had that sharp, birdlike expression; they were clouded with invisible images that overlaid the sea and sky and the gulls swooping past the carriage window. 'I slept in a chair that night beside Mama's body. The notice to quit the house had been delivered while I was out in the woods. I decided I would take the draught as soon as the funeral was over and Mary returned to Steventon. I had written a letter explaining it all. But as I walked to the post office there was Jane stepping down from the mail coach. She said she'd come to fetch me: to take me home.'

I murmured something like: 'What a blessing,' or some such inadequate remark. I couldn't help wondering why Martha's own sister had not offered to take her in. How awful, I thought, that this poor woman would have killed herself if Jane had not come to her rescue.

'Did you never think of it?' Martha turned her eyes on me. They were filmy with tears that she blinked away.

'No, I did not.' I heard the surprise in my own voice as I answered. It was true: in all the anguish that followed my father's death, all the horror of losing home and possessions, it had never crossed my mind that I would be better off dead. Now I asked myself what instinct had prevented such a possibility forming in my mind. Perhaps it was only that I knew of no quick or painless method of achieving it. Throwing myself in the Thames would, I suppose, have been the most obvious choice – but that might not have been quick; indeed, it might not have worked at all. What if I had had the kind of knowledge Martha possessed, though? Would I have swallowed poison as the bailiffs battered at the door?

'I'm glad of that.' Martha gave a wan smile. 'It's a wicked thing to contemplate. There is so much joy to be found in life; in other people.'

'Yes,' I said, 'though in the darkest times that can be hard to remember.' I was thinking of Jane as I said it; remembering how it felt when her hair touched my skin in the shadowy warmth of the hut with its wheels in the sea. Her parting words echoed in my head as the coach rattled through the streets of Rye and shuddered to a stop at the market cross.

Before she bade me farewell Martha said: 'Jane sets great store by your judgment, you know. She says she never came across anyone so aptly named as you.'

I feasted on this crumb of comfort as the coach trundled across the boundary between Sussex and Kent. Gratifying as it was to hear that Jane valued my intellect, it was adoration, not admiration that I craved. That much at least I knew.

As we drove through Ashford I realised that I must try to put Jane out of my mind and focus on what awaited me. I was longing to see Fanny, who had written half a dozen letters to me while I was away. Plainly she was bored. I wondered how she had been passing the days, with the three eldest boys away at school and only the little ones for company.

When the carriage bowled up the drive she came running out to greet me, despite the fact that it was nearly dark. Before I could step inside the house she dragged me off to see the new pets she had acquired in my absence. These were two young badgers, tumbling about like a pair of prize-fighters in a straw-lined box in a corner of the stables.

'Uncle Henry found them,' she said, plucking one out and

holding it up to my face. 'Can you see? Their mother was attacked by dogs. He brought them home in his hat.' She looked at me with big, earnest eyes. 'If they were left on their own they would die because they're not old enough to find their own food. I've been giving them bread and milk and Uncle Henry says I must dig up worms for them. He wants me to look after them until he comes back, then we're going to release them.'

'Oh,' I said, putting out my hand to stroke the wriggling creature, 'When did Uncle Henry find them?'

'Last Friday,' she replied. 'He was keeping Mama company till Papa came back from Chawton.'

She was looking at the badger cub, not at me, so I couldn't read her eyes as she said this. 'When will Uncle Henry return?' I asked her.

'After Christmas, I think,' she replied.

So, I had six weeks at least in which to plan my little speech; six weeks in which to fret over the right way to appeal to a man engaged in something so very far from my own experience that I struggled to put myself in his shoes. Whenever I tried to imagine him pining after Elizabeth I saw Jane's face, not his, in my mind's eye. I saw her walking through the streets of Bath – streets that I had never seen, only fancied – and then I would spy my own self, running behind her but never quite catching her up. This scene would come back to me in dreams, where I would be calling her name but no sound would come from my lips. When I awoke my heart would be hammering at my ribs and I would lie awake for ages afterward, wondering if she ever dreamed about me.

Chapter Thirteen

A s Christmas approached I tried to carry on as I had before the summer. My days were busy enough, teaching Fanny, helping Sackree with the younger children when she was tired and sometimes, if a servant was ill or absent, performing sundry duties about the house. My new spectacles meant that I could, once again, fill my evenings with reading. But nothing was the same. Jane's presence had sweetened my life like sugar in tea and now I must always feel the want of it.

'Bath is every bit as grey and dispiriting as I left it,' she wrote, a few days after our separation. We drove back in a fog that lingers in the streets like wet cobwebs. I ventured out yesterday to find the pastry shop in Milsom Street full of fat old men with crumbs in their whiskers. The widows, meanwhile, were devouring all manner of confections, concealing the act of mastication behind open fans. It is not their gluttony that shames them: they do it merely to conceal their rotten teeth. Mama may be similarly afflicted – having lost both teeth and husband – but you would never catch her simpering in pastry shops with a mouth full of lemon tart.'

With such delightful snippets she buoyed me up. But

beyond wishing I could see what she described for myself she expressed none of the longing I felt for her. I tried to keep my replies light, with no mention of my feelings – or of the forthcoming visit from Henry. She may have known of his plans but if she did she made no reference to him.

On the day before the solstice, when the servants brought the holly and ivy into the house, Fanny announced that her badgers had grown too fat for their box. 'I must build them a run,' she said. 'Will you help me? If Uncle Henry sees how squashed they are he will be cross. We have a se'nnight – do you think that's enough time?'

'Yes,' I said, aware of my heart quickening. In seven days it would be the twenty-seventh of December: Edward and Elizabeth's wedding anniversary. They were sure to hold a special celebration, as they had last year. Was Henry really planning to come on that day of all days? Was he really so careless of his brother's feelings that he would trespass on a day so sacred? And what of Eliza? What on earth must she make of this, I wondered? Unless, of course, he was planning to bring her too.

'Will Aunt Eliza be coming this time?' I reached out to stroke one of the badgers as I said it, trying to appear unconcerned.

'Aunt Eliza?' Fanny gave me a look of the utmost incredulity. 'How? She can only breathe London air – didn't you know that?'

'Oh, that's what Uncle Henry says, is it?' I had to smile, although there really was nothing to smile about.

'Not just him: Mama says it too. And Papa. I've heard both of them say that Aunt Eliza starts to sneeze the minute she crosses the Thames.'

I was not sure if this was a real ailment or some longstanding family joke. Whichever it was, it served Henry's purpose only too well. It occurred to me, as we crouched over

125

the furry bundles in the stable, that I could use it for my purpose too. I had been racking my brains for a way of initiating the conversation I meant to have with Henry: this would provide me with just the pretext that I needed.

Henry did not come on the day of the anniversary: he arrived at eight o'clock the morning after. This seemed to me to be so lacking in any kind of subtlety that I wondered Edward did not mark it. If he failed to, however, his daughter did not. She came to find me in my room, where I was to pass the day sewing and reading while the family continued their yuletide festivities.

'Uncle Henry must have set off when Aunt Eliza was still asleep,' she said. 'Do you think she minds him leaving her all alone in London when everybody else is enjoying themselves?'

I cast about for a suitable answer but could find none. I pretended to concentrate on threading my bodkin.

'Mama says Aunt Eliza loans him out like they do with the books in the circulating library at Ashford.'

The piece of thread I was moistening flew out of my mouth.

'What's the matter?' Her face was as straight as the needle in my fingers. 'Did I say something wrong?'

I couldn't decide if her expression was a mask of innocence or the real thing. Was she testing me out? Seeking confirmation of what she herself suspected? Or was she just a trusting little girl, repeating the words of her mother without reading anything into them? 'It seems a funny thing,' I said, 'to compare Uncle Henry to a book. What do you think he would say to that? Would it make him smile, do you think?'

'Well, I don't know,' she frowned. 'With a book that you borrow, you read it and give it back, don't you? You don't keep taking the same one out over and over again.'

'That is quite right, Fanny. We should find a better simile, shouldn't we? Let me see: if Uncle Henry was something other than a person, what would he be?'

She looked at me very solemnly for a moment. 'I think that he would be a cuckoo,' she said, 'because he likes our nest better than his own.' Without pausing for breath she bobbed down to kiss me on the cheek. 'I've got to go now: Grandmama Bridges wants me to play cards with her.'

She left me to my sewing, which I cast aside, too agitated to concentrate. If the things Jane and I had speculated about beneath the boat at Worthing were correct, Fanny's cuckoo analogy was bitingly accurate. Was this just a coincidence? Or had she been thinking along the same lines as me and her aunt? My resolve in the matter of tackling Henry – which had wavered in the weeks of his absence – was suddenly strengthened. Fanny's young mind was *my* responsibility: how could I stand by and watch this deceit take root in it?

It began to snow just after midday and Elizabeth's mother and younger sisters were forced to depart early for fear of their carriage becoming stuck in a drift on the way home. Edward took to bed after dinner with one of his increasingly frequent attacks of the gout and Elizabeth was called up to the nursery to sit with Louisa, who had chicken pox and would allow none but her mama to dab lotion onto the pustules. The older children took advantage of this distraction to scurry off to the stables to make sure that the badgers were cosy for what promised to be a bitter night ahead.

I saw Henry heading for the library and I decided to follow him. There were two fires burning in the long, lofty room and the curtains had been drawn against the twilight. On one of the tables at the far end a candelabra cast a pool of yellow light. Of Henry there was neither sight nor sound, until the soft thud of a book being closed up told me that he was behind a row of shelves that jutted out from the wall between the two farthest windows.

'Hello?' I called. My voice sounded very small in that

enormous room.

'Miss Sharp!' He emerged from the bookshelves with his hand shielding a single candle. The light threw deep shadows onto his face, distorting his smile and making him look much older. 'I'm sorry if I frightened you – did you think I was an intruder?'

'No,' I replied, thinking how appropriate was the word he had unwittingly used. I must not forget, I thought, that his presence in this house *is* an intrusion of the worst possible kind; I must not allow myself to be won over by his charm. 'Actually,' I lied, 'I thought one of the children might have strayed in here.'

'No,' he said, setting down the candle on the nearest table, 'there is nobody here but me, more's the pity. I was hoping to read *A Winter's Tale* to them all tonight but there is no one left to hear it.'

'Yes, it is a pity,' I agreed, desperate to recall the opening line I had rehearsed a hundred times. 'You…I mean your…er, *wife*…' My tongue tripped on the word. 'She…she was so gracious to me. When I stayed at your house, I mean…but Fanny tells me she is not well enough to accompany you: I am sorry to hear it.'

Deep frown lines appeared on his forehead. 'Not well? She was quite well when I left her.'

'Fanny said that she was unable to breathe the air here,' I went on, attempting a tone of innocent enquiry, 'She said that it would make your wife sneeze.'

'Oh! That old joke!' A black chasm opened in his face as he chuckled. 'Poor little Fanny takes everything so seriously!'

He had fallen right into the trap that I had fumblingly succeeded in setting. 'Yes,' I said, 'She does, doesn't she? Sometimes it's quite harmless to tell her half-truths but there are other things she really shouldn't know about.'

'What do you mean?' I heard the change in his voice. His

eyes glinted in the flickering light. I kept silent, hoping to increase his unease by making him wait for an answer. 'What should she *not* know about?' His voice sounded very loud in the quiet, book lined room.

'I think you know very well what I mean,' I said softly.

'Madam, I assure you I do not!' I felt his breath on my face. 'Explain yourself, I pray you!'

'Very well, I will spell it out if I must.' I was glad he could not see me very clearly, for I felt my limbs begin to tremble. 'Fanny showed me a note she found in her mama's card case.' I watched his face as the lie unfolded. 'She recognised the hand as yours and she wanted to know what it meant.' I paused for a moment to give my next sentence all the punch that it required: 'It was an extract from the "Song of Solomon": the words of a lover to his mistress.'

'Oh.' It was a small sound, like the useless puff of a pair of broken bellows. The fire nearest to us crackled and spat. The wind whipped the skeleton fingers of a bush against the window. In this broken silence I could almost hear Henry's brain grasping for some excuse, for some innocent explanation of the damning evidence I had presented.

'I'm afraid that you – and she – have fallen victim to another of our family jokes.' He pulled out a chair and sat down heavily. 'Elizabeth and I have perhaps allowed it to go too far but we are guilty of nothing more than that, I can assure you.'

'A joke?' The contents of my stomach turned to ice.

'Yes,' he said, 'It's been going on for as long as I can remember: a sort of game in which we try to outdo each other in finding the most obscure and inappropriate quotations to send to one another. It has amused us very much in the past but I can see, now, how easily it could be misinterpreted.'

I told myself that he must be lying; that such a game could not be concocted by innocent minds. But he said it with such conviction, with such a look on his face… *Oh God*, I thought, *have I got this all wrong?*

No, you have not. It was Jane's voice that replied. I saw her with my mind's eye, sifting the shingle through her fingers, telling me what she had seen on the night of the Canterbury ball.

Henry shifted in his seat. 'Tell me something: you and my sister Jane are very close, are you not? Have you spoken any word of this to her?'

'No, sir, I have not.' I clenched every muscle in my body, praying that I might convince him. 'She was not here when the note was found.' That at least was not a lie, I told myself.

'Very good,' he said, rising up again. 'We shall say no more about it tonight. But I would ask you to consider very carefully what I have said to you: consider it very carefully indeed. And now you must excuse me.' The smile he gave was no different to the one he had greeted me with at the start of the encounter. Like the sister whose features he shared, he was adept at putting on a mask. 'Goodnight, Miss Sharp.'

He took the candelabra from the table, leaving me nothing but the one guttering stub of candle and the glow of the coals to lighten the darkness. My legs suddenly gave way like saplings in a gale and I grasped the edge of the table for support. He had made it sound so plausible. Could Jane and I *both* have imagined what our eyes and our instincts told us? *How I wish that you were with me.* The breath my words drew forth put out the candle. Now there was only the fire. It flared and spat as the wind gusted down the chimney. *Stupid, stupid*, it hissed.

When I woke from fitful sleep in the grey light of the morning he had gone. The snow had not prevented him from riding his horse through the park to the Canterbury road. Fanny said she had heard the grooms talking when she went to see to her badgers. Apparently, Henry had been warned not to make the

130

journey but had ignored their advice. I was glad that I would not have to face him but I shuddered to think that I might now have his death on my conscience.

I did not have long to dwell on this thought, however, as I was summoned to Elizabeth's parlour soon after breakfast. I should have guessed what was coming but, stupidly, I did not. As I entered the room she gave me a look as cold as the north-east wind.

'I understand that you have been interfering in matters you have no right to interfere in.' She leaned forward like a cat about to pounce. I stood absolutely still, paralysed by the dawning horror of my situation. 'How dare you accuse my brother-in-law of such...' she tailed off, her icy eyes piercing mine. 'How dare you suggest that I—' She brought down her fist, sending tea cascading over the sides of the Wedgwood cup on the table beside her. 'What would Fanny say if she knew what evil, twisted thoughts her governess harboured?'

'I beg your pardon, ma'am, but it was for Fanny's sake that I spoke out.' My voice squeezed out of my chest as weak and puny as a newborn lamb.

'For Fanny's sake? For your own profit, more like! How much were you planning to extort from my husband's brother for this piece of wickedness?'

'Pray you, listen to me ma'am...you have it all wrong! I only—'

'You only what?' She cut me short. 'You only thought that you could get away with blackmail! And Henry, who has been so kind to you – who has put you up in his own home, no less – seemed like an easy target, I suppose!' She did not pause long enough for me to protest. 'I should have known you were not to be trusted! Edward foisted you on me and I should never have allowed it; your father disgraced himself and you have proved no better! Do you think I didn't notice the way you tried to worm yourself inside this family? Well, your precious Jane won't save you now! What do you think *she* would say if she knew what her so-called friend had tried to do to her favourite brother?'

By now I was quite unable to speak. I was going to lose everything. *Everything.* I began to tremble and my eyes would not focus. Elizabeth's face became a blur of eyes and lips. I could hear sounds from the courtyard below: the scrape of spades shifting snow from the cobbles; the voice of a dairymaid calling to the men as she tramped across to the kitchen. It seemed impossible that outside this room, everything was normal; nothing had changed.

I don't know how long we sat there in silence. When Elizabeth spoke again, I detected a change in her voice. 'I want you gone by the end of January,' she said. 'I would send you away this instant but that would require an explanation. I shall tell my husband that the spectacles have not improved your eyes; that you are finding book work too taxing and must seek a position that does not require much reading. No doubt you will find work of some sort. I will furnish you with letters if you need them.'

These words were spoken very quickly and quietly but to me their significance was profound. *She's going to lie to Edward about the reason for getting rid of me. Why would she do that if she were innocent?*

Chapter Fourteen

I don't remember the words I used as I left Elizabeth's parlour. Neither do I remember walking back to the schoolroom, nor the conversation I had with Fanny when I got there. I know that I attempted to teach her some French irregular verbs. I can still recall her voice as she recited them, struggling with the unpredictable endings. And I stood with my back to her, my eyes hot with tears, contemplating the hurt I was about to cause this child with the ending *I* had brought about.

I felt utterly wretched. My attempt to protect Fanny had backfired on both of us. Elizabeth's parting words had given me reason to believe I was right about what had been going on and if that were the case, it would have been difficult to remain at Godmersham even if she had not dismissed me. But I could not be *certain* I was right. I could not rule out the awful possibility that I had I sacrificed Fanny's happiness and my own future for a baseless case built on whispers and shadows.

I ached with regret for my arrogance. What a fool I had been to try to take on a man like Henry: a man who had made a fortune from his ability to manipulate rich and powerful men. I wondered if Elizabeth really believed I had been planning to blackmail him. Then it occurred to me that I could have tried to outmanoeuvre her with the very thing she had accused me of: I could have threatened to go to Edward and tell him what I suspected. But I had no reason to think he would believe me. The way he looked at her, his whole demeanour towards her, spoke of his devotion. Yes, I had seen him look at other women with admiring eyes, but I sensed that, in Edward's case, looking was all it amounted to. I think he loved Elizabeth as a starving dog loves a butcher: she was more than he ever expected; more than he thought he deserved. He was a parson's son and she was a baronet's daughter – and unlike Henry, I don't think he ever forgot that.

At lunchtime that day Fanny was given the same excuse Elizabeth had already given to her husband: that my eyes were beginning to fail me again and I could no longer continue as governess at Godmersham. Fanny came running into the schoolroom, tears streaming down her face, begging me to tell her it wasn't true.

'Please don't go!' She wrapped her arms around me, squeezing so tight I nearly lost my balance. I dabbed her eyes with a handkerchief still damp with my own tears. 'Your eyes can't be *that* bad,' she pleaded, when her sobbing subsided. 'You were sewing yesterday, weren't you? What's the difference between that and reading books?'

I made up some story about the letters on a printed page making my eyes go out of focus. I said that there was no knowing if they would get better and it was not fair on her to be without instruction while I waited for what could be many months for my sight to recover. She believed me, of course, and her solicitude made me cry more bitter tears. She came knocking on my door early the next morning, full of a plan to keep me at Godmersham.

'You can work in the dairy!' she announced. 'You don't need good eyesight to churn butter!'

I didn't want to tell her any more lies. I couldn't allow her to go on hoping like this. I told her as gently as I could that I would not be accepted by the servants if I tried to live among them, because I was educated and they were not. 'How would you feel,' I asked her, 'if you were a dairymaid and someone came to work alongside you who could speak French and wanted to talk about books you couldn't even read?'

'I would feel very stupid, I suppose,' she replied. 'And I would probably be envious.'

'Exactly. So do you see, now, why I can't stay?'

She gave me a long, sorrowful look, then a little nod. 'But who will teach me? All my other governesses have been either horrible or hopeless!'

I could give no answer to this. She didn't ask where I would go when I left her. She promised to write to me even if I could not see well enough to write back. *Write back?* Her words mocked me. In her innocence it never occurred to her that I had nowhere to go. How on earth was I going to find another position before the month was out? My nightmares were peopled with beggars and streetwalkers; I saw myself ragged and dirty with holes in my boots, huddling in some alleyway as snow drifted round my feet. I had no idea how to go about finding employment. The only certainty was that I would never be able to work as a governess again: Elizabeth's letter of reference, left in the schoolroom a few hours after my dismissal, made it clear to any prospective employer that the only work I was fit for was that which did not involve reading, writing or close work of any kind.

As that long, dreadful week wore on and the old year gave way to the new, another spectre rose up before me. I had not received a letter from Jane for three weeks. Usually she wrote once a fortnight. I had no reason to suspect Elizabeth of telling Jane what she had not told her own husband, yet I feared that somehow she had found out. Could Henry have told her, I wondered? I could just imagine him relating what had happened in the library: painting me as a waspish creature always ready to see the worst in people; a foolish woman who had been tripped up by a family joke. And I could picture Jane listening to him, saying nothing, because he was effectively making her choose between himself and me. There was no doubt in my mind of the result: he was, as Elizabeth had so smugly pointed out, Jane's favourite brother.

I tortured myself with this idea for many days and it came as something of a shock when Fanny brought a letter to me on the sixth day of January. 'Shall I read it to you?' she asked, 'It's from Aunt Jane – I recognise her writing.'

I sat down suddenly, my limbs weak with a mixture of hope and terror. I wanted to read it myself, whatever it may contain – indeed I was afraid of what it might say – and yet I must keep up the pretence about my eyesight for Fanny's sake. I sat there, paralysed, for a moment; at a loss for what to do.

'I wrote and told her you were leaving.' Fanny settled herself in a chair next to me and broke the seal on the letter. 'I thought you probably wouldn't be able to write to her yourself.'

The tender concern this act displayed moved me greatly. I swallowed hard, determined not to upset Fanny all over again. 'That was very kind of you,' I murmured. Whatever was in the letter, Fanny was going to have to hear it.

"'My dearest *Anne*,'" she arched her eyebrows, "'I was so alarmed to receive Fanny's letter. As you will probably have to have this one read aloud to you, I will keep it brief and to the point. I am terribly sorry to hear about your eyes. I suppose that you were so overjoyed at the prospect of being able to read again after six long weeks of abstinence that you have overtaxed yourself. It is to be hoped that your sight will eventually improve, but I quite understand that it would not be fair on Fanny for her to have to go without her lessons for the time that it may take for you to recover. In the meantime

I am most concerned about what you will do and where you will go. Perhaps you have already found some employment and I am being over-anxious – but if not, may I offer a suggestion? *The Times* has a list of situations vacant: employment of a respectable nature for both men and women. I know that Edward takes the paper and I'm sure that Fanny would oblige by reading this particular page aloud to you—"'

'Oh yes, of course I will!' Fanny broke off with a sweet, earnest smile. I pressed my lips together, struggling to contain my emotion.

"'I realise, of course, that you will be limited as to the nature of the employment you are now able to engage in,'" Fanny read on, "'But having cast my eyes over this column many times in the past, I believe you may find something suitable therein. I only wish that I could offer you a place with us here in Bath, but our own situation does not improve: we are to move to a smaller house very soon and we cannot even accommodate poor Martha any longer – she is to move to separate lodgings until we can settle on somewhere less expensive than Bath to call home.'"

'Oh! They are moving again – I didn't know that,' Fanny broke in. 'Sorry – there are just a few lines more: "Please let me know, via Fanny if necessary, where you will be going when you leave Godmersham. I shall send her my new address as soon as I have it and I cherish the hope that we will find a way of continuing to correspond, despite your predicament. Your letters mean so much to me: I can hardly bear the thought of their ceasing. I remain, dearest Anne, your most affectionate friend J. Austen.'

A wave of relief swept through me. She did not know what had taken place at Christmas: the warmth of her letter made that quite plain. *Your most affectionate friend.*' Her words fanned an ember of yearning inside me. I felt that I could bear the ordeal that lay ahead, knowing that she still cared for me.

'I'm going to fetch the paper this minute!' Fanny jumped out of her chair and bounded towards the door. 'It's not that I want you to find another job,' she glanced back at me, shamefaced, 'but Mama says I shall have a new pony to console me when you've gone.'

I was pessimistic about the chances of finding anything in *The Times* that Elizabeth's reference would not debar me from. But after weeding out all the advertisements for governesses, secretaries and clerks, Fanny came up with a species of employment I had never heard of before:

'"Companion required for elderly lady in Yorkshire. Must be well-educated, convivial and strong of body…" That's you!' She thrust the newspaper up to my face. 'Can you see it? It says you have to send a letter of application with a reference to Mrs Raike of The Bourne, Doncaster.'

I could see the advertisement quite clearly, though I had to make a pretence that it was difficult to decipher. 'But wouldn't she want me to read to her?' I said. 'She would find me a pretty useless companion in that case.'

'Just because she's old doesn't mean she is blind!' Fanny replied. 'It says "well-educated and convivial" – that means good company, doesn't it – so what she wants is a clever person she can talk to. And "strong of body" probably means she's a bit doddery on her legs, like old Mrs Owens the blacksmith's mother. She'll probably want you to carry her about like he does when she gets tired.'

I had to smile at this image she conjured of me heaving the poor old lady out of her chair and striding through the village carrying her like a baby, as the well-muscled Mr Owens was frequently seen doing. 'I may be tall,' I said to her, 'but I fear I'm not as strong as all that. Do you really think I should apply?'

'Of course you should! And anyway,' she swished the paper

against the arm of the chair as if she was swatting a fly, 'it's the only job in here that doesn't need someone with good eyesight.' She stood before me, hands on hips, like a mother chiding a wilful child. 'I'll get my writing things. You can dictate the letter to me and I'll make sure it goes off tomorrow.'

It was a great surprise when the old lady responded by return of post. Fanny had been uncannily accurate in her assessment: Mrs Raike was far more interested in the aptitude I had professed for discussing and debating a wide variety of subjects than my ability to read to her. She expressed the wish that I should commence my new employment at the earliest opportunity.

I went to see Elizabeth to ask if she would release me before the end of the month. I dreaded entering the parlour, certain that she would not let me leave without delivering a brace of parting insults. But I was in luck, for Edward was sitting beside her. I had not spoken to him since the news of my departure had reached him and he was full of concern for my 'predicament', as he called it. Listening to his kind words I felt fraudulent and ashamed, as I felt with Fanny. But I could not help noticing Elizabeth's face during the exchange between her husband and myself. She looked as if she had bitten into an apple and found a worm. I don't know if it was Edward's praise for my achievements with Fanny or his wish that I should continue my friendship with his sister that discomfited her most: I think that if she could have, she would have had me ejected from the house that very instant. As it was, we agreed that I should leave on the seventeenth of January – two weeks earlier than her original deadline.

Only Fanny and Sackree were there to see me off on that raw, dark morning. Elizabeth had avoided me completely during my last few days at Godmersham and Edward was away, visiting the estate in Hampshire. I had heard no mention of Henry from either Fanny or the servants. I wondered if he was biding his time, waiting until I was out of the way before resuming his intimacy with Elizabeth. For Fanny's sake I hoped he would stay away but I sensed that this was probably beyond him. I hoped, therefore, that he would at least conduct himself with more discretion.

The horses' breath plumed like smoke in the frosty air. I shivered when the footman took my trunk. Fanny took my gloved hands in hers and rubbed them hard. Sackree punched me on the shoulder and told me I had better get used to such weather, going so far up north to live among people she clearly regarded as little better than savages.

'Let's hope they'll fatten you up a bit with all them Yorkshire puddings,' she whispered in my ear. 'Men like something to grab hold of – 'specially on frosty nights – and there'll be plenty o' them where you're going!' I'm sure she meant there would be many cold evenings, not an over-abundance of lecherous males, but her words made me smile all the same. She was a curmudgeonly old thing but she had my best interests at heart: how could she know that a man's arms were certainly not something I would crave however chilly the bed?

The footman opened the door and I gave Fanny a last, long hug. 'I *will* see you again,' I said. 'Aunt Jane will make sure we all meet – not here, perhaps, but *somewhere* – so you mustn't cry, do you hear?' I was saying this to myself as much as to Fanny, fervently hoping for it to be true. The footman cleared his throat, impatient to be off and not willing to suffer the cold for the sake of a mere employee – or *former* employee, as I had now become. The faces faded into the darkness. The last image I had was of Sackree pulling the child to her, comforting her as she had always done. And there was some comfort for me in seeing it. Sackree had cared for Fanny from the time she was born and for her mother before her. Whoever replaces me, I thought, Fanny will always have her nurse.

The journey to Yorkshire took the best part of two days. The first part – from Godmersham to Ashford – was by far the most comfortable. After that I was on my own, Edward's splendid carriage replaced by a succession of mail coaches, all crowded, all stinking of sweat and stale breath. I slept at a coaching inn at Northampton, sharing a bed with a mother and daughter who made it quite clear that I was an unwelcome addition to the chamber they regarded as theirs, having arrived half an hour before me. They revenged themselves by snoring all night long. As I lay awake listening to this hogs' chorus, I tried not to dwell on what I had left behind and the unknown life that awaited me. The only way to push these thoughts from my mind was to imagine Jane. I relived all the best moments from our time together in Worthing. I conjured her face all lit up with sparkling droplets of seawater; the scent of her hair as I undid the buttons of her dress; the warmth of her skin on mine as we jumped into the lapping waves.

I must have fallen asleep at some point. I woke up thinking I was back in Worthing, with Jane just the other side of the wall. The sight of those unfamiliar faces, mouths open like fishes, brought me back to grim reality. *At least I will have my own room tonight*, I thought. I told myself that I should not fear my new employer: that there was no reason to suppose she would be as cantankerous as these bedfellows. *Just let her be civil*, I murmured, *that is all I ask.*

I was put down from the mail coach at Doncaster, having travelled the last few miles through countryside unlike any I had seen in Kent or Sussex. It was nearly dark when I alighted, so I had only a vague impression of the town itself.

A man had been sent to meet me. He stepped forward and grunted some kind of introduction. The only words I caught were 'Mrs Raike' and 'the Bourne'. These were enough to reassure me and I climbed into the carriage, spreading myself out in blessed relief at having the whole thing to myself.

This last leg of the journey was not a long one. The Bourne was a large stone-built house on the outskirts of the town, hidden from the road by woodland. To reach it we had to cross a tumbling stream by a bridge that was only just wide enough for the carriage. It seemed a very lonely spot. *No wonder she needs a companion*, I thought. My spirits dived just then, wondering what on earth I had come to.

The driver left me at the door. He did not trouble himself to wish me goodnight, merely unloaded my trunk and set it down on the doorstep before disappearing off into the darkness. I could see lanterns through the hall window. A young girl in cap and apron appeared at the door. As she pulled it open a wonderful smell of scones, still warm from the oven, wafted out to greet me.

The maid was as uncommunicative as the coachman. She took my things and showed me into the drawing room, where Mrs Raike – a tiny, birdlike woman with a patchwork blanket over her knees – was waiting. A fire blazed and a table beside her was set with teapot, cups and a mouth-watering variety of cakes.

'Welcome to the Bourne, my dear.' Clutching the blanket with a clawed hand, she raised herself with the aid of a walking stick. 'I thought you might be hungry after that long journey. Please, make yourself at home.'

If someone had told me when I alighted at Doncaster that I would not get to bed until after eleven o'clock that evening I probably would have climbed back into the mail coach. As it was, the cakes and the conversation with Mrs Raike so revived my spirits that when she asked me, two hours later, if I was tired I could honestly answer that I was not. Her voice belied the frail-looking body that contained it. And the opinions she expressed were surprisingly modern. If I had closed my eyes I could have fancied I was talking to someone my own age.

We dined at eight o'clock, served by the quiet little creature that had met me at the door. Mrs Raike explained that she was mute and had been so from childhood. 'Rebecca has lived here since she was a baby. She's the daughter of the coachman who brought you from Doncaster. She took over as cook and housemaid when her mother died and she and her father manage things so well between them I find I need no other help in the house.' She lifted her glass in a toast. 'To you, my dear: I hope you will be very happy here.'

After dinner she read aloud to me from the newspaper, stopping now and then to ask my opinion of this and that. She asked me nothing about my background or the life I had left behind, for which I was grateful. I went to bed that night in better spirits than I would have thought possible. I lay awake for only a short time, thinking of all that I had left behind. I pictured Fanny fast asleep – tucked up in bed with one of the younger children, no doubt, for that was what she always did when in need of comfort. Did I miss anything about Godmersham other than its younger occupants? Certainly I would not miss Elizabeth, who, in the two years I had bided there, had not displayed one ounce of the warmth Mrs Raike had shown me in a single evening. Neither would I miss Henry, whom I sincerely hoped I would never set eyes on again. But Jane was never far from my thoughts as I contemplated all this. I tried not to calculate the distance that now lay between us.

Will I ever see you again? My voice, though only a whisper, sounded very loud in that silent house.

*

Life at the Bourne soon settled into an uneventful but pleasant routine. Mrs Raike was not an early riser and the mornings were mine to spend as I pleased. For breakfast Rebecca brought hot chocolate on a tray to my chamber. I had the luxury of drinking it in bed whilst reading. I had to conceal both book and spectacles until after she had left me, of course, for I had to keep up the pretence about my eyesight for a while yet. I had not yet worked out how Rebecca managed to communicate with Mrs Raike but the smooth-running of the household suggested that she had devised some way. Mute she may be but her eyes spoke with great eloquence. I didn't want to give her any clue to the fact that I was deceiving her mistress.

On my fifth morning at the house Rebecca brought something extra on the tray. I could see that it was a letter and as she laid the tray down my heart leapt. The handwriting was Jane's. It was all I could do to keep from grabbing it and breaking the seal right away. But Rebecca was still in the room, pulling back the curtains and seeing to the fire. When she had gone I plucked the letter from the tray and stared at the blob of blood red wax that kept its contents from me. If I broke the seal Rebecca would know that I had read it. But how could I wait the three long hours before Mrs Raike presented herself downstairs? And how could I bear to hear Jane's precious words at second hand?

In a moment I had come up with a solution. I would tell Mrs Raike that my excitement at receiving a letter had made me open it and try to read the contents – which had proved impossible. I would hand it over to her and react as if I was hearing the words for the first time. And so, clumsy with anticipation, I broke the seal:

Dearest Anne, I hope that you are settling into your new home and that your eyesight is beginning to improve – but in case it *is not, I expect there is someone who will be kind enough to read this on your behalf (my thanks to this person, whose name I will perhaps come to know). It is a little early to be enquiring about holidays, I know, so I beg forgiveness from your employer for asking, but ask I must if you are to visit me in Bath before I quit it for good. Mama, Cassandra, Martha and me will be moving to Southampton in June. My brother Frank's ship anchors there and he is looking for a house for us all to rent. I do hope you will be able to visit before we leave here – it would be <u>so good</u> to see you again. Cass has agreed to go to Martha's lodgings for a few days if you are able to come, so there will be a bed for you. It will be rather a squash, as our room is very small, but if you don't mind that, all will be well.*

If you are still unable to write, please ask for help – I long for your answer! Yours ever truly, Jane Austen.

I hugged the letter to my chest. I could feel my heart thudding through my ribs. I read the sentence with the underlining a second time...*so good*. Those two small words had me bursting with joy. But what was I to do? She was leaving Bath in just four months' time. How could I ask for a holiday so soon? I counted myself far too fortunate to have found such an employer to make any such untimely request; and yet I longed with all my heart to see Jane.

It was Rebecca who brought a solution to this dilemma. When she came to collect my tray she passed me a note, written in capital letters. It was from Mrs Raike, who apparently marked the delivery of the post from her bedroom window: DO YOU NEED HELP TO READ YOUR LETTER? IF SO, DO NOT HESITATE TO ASK.

The boldness of this enquiry made me smile. Plainly she wanted to know who it was from but she had cloaked her curiosity with this seemingly innocent offer. In doing so she made it easy for me. I would simply revert to my original plan of handing the letter over and pretending I had been unable to decipher it. This would clear me of any offence Jane's request might cause.

I took the letter down with me to the drawing room, where Mrs Raike was already waiting. After reading it she smiled and said: 'Bath! What a wonderful idea! I've been meaning to go and take the waters ever since my poor husband passed away, you know, but the idea of travelling so far put me off. Now we shall go together! There will be no need to squash yourself into your friend's house: I shall take rooms for both of us at one of the inns. Fetch me a pen, dear – I shall write back to her immediately!'

Chapter Fifteen

My first sensation of Bath was the noise. As we bowled across the River Avon a cacophony of sound invaded the carriage. Above the thunder of wagons, heavy laden with baggage or produce, were the raucous cries of tradesmen and milkmaids, chairmen and fishwives. And accompanying these, like the drumming of hail on a window pane, was the endless rhythm of pattens on the pavements.

Living in a remote country house with not even the sound of children to break the silence, my ears were unprepared for such an assault. I alighted from the carriage in a daze, blinking in the bright sunshine as I took in my new surroundings. Mrs Raike had taken rooms for us at the White Hart Inn, chosen for its close proximity to the Pump Room. It stood opposite the Abbey churchyard, just a stone's throw from the river and, judging by the throng of people coming and going, was at the very hub of life in the city of Bath.

Poor Mrs Raike was almost knocked over when a stout gentleman in an ostentatiously caped coat shouted: 'Chair! Chair!' and half a dozen wicked-looking fellows with thick wooden poles in their fists descended like crows on a carcass.

'At your service, m'lud,' one shouted, only to be drowned out in his negotiations by another bawling: 'No! I was first!' and shaking his pole menacingly while a third man shoved him from behind. I had sometimes spotted sedan chairs in London but in Bath, I discovered, they were the favoured mode of transport. As we made our way to our rooms, Mrs Raike explained to me that they were narrow enough to pass through the doors of buildings, so that a person could travel to the baths in complete privacy, without the need to undress upon arrival. On the homeward journey they would be swathed in blankets to retain the heat and delivered to bed by the chairmen, who would then retire from the room to allow the occupant to sweat peacefully for an hour or two.

My room at the inn was small but comfortable, with a view of the river and the Pulteney Bridge. I would far rather have stayed with Jane, of course, but it would have been impossible to explain that to Mrs Raike without offending her. To my eternal gratitude she had arranged our visit to coincide with that of a cousin of hers, Miss Gowerton, and she had encouraged me to make what arrangements I pleased for the evenings, when she would take her dinner with this lady. It was almost the end of the season, so the time for balls and public entertainment was drawing to a close. Nonetheless, Jane had promised me the spectacle of fireworks in Sydney Gardens on my first evening, with many more treats to follow.

She had written in her last letter that Fanny might be in Bath at the same time as me – a prospect that filled me with a mixture of joy and trepidation. For Jane had not said whether Fanny was coming alone or with her parents. I had sent word of my plans to the child, but her reply had not reached me before my departure from Yorkshire.

Jane, of course, had no notion of how awkward it would be for me to see Elizabeth again. I was not sure what I would do if Fanny and her mother were invited to any of the outings

Jane had planned for me. I consoled myself with the thought that Elizabeth would find herself thrust into as awkward a situation as myself, for she would not be able to betray the animosity she felt for me, given that she had told the world that we had parted on amicable terms.

But it was not Elizabeth who made my visit to Bath uncomfortable. On that first day, as I sat beneath the gilded Corinthian columns in the Pump Room sipping cloudy, sulphurous water with Mrs Raike and Miss Gowerton, I caught sight of someone whose familiar profile froze my blood.

I shrank back, thankful for the breadth of the brim on my new cambric muslin bonnet. Miss Gowerton, who was of the same small stature as my employer but twice her girth, was holding forth about the deliciousness of Bath buns, and promising to take her cousin to Molland's of Milsom Street, which, she proclaimed, was the best pastry shop in town. As she described the heavenly confections to be found there, I stole another glance at the man in the pearl grey morning coat and hussar boots. It was Henry. And he was deep in conversation with a woman. The lady in question was neither Eliza nor Elizabeth, but a dark-haired, large-boned woman who had none of their delicate prettiness. As she angled her face towards me I saw that it was scarred by smallpox. And yet Henry had that unmistakable look about him as he leaned forward, one hand resting on a silver-topped cane: he was flirting with this woman – of that there was no doubt. And the simpering smile on her face told me that she was enjoying every minute of it.

I felt a tingle of triumph. Perhaps my confrontation with Henry had not, after all, been in vain; perhaps he had heeded my words and cooled his relationship with Elizabeth. Was this woman a new diversion? It certainly appeared so, and while I could not condone his seeking yet another affair outside his marriage, surely this must be the lesser of two evils?

'And the lavender cake, my dear! It simply melts in the mouth!' Miss Gowerton's high, piping voice cut across my thoughts. 'You really must come too, Miss Sharp.' I tried to affect an interest in what she was saying, nodding earnestly and murmuring my approval of her invitation, but my mind was firmly fixed on Henry and his companion. If he was here with her, it followed that Elizabeth was not in Bath; perhaps Henry had escorted Fanny from Godmersham, using the trip as an excuse for a rendezvous with this new *amour*? I wondered where he was staying. Not at Jane's home, I hoped, for I had been invited to dine there before the firework display that evening.

My eyes darted back to the couple. They were on the move, strolling back towards the entrance to the Pump Room. I saw Henry's hand move up to the woman's shoulder, touching her so briefly that he might have been brushing off a fly or a crumb of cake. She turned and batted her eyelashes at him, in what looked like a mixture of delight and embarrassment. I wondered who she was and where he had found her. Certainly she was not in the first flush of youth; I guessed that she was about my age – possibly a little older. I hoped that she was not married. But then, if she was single and had marriage on her mind she stood to be sorely disappointed. *Poor woman*, I thought, *if only she knew what she was letting herself in for*.

The rest of the afternoon passed pleasantly enough. I wheeled Mrs Raike the short distance to Milsom Street in one of the invalid chairs that were available for hire. This was not only cheaper than a sedan, but allowed the occupant an open view and a good deal more fresh air than the musty-smelling boxes on poles.

Milsom Street was all bustle and gaiety, the shops laid out as elegantly as any in London's Bond Street. There were tailors, milliners, confectioners and tobacconists; libraries, galleries and music shops. It was a veritable feast for the eyes, designed to satisfy the most fastidious appetite. Miss Gowerton was waiting for us in Molland's the pastry cook's shop, which appeared to rival the Pump Room as a place of gathering for visitors to the town. For one so delicate, Mrs Raike had a mighty appetite. She managed a Bath bun, a slice of rosewater cake and a macaroon, despite the fact that it wanted only a couple of hours until dinner.

Having seen her safely back to her room I made myself ready to walk across town to Jane's house. I forced all thoughts of Henry from my mind, concentrating only on the pleasure of seeing my friend again. If he was there, I told myself, I would just have to bear it as best I could.

Washing the sticky traces of cake from my fingers, I put on the new white dimity gown made for me by Mrs Raike's own dressmaker. I pinned on the same silver brooch I had lent Jane for the ball in Canterbury and tied a band of green silk around my cambric bonnet. A shawl of emerald kerseymere completed my outfit. With a deep breath I reached for my reticule and made for the door.

Dodging the chairmen waiting to pounce on every person who emerged from the White Hart, I crossed the street and passed under the archway. Jane's house was in Trim Street, and I had spotted the sign on the way back from the shops. It was but a short walk across Cheap Street and up Union Passage to reach it. Jane had warned me that her lodgings were far inferior to others they had occupied in Bath. Her letters said that Cassandra, in particular, detested Trim Street. But in the reduced circumstances in which they found themselves after her father's death, Jane said, there was little choice left to them.

She had made no mention of how she felt about me staying at the White Hart rather than with her. It was difficult for either of us to express our true feelings through letters at that time, knowing that our words would be read or written by

Mrs Raike. Living in so remote a place I had no hope of writing secretly to Jane: Rebecca's father was my only means of reaching Doncaster and as his brother was the postmaster, any correspondence written in my own hand would certainly have been noticed.

As I turned in to Trim Street I felt suddenly afraid. I had been living for this moment, aching for the sight of her face and the sound of her voice. I wondered if she had dreamed of me as I had dreamed of her. Did she truly miss my company or was she just being compassionate? Would she have invited me to stay if I had *not* lost my position at Godmersham? Was I someone she pitied rather than loved?

I had my answer the instant the door opened. She flung her arms around me and kissed my face. 'Oh, it's been such a long time! Come inside: I want you all to myself for a while!' I made no reply, for I was overcome with emotion. Fearing she would think me quite idiotic, I blinked back the tears that pricked my eyes and held out my hand, letting her lead me into the house like a tame animal.

'We have only one servant, I'm afraid,' she whispered as she took me down the narrow hallway. 'She is very old and smells of mothballs but she makes the best scotch collops I have ever tasted!' Then, as she ushered me into the parlour, she asked me how I liked Bath. I replied that what I had seen thus far had impressed me very favourably. 'Ah,' she said, 'it is vastly well to be here for a short visit but I can assure you, you would not want to live here.' She told me how much she had come to hate the place; how she despised the dandified gentlemen and rouged ladies who paraded up and down Royal Crescent and around the Orange Grove. 'And most of them are so *old*,' she said. 'Bath has become God's waiting room: full of retired admirals and whiskery widows.' She stepped forward, seizing both my hands in hers. 'How wonderful it is to see you! You look as fresh as a snowdrop.'

I gave her a wry smile for her compliment. 'Is your mama well?' I asked, 'and your sister?'

She nodded. 'They will be here presently. Mama is sleeping off one of her headaches and Cass has gone to fetch Fanny.'

'Oh! She *has* come, then!'

'Yes. She arrived yesterday. Henry brought her.'

I tried to look surprised. 'Where are they staying?'

'Fanny is with my Aunt and Uncle Leigh-Perrot at their house in the Paragon. My brother James is there, too, with his wife and children. There was no room for Henry, so he lodges at the Sydney Hotel.'

I breathed a small sigh of relief that he had not chosen the White Hart. *How convenient for him*, I thought, *to be out of sight of his family while conducting this new affair.*

'We have only half an hour before Fanny comes,' Jane said, 'I want to hear all about your Mrs Raike – is she really as saintly as your letters would have me believe? I suppose you *cannot* tell the whole truth when she writes them at your dictation. I beg to hope she has at least *one* odious habit. Does she keep a little dog that she feeds from her plate? Does she pick her teeth with her fingernails? Perhaps she does both at the same time...' she tailed off with a twisted grin.

'No!' I laughed, shaking my head at this horrible image, 'I will not allow you to mock her! I would not be here now were it not for her goodness.'

'Hmmm. Very well, then – we must drink to her health. Will you take a glass of orange wine?'

We fell swiftly back into our old, easy manner of conversation and so absorbed did we become that we failed to hear the front door opening and the footsteps in the hall.

'Miss Sharp!' A human whirlwind hurled itself across the room. Fanny was now thirteen years old and seemed to have grown at least three inches in the few months we had been parted. Cassandra was not able to get in a word of greeting to me, nor was

153

Mrs Austen when she came downstairs, for Fanny was intent on telling me everything that had happened to her since I left Godmersham. She had made only passing references to her new governess in her letters – mindful of my feelings, I have no doubt – but now she told me the woman had packed up and gone.

'Mama sent her away last week,' she said. 'She pretended she knew French but she was hopeless at it: even worse than me. Someone else is coming when I get back. I wish I could go to school like the boys. Mama went to school; I don't know why she won't send me.'

'I expect she had as bad a time as we did.' Jane glanced at her sister. 'Believe me, Fanny, you would not wish for school if you knew what it was like.'

'We went to two schools,' Cass nodded, 'both run by women who were very proficient with a needle but knew next to nothing about the modern languages or Shakespeare. There was not enough to eat and we slept five or six to a bed. Your Aunt Jane nearly died of a fever at one of them.'

'Were they really that bad?' I asked. I had never attended school, having had the good fortune to be educated by my father, who, for all his other faults, was an excellent teacher.

'They were terrible,' Mrs Austen replied. 'If we had known how bad they were we would never have sent the girls away.'

Fanny, of course, wanted all the details about these dreadful establishments. She was only halted by the ring of the dinner bell, and even then she had difficulty keeping quiet long enough to eat the steaming palpatoon of pigeons with marrow pudding and apricot fritters set out before us.

'You must forgive her,' Cassandra whispered as she topped up my glass, 'It is the first time she has travelled such a distance without her mother and she is over-excited. There is another baby on the way so Elizabeth has stayed at home.' I nodded silently. Jane had not mentioned a baby. *Perhaps,* I thought, *it is a subject still too painful for her to talk about.*

A little after eight o'clock we set out for Sydney Gardens, leaving Mrs Austen and Cassandra behind. 'Neither one of them can stand the noise of fireworks,' Jane said as we walked down Trim Street, 'I myself find it greatly preferable to the sound of singing, which, thankfully, will be over by the time we arrive. Why the organisers of these events insist on holding a concert first is beyond my understanding: you never heard such a caterwauling; such a scraping of strings and squeaking of reeds. Thankfully the gardens are very large, which is just as well for the poor souls caught unawares: it is just possible to get out of earshot without quitting the place entirely.' She stepped off the pavement to avoid a lamplighter, who was halfway up a ladder with his taper at the ready. 'James and Mary said they would meet us on the bridge over the canal. They're bringing Anna and James-Edward. Caroline is too young, of course.'

'I am grown taller than Anna now,' Fanny cut in, taking my arm as we crossed the river by the Pulteney Bridge. 'And she is jealous because my Mama is going to have another baby and hers will not.'

I set my gaze on the cobbles, fearful of catching Jane's eye. 'How exciting,' I said, trying to sound bright. 'Another baby! I wonder what it will be this time?'

'Well, if it's a girl she will be named Cassandra Jane, Papa says.' Fanny beamed up at her aunt. 'That's very pretty, don't you think?'

How very telling, I thought: Cassandra Jane, not Jane Cassandra. It was a clear indication of the way the two sisters were regarded by Elizabeth.

'Look!' Fanny gasped, pointing down Pulteney Street. 'Can you see the lights? Aren't they amazing?' As we drew closer I could see that the trees were hung with hundreds of tiny lamps with orbs of coloured glass that glittered like jewels among the foliage and blossom. Between the trees were strings of Chinese lanterns, glowing sunset red against the darkening sky. Throngs of people were gathered in the gardens, their clothes and faces dappled with a rainbow of colours.

'I can't see any sign of James,' Jane said as we approached the little bridge that spanned the canal. 'Will you stay here with Fanny, while I go and look for them?'

We watched her disappear into the crowd, which was growing larger by the minute. 'How do you like it at your great aunt Leigh-Perrot's house?' I said, batting away an insect that had settled itself on Fanny's bonnet.

'It's all right, I suppose,' Fanny replied, pushing out her lower lip. 'But Aunt L.P. spoils James-Edward to death. He is her favourite and she never tires of telling Anna and me that one day he will inherit all her money.'

'Oh?' I smiled, 'And is this aunt very rich?'

'Not quite so rich as Papa, I think, but very nearly: they have a place in the country called Scarlets which is nearly as big as Godmersham, but not so fine.'

'And how is it that young James-Edward will come into all this?' I asked, intrigued.

'Because Aunt and Uncle L.P. are very old and have no children.' Fanny spoke slowly and clearly, as if I was the child and she the adult. 'Uncle L.P. is Grandmama Austen's brother, so Uncle James, being her eldest, gets all the money when they die and he, of course, will leave it to his son.'

'Ah!' I nodded, 'What a fortunate young fellow!' I couldn't help thinking of Henry, growing up in the rectory at Steventon with the dawning knowledge that he had lost out badly in the lottery of life. If he had only been born first or second he need never have worried about money. Edward was rolling in it and James had the prospect of plenty to come – and before very long if Fanny's assessment of the Leigh-Perrots' advanced age was anything to go by.

'Oh, look!' Fanny cried, 'There they are! Aunt Jane must have missed them.'

Coming through the crowds was a slight man in a coat with a collar so high it almost touched the brim of his black beaver hat. He held his head as if there was a bad smell beneath his nose and wielded his crystal-topped cane like a weapon. Behind him was Anna in a pink muslin frock with a tight-fitting bodice that showed off her burgeoning figure. She held the hand of a boy of about eight years old. As they grew closer I caught my breath, for the child looked like an exact miniature of Henry.

'Where is Aunt Mary?' Fanny demanded.

'Just coming,' Anna replied. 'She stopped to buy some sweetmeats from a stall.'

'There she is!' The little boy turned and pointed to a figure in a pale, shimmering dress and black gauze cloak advancing across the bridge. Her bonnet shaded her features, but as she drew level with her husband the light from a Chinese lantern cast a red glow over her face. I stared at Mary Austen in utter confusion. There was no mistaking the masculine nose and jaw and the pitted marks on her skin. It was the woman in the Pump Room; the woman I had seen with Henry.

There was an explosion of what sounded like gunfire from the canal bank below us. Plumes of jewel coloured sparks lit up the night sky. A flotilla of punts sent up fiery cascades that burst overhead with a fearsome crackle. There were cheers and sighs of awe as faces turned to the heavens. My thoughts were all disordered. Each soaring sky-rocket, each fizzing Roman candle and whirling Catherine wheel was a merciful distraction. While the fireworks sparkled and spat I was relieved of the burden of making polite conversation with Jane's brother and his wife.

I stole a glance at them as the crowd *oohed* and *aahed* at a spurting, many-coloured volcano. She had taken his arm and, although taller than him by an inch or more, he was reaching across with his other arm to grasp her wrist, as if offering protection from the raging firestorm. What had I been thinking of, to imagine that this woman was Henry's latest *amour*? Was my judgement so awry that I saw flirtation where nothing more than familial friendship existed? What, after all, could be more natural than a man accompanying his sister-in-law to the Pump Room and keeping her amused while, perhaps, her husband took a warm bath next door?

My eyes fell on young James-Edward, who was jumping up and down to get a better view. Yes, he had a definite look of Henry: the same nose, the same eager, smiling countenance. He looked nothing like his father or his mother. But that was not so unusual, was it? I had come across it before, a child more closely resembling the brother or sister of one of its parents than either of the parents themselves.

As the firework display reached its finale, with a pergola of golden arrows arching across the canal, I determined to stop taking the least interest in anything involving Jane's family, other than what politeness demanded. *Let this be a lesson to you*, I said to myself, thinking what a mercy it was that I had not told Jane of the encounter in the Pump Room.

'Good evening Miss Sharp! I did not expect the pleasure of your company again!' The voice was behind me, so close it made me jump.

'Uncle Henry! I thought you weren't coming!' It was Fanny who saw him first and darted around me to claim him before the others spotted him.

'Well, Fanny, I wasn't going to – but when I heard that your dear old governess was come to town I thought I must come and pay my compliments.'

I couldn't see his face, for I had not yet turned around. But I imagined him looking the picture of innocence as he said it.

Chapter Sixteen

I could not be certain what was in Henry's mind that night. I suspected that he had come to get the measure of me, to judge whether I might be about to disclose something of the circumstances of my departure from Godmersham to his sister. He walked with us back to Trim Street, where Cass and Mrs Austen were already in bed. Showing no inclination to leave, he stole the precious time I would have had alone with Jane. It wanted but half an hour till midnight when he offered to escort me back to the White Hart. I had intended to take a sedan but he waved that idea away. To my relief Jane insisted on coming with us. I avoided his eye as we said our farewells, dreading what he might say to Jane on the way home. Would he give his version of events to forestall anything I might say?

The thought of this robbed me of sleep for many hours. It would be so easy for Henry to turn Jane against me. I knew just how persuasive he could be. He had all but convinced me of his innocence that night in the library at Godmersham. How much more willing Jane would be to swallow what he fed her: what sister would *not* want to believe that she had been wrong about such a thing?

I turned it over and over in my mind. I reminded myself that Henry could have done all this months ago if he had chosen to. Why wait until now to sabotage my friendship with Jane? Did he underestimate the strength of the bond between us? Did he think that once I had left Godmersham I would be out of the way forever? *Please,* I whispered, *don't take her from me!* I don't know who I was entreating – Henry or God above – but I prayed that night as I hadn't done since my mother died.

When at last I drifted off to sleep I dreamed not of Henry or Jane but of Mary Austen. She was with her sister Martha in the house at Worthing, stirring a pot that hung over the fire. When Martha turned away Mary dipped her finger in and smeared her lips crimson. They stretched wide open, revealing sharp white teeth like a cat's. I knew that she was saying something but I couldn't hear what it was. I had to guess the words from the shapes her lips were making. The painted mouth bunched into a tight red bud, slid out then gaped wide. *Don't tell Jane.* Again and again she repeated the phrase and each time her lips swelled in size, sucking me towards them. The moment I entered the dark cave beyond her teeth I awoke with a start. The counterpane of burgundy damask had fallen over my face in the night and the sunshine piercing the curtains had set it all aglow. I threw it off and ran to the window, taking comfort in the sight of milkmaids and lamp snuffers going about their business.

The dream came back vividly as I sat before the looking glass, arranging my hair. The foxing on its silver surface gave me Mary Austen's pock-marked skin. The reflection also held the pot of lip balm her sister had made for me. Without looking down, I reached for it and pulled off the lid. My finger touched the sticky red wax. *You have a dangerous imagination.* The voice in my head was as clear and alarming as the dream. I jumped to my feet, seized the little pot and ran to the window. The catch was stiff but I pulled with all my might. It gave with a shower of rust and I leaned out, hurling the pot as far as I could. It flew in an arc across the street and landed noiselessly in the still, blue shallows of the river.

I was too agitated to eat breakfast that morning. My stomach lurched every time the head waiter came near our table because I saw him delivering letters to other guests and I convinced myself he had a note for me from Jane. If Henry had done what I feared, Jane would lose no time in cancelling tonight's rendezvous with me. She would, no doubt, be tactful and polite about terminating our friendship. Perhaps she would pretend to be ill and unable to admit any visitor to the house in Trim Street. This illness would persist for the whole week of my stay then, when I was safely back in Yorkshire, she would pack up for Southampton and neglect to inform me of her new address.

But by eleven o'clock that morning no note had arrived. I began to relax a little and managed to drink the coffee served to us in the lounge. Mrs Raike was reading the front page of the Bath paper aloud to me. She had got as far as the column that announced new arrivals to the town.

'Oh,' she said, pausing as she read out the names, 'This man's wife is a very dear friend of Miss Gowerton. They were out in India together. She has asked them to meet us in the Pump Room at midday.'

'Who is the man?' I asked.

'Warren Hastings.'

'Oh, is *he* come to Bath?' I said, unable to conceal my surprise.

'It will cause quite a stir, I am sure,' Mrs Raike nodded, 'but we must remember, he was acquitted from that bad business. There is no stain upon his character. Miss Gowerton assures me that no one speaks of it now.'

She had no idea, of course, that I had any knowledge of Mr. Hastings apart from what had been written in the newspapers. I thought of telling her that I had once met Eliza, his god-daughter, but decided it was too slight a connection to merit her attention. In any case, she had moved onto the subject of her dip in the warm bath, which she would take in half an hour's time.

'I will take a sedan, I think, my dear. I know it is only a short distance but at my age one can't be too careful. I should not like to catch cold when I come out.'

That seemed a most unlikely eventuality, for when I stepped outside to hail a chair the brightness of the day made me blink. There were so many new buildings in Bath, all made from the same white limestone, that when the sun shone upon them the effect was quite dazzling. I shaded my eyes and scanned the streets, half afraid of spotting Henry lurking in some shop doorway, ready to pounce. But there was no one about save the hawkers and carriers. I told myself that my fears about him were groundless, that he must realise I had nothing to gain and much to lose by telling Jane the real reason for my departure from Godmersham. And that being the case, why would he risk telling her himself?

My errand accomplished, I hurried back upstairs to make Mrs Raike ready for her sedan. At a little before one o'clock she emerged from her sweating-in, all pink and smiling and ready for the rendezvous at the Pump Room. We spotted Miss Gowerton through one of the downstairs windows of the White Hart. She was standing on the steps beneath the colonnade, in conversation with a short, stout old gentleman whose coat buttons twinkled in the sun, and a woman in a bonnet for which at least half a dozen birds must have been sacrificed, so elaborately was it trimmed.

'Oh! They are come already! We must make haste!' Mrs Raike almost tripped on her gown, so eager was she to meet the man whose life, a decade earlier, had been chewed up and spat out for public consumption. 'They say the trial ruined him,' she whispered, as I took her arm to help her across the cobbles. 'Miss Gowerton says it has taken him seven years to recover some measure of the fortune he once had. Of course, he was fabulously wealthy when he lived in India. They say that he bought his wife from a German baron on a boat to Madras!'

'Bought her?' I looked at her, astonished.

'That is what they say, yes, and Miss Gowerton does not deny it, though, of course, she would be the last person to spread rumours about her friend. Apparently, they met when this lady entered his cabins by accident. Then Mr Hastings fell ill and she nursed him, staying at his bedside day and night. Before they reached Madras he was in love with her. So he summoned the husband, asked his price, and by the time they disembarked the bargain was made.'

'And this lady is his wife still?' This bizarre tale of romance on the high seas was very much at odds with the description Jane had given, of the greedy old dame who talked with her mouth full and pinched Eliza's servants black and blue.

'Indeed she is,' Mrs Raike replied. 'A strange way for a marriage to come about, I'm sure you are thinking, yet she has stuck to him through thick and thin.'

We were making our slow progress up the steps now and I could hardly wait to meet the woman with the aviary on her head. What must the young Eliza have made of her godfather's strategy for finding a new wife, I wondered? Had she taken her cue from him in cooking up her plan to marry Henry?

'They had no children of their own,' Mrs Raike went on, gripping me tightly as we took the last step. 'He adopted her two boys and they say he already had a daughter from an affair with a married lady in India.'

'Really?' I guided her around the colonnade and through the doors.

'The child is still living, I believe, although of course, she is not a child any longer. Miss Gowerton says she married a French nobleman who went to the guillotine.'

With a shock of recognition I realised that she was talking about Eliza. I searched my memory for what Jane had said: something about Eliza's mother being lucky to have a child because she had been married for many years when her daughter came along…

'It is a good thing you are so tall,' Mrs Raike was craning her neck, trying to see over the heads of the crowds of people in the Pump Room. 'Leave me in this chair and come back for me when you have found them.' I did as I was bid, although I had difficulty focusing on the sea of faces around me, so preoccupied was I with Mrs Raike's revelation.

After a while I did spot Miss Gowerton and her companions sitting round a low table in one of the alcoves. I managed to convey my employer across the room without anyone treading on her poor feet and, as we drew near, Warren Hastings stood up with a little courtly bow. When he removed his hat I saw that the top of his head was completely bald, with just a few wisps of white hair at the side. This, I thought, is a man quite devoid of vanity, a man who could hide his pate with a wig but chooses not to. His blue-grey eyes were heavily pouched and sat beneath a pair of bushy brows. He smiled a greeting but there was a very wistful look about those eyes: not surprising, I supposed, for a man who had spent six long years on trial and seen his money guzzled by greedy lawyers.

His wife was the very opposite of what I had expected. From the distance of the inn it had been impossible to discern her features, but I now saw that despite her age, which must have been close to sixty, she was remarkably beautiful. Her

164

hair, which peeped out from beneath the monstrous hat, was a rich auburn with not a strand of grey. She had wide slanting eyes of a striking emerald, and high cheekbones in a face that bore very few wrinkles. Yet when she smiled it was a cold smile; a snake's smile.

The introductions over, Mr Hastings helped Mrs Raike into a chair and pulled one out for me beside his own. The three older ladies fell into conversation immediately; Mrs Hastings fanning herself with a set of feathers plucked from the same unfortunate creatures that adorned her hat. I sat there feeling very awkward in the presence of a man who was so well known but of whom I had just received the most scandalous intelligence. He must have sensed my unease, for he drew me into conversation with a smiling enquiry about my impressions of Bath, responding to everything that I said with a warmth and sincerity that seemed entirely genuine. Whatever he may or may not have done in the past, I thought, this is a man who has borne suffering and emerged the better for it.

We had moved on to the topic of the recent victory of the English fleet at St Domingo when I spotted Henry Austen over his shoulder. He appeared to be alone this time. He turned towards us and I dipped my head but it was too late. He was coming across the room. Obliged to dodge sideways by a group of elderly ladies who stepped into his path, he approached from a different angle and must have been very surprised indeed when he saw who it was that I conversed with.

'Mr and Mrs. Hastings!' He covered it very well, pretending that it was the gentleman and his wife he had sought out in the first place, 'And Miss Sharp! What a pleasure it is to see you again! I had no notion that you were acquainted.'

I felt myself colour and my heart began to thud. I saw Mrs Raike's brow lift with the question I knew she must ask, if not now, then later. But she had no need, for Warren Hastings did it for her.

'My dear Austen!' he said, rising from his chair. 'How is my sweet Betsy?'

I gathered in the course of the conversation that followed that it was Eliza he was referring to. Then he turned to me with a smile and said: 'Now, tell me, Miss Sharp, how comes a lady of your intellect and refinement to be acquainted with a rapscallion like this?'

'We have met at Godmersham, sir,' Henry cut in before I could say a word. 'Miss Sharp was governess to my brother Edward's eldest girl.'

I was looking directly at him as he said this and I swear there was not the slightest hint of embarrassment in his countenance. Out of the corner of my eye I saw the plumes on Mrs Hastings' hat shift and shiver. She was whispering something in Miss Gowerton's ear. A moment later, Henry bid us all *adieu* and disappeared into the crowd.

'So, Miss Sharp,' Mrs Hastings snapped her fan shut and jabbed the air with it, narrowly missing Mrs Raike's left eye, 'You have met Mrs Henry Austen?' her accent put me in mind of a small, growling dog.

'I...I have met her...once,' I stammered, aware of the eyes of all the company upon me. 'I found her very charming and refined; a most elegant lady.' Mrs Hastings' eyes narrowed at this. I wondered what lay behind her enquiry. Was she party to the gossip Mrs Raike had repeated? Was she jealous of Eliza's place in her husband's affections?

'She is an excellent hostess, is she not, Mr Hastings?' She turned her snake smile on him and he nodded. 'The last time we were there, Miss Sharp, we met another member of the Austen family but it was not the one you worked for.' She emphasised the last two words as if to draw attention to my lowly status. 'It was one of the sisters, wasn't it?' She turned to him again. 'What was her name?'

'It was Jane,' her husband replied. 'Jane Austen. And we took her to the opera.'

'So we did!' Mrs Hastings flung her fan open and began beating the air. 'What a queer creature she was! I think she spent more time watching the people in the audience than the ones on the stage. On the hunt for a husband, I suppose, poor thing.' She gave me a smug look; the sort of look that only a woman who has had a surfeit of husbands could give.

Well, unlike you, madam, she'll not end by selling herself to the highest bidder. That was what I wanted to say. But of course, I uttered no such thing. I took a deep breath and said: 'You are quite right, Mrs Hastings, in observing that Miss Jane Austen is a truly original creature, but I fear you were mistaken in thinking it was *husbands* she was hunting at the opera: you see, she collects characters in the way that some people collect insects.' I smiled brightly into those cold emerald eyes. 'She pins down the vainest, the ugliest, the most ridiculously attired and stores them in her memory. Her powers of description and mimicry are such that when she brings her specimens out it is impossible to keep a straight face.' I tried not to glance at the hat, although it was hard to resist.

Mrs Hastings pursed her lips. Then, without another word to me, she turned to Miss Gowerton and Mrs Raike and started talking about a performance of *The Rivals* that she had seen at the Theatre Royal.

Mr Hastings leaned towards me and whispered: 'Pay no heed to my wife, Miss Sharp. She is a Russian, from a city called Archangel, where they spear fish for breakfast.' He gave a smile that crinkled the pouches under his eyes. 'She can be rather brutal without realising it.' I smiled ruefully back at him. I was thinking of the sisters with the bad breath; of the lady with the fat neck and the pink husband; and I was wondering if Jane's victims would use such words to describe her.

The Pump Room emptied at lunchtime. The vile-tasting spa water seemed to have had a miraculous effect on Mrs Raike, for no sooner had the Hastings and Miss Gowerton departed than she had me almost flying across the cobbles to the White Hart.

'Well, my dear,' she gasped as she sank onto a dining chair, 'What a drama! I knew the child was called Betsy, but I had no idea she had married again – and to the brother of your old employer!' She looked over her shoulder then, lowering her voice, said: '*She* is the one, you know: the one I was telling you about!'

I didn't want to snuff out her excitement by letting on that I had already grasped this, so I affected some surprise and said: 'Does Mrs Hastings know, do you think?'

Mrs Raike's eyes widened like a child spying sweetmeats. 'I think she must know the substance of it, even if her husband has withheld the details. According to Miss Gowerton it was the talk of all India.' She leaned a little closer. 'She told me that Lord Clive was so outraged by the behaviour of the *woman* that he forbade his wife from having anything to do with her when they returned to England.'

'Oh?' I said, 'And did Miss Gowerton reveal the name of this woman?'

Mrs Raike shook her head. *That is something, at least*, I thought. How awful for Jane to have her aunt's name bandied about in the Pump Room by the likes of Miss Gowerton and Mrs Hastings. 'Do you think Mrs Hastings resents her husband having this secret daughter?' I asked. 'She seemed very discomfited by my having met her.'

'I would say that she had no reason to be jealous unless there was a question of inheritance,' Mrs Raike replied. 'If Mr

Hastings were to leave Daylesford to his natural daughter rather than to his wife's two sons, then I should think she would be most aggrieved. My cousin says it's one of the finest houses in Gloucestershire.'

I could imagine the look in those snake eyes if such a thing came to pass. Then something occurred to me. 'Does *she* know, I wonder?'

'Who, dear?'

'Mrs Henry Austen. Does she know that Mr Hastings is her real father?'

Mrs Raike stroked her chin. 'I really have no idea. Miss Gowerton never said.'

Jane would know. This thought struck me suddenly and forcefully. Eliza had told Jane all about her mother sailing off to India to find a husband; she had told her things that, at the time, Jane was probably too young to know about. From all that I had heard, Eliza sounded like the sort of person who would positively revel in a secret of this sort, especially as she had hardly known the man she called Papa.

'I must lie down, now, dear.' Mrs Raike raised a shaky hand to her heart, which conveyed to me that she was fagged beyond endurance. 'Will you have some luncheon sent up to my room?' I concealed a smile as I helped her to her feet. However tired she was, Mrs Raike never liked to miss a meal.

When I had settled her I went to my own room, for I had no desire to eat alone in the dining room. No sooner had I closed the door than I heard knocking. It was one of the young boys the inn employed as porters.

'A message for you, Miss,' he said, thrusting a card into my hand with a saucy grin. 'The gentleman awaits you downstairs – shall I tell him you are coming?'

I turned over the card. The name Henry Austen Esq. stood out in bold black letters. My first instinct was to tear it in two and send the boy back with a tart reply. But I had seen enough

169

of Henry to realise he was unlikely to be deterred by that. No doubt he would bribe the boy to get me downstairs on some other pretext. Unless I was to spend the rest of the day imprisoned in my room, I had better go and hear what he had to say.

Chapter Seventeen

Henry had commandeered a private salon for our meeting, a little room tucked away at the rear of the inn, behind the public bar. As I entered he snapped shut the lid of a silver snuff box, which he tucked into the pocket of his morning coat as he rose from his seat.

'Good morning Miss Sharp.' The smile was at its most brilliant. His eyes shone like a fox at a chicken coop. 'Please forgive me for this intrusion: I hope that your employer has not been inconvenienced by my request to see you.'

'What an eager interest you take in my concerns, Mr Austen!' I seated myself by the window, in clear view of a couple of draymen rolling barrels across the yard. 'But what a pity that you have not always been so solicitous of my welfare.'

Avoiding my eye, he paced across the room to the fireplace, where he turned to address me, one elbow braced against the mantelpiece. 'You can be at no loss, Miss Sharp, to understand the reason for my wishing to speak to you alone. I was most alarmed to see you this morning in the company of Mr and Mrs Hastings. Pray tell me the nature of your connection with them.'

'*Alarmed*, Mr Austen? I should not have thought a character such as yours to be susceptible to such extremity of feeling.'

'Madam, if I have offended you in the past, I beg your pardon, but…'

'*If*? Would you feign ignorance of your part in my dismissal from your brother's house? Do not insult me with such dissembling!'

He hesitated a moment, then said: 'I beg you to consider the matter from the other side. How would you behave if you felt that you had been wrongly accused?'

His vulpine gaze shook my confidence, made me doubt myself again. 'Do you continue to deny it, then?' I spat the words out, determined that he should not get the better of me.

'I deny requesting your dismissal, yes. That was my sister-in-law's decision and one for which I can hardly blame her. The reason for this audience is to prevent you from damaging another member of my family with your fanciful ideas.'

I stared at him, incredulous. 'What on earth can you mean?'

He shifted his weight from one foot to the other, surveying me coolly. 'I asked you the nature of your connection with Mr Hastings. Are you aware that he is my wife's godfather?'

'I am,' I replied. 'I suppose that you fear my repeating the intelligence about you and your sister-in-law to him, so that your wife will get to hear about it.'

'No, Miss Sharp: as usual, you have it all wrong,' he said, with an air of weary disdain. 'My wife would not be the slightest bit interested in such accusations, I can assure you. The person I fear would be injured by your gossip is my sister Jane.'

'*Jane?*' This was beyond reason. 'What *are* you talking about?'

'I don't suppose she will have told you,' he said, in a very superior tone, 'for it is something she likes to keep within the family. My sister writes books. Novels, to be precise. She has completed three of them and hopes for publication. Thus far, her expectations have been raised only to be dashed by delay and prevarication on the part of those to whom she has applied. On her behalf, I have found another publisher and am currently at a delicate stage of negotiations.' Here he paused and nodded, seeing the effect his words had wrought on me. 'This publisher is a client of mine, an investor in my bank. He is not the principal backer, however. That accolade is shared by two other gentlemen: namely my brother, Edward, and Mr Warren Hastings.' My eyes skirted the room as I tried to make sense of what he was saying. The voices of the draymen pierced the silence, shouting oaths as a barrel slipped and thudded against the wall. 'Do you understand, Miss Sharp? If you were to suggest to Mr Hastings…if you were to give any hint of a scandal, of a possible lawsuit brought by my brother against myself…'

Now I comprehended it. His banking empire depended on these two men. If Hastings got wind of Edward pulling out, he would no doubt do the same. Henry's house of cards would come tumbling down, bringing his sister's dreams with it. And yet she had not said anything about these novels to me; all I knew of her writing was the glimpse I had had of *The Watsons* – a book she said was not good enough to show me. I wondered for a moment if Henry had concocted the idea of Jane seeking a publisher as a device to ensure my compliance. She herself had said she thought him capable of almost anything. As if reading my thoughts, he reached into the pocket of his coat:

'This is from one of the novels.' He crossed the room and placed the sheet of paper on the table beside me. 'I expect you will recognise the handwriting.'

I did, of course. The title was *First Impressions*. Years later I was to recognise this page as the beginning of *Pride and Prejudice*. I read the first few lines and smiled inside. But it felt wrong to see her work in these circumstances, like sneaking a look at a private journal. I thrust it away and averted my eyes.

'If you have any regard for my sister you will not tell her that I have let you in on her secret,' Henry said, taking the paper from outstretched hand. 'I pray you, Miss Sharp, guard your tongue when in company – not for my sake but for hers. Do not deny her the chance to fulfil a God-given talent.'

He had rendered me speechless. What was I to do? He had found my Achilles heel and pierced it. He knew that I loved Jane; perhaps he sensed what I was only just beginning to grasp: that my feelings for her went beyond what friendship would allow. I studied his face, brazen in victory, no hint of remorse in its expression. Barely able to contain my anger, I rose from my chair. 'You have said quite enough, Mr Austen. Please leave me now.'

'Certainly Madam,' he replied with a little bow. 'Forgive me for having taken up so much of your time and accept my best wishes for your health and happiness.' And with these words he hastily left the room.

I returned to my chamber in an agony of mind. My chief instinct was to run from the White Hart to Trim Street and pour out everything to Jane. But I was not foolish enough to give way to that impulse. How humiliating for her to know what her brother had done! I would not subject her to such torture for the sake of revealing Henry's machinations and calming the beat of my own heart.

I lay on my bed, his face filling the dark space in my head every time I closed my eyes. I saw him more clearly now than ever: saw that his easy, jovial air concealed a hard, ruthless side. That ability of his to spot vulnerability and to milk it for his own ends had obviously served him very well in the world of commerce. Now he was using it to command my allegiance.

That evening a picnic was planned. Jane and I were to walk to

Beechen Cliff, taking Fanny and Anna with us. At five o'clock the air was as still and hot as a bake house. Mrs Raike said it was the warmest May she could remember. She was off to the theatre with Miss Gowerton and groaned at the thought of being inside a building with no windows. Desperate as I was to see Jane, I felt I should offer to stay with Mrs Raike and fan her while she watched the performance. But in the next breath she said that if she could stand lying swaddled in hot towels under an eiderdown for an hour, an evening at the theatre should be child's play. And with that she shooed me off to Trim Street.

As I hurried through the town, passing chairs and peddlers, I carried an image of Jane before me. She was sitting in the library at Godmersham, her fingers stained black and a pen propped in the inkwell beside her. How I longed to ask her about the other novels she had written. How delightful it would have been to spend the evening talking of the characters she had created, the settings she had picked and the plots she had dreamed up. It hurt to think that she could have shown them to me but had chosen not to. Yet I remembered the excruciating agony of self-doubt I had experienced at the thought of showing my own half-written play to anybody else. How much worse it must be for her, I thought, to have come so close to getting published only to be fobbed off with false promises. No wonder she had kept quiet about it.

I had hoped to have Jane to myself for at least part of the evening but it was not to be. When I arrived at Trim Street Fanny and Anna were already there, helping their aunt and the cook to pack the picnic baskets. It was not until we were high above the gleaming white buildings and the lazy river that the girls left us behind, vying to outrun each other to the view point at the top of the cliff.

'How has it been today?' Jane asked, slipping her arm through mine. 'Did you have to endure the Pump Room again? Having to look upon those insufferable people is bad enough, but having to *smell* them as well – how very vile in this heat!' I laughed and told her that it had not been so bad. She was very much surprised when she heard to whom I been introduced. 'I read in the paper that he was here,' she said. 'Did he bring his horrid wife?'

I described the feathered accoutrements and the snake smile but left out the spiteful comments about Jane's want of a husband. I added that I had found Eliza's godfather quite charming and that he had actually apologised to me for his wife's bad manners.

'She is a harpy,' Jane smiled, 'but she snared him with her beauty, I suppose. She hates Eliza, you know: she is desperately jealous of Mr Hastings' regard for her.'

'Oh?' I affected surprise, for I had not told her of the encounter with Henry and the look Mrs Hastings had given me when she realised we were acquainted.

'She tried to marry Eliza off to her eldest son when the Comte went to the guillotine,' Jane went on, 'because she fears that Mr Hastings will leave Eliza all his money.'

'And Eliza refused?'

'Absolutely. Charles Imhoff is a cruel, talentless oaf. Henry served alongside him in the militia. He told me some awful tales of the way Charles treated his men.'

I thought of Eliza, resplendent in her gilded drawing room, showing off her home to the embittered Mrs Hastings, whose husband was now funding the man Eliza had chosen over her own son. No surprise, then, that the lady had made herself so disagreeable at the musical evening, pinching the servants and criticising the players.

I wanted to tell Jane what Mrs Raike had whispered on the way to the Pump Room: ask her if it was true that Eliza was the natural daughter of Mr Hastings. But my concern for her was far greater than my curiosity. If Jane was ignorant of the gossip, I reasoned, it would come as a terrible shock to her, and if she was not, it would be humiliating for her to know that her cousin was being whispered about in such a public place. But to my surprise, she raised the subject herself.

'I suppose that you will have heard, if Miss Gowerton is a close friend of Mrs Hastings, what they say about Eliza's parentage?'

I hesitated a moment before owning it, but she saw it in my face. She gave a little sigh as I repeated what Mrs Raike had said. 'Is it true,' I asked her, 'or just a spiteful rumour from a jealous tongue?'

'I don't know,' she replied. 'Nobody knows: not even Eliza herself. My Aunt Philadelphia would never discuss it, even when Eliza demanded to know. When she died Eliza found letters – not love letters, exactly, but enough to suggest a deep attachment.'

'What about Mr Hastings? Surely he could give her the substance of it?'

Jane shook her head. 'Eliza told me she is afraid to ask. It is a case, I think, of not wanting to kill the goose that lays the golden eggs.'

At that moment Anna came bounding up to us, Fanny trailing in her wake. Anna had matured so much since the previous summer that she could easily have been mistaken for a woman of twenty, though she was only three weeks past her thirteenth birthday. Her dark curls twisted over her pink cheeks as she hung her head, breathless from running. I thought how pretty she was. Difficult for the stepmother, I thought, for Mary Austen could never have been a beauty such as this, with her scarred face and her masculine jaw. I remembered what Fanny had said in the bathing machine: about Mary being grumpy and jealous during her last confinement. Beholding Anna now I could well believe it. It was unlikely that Mary's own daughter would grow to be such a beauty.

We settled ourselves on a patch of short grass sheltered by blossoming gorse bushes and began unpacking the picnic baskets. The sun was still well above the horizon, its golden glow not yet turned amber. Jane tapped Fanny on the wrist when she tried to pluck a sweetmeat from beneath the cloth that covered them. Leaning back on the rug with a pout, Fanny said:

'Aunt Jane, what is Criminal Conversation?'

Jane's eyes darted towards mine with a look of surprise tinged with suspicion. 'Why ever do you ask me that, Fanny?'

'I saw it in the Bath paper. Aunt L.P. lets me read it, you know,' she replied, with an air of self-importance. 'It said: "Lord Craigavon is suing Sir Frederick Sissons for Criminal Conversation with his wife, Lady Diana Craigavon, nee Archbold." What does it mean?'

'Well,' Jane said slowly, 'it means just what it says, doesn't it?' She glanced at me again but before I could think up anything eligible she said: 'Evidently Sir Frederick and Lady Craigavon have been talking about things that should only be discussed by husband and wife.'

I nodded vigorously and pulled the cloth off the hard-boiled eggs. 'Have one of these, Fanny dear,' I said. 'Would you like some cucumber with it?'

'But surely you can't take someone to court for just *talking*!' the child persisted. I saw her cast a sly glance at Anna. Apparently she had a pretty good idea what the term meant but wanted the sport of embarrassing her aunt. In this, however, she was to be disappointed, for Jane was about to deliver more than her niece had bargained for.

'Actually, Fanny, you can: although that is a different matter altogether and is called slander. What you have read about is something the Bible teaches. Do you know the Ten Commandments?'

'Er...yes,' Fanny blinked at her, uncertain now where this was leading.

'And what is the seventh commandment?'

Fanny glanced at Anna again, but her cousin was staring determinedly at the hard boiled eggs. 'Thou shalt not....' She bit her lip. 'Thou shalt not commit...*adultery*.' A deep blush was spreading from her neck to her cheeks.

'Exactly right!' Jane clapped her hands together in mocking applause. 'And can you explain to us all what that word means?'

'I...no...not really...' Fanny stammered, all confusion now the tables had been turned. I almost felt sorry for the child, although she had brought it on herself.

'Well I suggest you pay more attention when you are in church, then,' her aunt replied, 'for if it is human wickedness you are interested in, you will learn more from the Old Testament than from any newspaper.'

Fanny went silent then and everybody fell to eating. But after a few minutes Anna ventured a question on the same theme. 'What will happen to Lady Craigavon,' she asked, her lips shedding yellow crumbs of egg. 'Will she be whipped in the street?'

'I very much doubt that, as she is the wife of a Lord,' Jane replied. 'But I expect that her husband will divorce her when the trial is over. That is what wealthy men do if their wives displease them.'

Anna looked thoughtful as she swallowed the last of the egg. 'So then she can marry Sir Frederick?'

'Well...yes...if he does not have a wife already, that is.' Jane said.

'Well, if he does, his wife would divorce him, wouldn't she?' Fanny piped up. Both she and Anna were looking intently at their aunt, as if they had planned all along to bring her to this point.

'It is not that simple,' she replied, picking at a clump of daisies and scattering the heads. 'A man can divorce his wife

179

for Criminal Conversation but she cannot divorce him for the same reason.'

'What? Even if she is rich?' Fanny sank back on her heels, her arms crossed over her chest.

'She may be as rich as Croesus but she must find some other evidence that he is an unsuitable husband. She would have to prove that he has beaten her or committed some other act of immorality.'

The girls turned to each other with arched brows. 'That is not fair, is it, Aunt Jane?' Fanny said. 'Must a woman feign blindness to her husband's wrongdoing? Must she forgive him everything even if he makes her hate him?'

'When was the lot of a woman ever fair?' Jane shrugged.

'I know what I would do.' Anna looked all innocence but her voice was as treacherous as ice on a pond. 'If I married a man like that I would poison him. I would do it slowly and secretly, so no one would ever know.'

'Anna!' Fanny stared at her, open-mouthed. 'Then you would go to hell when you died.'

'What would be the difference?' her cousin replied. 'To be forced to live with someone you hated, with no prospect of escape, would be hell enough. But if you were clever, if you did not get caught, you could have many years of heaven on earth.'

'I do not know what books you have been reading, Anna, but I think your papa would be very shocked to hear you talk thus.' Jane sounded stern but if I was not mistaken, there was a glimmer of approval in her eyes. 'Apparently you have scant regard for what he preaches.'

'That may be true, Aunt,' the girl replied, with a glance at her cousin, 'but I am not the only one in this family who is guilty of it.'

Her veiled accusation hung as heavy as the gold-laden gorse boughs. Of whom was she speaking? Was it her stepmother?

Her uncle Henry? Aunts Elizabeth or Eliza? Jane did not ask and neither did Fanny. Perhaps each was afraid of what they thought she might reveal.

I busied myself with pouring out lemonade, trying to ease the tension with talk of the comings and goings at the White Hart Inn. Jane was quick to respond and before long the girls were absorbed in making daisy chains. Watching their intent, guileless faces it was hard to recall that other, shadow side that Anna had displayed so artlessly just half an hour since. I could not have known it then but the words she had spoken on that sultry spring evening would haunt me just as powerfully as the ghost that had followed me from Godmersham.

Chapter Eighteen

There was great excitement on the final day of my visit to Bath, for Jane had arranged that we would attend a ball – the very last one of the season. We were to be accompanied by Cassandra and Mrs Austen, by James and Mary and, of course, by Henry.

Fanny and Anna were desperate to go too, but were considered too young to take part in a public ball such as this. As a compromise they were to be allowed to dress themselves in all their finery and watch the opening dances before being escorted home in Uncle and Aunt Leigh-Perrot's carriage.

Mrs Raike very kindly arranged for my gown to be sent round to Trim Street so that Jane could help arrange my dress and my hair. 'Be sure not to run off with any beaux,' she smiled, as she bid me goodbye. 'Tell them I cannot spare you!' I laughed at the sheer absurdity of this. I had, as far as I knew, never attracted the admiration of any man. Neither would I have welcomed such attention. My parents had talked of marriage when I was about twenty years old, but seeing my disinclination for the subject, had let it go. They seemed content to keep me with them, and I wanted nothing more.

Their loss left a gaping void that I simply could not imagine being filled by a husband. It had not occurred to me that I *was* capable of the kind of love my parents had for each other. Only in these past few months had that become clear to me. But my version of that love could never be celebrated, as theirs was; it could not even be acknowledged. I was fearful of what Jane stirred up in me; I told myself I was an oddity; an aberration. To tell Jane how I felt would be to risk losing her forever.

When I arrived at Trim Street Jane ushered me straight up the stairs to her chamber. 'I have the irons ready for your hair,' she said, by way of explanation, 'so you must sit down and let me get to work.'

I sat very still as she applied the hot metal tongs and what I experienced was something close to torture. She did not burn me or pull my hair – she was far too deft for that – but the sensation of her fingers on my scalp was an agonising kind of pleasure. I craved her touch but dreaded the price I must pay for it, which was an overwhelming sense of self-loathing.

Unconscious of my anguish, Jane was absorbed in creating a coronet of ringlets that softened my brow and covered my rather large ears. She had procured a length of blue satin ribbon to match my gown, which she wound into my hair at the back in a most intricate style, finally fixing in three white ostrich feathers. She told me that when I stood up I must remember to bend my head to get out of the room, as the feathers gave me an extra foot in height.

Her own dress was white satin with a gold trim on the bodice and sleeves. Around her neck she wore a topaz cross, bought for her by her youngest brother Charles on one of his voyages in the Mediterranean. 'Will you fix my hair inside this?' she asked, taking a gold Mameluk cap from a bandbox. 'Cass says it makes me look like a Turkish pirate – what do you think?'

I thought that no pirate could ever hope to look as handsome as she did, with her smooth, olive skin and mischievous, sparkling eyes. She took a bottle of lavender water from her dressing table and dabbed some on either side of my neck at the collarbone.

'There! You are finished!' She leaned forward and kissed me on the cheek. My hands moved without my permission, reaching out to gather her up. A rap on the door sent them swiftly back down again. Mrs Austen entered the chamber – or rather two peacock feathers appeared from behind the door, with the old dame attached to them. The feathers had been sewn onto the front of a snug-fitting satin cap of the same purple hue as the eye of the peacock. Her gown was of a similar shade and she carried a reticule adorned with shimmering silver sequins.

'How well you look, girls!' She leaned back a little, her gloved hands on her hips. 'Do you know, Jane, it was forty-two years ago that I danced with your father at this very ball the week after our wedding?'

'Yes, Mama, you have told me,' Jane replied with a rueful grin at me.

'Ah! Those were the days! So many young men asking me to dance! Your poor papa was fighting them off!'

'And I suppose the young men today are nowhere near as handsome or gay, are they Mama?' Jane's face was all earnest inquiry, but her bosom quivered with suppressed mirth.

'No indeed!' her mother replied. 'Your brothers are sure to be the only ones worth looking at this evening, more's the pity. I don't expect there will be anyone young enough to catch the eye of Fanny or Anna, but I cherish hopes for you girls and for Cassandra.'

Jane looked as if she was going to burst. She put a handkerchief to her mouth and made a kind of muffled snort.

'You are not going down with a chill, I hope?' Mrs Austen

said. 'All that tramping about the countryside in the night air! I never did hold with evening picnics.' With that she made for the door. 'Make haste now, girls. Cass is ready and Henry has arrived.'

When she had gone Jane fanned her pink face and turned to me with a helpless shrug. 'Poor Mama! She never gives up!'

But what about you, Jane? I couldn't help wondering how she felt about her mother's all-too-obvious desire to see her married. It must have shown in my face for she said: 'Someone did make a proposal once, you know. He was a neighbour when we lived in Hampshire. His sisters were great friends of mine and he had a large house and a fortune…' she trailed off, staring at the rag rug upon which she stood. 'I'd known him since he was a little boy and I loved him almost as much as I loved his sisters. But I knew that I could never love him in *that* way.'

I could not see her face for her head was still downcast. What did she mean? I wondered for a moment if she felt as I felt; that men held no attraction for her. But her wistful voice suggested that she was not as I was; that she *did* like men but had fallen for the wrong kind: the kind for whom a parson's daughter with no money would not do, no matter how clever or captivating she may be.

I wanted to ask her if she had ever been in love but Mrs Austen bellowed from downstairs, urging us to hurry up. I forgot to duck and my feathers were a little lop-sided by the time I reached the hallway. I saw Henry's eyebrows lift at the sight of me. I was not sure whether he was suppressing a grin at my headgear or simply surprised to see me there at all. Perhaps he had thought to frighten me off with his visit to the White Hart. If that was the case, I thought, grimly, he had underestimated me.

The ball was held in the Assembly Rooms and we found ourselves part of a crush of humanity so dense it was difficult to move beyond the entrance without getting poked in the face by high feathers or elbowed in the ribs by some fan-wielding matron. Mrs Austen spotted a friend sitting on one of the high benches that edged the ballroom and, with some determination, managed to push her way through the throng and take a seat beside her. She beckoned Fanny and Anna to join her, which they did willingly, for it afforded the best view of the assembled crowd.

Fanny was wearing a new gown of pale green taffeta, but Anna was wearing the same rather tight-fitting dress she had worn to the fireworks. I noticed that her father and stepmother were both splendidly and expensively attired. Mary wore an open-fronted gown of fuchsia silk edged with lace, worn over a white satin petticoat. On her head was a hat of the same deep pink, lined with white silk and trimmed with tiny beads of jet. Three ostrich feathers curled from the front: two white and one dyed to match her gown. The soft brim of the hat flattered her face, casting a shadow over the pockmarks.

She seemed very much the master of her husband, summoning him to her side with a flick of her fan when he got caught up with someone of his acquaintance. He wore a mauve waistcoat with a matching silk cravat – chosen, Jane told me, to complement his wife's costume. Observing him at the fireworks display I had not been able to distinguish his face very well. I saw now that he had similar features to Jane and Henry but lacked the magic ingredient that lit up their faces. He had a look of bored resignation in his eyes, which, together with his unfortunate habit of walking about with his nose in the air, made him appear arrogant and irritable.

When the Grand March was called Mary took James firmly by the arm and propelled him to a place as near to the front of the procession as she could get. Henry escorted Cassandra, leaving Jane and I together. There must have been fifty couples at least, which made the business of walking around the room without treading on the hem of a gown very difficult indeed. As we reached the place where we must curtsey to the Master and Mistress of the Dance we turned to the left and I caught sight of Mrs Warren Hastings. She and her husband were only half a dozen places ahead of us but I could not see him because of the turban she was wearing. It was the size of a goodly pumpkin, but of a creamy hue, with a fountain of black feathers erupting from her forehead.

Jane had spotted her too. 'Her head looks like a half-plucked turkey,' she whispered, 'and she will tickle all her partners till they sneeze.'

We squeezed each other's arms in mirth when we saw Mr Hastings take out a handkerchief and wipe his nose. It happened during *The Duke of York's Fancy*, for which each person retained their partner from the Grand March. The next dance saw Jane and I separated, for her card had been marked by Captain Jenkins, an elderly gentleman who lived next door to the Austens in Trim Street.

'He smells of dogs and has only three teeth in his head,' Jane grimaced as she showed me her card. 'I rather hoped that he would ask Mama, but it seems that I am to be the lucky one!' As the captain rolled up to claim his prize I saw Henry leading Cassandra to a seat on the bench near her mother. Then he took Anna's hand and raised her to her feet. I saw a blush come to her cheeks and she would not look up, her long dark lashes attempting to mask the embarrassment her skin betrayed. I saw Henry beckon to his brother, who looked at Mary for approval before moving across the room to join his family. He took Fanny's hand and the two men led the girls to a little alcove off the ballroom as the music announced the start of *The Prince of Wales' Favourite*.

'Henry is such a darling!' Mrs Austen declared as I took the seat Anna had vacated. 'He knows how much those girls were longing for a dance and he has found the very spot: a place where they can hear it all but not be seen by anyone save the musicians.'

Mary did not look in the least bit impressed by this gesture of Henry's to her stepdaughter. She complained that he had taken James away for what was *her* favourite dance. Then she began to grumble about the price of the tickets.

'It is all very well for you, living here,' she said to her mother and Cassandra, 'but the expense of visiting such a place is not to be borne! Austen and I have had to have six new outfits each, not to mention James-Edward's new boots and coat and the baby carriage for Caroline…' she trailed off into a litany of moans and groans, culminating with the observation that the Leigh-Perrots would do well to give away some of their money while they were still alive to see the benefit it would give.

I stole a glance at Mrs Austen, for it was her brother and his wife that Mary was discussing so disrespectfully. Her face bore a version of the weary irritation I had seen in her eldest son. I was reminded of the words Madame Bigeon had spoken in the kitchen at Henry's house. Yes, I thought, James *is* married to a scold.

The dance ended and the girls returned from the alcove bright-eyed with excitement. Henry gave Anna a little bow as he released her and she flashed a shy smile at him. Then Mary was on her feet, getting between them and simultaneously seizing her husband by the hand.

'It is high time you were going home, girls,' she said, in a voice that defied any appeal that might be forthcoming. 'Clarkson is waiting for you over there. Off you trot!' With a wave of her fan she dismissed them. 'Now, James,' she went on, 'you must take your sister for the next. She pushed his hand towards Cassandra and took Henry by the arm. 'Brother, do you like *The Royal Meeting*?'

'I do indeed, Sister,' he replied with a wide smile, 'but I fear I cannot be your partner, for I have promised this dance to Jane.' With that he set off to claim her from the octopus arms of Captain Jenkins.

James was already on his way with Cassandra and Mrs Austen had gone to see Fanny and Anna off. That left me alone with Mary, who looked as peevish as a cat turned off a cushion. There was noise and movement all about but the silence between us was oppressive. I was racking my brains for some suitable topic of conversation when, to my great surprise, Warren Hastings appeared at my side.

'Would you do me the honour, Miss Sharp?' He was holding out his hand to me. From the corner of my eye I saw Mary Austen's frown deepen.

'Why, thank you Mr Hastings,' I said, grateful for this unexpected chance of escape. As he led me away I heard Mary Austen muttering to herself. I could not tell what she said but no doubt it was something spiteful.

For an old gentleman Mr Hastings was very light on his feet. Before long I spied his wife dancing with an admiral whose brass coat buttons looked as if they might fly off with the strain of holding his stomach at bay. He was not sneezing, although he did look very red in the face. She wore a fixed smile and was obliged to shift this way and that to avoid being bumped by his belly. She did not look happy.

After complimenting me on my gown and remarking on the exceptional weather, Mr Hastings revealed the motive for his act of chivalry to me. 'Tell me, Miss Sharp,' he said, 'how was my Betsy when you saw her?'

'Oh,' I replied, 'she looked very well to me. We spent a most pleasant afternoon together.'

'Was her husband there?' There was a flicker of something dangerous in his faded blue eyes.

'Not that afternoon, no,' I said, cautiously, 'but he dined at home in the evening.' I thought it best not to say that Eliza had left the house before he returned. I was mindful of Henry's warning about the implications for Jane of stoking any suspicions Warren Hastings might already have formed about the marriage.

'I suppose you saw him more often at Godmersham?' He smiled as he said it, but I was certain he was fishing.

'When I worked there, yes,' I replied.

'I hear that it is a very fine house indeed,' he went on. 'If I had a brother with such a place I daresay that I would be a very frequent visitor.' I said nothing in reply to this, hoping that a puzzled sort of smile would put him off. It did not. 'Did Betsy visit much while you were there?'

As luck would have it, the dance demanded a star formation at this point and I was required to turn away from him as we joined our right hands with the couple opposite. The circular walk we next performed gave me time to think of a suitably evasive reply. 'I'm afraid that I was not always aware of visitors,' I said, as we came together again. 'I did not enjoy very good health while I worked at Godmersham. I was sent away to convalesce for several weeks on account of my eyesight. That, in the end, was why I had to quit my post as governess.'

'Ah,' he nodded, 'I am sorry to hear it.' To my relief he abandoned the subject of Henry, having apparently decided that a woman with bad eyes was a hopeless sort of witness to interrogate. The dance ended and his wife was upon us in a moment, her feathers twitching like the feelers of an ant. She touched her hat with the folded tip of her fan in a gesture that perfectly conveyed her opinion of me and her impatience with him. He bowed and took his leave. As I made my way back across the floor I felt Jane's hand on my arm. I turned to see Henry standing beside her.

'Well, Miss Sharp – a distinguished partner indeed!' His

190

eyes searched mine. 'I trust that Mr Hastings did not overtax you with conversation? *The Royal Meeting* is such a vexing dance to perform correctly, is it not?' Just like Mrs Hastings with her fan, Henry's message was crystal clear.

'He was a most considerate partner,' I replied. 'Alas, I am not as practiced as he, but I was able to play my part without too much disgrace, I think.' I saw a smile of relief spread across his face. Jane saw it too and cast me a curious look. But before another word could be spoken James came bustling up to us.

'Where is Mary?' he asked, his face agitated. 'I cannot find her anywhere!'

His inquiry caused us all to go off in different directions, searching inside and out to no avail. When we came together at the high bench we found him talking to his mother.

'She came running out as the carriage was departing,' Mrs Austen said. 'She felt unwell and decided to go home with the girls.'

'What was wrong with her?' James frowned.

'She did not say,' his mother replied with a shrug. 'It is vastly hot in here: I expect she felt faint from the dancing. I'm sure that *I* should have felt so at five-and-thirty with a child not a twelvemonth old!'

I saw someone else approach our little party then. It was Warren Hastings, who had seen our confusion and wanted to know the cause.

'It was my brother, sir,' Jane told him. 'He had lost his wife.'

'Is that so?' Mr Hastings inclined his head very slightly and fixed his eyes on James. Then he looked at Henry. With a sage sort of nod he said: 'You Austen men really should take better care of your wives!'

Chapter Nineteen

I wish that I could dwell on the joy of dancing with Jane that last night in Bath, of breathing her in as I held her in *The Duke of Kent's Waltz*. I took a bottle of lavender water back to Yorkshire to remind me of the scent of her, and to relive the days we spent together during the long, dark months when work and family ties kept us far apart.

I wish, indeed, that I could continue this memoir as I originally intended it to be: an honest portrayal of Jane and her family and the depth of my attachment to her. But a few days after recording my memories of the ball I made a discovery that transformed my perception of the tragic events that unfolded in quick succession of my visit to Bath. Suspicion has weighed so heavy on my mind that I have been unable to write anything for a long, long time. In taking up my pen again there is a sea change in my motivation; a pressing need to clarify thoughts that are too dangerous to voice.

There was a brief lull before these calamities began, during which my life in Yorkshire continued much as before the trip to Bath. I decided that enough time had elapsed to claim an improvement in my eyesight and before long I was reading novels to Mrs Raike every evening. One night I happened to get up during the reading to close a window that had been left ajar and I spied Rebecca, tucked behind the door, listening. She ran off in tears when she realised I had seen her. It took me a while to comprehend what the matter was but, with the aid of a paper and pencil, I managed to persuade her to draw pictures of what troubled her. The explanation was quite simple: she could not speak but she could hear quite clearly – and she loved to listen to the stories we read aloud each night.

With Mrs Raike's encouragement, I began trying to teach her to read. It was more of a challenge than anything I had ever attempted but she was an eager pupil. Within a month she had mastered the alphabet and was able to draw pictures of a hundred words whose written shape she recognised. It was a wonderful thing for me to behold her progress. I had missed teaching more than I realised and Rebecca gave a new dimension to my life, a sense of purpose.

Before long she was able to write sentences as well as read them. She would sit alongside me sometimes when I wrote letters, copying passages from the Bible or a favourite book. Sometimes I read snippets of Jane's letters aloud to her, for if she found something amusing it seemed to stick in her brain all the better.

'It will be two months on Friday since we left Bath for Southampton,' Jane wrote to me in August. 'What happy feelings of escape! I do not think I told you what happened the night before we left: Captain J. came from next door to bid us all *adieu* but when he arrived Mama and Cass were still upstairs packing. I was forced to entertain him in the parlour while we waited. As I went to pour him a glass of wine he said: "Well, Miss Austen, I suppose this is my last chance?" whereupon he seized the bottle from my hand and tried to kiss it (my hand, not the bottle, I should say). I did not wish to wound the poor old gentleman – in body or in mind – but this surprise attack produced the strongest reaction from me. I swung my other hand at his head and caught him on the nose (which, being fat and purple, was an easy target). Mama and Cass appeared at that moment to find him bleeding all over Martha's rag rug. He told them he had tripped over it and banged his face on the mantelpiece. I did not want to add to his humiliation by contradicting this: I only hope that his new neighbours will not be a gaggle of husband-hunters – the excitement could prove fatal.'

I laughed with Rebecca over this, although I have to admit that the thought of anyone trying to claim Jane, however unlikely their chances, made me jealous. I squirreled away every fond word, every tender phrase that she bestowed on me. And when I wrote back I tried not to betray myself. Her letters were full of the other people in her life while I, with a much smaller cast of characters to draw on, filled up the page with my opinion of some new book or volume of poetry I had acquired. I itched for news of her novels but I dared not reveal what Henry had told me.

Of him there was no mention in her letters. I wondered whether she regretted confiding her fears about him to me and sought, by silence on the subject, to expunge it from my memory. The only intelligence I received about Henry in the months that followed was from my correspondence with Fanny and Anna and each of them referred to him only indirectly.

Anna wrote in her usual, direct fashion of her fury at missing a trip to London: 'I am so angry today I can hardly control my pen. Last week I received an invitation from Aunt Eliza. She said that Uncle Henry was coming to Hampshire on business at his bank and would like to bring me back with him for a fortnight's visit. She promised trips to the theatre and the shops, and, as you can imagine, I was only too eager to accept her invitation. But what do you think? My stepmother took it upon herself to write back on my behalf, turning the offer down flat. She said I had recently suffered a cold and was still weak; the excitement would be too much for me. This, of course, is utter rot. I am as strong as a horse.' Evidently Mary Austen's jealousy of Henry's wife burned as bright as ever.

Fanny, on the other hand, wrote me a very cheerful letter announcing that Uncle James and Aunt Mary were to visit Godmersham for the first time in ten years. 'I'm so looking forward to seeing Anna again,' she wrote, 'and it will be most interesting to see how James-Edward and little Caroline get on with my brothers and sisters. Uncle Henry is sure to come during their visit, so it is a good thing that Aunt Eliza cannot cross the Thames, for there would certainly be war in our house if she and Aunt Mary found themselves under the same roof.'

The next letter I received from Fanny described all the fun the children had had together, although she did not include herself and Anna in this description as both were now in their fifteenth year and thought themselves young ladies. 'Papa took Aunt Mary and Uncle James to Southampton at the end of their visit,' she wrote. 'They all spent a week with Grandmama Austen and Aunts Jane and Cassandra. Uncle Henry stayed behind to keep Mama company.'

I raised my eyebrows at this, conscious of the fact that Fanny had made no attempt to qualify this arrangement: on the contrary, she had stated it quite baldly when she need not have mentioned it at all. Alarmingly, the letter following this one informed me that her mother was expecting yet another child. Her last-born, Cassandra Jane, had not yet reached her second birthday. Once again I had to wonder if Henry was the natural father of this coming baby.

A few months later I went to stay with Jane in Southampton.

I anticipated the visit with a mixture of excitement and trepidation. Jane had written that Cassandra, her mother and Martha Lloyd would all be away when I arrived, so we could spend the whole week together undisturbed.

'The wind from the sea makes the house rather cold, I'm afraid,' she added, 'but we can share my bed if you like.' I had shared a bed many times with my cousins. The memory of Catherine and Constance laughing with me late into the night was something I cherished. But the thought of lying beside Jane was as far from that image as the moon is from the sun. I had no idea how it would feel; how it *should* feel.

Jane's bed was a wonderful tented creation of white dimity which, with the curtains drawn, reminded me of a ship in full sail. When I climbed in beside her I was trembling and, thinking I was cold, she wrapped her arms around me. I lay there very still until she said: 'Are you asleep already?' She tickled me and made me laugh so much I forgot to be afraid. Then we lay with our arms entwined, talking until the bell in the castle square rang two o'clock.

The next two nights followed a similar pattern. I began to feel easy enough to stroke her hair as she stroked mine, to kiss her when we said goodnight. For that brief time I allowed myself to believe what I wanted with all my heart to be true. If what I felt inside was a sin, then I was prepared to face hell and all its demons. The words spoken by Anna at the picnic in Bath came back to me as I lay in her arms: *You could have many years of heaven on earth before that.*

But on the third night, with a single sentence, Jane snuffed out that flickering hope. 'I have loved only two men in my life.' She was lying on her back, her profile a barely discernable silhouette in the dark space we shared. 'The first was called Tom. He was Irish, the cousin of our friends the Lefroys. We were both twenty years old and we met at a ball in Hampshire.'

196

'What happened?' My question floated up to the canopy. I felt as if my soul was taking leave of my body.

'We flirted outrageously.' I could not tell if she smiled as she said it. 'It went on for about a week, until his aunt put a stop to it.'

'Why?'

'Because I had no money and he had a tribe of dependant sisters. They packed him off to London and I never saw him again.'

'Oh.'

'Oh, indeed.' I heard her give a little sigh. 'I hear of him sometimes. He married well and had three children, I think, at the last count.'

I hesitated a moment, trying to gauge her mood. He breathing was regular. Was she upset by this memory? Did she still yearn for this lost love? I could not tell. 'What about the second?' I ventured.

'I met him on holiday in Sidmouth,' she said. 'It was the summer after we left Steventon. He was a curate and he had a brother who was a doctor. They were visiting the town together.' She did not reveal his name and her voice told me that it still pained her to think of him. 'We made an arrangement during the holiday,' she said. 'We were going to meet there again the following year.'

I was afraid to ask what happened next. I lay there in silence, waiting for her to go on.

'Papa had a letter from his brother a few weeks after we parted,' she said at last.

'What did it say?' I held my breath.

'That he was dead,' she said simply. 'I want no husband now.' She reached for me in the darkness, her hand finding mine and squeezing it tight. 'A little companionship and a dance now and then will suit me very well.'

I kissed her cheek and found it wet with tears. I wiped them dry with the sleeve of my nightgown. Then I told her that I had never loved a man; that I had never truly thought of marriage. I did not tell her about the client of my father's who had thrust his hand under my skirts as I reached for a book he had requested from the highest shelf; I did not describe the revulsion and self-loathing this had caused me, nor the dread it had engendered of any man's touch. I have no doubt that such a confession would have provoked the most sincere and tender concern from Jane– but it was not her sympathy I wanted. It was clear, now, that she did not crave what I craved. If I was to keep her close, I must never, ever, give away my true feelings.

'You are so wise,' she whispered. 'When I look about me and see what slaves most women become I think that though I will never be rich, I am happier than many. What an awful thing it must be, to await a confinement: to write those parting letters to friends and family.'

'Yes,' I murmured, thinking of the letter Elizabeth had entrusted to me: the letter that had shamed me with its heartfelt expression of love and intrigued me with its postscript about Henry. I wondered if she wrote such letters anew each time a lying-in approached.

Echoing my thoughts, Jane said: 'I imagine that Elizabeth must have a whole cupboard full of them.' When she uttered these words, she could not have known of the dreadful event that had occurred just hours before.

She had informed me, upon my arrival, that Elizabeth had been safely delivered of her child, a boy, who had been named Brook-John. There was no reason to suppose that the confinement had been anything other than satisfactory and the mother was evidently recovering well. But on the fourth morning of my visit a letter arrived by express, informing us that Elizabeth had fallen violently ill after eating her evening meal and within half an hour of her collapse she was pronounced dead. She was but thirty-six years old.

The letter had been sent by Cassandra, who had gone to Godmersham to assist with the birth. The following day we received another, which described the terrible suffering the death had wrought on the family. Edward was beside himself with grief, saying that he could not bear to attend the funeral and see his beloved wife laid in the ground. Poor Fanny was clinging to her aunt for comfort while trying to be a mother to the little ones. And then there was Henry, who had apparently arrived within twenty-four hours of Elizabeth's death. When Jane told me this I had to look away for fear of showing my expression. How on earth could Henry have got there so quickly? It suggested that he had one of the servants in his pocket, primed to inform him of any sudden turn of events. *Highly likely*, I thought, *if he had a personal interest in the birth of Elizabeth's child.*

Jane's reaction to the death of her sister-in-law, once the shock had subsided, was not quite what I expected. Evidently she was uncertain how to respond, for as we sat writing letters of condolence, she asked me for my opinion of the reply she had made to Cassandra. In it she expressed concern first of all for the children, but after just four sentences she asked if Cassandra had seen Elizabeth's dead body. 'I suppose you see the corpse,' she wrote, 'how does it appear?' I wondered why she should ask such a thing but I did not want to make what had no doubt been a difficult task harder by querying her words. I suggested she might add a few lines in praise of her late sister-in-law, but this she rejected outright.

'How can I eulogise a woman who despised me?' she demanded. 'That would be hypocrisy indeed!'

In the end she added a sentence about Elizabeth's devotion to her children. I thought she had written more than that, but when she gave it to me I saw that most of the new paragraph was about her concern for Edward, and whether or not, when it came to it, he would attend the funeral after all. Then

Henry's name caught my eye. 'Of Henry's anguish, I think with grief and solicitude,' she had written, 'but he will exert himself to be of use and comfort.'

Anguish. With that one word she had acknowledged Henry's special place in Elizabeth's heart. What would become of him now, I wondered? If any of those children were his, he would certainly wish to keep up his frequent visits to Godmersham – but how painful for him, with her gone! In spite of everything that had passed between us, I could not help but feel for him.

But it was Fanny, of course, whose feelings were uppermost in my mind. I could hardly bear to think what it must be like for her, grieving for her mother while having to put on a show of fortitude for her younger brothers and sisters. It was a mercy Cass was there, I thought; between them, she and Sackree would get Fanny through this awfulness.

It never occurred to Jane or to me to question what had happened to Elizabeth. There was nothing unusual about a woman dying in childbirth, even if she had come through many previous confinements without mishap. With hindsight I can see that to murder a woman in the days following her lying-in would be shockingly easy – both in the execution of the crime and its concealment. If someone had asked me at the time if Elizabeth had any enemies, anyone who hated her enough to wish her dead, only one name, I think, would have sprung to mind. And it would have been the wrong one. I have to repeat that to myself in the darkness that descends on me so often now; I have to tell myself that even if I had suspected something was not right, I could not have prevented what followed.

Chapter Twenty

With much regret I left Jane the next day, for she was to take charge of Edward and Elizabeth's older boys, who were away at school in Winchester when their mother died. Her next letter told me of her very inventive ways of attempting to keep their spirits up at such a dreadful time. One afternoon, she reported, she had taken them up the river Itchen in a boat. 'Both boys rowed a great part of the way,' she wrote, 'and their questions and remarks were very amusing: George's enquiries were endless and his eagerness in everything reminds me often of his Uncle Henry.' She had underlined the last four words.

What was I to think of this? After two years of total silence on the subject she clearly wished to resurrect it. There was no more about Henry in that letter, though, for she launched straight into a piece of news that was to bestow boundless benefits. It seemed that Edward had suddenly decided to give his mother and sisters a permanent home on his estate in Hampshire. They were to move into the old bailiff's cottage in the village of Chawton the following summer. This intelligence gave me even greater cause for wonder than her comment about young George. For Jane and her female relatives had been moved from pillar to post for the better part of a decade, forced to accept smaller and poorer lodgings with each advancing year. Why had Edward waited until now to give them a home of their own? I had a feeling that Elizabeth had stopped him; that her dislike of Jane had led her to talk Edward out of doing what he could so easily have done when their father died. It seemed both petty and mean but I could think of no other explanation for this act of generosity coming so swiftly after her death.

To say that Jane was happy is an understatement. The pretty house with its view of all the comings and goings at the coaching inn across the street was the perfect place for her: the place in which she truly blossomed as a writer. Nothing had been said of the novels Henry had hinted at and I had begun to wonder if he had lied to me that day at the White Hart, but within two years of the move a signed copy of her first published book, *Sense and Sensibility*, arrived at the Bourne, much to the excitement of Mrs Raike and Rebecca.

I remember unwrapping it and running my fingers over the smooth skin of its spine; breathing in the aroma of new leather and printer's ink. It triggered a strange mix of emotions. There was the elation at Jane's achievement and a thrilling sense of anticipation of what the pages held. But there was also a pang of envy, for this book was a stark reminder of my own buried dreams.

Determined to banish such an unworthy sentiment, I plunged into the world of the Dashwoods. How I smiled when I encountered the character called Fanny, for she behaved in a way that reminded me very much of Martha Lloyd's description of her sister: Fanny Dashwood's meanness over the china at Norland mirrored what had happened when Jane and Cass had to quit the rectory at Steventon. This, I thought, is Jane's revenge on Mary.

We celebrated in great style when I visited Chawton that year, with several bottles of Martha's elderberry wine. I did not have the bitterweet pleasure of sharing Jane's bed, as she and Cassandra occupied the same room. I was put in Martha's room, as she was away from home, and we spent the better part of each night in there. During the early part of the evening we would read Jane's book aloud to each other or discuss the next one to be published. She confirmed what Henry had already let out: that she had written three novels before she turned thirty. The third one had been accepted for publication with a small advance paid, but four years on had still not appeared in print. Weary of waiting, she had revised her first novel and sent it to another publisher. This, I assumed, was the client Henry had told me about.

Jane was just beginning to write *Mansfield Park* when tragedy struck her family again. This time it was her cousin Eliza. The death was painful and lingering. She was thought to be suffering from the same condition that killed her mother, but the doctors could not be certain. Jane was with her when she died. She sent me a long letter from Henry's London home.

'Eliza has died after a long and terrible illness,' she wrote. 'Henry long knew she must die and it was indeed a release at last.' She described the great sorrow of Madame Bigeon and her daughter, who had become like family to Eliza. But of Henry she said: 'His mind is not a mind for affliction. He is too busy, too active, too sanguine. Sincerely as he was attached to poor Eliza he was always so used to being away from her that her loss is not felt as that of many a beloved wife might be.'

What a sad epitaph for the vivacious dark-eyed beauty who had dazzled the salons of Paris and London. What would Henry do now? He was forty-two years old and free to marry again – unless, of course, he chose to pursue another married woman. It occurred to me that for Henry, forbidden fruit was very likely the sweetest. Those long years of intrigue with Elizabeth must have left their mark. Such a man would no doubt be partial to the thrill of subterfuge.

When Jane sent me *Mansfield Park* I was quite amazed by her boldness. Henry and Mary Crawford were the very essence of Henry Austen and his late wife. The character of Henry Crawford, with his good looks and charming, devious ways, was unmistakable, as was the lively, dark-eyed Mary, who was so like Eliza that she even played the harp. Was this how Jane had perceived the Henry Austens' marriage, I wondered? Something more akin to a brother and sister, both free to pursue others while residing under the same roof?

I could not help spotting another familiar character on the pages of the new book: Maria Bertram put me very much in mind of Elizabeth Austen. She was the beautiful, self-regarding daughter of a baronet and Jane had even gone as far as to give her a surname that began with the same initial as Elizabeth's maiden name. I thought I perceived some further, more subtle trickery in the use of two names so very similar – Maria and Mary – which echoed Henry Austen's involvement with two women who bore the same Christian name.

I have mentioned before that I believe *Mansfield Park* was a channel for Jane's suppressed rage at her brother's behaviour. Watching her cousin die could only have inflamed her anger, and yet she could not hate Henry; on the contrary, she found it impossible not to go on loving him as she had always loved him. And so she meted out imaginary justice on the pages of her novel. Let Henry Crawford be exposed as the wicked seducer of a married woman; let Maria Bertram be cast out from respectable society for betraying her husband. For in fiction the righteous must triumph and sinners always get their just deserts.

Jane's letters reported that the real Henry continued to live a gilded life, although there were some who proved impervious to his charm. A few weeks into his widowhood he went to see Warren Hastings. It seemed that the extravagant lifestyle led by Henry and his wife had left him in a precarious state. Jane wrote that he had already tried – and failed – to claim back the lands that had once belonged to Eliza's late husband, the Comte de Feuillide. Now his only hope was to discover whether Mr Hastings had made a will in Eliza's favour and, that being the case, whether the money would revert to him on the old man's death.

It seemed that Henry had used Jane's books as a pretext for the visit, for she reported her delight at the comments she received about *Pride and Prejudice*.

'Henry has told Mr Hastings who wrote it, even though it was supposed to be a secret,' she wrote, 'but I am quite delighted with what such a man writes about it. His admiring my Elizabeth so much is particularly welcome to me.' The next paragraph made it clear that Henry's thinly disguised strategy had failed: 'Mr Hastings never <u>hinted</u> at Eliza in the smallest degree.' The underlining spoke volumes. Apparently, Warren Hastings was not going to acknowledge Eliza as his natural daughter, which meant there was unlikely to be any will in her favour. Henry's hopes of the golden goose were come to nought.

Remembering the questions the old gentleman had asked as we danced in Bath, I wondered if he had since gleaned some intelligence that had fixed his opinion of Henry. Had Warren Hastings read *Mansfield Park*? No one acquainted with Henry and Eliza could fail to recognise them in the personages of Henry and Mary Crawford. Had Jane's book revealed more of Henry Austen than Mr Hastings had been able to stomach? If Eliza really was his daughter, it was not difficult to imagine how such a revelation would make him feel – especially if his money had made Henry the gentleman-about-town he could never otherwise have been.

As Jane's star climbed ever higher, Henry's was about to fall from the firmament. The autumn of eighteen-fifteen was Henry's final season as a man of wealth and distinction. It was also the last time I saw my dearest Jane alive.

Chapter Twenty-One

I made the journey to Jane's village in the last week of September, having left Mrs Raike in London at the home of her cousin in Cheyne Walk. There was not much to see as the mail coach crossed the border into Hampshire, for a veil of low cloud hung over the trees and hedgerows, blurring the autumn colours. The horses slowed to walking pace as we drew near to Chawton. The Winchester road was a mess of mud and fallen leaves and a mizzle of rain had turned the roofs of the houses a darker shade of gold. Jane was at her usual post in the front parlour, where she was making some alterations to *Emma*. She spied me through the window and came running out of the cottage as I stepped down.

'You look so well!' She held me at arm's length, her eyes fixed on mine. I caught my breath, for I could not return the compliment. She looked different in a way I couldn't quite define: thinner in the face, perhaps; a little paler than usual. I put it down to the poor summer we had had and the strain of completing yet another novel.

Her writing slope was on a little table with the manuscript piled on top and I begged for a glimpse of the new book.

'Later,' she chided, steering me to a chair beside the fire. 'You must get warm first: your fingers feel like dead eels.' I frowned at my big, ugly hands, which were indeed white with cold. I wondered if they disgusted her. She saw my face and drew me to her, kissing me on my nose and forehead. 'I have missed you,' she whispered. 'And Cass is going to Scarlets tomorrow so you shall have her bed.'

I murmured a silent prayer of thanks to the Leigh-Perrots for inviting Cassandra to stay this week of all weeks. I was sorry that I would see her only briefly, for she was good company and never jealous of my friendship with her sister, but the prospect of waking up with Jane each morning was as wonderful as it was unexpected.

The creaking hinges of the parlour door made us jump apart. A girl appeared with a tray of tea. She was a new maid called Jenny Butter, who blushed to the roots of her fair hair when Jane introduced us. 'Miss Cassandra sent a note by William Parry,' she said, backing out of the room with the tray. 'She and Miss Martha are held up at Wyards with Mrs Lefroy. Nothing to worry about, she says, and she'll be back in time for dinner.'

'I still can't get used to Anna's new name,' Jane said when the maid had gone. 'It makes me feel very ancient, having a married niece. I shall be Great Aunt Jane in a few weeks, you know.'

I did know, for Anna had written to tell me of her pregnancy. She had been married a little less than a year. When the engagement was announced I couldn't help wondering what Jane must feel, knowing that her niece was about to become what she had once hoped to be. Ben Lefroy was a young cousin of the Tom Jane had told me about; the handsome Irishman she had fallen in love with at twenty.

'It's such a pleasure to have her living so near,' Jane went on. 'She gets books from the circulating library and brings them here to read aloud. We have such fun, making the characters as ridiculous as possible: Cass laughs so much she has to beg us to stop, for she cries all over her sewing.'

I felt a momentary pang of envy. Anna had taken the very part I would have liked to play in Jane's life. Rather spitefully, I said: 'I suppose she will not be able to do that when the baby is born.'

'No, poor animal! I fear she'll be worn out before she's thirty. But it's all still too new for her to fear what the future may bring.' She paused, pursing her lips. 'I wasn't sure about Ben at first; I never thought of Anna as a curate's wife. He is as serious as she is saucy – but they don't seem any more miserable than most married people.'

I returned her wry smile with a click of my tongue. 'I was quite concerned when she told me she was getting married. I thought perhaps she was being a little hasty.' I kept back what else had crossed my mind: that Anna was marrying the first eligible man who came along to get away from the stepmother she hated.

'She was rather young,' Jane nodded. 'Ben doesn't have much money and she spends it on the silliest things – but that will all have to change when the baby comes. Anyway,' she leaned forward to top up my teacup, 'we are all dining at the Great House tonight. Edward and his harem are staying there at the moment.' I raised my eyebrows at this and she gave a little snort and a shrug. 'He never travels without at least three female relatives for company,' she said. 'There is Fanny, of course, who has been like a mother to the little ones since Elizabeth died. Then there is Louisa Bridges, Elizabeth's sister – do you remember her? Well, she lives at Godmersham now. And there is another addition to the Kent clan – her name is Charlotte and she is the widow of one of the Bridges brothers. The whole party arrived here last month, bringing the four youngest children, the governess and nineteen servants.'

I shook my head, although I was not surprised by the size of the entourage. 'Has Edward never talked of marrying again?'

'Why settle for one wife when you can have three?' She gave me the kind of look I had seen at the ball in Bath when she spotted Mrs Hastings in her turkey hat. 'He says that Fanny wouldn't like it if he brought another woman in as stepmother to the children. But as it stands, he has her in that role and one of the aunts on his arm for everything else. Perhaps he will think about marrying when Fanny takes a husband – as she surely will before long – but he seems quite content with life for now.'

And what of Henry, I wanted to ask. She would have written to tell me, of course, if he had taken a new wife. It was more than two years since Eliza's death and he was not the sort of man to be without a woman for any length of time. But I bit my lip as the question formed. A decade had passed since that summer of intrigue at Godmersham but Henry's heart, I sensed, was still a slippery subject.

I heard the distant sound of bells from the village church and Jane's hand went to the pocket of her gown. She pulled out a slim gold fob watch on a delicate chain and flipped it open to check the hour.

'What a pretty thing!' I leaned forward to take a closer look. The back showed a tracery of twisting roses with her name engraved in the centre. 'Where did you get it?'

She hesitated a moment. 'It was a gift to mark the publication of *Mansfield Park*,' she said.

'A generous gift indeed!' I replied. 'Did the publishers send it?'

'No.' she snapped the case shut and put it back in her pocket. 'It was Henry. He bought it.' She looked at me and blinked, as if she was bracing herself for an interrogation.

'Well,' I said, rather taken aback, 'that was very kind of

him, I'm sure.' I wondered if this gesture had been made in memory of Eliza, who would certainly have been thrilled to the core by her cousin's success. I was about to ask when Jane's face warned me against it. There was an odd look in her eyes, like a dog guarding a bone. I turned my face to the window and made some stupid remark about the weather. When I turned back she was on her feet, halfway to the door.

'I'm just going to rouse Mama,' she said, 'She'll be so cross that she was asleep when you arrived – she's been longing to see you.'

I had only seen the Great House from a distance. It lay at the western boundary of the village, surrounded by acres of pasture and woodland. To reach it we crossed the meadow that lay between the cottage and the barns flanking the estate. The light was beginning to fade but I could see the pattern of flints in the brickwork of the ancient building, with a cluster of late blooming roses hanging over the north door.

'You'll find it very different from Godmersham, won't she Mama?' Jane turned to help her mother as we climbed a narrow path that skirted the largest dovecote I had ever seen. 'It's all dark wooden panelling and Jacobean hanging staircases.'

'Some of the chambers *are* rather dark,' Mrs Austen nodded, panting a little, 'but the dining room is splendid with a fire.' A chorus of cooing broke out behind us, as if the pigeons were all in agreement about this.

'It's such a shame about the weather.' Cassandra linked her arms through mine and Martha's as Jane and her mother fell behind. 'The parkland is so beautiful at this time of the year when the sun shines on the changing leaves: we must take you for a walk tomorrow, if the rain keeps off.' She led us through a cluster of laurel bushes, which showered us with raindrops as we brushed past. 'It's rather dirty, this way, I know,' she said, clicking her tongue at the rising tide of damp on the hem of my gown, 'but it's so much quicker than walking along the drive.'

I told her that it didn't matter, that I would soon dry out by a good fire. But I was worried about Jane. She was shivering by the time we reached the steps that led through the stone arch to the front door. Cass had noticed it too. With a glance at Martha and a murmured apology to me she withdrew her arms and removed her shawl. Martha went over to Mrs Austen and engaged her in talk of Edward's children while Cass took Jane aside and wrapped her up. Jane might have been her child, standing there still and uncomplaining, as this was done. I saw it more clearly than ever, then: that these were the roles they had slipped into; that Cass's fulfilment in life came from nurturing her sister, whether it was Jane's health or her writing that required it.

As we stood in the draughty vaulted porch waiting for admittance there was a clatter of hooves and a crunch of gravel. A carriage and four bowled up to the steps and as the driver reined in the horses I saw Anna's face pressed against the window. I quite expected her to leap out, as she would certainly have done in years past, but I had forgotten her condition. When the footman came to open the door I was shocked at the change pregnancy had wrought on her body. I suppose I still thought of her as a child, so to see her like that, barely able to walk for the weight of her belly, made me catch my breath.

She had to stand sideways on to kiss me. Then she introduced me to her husband, who was dark-haired, stick-thin and very earnest. Someone was getting out of the carriage behind him. It was little Caroline, the half sister who had been born the year Jane and I met. At ten years old she was not as pretty as Anna had been; I saw that she had the same strong jaw and large frame as her mother, who was following her up the steps.

At that moment Edward's voice boomed out from behind the door. The years had not been kind to him. Close to fifty now, his face was grown ruddier than ever and he looked almost as broad as Anna round the waist. I recognised the woman at his side as Louisa Bridges. Her eyes were very blue, like Elizabeth's but she had a very different air now; quite prim in a plain grey gown with a white lace tucker covering her neck and shoulders.

Waiting in the Great Hall was another member of what Jane had so wickedly described as Edward's harem. This woman I did not recognise, but Martha introduced her to me as Mrs Charlotte Bridges, wife of the late Reverend John Brook Bridges. She had red hair and a sprinkling of freckles and I was struck by how young she looked: not very much older than Anna, I thought. She seemed rather unsure of herself as she greeted me. I saw her smile at Edward as he handed Jane a glass of mulled wine and ushered her towards the roaring fire. Louisa was at the other end of the room, instructing one of the servants. I wondered how they got on, these two single women with their wealthy male protector.

'She was married only two years when he died,' Martha whispered as we moved away. 'No children, sadly. But she dotes on Edward's.' I wondered then if Edward was grooming Charlotte to fill the role Fanny would have to forsake when she married and started a family of her own.

'Where is your father?' Mrs Austen's voice startled me. She was standing behind me, and like many elderly people who are a little deaf, tended to speak very loudly in a crowd. Her question was addressed to Caroline, who was perched on a little stool so close to the fireplace she was almost in it.

'In bed,' the child replied. 'Mama says he has one of his stomachs.'

I had to suppress a smile at this, for she had made James Austen sound like a cow, with several digestive organs at his disposal.

'What have you been feeding him, Mary?' Mrs Austen fixed a beady eye on her daughter-in-law, who was tugging at the shoulders of Anna's gown in a bid to cover up her swelling bosom.

'Feeding him?' She frowned as she plucked a hatpin from her reticule. 'Why, nothing at all! He won't eat a thing: says the very thought of food makes him feel bilious.' With a sudden stabbing movement she stuck the pin through the back of Anna's bodice. 'Don't move!' she hissed, as the girl flinched. 'There! Now you look decent at last.' Turning to her mother-in-law she said: 'I told him, you know: "Your daughter is the one who is supposed to be bilious, not you," I said. Such a sensitive soul, poor Austen: always was and always will be. He thinks it's him having the baby, not her.'

Mrs Austen looked askance at this description of her eldest son. She opened her mouth but was prevented from delivering any kind of reply by the arrival of Fanny, who was a few minutes behind her father in coming to greet us. She looked very fine in a white sarsnet gown trimmed with silver and a silver ribbon braided through her hair. Seeing her beside Anna it was harder than ever to believe that they were of an age. Apart from gaining a few inches in height, Fanny looked much the same as she had at thirteen. She was not a beauty like her mother but her skin had all the fresh bloom of youth and when she caught sight of me her face lit up with a dazzling smile.

'Miss Sharp! Is it really you?' She put her arms round my neck and hugged me in just the same way as when she was a child.

'Oh dear,' I said, 'Have I changed so much?'

'Not a bit!' she said kindly, 'But I hope I have! And what do you think of Anna? A wife already and soon to be a mother!' If she was envious of her cousin's new status she hid it very well. We became so engrossed in catching up on the years that I failed to notice when the door of the Great Hall opened again.

'Good Lord, Henry! What are you doing here?' Edward gave a throaty chuckle as he clapped his brother on the back. I saw Fanny's brow tense into a row of fine lines I hadn't noticed before. She was looking at the new arrival, as was everybody else in the room. The only one who did not look surprised was Mary.

Henry was ushered towards the fireplace. I overhead him telling Edward that some unexpected business with the Alton branch of his bank had brought him to Hampshire on horseback. He had called at the cottage to find no one but the cook, Hannah Pegg, at home. It was she, he said, who had told him of the gathering at the Great House.

'Trust you to arrive just in time for dinner!' Edward was smiling broadly. 'We shall have some sport tomorrow, if you can keep away from the counting house for a few hours: I took a brace of pheasants from Knickernocker Copse this morning.'

They fell to an earnest discussion of the relative merits of the shooting to be had at Chawton and Godmersham, upon which I eavesdropped with some amazement. There seemed to be no edge to the conversation; nothing to suggest that they were anything other than the best of friends. Apparently Edward had no suspicion that Henry had been anything other than a favourite brother-in-law to his late wife.

Their conversation was brought to an abrupt halt by the summons to the dining room. As we were eleven females and just three men, Henry and Edward were required to sit at opposite ends of the huge table. Ben Lefroy was seated in the middle, opposite Anna, who could barely get her chair close enough to eat in comfort, and the rest of us were arranged around them. Louisa Bridges was seated at Edward's right hand and Fanny on his left. Charlotte Bridges was on Henry's right and Mary Austen sat to his left. Jane and Mrs Austen were either side of Anna, with their backs to the fire, and Martha and I were opposite, with Ben in between us. Caroline squeezed in between Martha and her mother and Cass took a seat beside Jane.

Sitting in that room was like being transported into the imaginary world of *Sense and Sensibilty*, for the house reminded me very much of Colonel Brandon's Delaford: *a nice old fashioned place, full of comforts and conveniences.* The gilded frames of portraits of Edward's adopted ancestors reflected the warm glow of the fire; the polished mahogany table glimmered beneath the light cast by three towering candelabra. Nine steaming silver platters were arranged in a diamond formation, the largest one in the centre. The combined smells of buttered crab, stewed hare, roast goose and boiled oysters wafted around the room as the pot-bellied covers came off.

Anna announced that she was starving and her plate was soon piled high with crab and pickles, for which she said she had a particular craving. As she went to spear another morsel of claw-meat she knocked her butter knife off the table. It landed with a clatter somewhere between her chair and Mrs Austen's. She bent to retrieve it, but her figure prevented it. Mrs Austen reached down but Henry got there before her. He bowed low to pick up the knife and from my vantage point directly opposite, I saw his eyes glide over Anna's body as he straightened up.

'We can't have you and Mama cracking heads,' he grinned. 'Where have all the servants gone, Edward? Have you given them the evening off?'

During the genial banter that followed I glanced around the table, wondering if anyone else had caught what I had seen.

Ben seemed unperturbed, and was well on the way to clearing his plate of the great mound of stewed hare heaped upon it. Jane was the wrong side of Anna to have noticed anything and so was Cassandra. Fanny was fiddling with her napkin and her eyes were downcast. Mary Austen was picking at the oysters on her plate but every so often she would steal a furtive glance at Anna. Was that resentment or concern in her eyes? I could not tell.

Henry was regaling Charlotte Bridges with some incident that had befallen him on the ride from London. Leaning back in her chair and fanning herself, she looked like a delicate flower that might wilt under the power of his beaming smile. At the opposite end of the table Edward was deep in conversation with Jane and Louisa about a review he had read of *Mansfield Park*. Louisa wanted to know when the next book was coming out and what its title would be. 'Will there be a character with my name in it?' she asked. 'I should *so* love it if there was!' Jane arched her eyebrows and said that she would just have to wait and see.

'Beware of what you ask for,' Edward said, wagging a finger at Louisa and cocking his head towards his daughter. 'She might make you someone impossibly good, like Fanny Price.'

Fanny's eyes narrowed at this. 'Better to be impossibly good than truly vile, like Henry Crawford!' Her head shifted just a fraction of an inch towards the other end of the table and her father roared with laughter.

'Oh yes! Poor Henry! I had quite forgotten about him.'

Louisa was laughing too, now, and Cassandra, who had been talking across the table to Ben Lefroy, wanted to know the cause of their merriment. I watched them all in fascination. Jane, for once, seemed lost for words and Fanny was sitting back, arms folded, with a rather supercilious look on her face. *How can Edward laugh?* I thought to myself. *Is he blind? Did he not recognise his brother on the pages of Mansfield Park?*

If Henry overheard the conversation at the top of the table he affected not to notice. He had drawn Mary, Anna and Mrs Austen into his conversation with Charlotte, having hit upon possibly the only thing the four women had in common, which was that all either were or had been married to men of the cloth.

The hubbub at Edward's end soon died down and Jane, I thought, looked relieved when Louisa started talking about plays instead of books. After several unsuccessful attempts at engaging Ben in conversation, I finally found some common ground in the subject of the education of young people, whereupon he told me at great length of his plans for the instruction of the new baby, who, it seemed, was going to be read extracts from the Bible as soon as it drew breath. It was a relief to me when Edward got to his feet and drank a toast to the ladies, which was our cue to withdraw upstairs.

Mrs Austen made a beeline for the fireplace, where she settled herself in an armchair and promptly fell asleep. The others gathered round the coffee tray – all except Fanny, who took herself off to a little alcove at the far end of the room. She stood at the window with her back to everyone, as if she was searching for something in the darkness.

'Not much to see out there tonight,' I said, setting a cup down for her on the window sill. There was no moon nor any stars in evidence, for the thick cloud had not dispersed. The drive was a ribbon of charcoal in a black landscape; even the tower of St Nicholas' church, just a hundred yards distant, was hard to distinguish. I heard Fanny draw in a slow, deep breath, but she said nothing. I remembered this little routine. It meant that something was bothering her; something she wanted to talk about but wouldn't unless she was pressed.

'You don't seem quite yourself this evening,' I began. Another heavy sigh. 'Has someone done something to upset you?' Silence. I tried another tack. 'It must be hard for you, being the eldest; having always to set an example to the little ones.' I paused a moment, then said: 'It must seem very unfair: Anna has had none of your responsibilities; if I was you I'm sure I would resent her.'

'It is not *Anna's* fault!' Fanny's voice was a hissed whisper. Ah, I thought, now we are getting somewhere. I fixed my eyes on the window pane, waiting for her to spill it out. 'Didn't you notice him? He was all over her! He can't help himself, you know.' There were only two men she could be talking about and I was pretty certain it wasn't Ben Lefroy. 'Don't tell me you didn't see it,' she went on, 'His eyes were out on stalks! There's something about women when they're with child: he was always hanging around my mother, you know – and Anna tells me he was just the same with Aunt Mary when she was expecting Caroline.'

'Yes, I did see it,' I said, trying to keep my voice neutral. Her words had sent a chill through my heart. I turned my face towards her but avoided her eyes.

'Why do you think he does it?' I saw her jaw flex as she clenched her teeth. 'I've tried to make allowances because he's my uncle and I'm meant to love him. I say to myself: He has no children of his own – and that *could* be the reason, I suppose, but I just find it so… *revolting*.'

I glanced over my shoulder before reaching out to squeeze her hand. The others were all looking at something Louisa was passing round. It looked like a miniature or a silhouette: from that distance I couldn't tell. 'I don't think he realises he's doing it,' I whispered. 'I'm sure you're right about the reason: it's a shame that he and your Aunt Eliza were never able to have children – he would have loved to be a father, wouldn't he?'

'Yes, I suppose he would,' she sighed. 'Why doesn't he just marry someone else, though? Somebody younger than Aunt Eliza who could give him a child?'

There she had me. I murmured some platitude about grief taking a long time to heal, which, in Henry's case, I did not truly believe. She had presented me with an entirely new reading of her uncle that disturbed me greatly. If her observations were correct, Henry was either a vile pervert whose obsession extended to his own niece, or a man of deep feeling whose own sense of loss made him overly attentive. I had to question every assumption I had made about him. Could I have mistaken what I saw that night at Godmersham for brotherly affection? Elizabeth had not looked as if she was with child at the time, but she might have been; for all I knew she could have suffered a miscarriage before it was generally known that she was expecting. Could Jane have mistaken the look that had passed between them that same night? Had Elizabeth been telling him of her condition as he helped her into the carriage? If a man wanted a child so badly, might his face display that kind of intensity, that kind of longing, when told of such a thing?

'I'm surprised he hasn't proposed to Aunt Charlotte.' Fanny shook me out of the web of speculation I was spinning. 'She's only two years older than me, you know,' she muttered, glancing over her shoulder. 'She has those ugly freckles, of course, but she has pretty hair, don't you think?'

'Oh…er, yes,' I stuttered, struggling to take in this new, unexpected twist. 'Do…do you think they like each other?'

Fanny shrugged. 'She's very shy and quiet and he always tries to make her laugh when he comes to stay, which is nice, I suppose. But he's *nice* to everyone, isn't he? *Prince Charming.* That's what Caky calls him.' There was more than a hint of resentment in her voice.

'Do *you* like Charlotte?' I asked.

'She is all right, I suppose.' Fanny stuck out her bottom lip in the way I remembered so well. For a moment she was a sulky twelve-year-old again, not a woman of two-and-twenty.

'The children seem to like her, although Lizzy doesn't. But Lizzy doesn't like anybody very much at the moment: that is why Papa sent her away to school.'

I was not surprised at this. Lizzy was the sixth of Edward's children – the next eldest daughter after Fanny. I calculated that she must be almost sixteen now. She had been a little tomboy when I was at Godmersham; it wasn't difficult to imagine her kicking against any new woman brought into the household after her mother's death.

'She's at Mama's old school in London,' Fanny went on. 'Uncle Henry takes her out sometimes, to an exhibition or a play.' She gave me a sideways look and pursed her lips, as if to say: 'Why can't he find someone *outside* the family to go about with?'

'Fanny, dear, you must come and have a look at this!' Louisa was beside us. With a conspiratorial glance at me she took Fanny's arm and tugged it. The girl followed her unwillingly across the room, where the others were waiting with smiles on their faces. I saw Cassandra hand the picture they had all been examining to Fanny. She frowned for a moment and passed it on to me. It was a miniature of a man with wide, rather vacant-looking eyes and a Roman nose. His brown hair was styled in the current fashion but it was tinged grey at the temples.

'Who is he?' Fanny asked.

'Sir Edward Knatchbull,' Louisa replied. 'He is the eldest son of a baronet and he is looking for a wife.'

'He looks very *old*.' Fanny wrinkled her nose. 'He must be even uglier than he is painted if he has not managed to find a wife by now.'

'I would not call four-and-thirty old, would you, Jane?' Louisa was trying not to smile too broadly as she said this: she and Jane were almost the same age, which was half a decade more than this gentleman. 'Anyway,' she went on, 'he did have a wife but she died last year.'

'Oh?' Fanny looked hardly more interested than before. 'I suppose he has a gaggle of children, then?'

Louisa folded her arms across her chest. 'I believe there are children, yes.' Her face told me that his wife had probably died giving birth to the youngest. She would not say so, of course, for fear of upsetting her niece.

Fanny let out a great sigh and turned to me and said: 'You see what they are trying to do to me?' She looked about her. 'How many are we in this room? Ten women altogether. And how many of us have husbands?' She glanced at Mrs Austen, who was snoring gently in her armchair, then at Mary, who was staring into space. Her head moved slowly from left to right, taking us all in before she fixed her eyes on Anna. 'Just two out of ten live in the married state. What do you say, Anna? If you could turn the clock back by one year, would you marry Ben again? Or would you choose a single life?'

Anna, who was already flushed from the food and the heat of the fire, turned a deeper shade of red. 'How can you ask me such a thing?' she said, spreading her hands over her stomach. She looked about her for some word of support but an uncomfortable silence had fallen over the room.

'I'm sorry, Anna.' Fanny swooped down and kissed her cousin rather roughly on the forehead. 'I shouldn't have. But I just can't help feeling I'm being pushed out of this family by people who haven't the courage to do the thing they are urging *me* to do!' With a glare at her aunts she stomped out of the room, slamming the door as she went.

'Was that a gun?' Mrs Austen sat bolt upright, her eyes wide with fright and her toothless mouth gaping. The others fussed round her, glad, I suppose, of the distraction.

'Should I go after Fanny, do you think?' I whispered to Jane.

'She's better left alone,' she replied. 'The problem is that she *wants* to marry but she's terrified of having children. She'll go up to the nursery now and climb into bed with little Brook-John or Cassandra Jane and cry herself to sleep.'

There was no chance to talk to Jane alone that evening, but the next night, when Cassandra had gone away, we sat before the fire in Jane's bedroom, discussing the occupants of the Great House. We talked mostly about Fanny, whose outburst had greatly disturbed me. 'She's so grown-up in some ways, isn't she,' I said, 'but I suppose it's a terrible strain for her, having always to be an example to the others.'

Jane leaned forward in her chair and poked the fire. A tongue of orange light shot up the chimney. 'You know that she actually saw her mother drop down dead at the dinner table?'

'No, I did not.' *Little wonder, then*, I thought, *that the girl has such a morbid fear of giving birth: how awful to see your own mother collapse and die while you, a helpless child, stood watching it happen.* 'It must have been very hard for her,' I said, 'stepping into her mother's shoes at such a young age. I'm sure it would be a terrible wrench for her to have to leave the family before they are all grown. But Louisa seems very keen to marry her off.'

'I know what you're thinking.' Jane stretched out her hands to the flickering coals. 'But I don't believe Louisa has designs on Edward. I think Fanny's observation was quite astute, actually: Louisa has never struck me as the type who would marry. I think she has the perfect situation at Godmersham – all the trappings of married life with none of the encumbrances.'

'It would not be very seemly, anyway, would it, for him to marry his dead wife's sister?'

'I'm sure James would not approve: I've heard him give at least one sermon about the immorality of such things, although I don't see the harm in it myself: who better to take

223

on the care of motherless children than their own aunt? And why should that aunt be forbidden from marrying her brother-in-law because of some arcane verse in the Old Testament? It's not as if it was enshrined in something weighty, like the Ten Commandments.'

I nodded agreement. 'It leads to so much pretence, and there is enough of that in the world already,' I said. 'I suppose that if Louisa is happy with things as they are, she has a vested interest in keeping Edward from marrying anybody else.' I leaned closer to the fire, my outstretched hands casting shadows that swallowed the ones she made. 'Was Louisa playing a game with Fanny?' I asked, 'Championing Sir Edward Knatchbull because she knew her enthusiasm would have the opposite effect?'

'I wouldn't be at all surprised:' Jane replied. 'Louisa is much deeper than she looks. Ten years ago she was a poor, shy little thing; a pale imitation of Elizabeth. But look at her now: she has everything that once belonged to her sister.'

'Yes, I suppose she does,' I frowned. 'What about Charlotte, though? Is she interested in your brother, do you think?'

'Not that one.' She turned onto her side, propping her head on one hand. I couldn't see her eyes, for they were cast in pools of shadow. 'She has had a lucky escape, I think. Elizabeth's brother died before he managed to get her with child. Otherwise she might have become another poor animal.'

'Is that the way she sees it, do you think?

'She has never said that, exactly, but when I watch her in company I see someone who shies away from men as if they carried some dangerous disease. Edward is the exception: with him she feels safe, because of his loyalty to Fanny. And in that respect, she and Louisa are exactly alike.' She moved her hand to her chest and coughed a little. Then she bent over and rubbed her legs. 'I don't know why it feels so cold in here. It would be warmer, I think, if we got into bed.'

I hung back as she eased herself out of the chair. I watched her untie the dimity ribbons that held back the drapes, uncertain what she wanted me to do. I saw her reach under the pillow for her nightgown. 'Will you undo my buttons?' she said, turning her back to me. 'Cass usually does them for me, but...' she trailed off, standing there, patiently waiting. *Like a child*. The thought intensified the guilt I felt in wanting her beside me. I fixed my eyes on the ceiling as the dress slid from her body; turned away as she stepped out of her underclothes. I heard her shiver as she pulled on her nightgown. I took a step towards Cassandra's bed. Then I felt her hand on my arm. 'Hurry up and get undressed,' she whispered. 'I need you to warm me up.'

I could have refused, I suppose: made some excuse about being too tired to stay awake. But I didn't *want* to exile myself to that other bed – even if the agony of her closeness kept me awake all night.

'My legs are like icicles,' she said, as I slid under the covers. 'Will you rub them for me?' She winced as I touched her. Her skin was very cold; unnaturally cold, I thought, for one who had spent the evening next to a fire. She lay on her back as I worked away. 'What wonderful hands you have,' she sighed, 'so strong and warm!' She could not see the wry expression her words provoked. Nor could she have guessed what torture it was to rub her limbs like a butcher salting meat when what I wanted was to caress them.

After a few more minutes she said she felt better and I settled down onto the pillow, forcing myself to turn away from her. I felt her hand go round my waist as I tucked my back into the curve of her body. She was quite unaware of the powerful sensation this caused. As I lay there, stock still, the image of that other hand, encased in its white glove, swam before me in the darkness. It stayed with me as I drifted in and out of consciousness, twisting and stretching and melting into a face. It was a woman's face, and she was trying to tell me something. I remember nothing more, for sleep took me to a place where there was no one but Jane and me; a place where we could lie like this for all eternity.

Chapter Twenty-Two

The next day Jane and I were out in the garden after breakfast. The rain and low cloud had gone and the sun felt warmer than it had all summer. Mrs Austen was in her customary garb of labourer's smock and stout boots, digging up potatoes and onions.

'She's marvellous for her age, isn't she?' Jane said with a wry smile.

'How old is she, exactly?' I whispered.

'Seventy-six, I think, although she will only ever admit to being over sixty. She won't let anybody else help with the garden, you know. I think she prefers vegetables to people nowadays – certainly she stays awake longer in their company than she does in ours.'

Martha came out to us then. She was carrying large bunches of dried flowers, which she had unhooked from a rack suspended over the range in the kitchen. She told us the names, but I can only remember one or two. There was feverfew and marigold, the one for headaches and the other for stopping infection in a cut, she said. And I think she mentioned pennyroyal, which is, I believe, principally used for what they call 'procuring the menses': in other words, you take it if you think you are with child and do not wish to be.

'Will you come for a walk with us?' Jane asked her. 'We're going up to the Great House to see the park.'

'I will if I can,' she replied. 'I have to put these to steep, though; the weather has been so damp they've taken longer than usual to dry. Don't wait for me – I'll come and find you.'

The meadow was full of sheep that morning. They scattered as we approached, their feet rumbling like thunder. Chickens were pecking about outside the barns and a sudden rustling in the hedgerow heralded a pheasant, which came scuttling across the path in front of us. The sound of a shot made us both start. The bird had had a lucky escape, for a few moments later Edward emerged from a thicket above the dovecote, his gun slung over his arm and a brown pointer bitch at his heels.

'I'm not going to kiss you in case you kill me by accident,' Jane gave him a little shove as we drew level with him. 'Have you slaughtered very many yet? I suppose we should take cover: no doubt Henry will come charging out of the bushes any minute with both barrels blazing.'

'He's not here,' Edward replied, rubbing a splash of mud off the barrel of his gun with the sleeve of his coat. 'He went off with Mary to Steventon last night: said he had some business to sort out with James before he goes back to London.'

'I thought James was ill,' Jane frowned. 'Was Henry planning to drag him from his bed at midnight to talk about money? I hope he wasn't after a loan: he'd get short shrift from James if he was.'

'Who knows what goes on in that mind of his,' Edward shrugged and shook his head. 'I was surprised, I must say, for no one loves a day's shooting like Henry. It must be something weighty, to take him away from these beauties. Excuse me, ladies!' He wheeled round and took aim, felling a bird which had taken the same route across open ground as the one we had seen earlier. 'Stupid thing! They really don't deserve to live, do they?' He whistled to his pointer, who went bounding off to collect it.

Jane shuddered at the sight of the dog returning, blood dripping from the limp creature held in its jaws. 'Come on,' she said, 'I love to eat them but I can't bear to see them killed. They look so pathetic, somehow, in all their finery.'

As we came in view of the house she stumbled a little. I caught hold of her arm and held it as we squeezed through the gap in the laurel bushes. 'Are you sure your legs are better?' I asked her. In bed that morning she had told me that the numbness had gone; that she was feeling like her old self again. Now I wondered if she was telling me the truth.

'I'm fine, really,' she replied. 'It was a stone or a wet leaf or something: my foot just slipped.' To show me my fears were displaced, she strode out ahead of me, past the east porch and round the side of the house to the terrace. 'I want to show you the Wilderness,' she called over her shoulder. 'I used it in *Mansfield Park*.'

Martha waved to us across the lawn as we emerged from the dark, silent copse with its hidden pathways cut through groves of ancient ash and beech. 'Fanny is waiting for you at the Great House,' she said when she caught up with us. 'She thought you might like some lunch after your walk.' She was looking at Jane with an expression of undisguised concern, reinforcing my suspicion that Jane was underplaying the seriousness of whatever it was that ailed her.

'Is it that time already?' Jane pulled out her gold watch and consulted it. 'We were going to see the deer park and the kitchen garden.'

'There'll be plenty of time for those another day.' Martha took her by the arm and steered her towards the house, with an apologetic glance at me. I got the impression that she and Cassandra had a sort of pact between them: Martha, it seemed, took on the role of mothering Jane in Cass's absence. There was no word of protest at this treatment. Once again, Jane silently complied; surrendering her body to the will of others like a bird with a broken wing.

Fanny was all smiles when she came to greet us, hardly recognisable as the girl who had flounced out of the ladies' withdrawing room the night before last. 'Would you like to see the children?' she asked me. 'They're with Caky in the nursery. Marianne has been asking after you. I didn't think she would remember – she was only about five when you left, wasn't she? But she said: "Was Miss Sharp the one with the big hands, who used to hide hazelnuts behind her back and make us guess which one they were in?"'

I laughed at this. *Yes*, I thought, *my hands really are the only remarkable things about me.* But I felt unaccountably nervous as I climbed the stairs in Fanny's wake. Marianne would be fourteen now and baby Louisa a girl of twelve; Cassandra Jane would be nine and Brook-John on the brink of his sixth birthday. As the nursery door opened the source of my unease hit me: I feared seeing Henry in their faces.

The person I saw first, though, was not one of the children. It was Sackree, bent over some mending, sitting by the window to catch the light. Well into her fifties now, she had hardly changed at all. Still in mourning black for the husband she had lost twenty years since, and still with that hawkish look in her eyes, even though it was a piece of muslin she was attacking.

'Oh, you've come then,' she said, without looking up. She might as well have said: *Good day to you, Lady Muck: I suppose you think you've grown too fine for the likes of us?*

Fanny's face fell. Then she saw that I was smiling. I marched across the room and planted a kiss on Sackree's forehead. 'There, you old battleaxe,' I said, 'am I forgiven, now?'

230

Sackree rolled her eyes. 'Pull that up,' she said, gesturing to a child's stool standing near the fireplace. 'Make yourself comfortable, why don't you?'

'Where are the children?' Fanny was puzzled by our performance, never having been party to the banter we exchanged in my Godmersham days.

'Gone to the kitchen garden to pick flowers for madam here,' Sackree replied. 'A nice little bunch of Deadly Nightshade and Old Man's Beard.'

With a little gasp of exasperation Fanny turned on her heel. 'I'll go and find them. Try to be civil to each other while I'm away.'

Sackree gave me a sly look when the door closed. 'Well, Sharp, I see that your nose hasn't got any smaller and your bosom hasn't got any bigger.'

'And I notice that you are as fat as ever, my dear Sackree.' I leaned forward to pinch her arm and fell off the stool, landing in a heap on the carpet. She was shaking with laughter by the time I picked myself up. We both took deep breaths then in a bid to subdue the hysterics that overtook us each time one of us tried to say something.

'I'm glad to see you looking happy,' she managed at last. 'I always thought you seemed so lost in that great big house.'

'I was.' I said, wiping my eyes. 'I'm quite content in my new situation although I miss the company of children.'

She nodded and her face clouded. I asked her if she still missed her husband.

'Not really.' She tugged at the black collar of her gown. 'I wear this for her, not him.' Catching my blank look she said: 'It's for the mistress. I loved her like she was my own child.' I had never seen such a look as she gave then; I swear her eyes changed colour, from pale blue to grey-green, like the sea on a showery summer day. 'She was only two years old when I first had the care of her: I was thirteen and come to Lady

231

Bridges as under nursery maid. I remember the first time I ever set eyes on her: such a beauty she was: like a little fairy, that's what I thought.'

'She *was* very beautiful.' This I could say honestly, knowing I could not bring myself to utter any other compliment.

'When she married and young Fanny was born she begged Lady Bridges to let me come to her.' She let out a deep sigh and a single tear escaped her left eye, trickling down the side of her nose to land with a splash on the black bombazine bodice. 'I never thought to lose her at six-and-thirty. She might have looked like a fairy princess but she was as strong as an ox in her confinements; I never saw such a brave one as she.'

I was framing some response about the awfulness of Elizabeth's death when the door flew open and a little boy marched into the room with a huge bunch of chrysanthemums held out in front of him like a shield. I could not see much of his face, for the flowers obscured it.

'Go on, Brook-John: give them to Miss Sharp!' A pretty blonde-haired child, the very image of Elizabeth Austen, stepped round the door behind her little brother. She looked about eleven or twelve and I guessed that this must be Louisa. Following behind her was another, older girl, whom I recognised from her dark curls as Marianne, and an impish little redhead who could only be Cassandra Jane. Louisa, I noticed, had the distinctive Austen mouth; small and rosebud-like, and an aquiline nose. The other girls had wider lips and smaller noses. Brook-John, when he lowered the flowers, revealed a chubby face with eyes just like Jane's. *When he loses that little-boy softness*, I thought, *he will be another Henry*.

'These are for you, Miss,' he said and with a little bow he handed the chrysanthemums to me. The others stood awkwardly in the doorway until Fanny shooed them forward.

I reached for my reticule and, to my relief, saw that there was a shilling amongst the coppers that weighed it down.

'Are you big enough to walk all the way to Alton, yet?' I asked him.

'Oh yes, Miss,' the hazel eyes widened. 'I went to the fair last week with Aunt Cass and Aunt Jane.'

'Then you can buy some sweets for your sisters, can't you?' I pressed the silver coin into his hand and was rewarded with a smile that made my heart lurch in my chest.

We left the Great House in high spirits, for the children had Fanny and me racing each other around the courtyard with hoops and sticks. I was quite touched to hear them cheering so loudly as I took the lead, until I realised that the racket was made on purpose to provoke Sackree into tipping a jug of water from the nursery window.

'Is your gown very wet?' Jane was trying not to smile as we walked down the drive. 'I should have warned you about them: they're little devils. Edward's decided to take them off to Paris tomorrow. He says he's tired of all the rain and the mud.' She reached for my arm and linked hers through it. 'I don't know why he thinks Paris will be any better; Madame Bigeon says the weather there is hardly any different to London.'

As we reached the end of the drive I saw someone waving over a garden wall. It was a man who looked about Edward's age, but much thinner and longer in the face. He didn't call out or come any closer, but carried on doing whatever he was engaged in, which, from the way his mouth opened and closed, appeared to be talking to his laurel bushes.

'That's Reverend Papillon,' Jane hissed as we passed by. 'He likes to rehearse his sermons in the garden. I am to marry him, you know.' I turned to her, horrified. Seeing my face she snorted into her handkerchief. 'I'm sorry,' she mumbled, 'I didn't mean to alarm you. It's been a joke in the family ever since we moved to Chawton. He lives with his maiden sister and I don't think he would marry me if I was the last woman on earth.' She winked at me over the white lace of the handkerchief. 'I shouldn't be mean about him: he actually went out and bought his own copy of *Sense and Sensibility*. After church the other day he asked me if he was the inspiration for Edward Ferrars. I didn't have the heart to tell him I wrote it fifteen years before we came to live here.'

The cottage was just a few yards away now and I could see Mrs Austen walking up the path with a basket of carrots. I couldn't help imagining how happy she would have been to see her daughter married to a parson, however laughable Jane made it sound. And to my shame I realised that I was jealous of the Reverend Papillon, for no other reason than that he was a man and I was not.

Chapter Twenty-Three

To my surprise and delight Jane was sitting beside me when the mail coach carried me away from Chawton at the end of the week. Her publisher had written to ask for a meeting to discuss the changes she had been making to *Emma*. We spent the evening before our departure planning all the things we could do together in London.

'Do you think dear old Mrs Raike will let you out?' Jane was propped up on her elbows on the bed watching me undress in front of the fire.

'I'm sure she will, as long as Miss Gowerton is there to keep her company.' I hesitated a moment. Her colour had not improved during my stay and I was worried about the stiffness in her limbs that she complained of. I longed to have her with me in London but I feared the trip might be too much for her. Eventually I said: 'Are you sure you won't be too fagged? The roads are very bad at this time of the year and London is such a frantic place.'

She laughed as if I had said something quite insane. 'I'm not an invalid! If my legs are a little weak it's because they are far too idle: walking about London will do me no end of good!'

'Well, if you are certain…' I slipped into bed beside her, all too ready to accept this assurance. I rubbed her cold feet while she read the final chapter of *Emma* aloud to me. We had been reading it together during the week and now she wanted my comments on it before the meeting with her publisher.

'Well,' she said, leaning back on the pillows, 'I want your honest opinion. You are the only one I really trust, you know. My family are far too afraid of my bad temper.'

'And you think that I am not?' I poked her gently in the ribs.

'No,' she laughed, wriggling away, 'but you do not have to live with me – that is the difference.'

I fell silent then, for I would have given the world to live with her, temper or no temper.

'Come on,' she coaxed, 'what did you think of it? Does it match up to *P. & P.*? Is it better or worse than *Mansfield Park*?'

I took a deep breath. 'I like it better than *Mansfield Park* but not so well as *Pride and Prejudice*. Emma is a very original heroine and Mr Knightley is really delightful; Mrs Elton is wonderfully wicked and Mr Woodhouse endearingly silly; my only real dissatisfaction is with Jane Fairfax: she doesn't strike me as the sort of person who would have the courage and boldness for a secret engagement to a man like Frank Churchill.'

To my relief, Jane laughed at this. 'I knew it! I felt it in my bones as I was writing but nobody would tell me: no one else is courageous or bold enough, you see! And you, above all others, know what a governess should be like.'

After much heated discussion about how Jane Fairfax could be altered, we agreed to await the comments of Mr Murray, Jane's publisher.

The next day, as the mail coach neared London, she told me of her plans for the next novel.

'I'm going to begin writing it as soon as I get back,' she said. 'I shall set it in Bath and Lyme Regis and you will be in it, but I shan't tell you who you will be: you'll just have to wait until it's finished!' Of course, I couldn't let her get away with that. I quizzed her all the rest of the way to London, although it did me no good. I was none the wiser about my role in the new book when she took her leave of me. 'I'll see you tomorrow,' she squeezed me tight and planted a kiss on my cheek. 'Come to Hans Place at about six: I'll ask Henry what's worth seeing at the theatre.'

It was nearly dark when I arrived the next evening. Henry's new house was in Chelsea, not far from Miss Gowerton's in Cheyne Walk. Jane had not said why he had moved: I suppose it was because his old home held too many memories of Eliza. Number twenty-three Hans Place looked even grander than the house in Brompton.

Madame Bigeon flung her arms around me when she opened the door. 'Mademoiselle Sharp! *Vous nous avons bien manqué!*' Marie Marguerite came running down the hall after her. She was just as affectionate to me as her mother, but I could see from the glances they exchanged that something was wrong.

'It is Monsieur Henry,' the daughter said when I pressed her, 'He came home from the bank yesterday feeling unwell – and now he is much worse. The doctor is here and Jane is with him.' She told me that it had started as nothing more than a cough but now it had developed into a fever. I asked if she thought I ought to leave but she urged me to stay: 'Jane wants to see you very much. Please, let me take your cloak.'

I waited in the parlour until the doctor had gone. When Jane walked into the room she looked more tired than I had ever seen her. Her face was chalk-white and she leaned on the handle of the door for support as she closed it. I jumped out of my chair and ran to her, gathering her up and half-carrying her to the fireside.

'The doctor says he might die,' she whispered. 'What am I going to do?'

'Does Cass know,' I asked, 'or any of the others?'

She shook her head. 'I didn't want to worry them.'

'We must write to her immediately. You can't bear this burden alone: she wouldn't want you to. Martha can look after your mother for a while longer, can't she?'

'I suppose so.' She looked like a frightened child.

'What has the doctor given him?'

'Not much. He bled him this morning and told me to feed him nothing but water.' She closed her eyes. 'I'm afraid to leave him: he cries out and says things I can't understand. Madame Bigeon and Marie Marguerite are angels, I know, but I feel I should be with him all the time.'

'Then I will stay with you,' I said. 'I'll send a note to Mrs Raike – she won't mind, I'm sure, when she hears the reason.'

'But you—'

I held up my hand. 'Don't say anything. I'll stay until Cass gets here. We'll sit in his room together and if you need to sleep a little I'll watch him.'

The next two days reminded me of the dreadful vigil at my mother's deathbed. Seeing Jane so distraught I relived all the anguish, all the helplessness I endured the night before she passed away. It was deeply disturbing to see Henry so altered: the handsome, urbane charmer had been replaced by a dishevelled, tossing creature beaded with sweat who moaned like an animal in pain as he slipped in and out of consciousness.

After the first night had passed and dawn was breaking, I roused myself from the doze I had fallen into to see Jane uncorking a bottle and pouring a measure into a glass. I thought it was something the doctor had prescribed for Henry but to my surprise she drank it down herself.

238

'What are you doing?' I hissed.

'Fortifying myself.' She gave me a weak smile. 'It's Martha's tonic wine: I never travel without it these days. Would you like some?'

I shook my head, relieved that she was not so dazed with lack of sleep that she had drunk her brother's medicine by accident. Henry looked quite peaceful at that moment but a few minutes later he let out a blood-curdling cry that brought Madame Bigeon and Marie Margeurite rushing into the room in their nightgowns. Between us we quietened Henry and made him a little more comfortable. I don't think that he had any idea of who was in the room but Jane's voice seemed to have some power over him. When he was lying still we held a hasty conference outside the chamber.

'There must be something more we can do for him!' Jane wrung her hands. She looked absolutely wretched; her skin transparent and her eyes red and puffy. 'Do you think we should call in another doctor?'

'Don't you have faith in the one that came last night?'

'If I am honest, no. He was so unfeeling in the way he behaved. You should have seen him pulling off the leeches: there was blood everywhere; and he spoke of the risk to Henry's life with no more compassion than a farmer losing a chicken to a fox.'

Her fingers had flown to her cap and she was pulling at her curls; twisting them round and round till they stuck out like horsehair from a mattress. I reached out for her hands and drew her to me, saying: 'Is there any other doctor that you know of?'

I felt her head move against my shoulder. 'There is someone,' she replied. 'He's very expensive but Henry can afford it. His name is Doctor Baillie; he is one of the court physicians.'

We waited three tense hours for the arrival of this new doctor. Henry had begun raving again, throwing out his arm as if he was pointing to some evildoer who was about to attack him. We could not tell what he was saying, although I thought I heard the word 'notes' at one point and an oft-repeated phrase that sounded like 'mustn't tell him'. Doctor Baillie managed to get some sort of sleeping draught down him and he advised both of us to get some rest while we could. He said that until the fever broke there was no way of telling which way Henry would go, and it could be another twenty-four hours before the crisis came.

I suggested to Jane that we should take it in turns to watch Henry so that each of us could sleep in a proper bed rather than a chair. I said I would take the first turn, so that she could be with him when the effects of the drug wore off. She reluctantly agreed to my plan, although she would not leave the chamber until she was sure that he was sound asleep.

That evening, as she lay sleeping, we received an unexpected visitor. It was Lizzy, Edward's fifteen-year-old daughter, who had apparently been allowed out of school for an evening at the theatre with her uncle and was quite unaware of his illness. Uncertain what to do with her, Madame Bigeon came to tell me that she was waiting downstairs and had begged to be allowed to see Henry, even though he was sleeping. I decided that there could be no harm in it and bid the housekeeper show her upstairs as long as she cautioned the girl to be quiet.

Lizzy had been just five years old when I last saw her, so I hardly knew the beautiful creature who came tiptoeing round the bedroom door. Her dark brown curls were just like Jane's and she had the most enchanting eyes; not hazel but a pure shade of emerald. She gave me a worried smile of recognition then crept across to the bed. She lowered herself slowly onto the chair Jane had vacated and stretched out her hand to stroke Henry's arm, which hung over the side of the bed. I held my breath for a moment, worried that she might wake him, but he slumbered on quite peacefully.

'Go and rest a while,' she mouthed at me. 'I'll stay with him.'

At this point I had been without proper sleep for nearly forty hours. I declined her offer at first, but soon found my eyelids beginning to droop. My head slumped forward and I almost fell out of my chair, making a noise that startled Lizzy and brought me to my senses. Henry moved his head on the pillow but, mercifully, did not open his eyes. I decided then that I should quit the chamber for fear of undoing Doctor Baillie's good work.

I slipped into bed beside Jane, moving as slowly and quietly as I could. I need not have worried. She was in a deep sleep, having been awake the best part of three days. I lay there a while, unable to drop off despite my fatigue. I must have slept eventually, for when I opened my eyes the candle I had left on the bedside table had burned down to a stub. Jane had her back to me, her breathing slow and regular. I decided not to wake her, but crept out of the room, back to Henry's chamber. As I neared the door I heard a young voice talking in a conversational way about a meal enjoyed at some London restaurant. It was Lizzy. She was addressing Henry, who was sitting up in bed with a sort of bemused smile on his face and a faraway look in his eyes. As I stood on the threshold I heard her say: 'James-Edward is very clever, you know; he's going up to Oxford soon. When he took me out to lunch he said I could visit him there next year, if I wanted.'

She turned then and saw me standing there. With a smile she beckoned me in. If Henry was aware of my presence he showed no sign of it. 'He's in a world of his own,' Lizzy said softly, 'but he seems quite composed; do you think he's getting better?' I replied with my eyes rather than my mouth, still fearful of breaking the tranquil spell the doctor had cast. We sat in silence then for a while and eventually Henry closed his eyes and slid back onto the pillows. 'I should go now,' Lizzy whispered. 'It's quite late, isn't it?' I nodded, though I had no idea what the time was. She said that she would call again soon and asked me to give her regards to her aunt. After a few minutes I heard the clatter of hooves in the street below.

I went to straighten the covers, which had fallen to one side of the bed. As I did so, Henry gave me a fright by suddenly opening his eyes and grasping my wrist. He stared wildly at me for a moment, as if he couldn't fathom who I was. Then, in a perfectly clear voice, he said: 'Keep her away from him! Do you hear me? Don't let him touch her!'

I crouched over the bed, afraid to move a muscle, for I really feared that he was going to strike me. But suddenly he loosed his grip and his arm fell away from mine, as if he had lost the use of it. His eyes closed and his breathing slowed until his chest was rising and falling quite peacefully again. I tiptoed back to my chair, wondering what on earth had prompted this alarming episode. The drugs, most probably, I thought; no doubt they had sucked up some long-buried memory that burst from his brain as a fragment of lucid speech.

I didn't mention it to Jane when she appeared at the door an hour or so later. I went off to bed and slept soundly until the doorbell woke me next morning. It was Cassandra, who arrived at the same time as Doctor Baillie and quickly took over the duties Jane and I had shared. The next night I was back with Mrs Raike in Cheyne Walk and by the end of the week Jane sent me a note to say that Henry seemed to be over the worst. We were due back in Yorkshire the following Tuesday but she asked if I would come and take tea with her before I departed.

She looked a little less tired than when I had last seen her, but she had recovered none of her colour. Madame Bigeon fussed over her when she brought in the tea things, telling me what a marvel she had been, and how lucky Henry was to have two such devoted sisters. When she had gone Jane gave a wry smile.

242

'The French are wonderful cooks but they do exaggerate so,' she said. 'She paints me as a selfless nurse when, in fact, I have benefited enormously from poor Henry's misfortune.'

'Whatever can you mean?' I asked.

'Do you remember me telling you that Doctor Baillie is one of the court physicians?'

I nodded.

'Well, on his third visit, when Henry seemed to be recovering a little, he asked me if I was the author of *Pride and Prejudice*. I was very surprised that he had heard of it – and even more amazed when he told me that the Prince Regent admired it greatly.'

'*I* am not surprised,' I clapped my hands with delight, 'but it is a wonderful compliment, all the same.'

'You'll never guess what: he wants me to dedicate *Emma* to him – the Prince Regent, I mean, not the doctor – and I've been invited to the library at Carlton House!' We rolled about at this, for she had always reserved her wickedest barbs for the Prince Regent, whom she despised for his gluttony, his extravagance and his shameless adultery.

'Will you still speak to the likes of me afterwards, I wonder?' I was pleased to see that laughter had brought a little colour back to her cheeks. She swiped at me with her tea plate, sending a shower of cake crumbs onto my lap. For this she attempted to apologise and ended up on her knees, brushing at my gown in a fit of helpless giggles.

The sound of Henry's voice put a sudden stop to her mirth. He was calling from the landing, asking Cassandra to fetch him the newspaper. Jane stuck her head out of the parlour door. 'It's all right,' she said, glancing back at me over her shoulder, 'Cass is on her way up now.'

'He sounds much better,' I replied, 'quite like his old self.'

'Yes, he is.' She settled herself back on the sofa beside me. 'I was so worried, though: that night when Lizzy called and I

243

was asleep – do you remember – that was the worst. When you went to bed he started raving again. I really thought he was going to die. He was staring at me as if he didn't have a clue who I was, then he'd shout out; the same thing again and again: "Keep her away from him! Don't let him touch her!" It was horrible. I told the doctor the next morning and he said it was the laudanum – but Mama takes that all the time and I've never heard her raving; not like that, anyway.'

I told her he had said exactly the same thing in my hearing. 'It was just after Lizzy left,' I said. 'I was worried that she'd disturbed him when she sent me off for a rest.' I related what had happened, and how I had returned to find her talking to Henry.

'What exactly was she saying to him?'

'Oh, just ordinary things: she was telling him about a restaurant she'd been to for lunch. She mentioned James-Edward; he took her, I think. And she said something about going to visit him when he goes up to Oxford. That was all I heard.'

She was staring at me intently, as if devil's horns had sprouted from my forehead.

'What's the matter, Jane? What have I said?'

'Nothing.' She shook her head violently, as if she was casting out an idea she wouldn't own. 'It must have been the laudanum, like Doctor Baillie said.'

Chapter Twenty-Four

The memory of the way Jane had looked at me that afternoon in the parlour at Hans Place came back to me many times over the next few months. I would have pressed her for an explanation had not Cassandra come into the room with the news that Edward and the family were going to call in on the invalid on their way home from Paris. As it was, I had to take my leave of her without discovering why the mention of Lizzy's developing friendship with her cousin had disturbed her so.

On the journey back to Yorkshire I began to form my own theory. While Mrs Raike dozed fitfully, her head tipped back against the velvet banquette, I pieced together everything I could remember about James-Edward and his parents. I could not help recalling my first glimpse of his mother in the Pump Room at Bath; my instinct then had been that Mary and Henry were lovers and the sight of her son later that same day had intensified that feeling. Henry's stinging warning at the White Hart Inn had strengthened my resolve to keep my nose out of the affairs of Jane's family. But what if I was right? What if Henry had been dallying with not just one sister-in-law but two? What if the reason James-Edward looked so much like Henry was because he was his natural son? Had Henry fathered bastards on *both* of his elder brothers' wives?

It sounded preposterous, but it would explain Henry's violent reaction to the news that James-Edward and Lizzy were becoming close. What if they were to marry, as cousins so often did? The union would be that of a half-brother and half-sister. No wonder Henry had clung to me like a drowning man when Lizzy left the room. I would have dismissed his anguished pleas as the senseless ranting of a fevered brain had it not been for one thing: Jane's reaction. She must have suspected what I was now thinking.

I began remembering other little details: Mary's annoyance when Henry declined her invitation to dance at the ball in Bath and her subsequent hasty departure; her lack of surprise when he appeared unexpectedly at the Great House in Chawton; his decision to go and spend the night at Steventon, where James was confined to his sick bed. All these things seemed to point to just one conclusion: Mary and Henry were engaged in an illicit liaison that had been going on for many, many years. No wonder he does not choose to marry again, I thought: It is as I suspected – he is only interested in forbidden fruit.

As the coach rattled along, leaving London far behind, I attempted to divine the workings of Henry's mind. Was there some peculiar attraction in seducing the wives of his brothers, as opposed to the wives of any other men of his acquaintance? Was there an element of jealousy involved? I reminded myself of the relative fortunes of Jane's older brothers; of the fact that Henry had seen Edward plucked from obscurity to be showered with all the advantages money could buy, while James had the automatic right to their father's living and the family home, with the promise of great riches to come when the Leigh-Perrots died. It wasn't hard to imagine a bitter resentment taking root in Henry's heart. Was it a kind of revenge, I wondered, to pursue the women his brothers chose to marry; to defile what they held most dear?

I longed to know if my theory was correct but it was the kind of subject that could only be embarked upon with the greatest subtlety and in the utmost privacy. Certainly I could not *write* to Jane about it. I knew that it must wait until our next meeting, which I hoped would occur soon after the publication of *Emma*. I decided that I would use the gold pocket watch as a starting point. She had been so reluctant to tell me that it was a gift from Henry and it struck me that there may have been an ulterior motive for his generosity: I could never believe Jane to be susceptible to a bribe, but I could imagine the watch being presented as a sort of peace offering…his way of saying that the thing she had accused him of would not be repeated.

The first letter I received from Jane after my return from London contained some shocking news. It seemed that the sudden breakdown in Henry's health had not been due merely to a chance infection: his business empire had crumbled, leaving him bankrupt and his backers with monstrous debts. The signs of impending disaster had been evident for several weeks, Jane said, but he had kept his fears to himself. On the afternoon we had arrived in London he had received devastating news – the exact nature of which he still could not bring himself to divulge – and had literally collapsed under the weight of it.

'Nearly everyone in the family has lost money,' she wrote. 'Edward must bear the brunt of it, of course: he has lost twenty thousand pounds himself and the Crown has ordered him to pay twenty-one thousand in installments on Henry's behalf over the next twelve months. Uncle Leigh-Perrot is similarly afflicted: he lost ten thousand and must pay the same amount as Edward in installments to the Crown. James lost several hundred pounds, as did my brothers Frank and Charles. Cass had invested one hundred and thirty-two pounds of the legacy left to her by her fiancé and I put in twenty-five pounds and seven shillings, which was my profit from *Mansfield Park*.'

The losses meant that her mother would no longer receive the allowance her brothers had been making to keep them in comfort at Chawton Cottage, so any plans for travel had had to be curtailed. We had talked of her coming to stay in Yorkshire in the spring but that would not now be possible.

'Henry has had to give up his house and move in with us,' the letter went on. 'Poor Madame Bigeon and Marie Margeurite have returned to France, although they are very despondent about their prospects there. Henry feels wretched about them, of course, but despite everything that has befallen him he has come to Chawton as cheerful as ever. He talks of taking Holy Orders and has already written to the Bishop of Winchester on the subject. He hopes to get the living of curate at St Nicholas, which would give him a stipend of fifty-two guineas a year and allow him to keep a horse.'

The old Jane would have made some joke about the absurdity of Henry's new-found vocation; the fact that she did not revealed just how sombre was the mood at Chawton Cottage. I wondered why, with all the chambers at the Great House, Henry did not reside there. I could only conclude that the jovial brotherly relationship I had witnessed on my last visit had been brought to an abrupt end by the collapse of Henry's bank.

Subsequent letters from Jane and other members of the family gave few clues as to the cause of Henry's misfortunes. Fanny hinted that the crisis had come about because a major backer had suddenly pulled out but she did not name the man nor state the reason why. I wondered if it was Warren

248

Hastings, whom Henry himself had named as one of his chief investors. It wasn't difficult to imagine him harbouring a grudge towards Henry in the wake of Eliza's death, a grudge that might turn into outright war if he received some solid evidence of Henry's misdeeds.

Fanny's letter made clear her annoyance at Henry's apparent ability to bounce back from disaster with a beatific smile on his face: 'The idea of his becoming a curate worries me,' she wrote. 'I can think of no one less suited to the role of guiding the spiritual life of other people, yet the Bishop accepted his application without the slightest objection, not even bothering to test his competence in Greek – which, I'm sure, must be very rusty indeed.'

Anna was a little less sanctimonious: 'Uncle Henry will no doubt be as charming in the pulpit as he is elsewhere. My father and stepmother have invited him to stay at Steventon in the coming weeks so that he may observe the running of a parish at close quarters. It is to be hoped that Reverend Papillon will reap the benefit of this when Uncle Henry returns to Chawton as curate – which he hopes will happen before next Christmas.'

So Henry is under Mary's roof again, I thought. Would she find him quite so attractive now his money had gone? I wondered if his dramatic fall from grace had chastened him. Did he see it as divine retribution? Perhaps it was not just the promise of a living that led him to embrace the church with such enthusiasm: perhaps Salvation was his quest.

The next letter from Jane brought more bad news but this time it was about her, not Henry. She reported that she was feeling sick and faint and had been confined to bed for a week. She was trying to finish her new novel but found that the slightest exertion fatigued her. 'Forgive me for making this so very brief,' she wrote. 'I promise to write again as soon as I am recovered.'

I had begun writing a reply when a loud cry summoned me to Mrs Raike's side. She was doubled over on the sofa, clutching at the bodice of her gown and fighting for breath. Rebecca, who had heard it from the kitchen, was beside me in a moment. She didn't need me to tell her how serious it was. She ran outside to send her father for the doctor.

For the next six weeks I hardly left Mrs Raike's bedside. The doctor said she was not strong enough to recover from the attack and he doubted if she would live to see Christmas. Sadly, he was right. Rebecca tried to tempt her with all manner of tasty morsels but we could not get her to eat enough to keep a bird alive. I watched her fading before my very eyes.

The weather was bitterly cold and we kept a fire burning constantly in her room, hoping its warmth would revive her enough to sit up and eat a proper meal. On the morning of Christmas Eve she opened her eyes for a moment when Rebecca drew back the curtains. We thought she was trying to get up. But she slipped back onto the pillow and fell into a restless slumber, her breathing slow and rasping. I had heard that sound the night my mother died. As the pale winter sun dipped below the frozen fields, Mrs Raike passed away.

I had been her companion for eleven years and she had become like another mother to me – although in practical terms it was I who had done the mothering. Rebecca, her father and I spent a sad Christmas together, trying to put her things in order and making the house ready to be sold, wondering all the while what we would do for employment now. It came as a great surprise when her solicitor came calling one day in the first week of January to tell me that Mrs Raike had left me a considerable bequest.

He sat me down at the dining room table and read the Will aloud: 'To Miss Sharp, who has not only been a loyal and compassionate companion to me but also a patient and devoted teacher to my servant, Rebecca, I leave the means to further a talent that deserves wider expression.' He looked up and, seeing my welling eyes and uncomprehending face, explained what the bequest meant. I was to take possession of two houses owned by Mrs Raike. They lay beside the River Mersey in Liverpool, he said: adjacent properties that formed part of a terrace of villas in a district called Everton. Her wish was that I would transform the houses into a school for girls, with myself as headmistress and Rebecca and her father as housekeeper and caretaker. She had left me an additional sum of money to execute the necessary work.

I wrote to Jane the same day, wishing with all my heart that I could sprout wings and fly to Chawton to deliver the news in person. I began to entertain all manner of foolish fantasies, the chief of these being that Jane could come and live with me, writing in a room overlooking the river while I taught in the schoolroom below. It *was* foolishness, of course, for I knew that Jane would never leave Cass and Mrs Austen, even if she wanted to, which I doubted. Her last letter had been full of optimism; she felt much better, she said and was able to walk into the town of Alton – some three miles distance from the cottage – although she was not yet strong enough to make the journey there and back on foot. She had finished her latest novel, for which she had still to settle on a title, and was longing to read it to me. She added as a postscript that Anna had just given birth to her second child – another girl – and Henry had been ordained in Winchester. The whole family had been to hear him preach his first sermon at St Nicholas on the Sunday after Christmas.

I wrote to tell her that I would come to see her as soon as I had settled in Liverpool and got the scheme of work for converting the houses underway. If Cass and Martha were both at home when I visited I proposed to take a room at the Greyfriar Inn across the road. It gave me a huge thrill writing those words: Mrs Raike's generosity had made me a woman of independent means.

I was a little surprised that Jane did not write back straightaway. The time soon came for me to leave Yorkshire and still there was no word from her. I wrote again the week after my arrival in Everton, thinking that she had perhaps sent a letter to the temporary lodgings I had taken in Doncaster when Mrs Raike's house was sold. It was not until the end of May, when work on the new school had begun, that I received an envelope bearing her familiar hand. I frowned at the postmark, which was not Chawton but Winchester:

Your kind letter found me in bed, for in spite of my hopes and promises when I wrote to you, I have since been very ill indeed. An attack of my sad complaint seized me within a few days afterwards – the most severe I have ever had – and coming upon me after weeks of indisposition, it reduced me very low. Now I am getting well again and indeed have been gradually though slowly recovering my strength for the last three weeks.

My looks have improved a little, for my face was black and white and every wrong colour. I must not depend on ever being very blooming again. My chief sufferings were from biliousness, weakness and languor and as our Alton apothecary did not pretend to be able to cope with it, better advice was called in. The applications of Mr Lyford from the Winchester hospital have gradually removed the evil and I am about to go and reside in a house there for several weeks to see what he can do farther towards re-establishing me in tolerable health.

I am now a very genteel, portable sort of an invalid. The journey is only sixteen miles and Cass and I are to be conveyed there in my elder brother's carriage, which will be sent over from Steventon on purpose. Now, that is the sort of thing which

Mrs James Austen does in the kindest manner! But she is in the main not a liberal-minded woman, despite the recent death of my Uncle Leigh-Perrot bringing vast wealth ever closer. It is too late in the day, I fear, for her character to be amended.

I have not mentioned my dear mother: she suffered much for me when I was at the worst, but is tolerably well. Martha, too, has been all kindness. In short, if I live to be an old woman I must expect to wish I had died now, blessed in the tenderness of such a family and before I survived either them or their affection. You would have held the memory of your friend Jane in tender regret also, I am sure. But the providence of God has restored me and I may be more fit to appear before him when I am summoned than I should have been now! Sick or well, believe me your ever attached friend,

Jane Austen

Thank God, I breathed, as I set the letter down. Clearly she had been very ill but she was getting better. How sensible of Cass, I thought, to take her to Winchester, where she could convalesce under the watchful eye of Mr Lyford, the man who had cured her. I sat down immediately to reply, writing of my great joy at her recovery and the plans I had for the school, which I hoped she would be able to visit when she was feeling stronger.

But when the next letter arrived from Winchester I didn't recognise the hand. My stomach lurched as I broke the seal and saw Cassandra's name at the bottom edge of the paper. Cass and I did not correspond in those days, so I knew straight away that she had written in her sister's stead. Jane must be taking longer than expected to recover her strength, I thought; perhaps the doctor has told her not to overtax herself while she convalesces. The address at the top of the letter was

Chawton Cottage. 'They are home then,' I said aloud, the wave of panic ebbing a little. My eyes darted down the page:

I grieve to write, dear Miss Sharp, what you will grieve to read. My darling sister Jane, the sun of my life, the gilder of every pleasure, passed away at Winchester in the early hours of the eighteenth day of July. Though she suffered much in her last weeks on this earth she never once complained. She was the soother of every sorrow, always composed and cheerful. It is as if I had lost a part of myself—

Chapter Twenty-Five

My first instinct was to throw the letter through the window into the swirling grey depths of the Mersey. I told myself it wasn't real; it wasn't true. I doubled over as I lurched towards the casement, retching and gasping for breath. Then, with trembling hands, I read it again. The loops and curves of the words began to writhe like snakes. I felt the same suffocating sense of panic I had felt when my mother died: the thought of never being able to see or talk to Jane again was unbearable. I felt as if my heart had been ripped from my chest.

My next impulse was to leap onto the first mail coach heading south. Despite the evidence I held in my hand, I simply could not accept that she was gone unless I saw her lifeless body with my own eyes. But Cass's letter was dated the thirty-first of July: she had been dead for *two weeks*. Her funeral must have taken place already – they had buried her without telling me – I could not see her, even in death. How could they do that? Did they not know what she meant to me?

Of course they didn't: how could they? The answer came from within; from that part of my brain that saw things as the outside world would see them: a world that would not understand nor *wish* to understand the nature of my love for Jane.

The wave of nausea surged through me again. I slumped against the nearest piece of furniture, causing it to thud against the wall. Rebecca must have heard it, for she came running up the stairs to see what had happened. I tried to tell her but the words would not come out. I gave her the letter to read for herself and she cried with me when she realised that the woman whose books she loved above all others was dead.

I have little memory of the days that followed. Somehow I collected myself sufficiently to write letters of condolence to Jane's family. I said nothing, of course, about the hurt I felt at not being able to pay my last respects, for I could well imagine the state of shock Cass must have been in at the time, cut off from the person who was dearer to her than anyone in the world. About a week later Cass wrote back. She sent me two precious mementoes. These were a silver bodkin, which Jane had used for her needlework, and a lock of her hair, a portion of which I fashioned into a tiny plait. I had it mounted in a gold ring, encircled in stones of moss agate, the colour of her eyes. I wear it on the third finger of my right hand and in the mirror it becomes a wedding ring.

It was early September when I made the journey to Hampshire. The school was ready to open its doors but the first pupils were not due to arrive until the fifteenth of the month, so I seized the chance to do what I dreaded and yearned for in equal measure.

The mail coach from Liverpool was hot and airless. By the time it rolled into Winchester the sky had turned a sulphurous yellow-grey. I had two hours to spare before boarding the coach that would carry me to Chawton; time enough to find the place I had visited every night in my dreams for the past six weeks. Cass had offered to accompany me but it was something I needed to do alone.

The cool, dark interior of the cathedral was a welcome relief from the heat outside. The scent of burning tallow and a whiff of incense hung in the air. As a child, I had found the smell of churches comforting but I felt no such sensation now. There were few people about; just a handful of curious visitors come to see the tombs of ancient kings and queens. It didn't take long to find the tablet of black marble, newly laid in the north aisle of the cathedral. The sight of her name carved in stone paralysed me. It was a while before I could bring myself to move close enough to read the inscription properly:

In Memory of
JANE AUSTEN
youngest daughter of the late
Revd. GEORGE AUSTEN,
Formerly Rector of Steventon in this County
she departed this life on the 18th July 1817,
aged 41, after a long illness supported with
the patience and the hopes of a Christian.

The benevolence of her heart,
The sweetness of her temper, and
the extraordinary endowments of her mind
obtained the regard of all who knew her and
the warmest love of her intimate connections.

Their grief is in proportion to their affection
they know their loss to be irreparable,
but in their deepest affliction they are consoled
by a firm though humble hope that her charity,
devotion, faith and purity have rendered
her soul acceptable in the sight of her
REDEEMER.

'What about her books?' I said the words aloud, as if the family were gathered there before me. The sense of injustice I felt at this glaring omission temporarily numbed the pain of seeing her grave. Then the enormity of it hit me: her body was lying there, beneath that stone, just inches from my feet. I sank onto a nearby pew, my breathing too fast and too shallow. I tried to calm myself, but my eyes were drawn back to that black slab with its dreaded affirmation of death. Shutting out the sight, I slumped onto the kneeler.

My relationship with God had not been close since the death of my parents; I was the kind of Christian who went through the motions but found it impossible to believe that a benevolent, all-powerful spirit watched over me. But the prayer that I sent up now came straight from my heart: *Oh God, if you truly do exist, grant me some sign that she lives on: give me some hope that I might see her again in the hereafter.*

I crossed myself and opened my eyes, steeling myself for the empty nothingness I expected. But up ahead something was moving. I could see a woman and a child, hand in hand, coming down the north aisle towards me. The child – a dark-haired girl of about six years old – suddenly broke away and ran ahead. I watched, spellbound, as she came to an abrupt halt right in front of Jane's tombstone. Kneeling beside it, she traced the letters with her finger. 'Look Mama,' she said, as the woman caught up, 'it's my name!'

I had to fight back the urge to jump up and hug her. With tears blurring my eyes, I shuffled along the pew in the opposite direction and made my way out into the stifling heat of Cathedral Close. I walked in a sort of daze through Kingsgate to College Street, where I stopped and sat down on a low wall. It was very peaceful there, away from the main thoroughfare. All I could hear was the cawing of rooks in the tall trees that shaded the little street. When I had recovered myself I walked slowly past the houses, searching for number eight. This was the house where Jane had spent the last few weeks of her life.

When I found it I stood for a while on the pavement opposite, looking up at the first floor windows. I wondered if one of these had been Jane's bedroom. I had planned to knock boldly on the door; ask to see the chamber where my friend had taken leave of her mortal self. But somehow it seemed unnecessary; I felt as if she had stepped from her grave and was standing beside me.

I could see someone working away in the garden as the coach pulled into Chawton. I thought it was Mrs Austen, digging away as usual in her vegetable patch, but as I walked towards the house I saw that it was Cass. I called her name and she straightened up, wiping dirt-streaked hands on her overall.

'Oh, I'm so sorry!' She fanned out her hands in a helpless gesture at her clothes. I noticed that she wore a ring on the same finger as me, tiny pearls encircling the braided hair within it. 'Was the coach early? I wasn't expecting you for another half an hour.'

She settled me down in the parlour and went off to change. The house was silent, then, for Mrs Austen was in bed with a chill and Martha had gone off in the donkey cart to visit her sister in Steventon. As I glanced around the room, I caught my breath. There was a new picture on the wall: Jane's face, with that funny, sharp look I remembered so well, captured in pastels. Cass's work, I guessed. I went across to the portrait and stood in front of it. Her eyes were on a level with mine but looking past me, towards the door; and that small mouth was set firm as if she had spotted an unwelcome visitor come to interrupt her work and was about to mutter some needling remark.

'Why did you leave us, Jane?' I whispered. 'Why didn't you tell me you were dying?'

I wheeled round at the sound of the door, jumping away from the picture like a child caught stealing cake.

'It's not very good, I'm afraid,' Cass smiled. 'I wish we'd had her painted in oils by a real artist.'

'You're too modest. You've captured her perfectly.'

'I can make a copy for you, if you like.' She sank down on the sofa and I saw that her eyes were brimful of tears. I went to hug her but that only made things worse. In a moment we were both wiping our eyes and trying to compose ourselves.

'I still can't talk about her without weeping,' Cass shook her head, as if her grief was an unpardonable weakness. I nodded, although I ached to know what had happened in those last weeks of Jane's life. My head was full of questions but I had no wish to upset Cass further. So I deliberately changed the subject, asking after Anna and her babies.

'She's longing to see you,' Cass said. 'She said I was to send you over to Wyards as soon as you had unpacked. The little girls are real beauties, although they're wearing her out at the moment.'

'Is it far?'

'Only half an hour on foot. I'd take you myself but I can't leave Mama.'

'I'm sure I'll find it,' I said. I was pleased to be going alone, for it would give me the chance to talk to Anna without the fear of upsetting Cass. After a bite of lunch I made my way through the village, turning off the Winchester road into a narrow lane. The sky had lightened a little, sending shafts of sunlight on the tufts of cow parsley that stuck out from the hedgerows like bristles from an old man's chin. Jewelled clusters of blackberries were turning ripe and I couldn't help imagining Jane, her fingers stained with juice instead of ink, dancing up the lane ahead of me.

It wasn't long before I spotted Wyards, a farmhouse set back from the road at the end of a muddy track. Anna and

Ben lived in half of it and the line of baby clothes strung between two trees told me which side was theirs.

'I'm sorry the house is such a mess.' Anna shrugged as she showed me into the parlour. I saw that her mourning gown was smeared white at the shoulder. And her stomach bulged under her bodice. I wondered if she was with child again. Jane's words came back to me very clearly: *She will be another poor animal.* I hoped very much that it was not another pregnancy, just extra weight put on after the second baby.

Julia, her youngest, was asleep in a basket in the corner but little Jemima began scrambling all over her mother's lap the moment she sat down. I tried my best to distract the child with a toy I had bought: a doll with horsehair plaits that could be undone and brushed out with a tiny tortoiseshell comb. After a while she settled on the floor at my feet and Anna began to tell me what Cass had been unable to relate.

'The last time I saw Aunt Jane was on Easter Sunday.' As she said it a tear rolled down her cheek to join the beads of perspiration on her upper lip. She drew the back of her hand across her mouth. 'Caroline and I walked over to the cottage to see her after church. She looked very much altered in the face and she was so weak – she had not the strength enough even for talking very much.'

'But she wrote her last letter to me in the third week of May,' I said, 'and she sounded in such good spirits; she said she had not been well, and that she was going to Winchester for treatment, but there was no hint of her being seriously ill.'

'She did seem to improve,' Anna sniffed. 'My father called in on me after visiting her at the end of April and he said she looked much better. I couldn't go myself because Jemima and Julia had chicken pox, one after the other.' She paused and glanced over her shoulder at the basket, where the baby lay, pink and motionless. 'My stepmother was Aunt Jane's most frequent visitor: she called at the cottage nearly every day with new-laid eggs and milk from her own cow for Martha to make into possets; and when the time came to go to Winchester she offered their carriage to transport her.' The tilt of Anna's eyebrows betrayed her feelings about this; evidently she was as surprised as Jane had been at Mary's uncharacteristic generosity. 'She was with her right up until the end, you know,' she went on. 'She said it wasn't fair to expect Aunt Cass to nurse Aunt Jane all alone.'

'But what about Martha?' I bent to pick up the doll, which Jemima had thrown across the floor with a chuckle of delight. 'Couldn't she have gone to Winchester with them?'

Anna shook her head. 'Grandmama was feeling unwell too, so Martha had to stay in Chawton.'

'That was very kind of your stepmother, then, wasn't it?'

Mary Austen had not struck me as the kind of woman who would willingly spend six weeks at the bedside of a sick in-law – especially as her relationship with Jane had been one of ill-disguised dislike on both sides. 'Had she and Jane become closer, do you think? I always got the impression there was not much common ground between them.'

'There wasn't. Aunt Jane despised my stepmother for having no interest in books and she thought the marriage had altered my father's character for the worse. She said he'd become grumpy and intolerant, which is quite true, actually: he can be very difficult when the mood takes him.' She leaned forward to retrieve the little comb, which Jemima had tucked into the side of her slipper. 'My stepmother, for her part, was always running Aunt Jane down. She said she lived an idle life, because the only thing she was expected to do around the house was make breakfast. She didn't count writing as work.'

'So why was she so compassionate to Jane at the end?'

'I don't know,' she shrugged. 'Perhaps she just felt sorry for Aunt Cass, who says she doesn't know how she would have managed without her. I would have given anything to be able to help, but...' she tailed off with another shrug as Jemima spun the doll round by one of its plaits.

'Were you able to see her when she...before the funeral, I mean?' I couldn't say it properly: it seemed an unseemly thing to ask, but I couldn't help it. I wanted to know if Jane had looked serene in death the way my mother had; I wanted to hear that she had regained the sweet countenance her letter said had been so altered by the illness.

'No.' Anna blinked back more tears. 'Uncle Henry organised everything. Uncle Frank was able to get there and Uncle Edward came over from Godmersham. Papa wanted to go but he felt too unwell, so James-Edward went in his place.'

'You father is still unwell?' I stood up to catch hold of Jemima, who was climbing on a chair next to the open window.

She gave a small sigh: for her father or the child – I was not sure which. 'James-Edward called by yesterday to tell me that Papa had taken to his bed, seized with a pain in the bowels.'

I didn't want to worry Anna by remarking on it, but I wondered if her father was suffering from the same complaint as Jane. She had talked of problems with her stomach in her letters.

'Uncle Henry has gone to Steventon to take over some of Papa's duties,' Anna went on. 'James-Edward says he's serving Sherborne Saint John.' Hearing Henry and James-Edward mentioned in the same breath reminded me of the question mark that still hung over the young man's parentage. I wondered if I would ever know, now, whether my suspicions about Henry's affair with Mary were correct. And what of Lizzy, I wondered? Were she and James-Edward still close? Had she been to visit him at Oxford or had Jane somehow intervened to nip their mutual attraction in the bud? I guessed that even if such a thing had been in her power, the debilitating nature of her illness would have prevented it.

263

Anna was not able to tell me any more about her aunt's death, for the baby awoke suddenly with a loud, urgent cry. I took Jemima by the hand, intending to take her into the garden while Anna attended to Julia, but as we stepped outside I saw her husband riding up the track to the farm. I judged it best to take my leave then, and walked back to the village with a heavy heart.

Chapter Twenty-Six

As I drew near to Chawton Cottage I caught sight of Martha guiding the donkey cart through the side gate. There was someone sitting beside her; a woman whose face was obscured by her bonnet. When they came up the path from the stable I saw that it was Mary Austen.

I had a sudden, inexplicable urge to hide from her. I dodged into the kitchen, where Cass and Hannah Pegg were about to haul a rib of beef up the chimney to hang. I asked if I could help, but Cass shooed me out with instructions to go and put my feet up in the parlour after my walk.

Mary's mouth twitched when she saw me. It was not a greeting, exactly; certainly not a smile. Having acknowledged my presence she turned back to Martha, who was showing her some needlework. But on seeing me Martha dropped the sampler and rushed across the room to hug me. As she drew back she shook her head and clicked her tongue.

'Oh, Miss Sharp! Such sad times!' She pressed her lips together as if she could not trust herself to speak on. She patted a cushion and waved me towards it. 'I'll fetch some tea,' she whispered. 'Back in a moment.'

An awkward silence fell upon the room. It reminded me of the ball in Bath, when Mary and I had been left together on the high bench watching the dancers. But this time there was no Mr Hastings to rescue me. She had picked up Martha's needlework and was pretending to examine it. Apparently, she felt as uncomfortable in my presence as I did in hers. Remembering what Anna had said about her devotion to Jane in those last few weeks of her life I told myself that she couldn't be all bad. Maybe she is just shy, I thought; perhaps she is self-conscious of her face and feels embarrassed to be seen by people outside the family.

'I hear that you were very attentive to Jane in her illness,' I began. 'She mentioned you by name in the last letter she sent me.'

She looked up and blinked. Then she gave me a dazzling smile. 'I tried my best,' she nodded, 'and it is a comfort to know that I was able to make things a little easier for them.'

I thought how very different she looked when she was smiling; there was an eagerness about her, like a sulky dog let off a leash to chase rabbits. 'It must have been very hard for you and Cass, nursing her all those weeks,' I said. Despite the pain I knew it would cause me I wanted to hear it all; every detail of those last days.

'It was,' she replied. 'At first we thought she was getting better: we used to have her taken about Winchester in a sedan chair and in the evenings she would sit at table with us and manage a bite or two of her dinner. But then she suddenly went downhill again and Mr Lyford said there was nothing more he could do.'

'What exactly was she suffering from? She never said in her letters.'

'Mr Lyford never gave it a name.' Mary gave a little shrug that made the black bead trim on her bodice jiggle. 'She had all kinds of symptoms: biliousness and fevers, mainly, along

266

with fainting spells and weakness of the limbs. The medicine he gave her seemed to work at first but about a month before she died he told us there was nothing more he could do. I was sitting with her the day before she died. It was about five in the afternoon and Cass had gone to the shops for some food. Jane suddenly let out a terrible cry and writhed about in the bed. There was blood gushing from her mouth and it went all over the sheets.' Her lower lip twitched at the memory of what must have been a terribly distressing thing to witness. 'I thought she would die then,' she went on, 'but she did not. When Mr Lyford came he said a large blood vessel had given way. He gave her laudanum and she fell into a sort of sleep. Cass was back by that time and she sat with Jane's head cradled on her lap. Every so often Jane would cry out. Once Cass asked her what she wanted and Jane replied: "Nothing but death."'

I turned away at this, no longer able to contain my emotion. Seeing my tears, Mary paused. 'Please...tell me all of it,' I mumbled, 'It helps to know – really it does.'

She took a deep breath. 'Well, she didn't say much more after that. She begged us to pray for her and we did pray all that night. At one in the morning I told Cass she must rest, because she had been sitting like that, with Jane's head in her lap, for six hours. She came back two hours later, and an hour after that Jane was dead.'

'So her sister was with her when she died; that must be a comfort to her, I'm sure.'

'Yes. She was able to close Jane's eyes herself and wash her body before it was laid in the coffin. We kept her in one of the upstairs rooms until the funeral, so that the family could come and see her. There was such a sweet, serene air over her countenance: everyone remarked on it.'

That, at least, was something to be thankful for. 'I would have come to see her if I had known,' I said, dabbing my eyes and swallowing hard. 'But I suppose her sister was overwhelmed with grief; it's not surprising that she was unable to write letters until the funeral was over.'

'She was quite calm, actually,' Mary replied. 'I was surprised how well she managed to control herself. We had to wait six days for the service to be arranged. Henry organised it: he knows the Bishop, of course, and it was because of his connection that permission was given for burial within the cathedral. Jane is very lucky – only three people have been granted such an honour this year.'

I glanced at her over my handkerchief. She was smiling again, as if it was the proud achievement of one of her children she was describing. I suppose she *is* proud, I thought, for it was indeed an honour to be laid to rest in such a place, although I had a feeling that Jane would rather have been closer to home, in the churchyard at St Nicholas.

'It was Henry's idea to ask for a place in the cathedral,' Mary went on, 'and he composed the inscription on the stone: it is very moving – have you seen it?'

I replied that I had. 'But there is no mention of her books,' I couldn't help saying. 'Why is that?'

'Henry wanted a line about that but James and Edward talked him out of it. They always thought it rather unseemly that she was known to be a writer of *novels*.' She raised her eyebrows as she spoke the word, as if it was a dirty secret. 'That was Henry's fault, of course: he was so proud of her he simply couldn't keep it to himself. Everybody seems to know now, even though her name never appears on the books. Evidently the Bishop has read *Pride and Prejudice* and liked it very much, which must have helped persuade him to grant the burial, I suppose.' She went on at some length then, describing Henry's continuing efforts on Jane's behalf; his determination to get her last novel published along with the one she had written many years earlier but never seen in print.

'Did you know that Jane left him fifty pounds in her Will?' She gave me a guarded look and I wondered if she thought I had been hoping for something myself. 'She was so sorry for what had happened to him, you see. He was the only member of the family, apart from Cass, of course, that she left money to.' She chattered on about the sterling service Henry was providing at Sherborne St John, and how 'poor Austen' – as she always called her husband – was so lucky to have such a reliable substitute. I thought that she was a little too enthusiastic, a little too effusive about Henry. She is doing what people do when they are in love but won't own it, I thought: she mentions him at every possible opportunity; she veers to and from the main topic of conversation for the pleasure of uttering his name.

I wanted to steer Mary back to the subject of Jane's illness, for I yearned to know what she had spoken of in those last weeks of her life, but we were interrupted by Martha bringing in a tray of tea. Cass followed close behind her with a seed cake, so all talk of Jane came to an abrupt halt. Mary left soon afterwards. She was collected by her son, James-Edward, who was returning from a trip to Winchester in the family carriage. He stayed only briefly at the cottage but I was struck anew by his resemblance to Henry – not just in looks but in his manners, his mode of speech, even the tilt of his head as he bid us all goodbye. At eighteen years old he looked every inch the gentleman-about-town.

I wondered if Mary had any inkling of what had gone on at Godmersham. Unless Henry had confessed to a liaison with Elizabeth she would have no reason to discourage her son's attraction to young Lizzy. It beggared belief that Henry would allow her to continue in ignorance of the terrible consequence of such a union. I heard that warning voice again, the same that had whispered to me in the bedroom at the White Hart: *You think of this as if it was a fact, yet it exists only in your mind.*

269

When Mary and her son had gone I went into the garden with Martha to help pick apples for a pie. I soon discovered that she was just as prone to tears as Cass when Jane's name was mentioned. So, casting about for some safe topic of conversation, I asked how long she and Cass had known each other.

'Goodness,' she replied, 'it must be nearly thirty years!'

'How did you come to be friends?'

'Well, it wasn't long after we'd moved to Hampshire. My father had died and we were renting Deane parsonage from Reverend Austen. He invited us to Steventon and we met the whole family. Cass was only about sixteen then and I was in my early twenties.'

Quite unconsciously my brain jumped back to Jane, calculating that she would have been thirteen or fourteen at the time. I almost said this aloud but checked myself just in time. Instead I asked how old Mary had been when they arrived in Hampshire.

'She was the same age as Cass,' Martha replied. 'I hoped they would be friends, because Mary was very shy in her teens. She had smallpox when she was ten and it knocked her confidence terribly.' She gave a small sigh as she reached up into the apple tree. 'She once told me she overheard the doctor telling our mother that she might as well forget about marriage because her face was quite ruined. But she seemed to blossom when we moved to Deane; she started going to balls and became very friendly with all the Austens. Of course, we had no idea then that she would end up as wife to James.'

'I suppose he was already married to Anna's mother when you arrived?' I bent to pick up an apple that had fallen from the branch she was pulling on.

'No,' she replied, tossing another apple into the basket, 'none of the Austen brothers had wives when we first came to

270

Deane. But it was only two or three years later that James married Anne Matthew. That was difficult for us because James got the living of Deane on his marriage and we had to move out. We went to Ibthorpe, which was eighteen miles away and not nearly so pleasant.' She paused to wipe her brow with the skirt of her pinafore then reached up into the tree again. 'Mary used to visit them often – more because she missed the place than because she liked James' wife, I suspect – so when Anne died it seemed natural for James to ask her to be mistress of the house.'

Yes, I thought, *but only after Eliza had turned him down*. No wonder Mary had refused to have the woman under her roof, when she had so very nearly deprived her not just of a husband but of the place she thought of as home. I could just imagine the ten-year-old Mary, lying in her sick bed as snatches of the doctor's conversation with her mother reached her from beyond the bedroom door; I pictured her poor, blistered face as his words rang out like a death knell. I wondered if, rather than leaving her bereft, his pronouncement had forged an iron determination to prove him wrong. It occurred to me then that Mary might have set her sights on Henry first; perhaps she had singled him out long before James, merely settling for the older brother when the real object of her desire made it clear that he would only marry money.

Once again my thoughts returned to Jane, remembering what Martha had told me years before, in Worthing, about the bitterness caused when James and Mary took over the rectory at Steventon. Mary had apparently shown the same disregard for the feelings of Jane and Cass as she felt had been shown to her by their brother and his first wife. Seen in this light, her meanness was harder to condemn.

Over the next few days Mary was a constant topic of conversation at the cottage – or rather her husband was – because Anna called with the children to tell us that he was very ill and James-Edward had ridden to Winchester to call for the assistance of Jane's physician, Mr Lyford.

By the time I left Chawton we had received better reports of him, but a few months later he seemed to have suffered a relapse. Anna wrote to say that he had been too weak to attend the christening of her new baby boy, George. She added as a postscript that her cousin Lizzy was to be married. My heart skipped a beat at this, but the next paragraph informed me that her fiancé was not Anna's half brother, James-Edward, but Edward Royd-Rice, the wealthy young son of a sea captain, whom she had met at a ball in Paris.

I breathed a sigh of relief, thinking of Jane's face that last day I saw her at the house in Hans Place. If anything had gone on behind the scenes to keep Lizzy and her cousin apart, it appeared to have worked. Whether she had had any hand in it I supposed I would never know.

At Christmas Anna wrote to me again. This time the paper was edged in black. 'My dear father died, after a long slow decay, at Steventon,' her letter said. 'Uncle Henry is to replace him as Rector. My stepmother and Caroline must leave the house by the middle of January. They are to go to Bath until they decide where to settle.'

How ironic, I thought, that Mary is to be turned out of the home she took so smugly from Jane twenty years ago. It occurred to me that now she and Henry were both widowed the illicit union – if there *was* one – could be legitimised. As a man of religion, Henry would be setting a rather bad example by marrying his dead brother's wife, but such a thing was not unheard of, even for a parson. Perhaps Mary would not be losing her home after all; perhaps she had simply gone to Bath to wait for the dust to settle.

But a letter I received from Fanny in April that same year put paid to any such possibility. 'You will never guess what–,' she wrote, in her usual breathless style, 'Uncle Henry has surprised and shocked us all by taking a new wife. Her name is Eleanor Jackson and she is only six months older than me. She is the niece of the Reverend Papillon. Do you remember him? He lives at the rectory in Chawton, right opposite the Great House.'

Fanny went on to describe the visit she had made to the newlyweds while staying at the Great House with her father: 'Miss Jackson has a good pair of eyes,' she wrote, 'but I fear she is not strong. She cannot go for walks by herself: Uncle Henry pushes her about the village in a wheelchair, which seems rather strange when one considers that he is close to fifty and she twenty-eight.'

The rest of the letter was taken up with Fanny's own wedding plans. She was to marry the man in the miniature, Sir Edward Knatchbull, who, she told me, had six children under ten years old. Poor little Fanny, I thought. Perhaps she believes he will not be interested in fathering any more.

As I folded the letter and put it away I could not help thinking of Mary, kicking her heels in Bath. If my instincts about her were right she must be incandescent with rage: not only had Henry passed her over, he had chosen someone young enough to be her daughter. Perhaps now that Mary was available she was no longer desirable. I wondered if what Henry really wanted was a child: a *legitimate* child. If so, Mary was unlikely to be able to provide him with one at forty-two years old. Was that the reason for him choosing young Miss Jackson? If Fanny's description of her was anything to go by she did not sound an ideal candidate for motherhood. Perhaps there was another attraction then: did this new bride come with money, or the promise of it?

I took a little cloth from my desk to polish the ring on my finger. 'Well, Jane,' I whispered, 'What do *you* make of it?'

273

Chapter Twenty-Seven

Jane shared my new home in Liverpool in a way that would never have been possible in life. I spoke to her every day, out loud when I was in private or in my head when there were other people about. Sometimes I would consult her about the running of the school or my concern for one of the pupils; another day I might tell her how the Mersey looked as it flowed past my window to the sea. She became a constant presence in my life and although my evenings were often spent alone I never felt lonely, for I had her books and her letters all about me.

It wasn't long before I had her face to look upon as well. True to her word, Cass copied the pastel drawing and sent it to me, along with first editions of *Northanger Abbey* and *Persuasion*. In the days that followed it was as if Jane was sitting beside me, reading the words herself. I have to confess that of all her books, *Persuasion* is my favourite, because its voice is the voice of the Jane I got to know at Godmersham; the Jane who knew what it felt like to suffer for love but could summon delight from the most hopeless of circumstances. *Persuasion* felt like her gift to me – a promise of fulfilment at last, made all the more precious by a heroine named Anne.

I was invited to stay at Chawton many times over the next few years. Being with Cassandra and Mrs Austen fed the flame in my heart. And I would catch glimpses of Jane in the faces of Anna's children. Julia had her eyes; Jemima had her sharp tongue and little George once told me very solemnly that he could not decide what he loved best: reading or dancing.

In all those years it never occurred to me that Jane's death had been anything other than the tragic result of some unidentifiable illness. It was not until 1827 – a few months before the tenth anniversary of her passing – that I came across something that led me to question that assumption.

In the last week of January I received the sad news that Mrs Austen had breathed her last on the eighteenth day of that month, at the ripe old age of eighty-seven. Like many of those who claim a weak constitution, Jane's mother had outlived most of her contemporaries and several of her younger relatives. One of the last things she ever said to me, as I bid her farewell the previous summer, was: 'I think God has forgotten me.'

It was Anna who wrote to tell me of her passing. 'The vigour of her constitution even at her great age made the battle between life and death severe,' she wrote, 'but the last hours were tranquil and free from pain, and when it was over the very wrinkles seemed smoothed out of her face and the beauty of youth restored to it – her nurses were Aunt Cassandra, Martha Lloyd, and the two maids, who took their full share and proved themselves most faithful and kind.'

Two days after Anna's letter arrived there was a notice in the *Times*. It was short and to the point, noting that she was the mother of the late novelist, Miss Jane Austen, and had been buried in the graveyard of St Nicholas in the village where she had spent the latter years of her life. As I turned the page I was talking to Jane, asking her how she felt about her mother's grave being so far away from her own. I was staring at the newspaper without seeing the print but as my eyes came back into focus they alighted on an extraordinary headline: 'Woman poisons husband and two children.'

It was a report of the trial of a person from the north of England who had been accused of murdering her spouse and stepchildren for the insurance money their deaths would bring her. Her crimes had apparently gone undiscovered until she attempted the same method of disposing of her second husband, whose doctor spotted the tell-tale symptoms of poisoning. I stopped short when I read what the doctor had said in court: 'The patient's skin displayed a distinctive discoloration. It was blotched black and white, which is a clear indication of the ingestion of arsenic.'

Jane's last letter leapt into my mind. 'My face is black and white and every wrong colour...' Those were her exact words. My heart lurched. Was Jane poisoned? I searched my memory for everything I knew about arsenic. Like most people, I have some in my own kitchen cupboard, used whenever rats are spotted rooting around in the alley at the side of the school. Had there been some accident? Had someone mistaken it for an ingredient that was mixed into something Jane ate?

I remembered the episode with the eye wash, described to me by Jane herself, when her mother had mistaken ground hen's dung for pepper and put it in an oyster pie. But that had been a joke, hadn't it? And besides, if arsenic had got into the food at Chawton Cottage, other members of the family would have fallen ill too.

I cast about for another explanation. Arsenic was often prescribed by doctors. It was used to treat all manner of ailments. Had she been given too large a dose? The other possibility was too wild an idea to contemplate: that someone had deliberately poisoned her. I dismissed it immediately. 'Who in the world,' I murmured, 'would want to murder such a creature as you?'

I went back to the newspaper article, searching for any small detail that would dispel the thoughts taking shape in my mind. But what I saw only increased my disquiet. There was a paragraph about a former neighbour of the accused woman who had been called to give evidence. She reported that the stepchildren and first husband had all 'gone a funny colour in the face' in the weeks leading up to their demise. My heart thumped so hard I thought it would burst out of my ribs. Was it wrong to make a connection between this case and Jane's death? Was I being as fanciful as Catherine Morland in *Northanger Abbey*? I blinked at the words on the page before me. *No, you are not. There it is in black and white. Black and white!* Jane's voice was as clear and strong as it had been in life.

Over the next few weeks I buried myself in medical books. First of all I wanted to know if anything else could have caused the facial discoloration. I found diseases that turned the skin yellow, red or blue, but nothing that gave the patchy black and white effect she had described.

Then I read everything I could find about arsenic. The more I learned, the more I was convinced that Jane's illness was not an illness at all, but the result of her system being poisoned. She had reported stomach problems; sickness; weakness in the limbs: all were typical of chronic exposure to arsenic. I read of people who had been accidentally poisoned by arsenic in the wallpaper of their homes, or by working in factories that manufactured paint and dyes for cloth, both of which processes involved handling the deadly compound. But every innocent, accidental explanation I sought brought me back to the fact that those who lived with her had not been similarly afflicted. Cassandra and Martha were still alive and well; so were the two servants, Jenny Butter and Hannah Pegg. Even Mrs Austen had survived her daughter by nearly a decade and had, in Anna's words, looked quite beautiful in death.

I read that there were two ways in which people could die from ingesting arsenic. If small amounts were taken over a long period of time, the victim would not die at once but would develop symptoms which mimic those of cancer of the stomach or the bowel. If the amount is then increased by even a little, the body, already so weak, will experience major organ failure, with death occurring quickly after. The second type of death results from ingesting a single large dose of the compound. In this instance, the person suffers a sudden, violent death.

By now my head was tumbling with questions. The chief of these was the matter of Jane's medical treatment. Had she been given arsenic as a cure? If so, her symptoms could be attributed to accidental overdose or malpractice on the part of the doctor. This was not the sort of question that could be asked in a letter to Cassandra. It would have to be done with great subtlety on my next visit to Chawton. But when would that be? I could hardly invite myself, especially with Cassandra in mourning for her mother.

In a fever of uncertainty, I hit upon a plan. I wrote to Martha Lloyd with a request for advice, pretending that one of the girls in my charge was suffering from a condition that had so far defied diagnosis, but reminded me of the symptoms Jane had described to me in her letters. I told Martha that the doctor was inclined to administer arsenic, but I was not sure that this was the right course of action. Did Martha know if Jane was given such treatment, I asked, and what was her opinion of it?

I awaited her reply with a mixture of trepidation and guilt. I was desperate for the answer but it felt wrong to manipulate a good woman like Martha Lloyd in this way. To my shame the letter arrived with a package. Martha had taken the trouble to prepare a special remedy for the non-existent sick girl, along with detailed instructions as to its use. As for the arsenic, she dismissed it in a single sentence. She herself had advised Jane against its use, for in her opinion it was a harsh remedy with many dangerous side effects.

I had no doubt that Jane would have heeded her advice, for although she often teased Martha about her potions, she had recommended them to me on more than one occasion. All the occupants of Chawton Cottage regarded a visit to the doctor as a last resort and Martha was the one they trusted most when illness struck. So if Jane had not taken arsenic as a medicine, where had it come from? Was there one thing she habitually ate or drank that no one else in the household ever touched? Was it possible that whatever this was could have become contaminated with the poison? It seemed highly unlikely. But that left only one other conclusion: that somebody had deliberately administered the arsenic because they wanted her dead.

I had dismissed this idea at the outset but now I was not so sure. I was not privy to everything that went on in her life: she was apt to offend some people with her sharp remarks. Had she gone too far? Upset one of the servants, perhaps, at the cottage or the Great House? For if it was deliberate, the perpetrator would have to have been close enough to have the opportunity, over a period of many months, to bring about their evil scheme.

As the school year drew to a close I became quite desperate to get to Chawton. Cassandra's letters became brighter and more optimistic as another Christmas approached, but contained no invitation to visit. In the end it was Martha Lloyd who came to my aid once again. She wrote to tell me the amazing and wonderful news that at the age of sixty-three she was to become a bride. Her fiancé was none other than Jane's brother Frank, the sea captain, whose wife had recently died leaving him with six children still at home. She had agreed to take charge of his house and family in Portsmouth and would soon be leaving the cottage at Chawton. Would I be able to manage a trip to Hampshire, she asked, to attend the wedding?

Within an hour of receiving her letter my reply was written. 'You will help me, Jane, won't you?' I whispered as I sealed it up.

Chapter Twenty-Eight

I set off for Chawton in the third week of July, the day after the girls had left school for the summer holidays. On the journey I caught my first glimpse of Mr Stephenson's famous locomotive, *The Rocket*, which was being tested on the new railway that an army of labourers were laying down between Manchester and Liverpool. The bitter smell of burning coal seeped in through the closed doors of the stagecoach and my stomach, already churning at the prospect of the quest that lay ahead, was turned to ice by the shrieking of the great engine as it flew past.

The thatched roofs and lush meadows of Hampshire belonged to a different world from the one I now inhabited: a world of slow, steady rhythms and old-fashioned ways. Stepping down from the coach to nothing but the sound of birdsong and the panting of horses, it was hard to believe that anything sinister could happen in such a place. I felt suddenly foolish. What was I thinking of, coming here with a hidden motive? Then I remembered something Anna had said on a hot May evening more than twenty years distant: *If I had a husband like that I would poison him slowly...* I reminded myself that she lived in this very county, the respectable wife of a parson with a brood of seven children now. Dark thoughts will grow in any soil, I thought.

It struck me that Anna was the only person I had ever heard utter such a thing. Why, then had I not thought of it before? The answer came swiftly, in Jane's voice. *Anna loved me.* It was beyond doubt that Anna had adored her aunt. Jane had cared for her when she was small and had continued to be the most special woman in Anna's life, more of a mother figure than Mary Austen had ever been. I could no more suspect Anna of poisoning her aunt than murdering one of her own children.

I started counting all the people I could think of who visited the cottage on a regular basis, and could, therefore, have had an opportunity to introduce arsenic into something Jane ate or drank. When I included all the family members and servants who had stayed at the Great House during the year before she died, the number exceeded thirty. I wondered how on earth I was going to investigate so many potential suspects, especially as I knew of no reason for any of them wanting Jane dead. Cass and Henry were the only beneficiaries of her Will and the amounts she left were trifling, despite the success of her books. Cass, I was certain, would rather have died herself than see any harm befall her sister. Henry was a different character altogether: I had seen his ruthless side at close quarters. He had lost his fortune, of course, but was he really capable of murdering his own sister for a little less than a curate's yearly stipend?

Fanny and Anna never mentioned him in their letters now. Cass had given me the occasional bit of news. There had been talk of him taking up a chaplaincy at the British embassy in Berlin, then news of him moving instead to a parish in Colchester. 'He and Eleanor have little in the way of material wealth but they seem very happy,' Cass had written a year or so ago. She had made no mention of any baby being born to the couple. It appeared that Miss Jackson had brought Henry neither children nor money.

I heard my name called and looked up. Still, after all these years, I had a fleeting sense that the figure waving from the window was Jane. It was Cass, of course, and soon she was out of the door and coming along the path, hands outstretched in greeting. I saw that she was still dressed in black, like a widow in mourning. When she smiled at me I saw that she had lost two of her front teeth, just like her mother. As she led me back to the house I half-expected to see Mrs Austen bending over the cabbages in her boots and workman's smock. I had to remind myself that, like Jane, she no longer walked this earth.

Jane's face was the first thing that I sought when I entered the parlour. I noticed that there was something hanging on the wall beside it: a piece of writing in a gilt frame that matched the one containing her portrait. 'What's this?' I asked Cass.

'It's a poem,' she replied. 'The very last thing that Jane composed. She dictated it to me two days before she died.' She glanced away. 'I've had it in a drawer for ages but I thought it ought to go on display.'

I took a few steps closer until I was able to make sense of the letters. '"When Winchester Races – a poem for St Swithin's Day,"' I read aloud.

'She wrote it on St Swithin's Day,' Cass explained. 'I don't know why she chose that subject – it seems an odd thing to be thinking about when you're….' She bit her lip.

'Would you mind if I copied it? I should like to be able to read it to myself sometimes, when I'm back at home.'

'Of course I wouldn't mind,' she smiled. 'You can do it now, if you like, while I make you some tea.'

She brought me paper and a pen and ink. I sat quite still for a moment, reading the poem through, with nothing but the ticking clock intruding on my thoughts. It was a strange poem about the saint taking revenge on the people of Winchester for having the nerve to hold their races on his holy day. I don't know what I was hoping for: it was quite unlike anything else of hers that I had ever seen. There were six verses and every so often a word was underlined – presumably Jane had instructed Cass to do this – but the choice of emphasis seemed quite random. Nevertheless, I set to copying it.

'Where is Martha?' I asked when Cass returned with the tea.

'Gone to Winchester,' she replied. 'She and Frank have to finalise the arrangements for the service. She'll be home in time for dinner.' A fragment of her voice broke away with those last few words and I asked her what the matter was. 'Don't mind me,' she said, 'It's just foolishness. I'm as happy for Frank and Martha as anyone could be. It's just that…' she tailed off, picking at the lace on her collar.

'Just that what?'

'They're getting married in the cathedral. Where…' She didn't need to finish the sentence. Now I understood. I had wrongly assumed that the wedding would take place at the village church.

'Why did they choose it?' I asked.

'The Dean is a friend of Frank's from his schooldays,' she replied. 'He married him the first time and took the funeral service for his poor wife. Frank says he would be offended if his wedding to Martha took place anywhere else.' She looked away then, fishing in her pocket for a handkerchief. It grieved me to see her tears but I blinked back mine, afraid of upsetting her even more.

'Do you talk to her, Cass?' My voice sounded very loud in the little parlour.

She searched my face for a moment. 'Yes, every day. Do you?'

I nodded. 'I have the drawing you made hanging in my

study, over the desk. I sit for ages, sometimes, just staring into her face, and after a while I hear her voice in my head. It seems so real to me; as if she's standing right beside me.'

'I get that too,' Cass smiled. 'It's usually when I'm in the garden, though, not in the parlour. I don't look at the portrait very often because it pains me to remember how she changed in those last months. Her face was so lovely, but it was ruined by her illness.'

I felt a prickle of apprehension. I wanted her to go on, to describe exactly what Jane's face had looked like at the end, but now the opportunity had arisen I found I didn't have the stomach for it. I stared at her stupidly, trying to think of something else to say.

'It was horrible, what it did to her.' Cass shook her head. I held my breath. 'It was as if someone had taken a paintbrush to her face and dotted it all black and white. They say the state of our skin reflects the state of the internal organs, don't they?' She glanced at me and I gave a quick nod. 'I suppose it was a manifestation of the disease inside her stomach. It was the same with my brother James, you know.'

This took me so much by surprise I could not frame a sensible response.

'His face turned a horrible colour.' She made a sound like green wood in a fire. 'I remember going to visit him the week before he died. I hadn't seen him for a while because Mama had been ill and I couldn't get to Steventon. Martha was helping Mary to nurse him – she'd tried everything she could think of to make him well, but nothing worked – and she warned me not to be shocked when I saw him. I suppose she knew it would remind me of Jane. It did, of course. I knew then that he must be dying.'

The air inside the room seemed to have liquefied; the furniture was melting and changing shape. Had Cass really said what I thought she said? I opened and closed my mouth like a goldfish. 'Was he…er, I mean… Did Mr. Lyford say what ailed him?'

'He told Mary he couldn't be certain what it was. He mentioned cancer of the bowel and he said there was probably a weakness of the digestive system in our family.' She paused, frowning, and said: 'Mama did not have it, though; she ate like a horse until the last week of her life and her skin was quite lovely when she died. I remember thinking it was as if the years had suddenly fallen away.'

I was nodding as she spoke, but my mind was racing ahead. Why had James displayed the same discoloration of the face as his sister? Could it be that *both* of them were poisoned? Or was Mr Lyford's conclusion the correct one? Had Jane and her brother died of some mysterious digestive disorder not mentioned in the textbooks I had read? A condition that affected some members of Jane's family but not others?

'What about your father?' I asked. 'Did he have problems with his stomach?'

'No,' she replied. 'He never had a day's illness in his life: he was absolutely fine one day, then the next he collapsed. They said it was a stroke.' She stared into the empty fireplace. 'The only other person I've seen with a face like that was Elizabeth, but of course, she was only a relative by marriage.'

'Elizabeth?' I stared at her, incredulous. 'Surely *she* died because of giving birth?'

'Yes, she did,' Cass replied. 'It was ten days after poor little Brook-John was born. We all had dinner together and suddenly she fell to the floor, just writhing in agony, poor thing. And black patches appeared on her face, before our very eyes.'

Something swam up from the depths of my memory: a line in a letter Jane had written at the time of Elizabeth's death: *How does the corpse look?* I remembered it because it had puzzled me greatly when she showed the letter to me. It dawned on me now that Cass must have mentioned the condition of Elizabeth's face when she wrote to tell Jane of the tragic event at Godmersham. No doubt Jane, with a writer's fascination, had been curious to know whether Elizabeth's complexion had reverted to its beautiful, unblemished state after death.

This revelation of Cassandra's, coming hard on the heels of the news about James, sent me into a flurry of speculation. What if Elizabeth had been poisoned too? Her death was exactly like the descriptions I had read of victims of a single, large dose of arsenic, where an apparently healthy person suffers a sudden, violent end. Could it be that one person had killed all three members of the Austen family? If so, what was the motive?

The first question to consider was who might benefit from this series of murders, if murders they were. Henry's name sprang to mind once again: he had inherited money from Jane and a living from James. But surely he was the last person to have wanted Elizabeth dead? I considered it for a moment. What if Elizabeth had grown tired of all the subterfuge and deceit? What if she had wanted their relationship out in the open, with a divorce from Edward? How would Henry have reacted to that? His fortune was still intact at the time, but to incur Edward's wrath would have been financial suicide: not only would Edward have pulled out as a major backer, he would have sued Henry for thousands of pounds in damages in the Criminal Conversation case that would surely follow. *Men have murdered for far less*, I thought.

The second question was one of opportunity. If my theory about Jane, James and Elizabeth was correct, the perpetrator must be someone who had access to the homes of all three. Henry was a regular visitor to Chawton, Steventon and Godmersham. He was not at Godmersham when Elizabeth died but he could have bribed one of the servants to put arsenic in that last meal. So many staff went in and out of that great kitchen that it would have been very difficult to pin the crime on any individual, even if poisoning had been suspected. And Henry had been a very rich man at that time: it wasn't hard to imagine some footman or groom or scullery maid taking a risk like that for the kind of money he could offer.

The fact that Henry had arrived in Kent within twenty-four hours of Elizabeth's death was in itself most unusual, given that he lived sixty miles away. This eagerness to attend a scene of death was a consistent feature of Henry's behaviour: Mary had told me that he was the first member of the family to arrive at the house in College Street following Jane's passing. He was actually residing at Steventon rectory when James died and had subsequently taken over the place with what many would consider indecent haste.

Once set on this path, my thoughts began to run away with me. What if there had been more to be gained from Jane's death than a mere fifty pound legacy? What if he was creaming off the profits from the two novels published after her death, along with the profits from any new editions of her earlier books? Without Jane to keep a watchful eye on the accounts, there was no knowing what he might get away with. Cassandra was not the sort of person to question her brother about the money Jane's estate yielded: no doubt she was grateful for whatever she received.

It was next to impossible to shake off these ideas. Cass asked if I would help her in the kitchen and though my body did her bidding my head was miles away. Hannah Pegg had gone to the Great House, where preparations for the wedding breakfast were being made, so Cass and I were soon up to our elbows in eggs and sugar, making dainty offerings to add to the feast. My task was to whisk twenty egg whites for thirty minutes and though my right arm ached with the effort, thoughts of Henry made me beat all the harder. I was gathering up all my memories of him, holding them up for inspection like fallen apples. Was he *really* capable of such heinous crimes? Could a man who sought out the prettiest, most expensive muslin for his sister also be capable of killing her for money? Could a man who cradled a baby in his arms and sang it to sleep think of murdering its mother?

'Would you fetch me some vanilla pods?' Cass's voice broke into my thoughts. 'They're in the pantry, next to Martha's wine.'

I glanced at the egg whites, which were stiff enough by now for a whole family of mice to run across. Laying down the whisk I set off down the passage that led to a little room that smelt of cheese and vinegar and smoked meat. I had no candle, so it took me a while to locate the jar containing the vanilla pods. The first thing I put my hand on turned out to be a draught for curing piles and the label on the second jar I scrutinised was a remedy for gout. Eventually I spotted what I sought on a low shelf bearing a row of demijohns. As I tucked it under my arm I heard the clatter of hooves through the wall. I wondered if it was the stagecoach pulling up outside the inn but as I made my way back towards the kitchen I heard a familiar voice.

'Cass! Where are you?' It was Henry. I froze in mid-stride. From the passageway I could see into the kitchen through the door, which I had left ajar.

'In here!' Cass called over her shoulder.

Henry strode into the room. I observed him in profile as he bent to kiss his sister then stuck his finger in the mixture she was stirring and licked it. 'Mmm! Delicious! I wasn't sure there'd be anyone at home: thought you might be up at the Great House. I'll go and fetch Eleanor.' With that he made a swift exit and I darted into the room with the vanilla.

'Henry and his wife are here,' Cass said when she saw me. 'Would you mind taking these into the parlour while I make another pot of tea?' She took gingerbread biscuits from an earthenware jar and arranged them on a plate. As she did so I glanced out of the window. There was a gig parked by the donkey shed and Henry was lifting a young woman out of it. She was pale and slight with wisps of blonde hair poking out from under a straw bonnet. He did not set her down, as I expected, but carried her all the way up the path that led round the side of the house. She had her arms around his neck and when I glimpsed her face I saw a look of adoration in her eyes. So this is Reverend Papillon's niece, I thought. She did indeed look like an invalid, albeit a very young one. Henry looked like a father carrying his sick child.

I reached the parlour before them and set the plate of biscuits down on the table. Henry didn't notice me at first. He was puffing slightly with exertion as he set his wife down on the sofa. He kissed her forehead, murmuring: 'There you are my love. Do you feel quite well? I hope the journey hasn't taxed your strength.'

'I'm fine, my darling,' she replied. 'It isn't far, really, is it? And I have a whole day to rest before we go to Winchester.'

Henry caught sight of me as he straightened up. 'Good gracious! How you startled me!' He gave his customary beam. At this distance I could see the march of the years in his face. There was a row of wrinkles across his forehead and fine lines either side of his mouth, noticeable only when he smiled. At seven-and-fifty he was still a handsome man and appeared not to have put on an ounce of extra weight.

'Allow me to introduce my wife,' he said. 'Eleanor, this is Miss Sharp: she is an old friend of my sister Jane.'

I felt very old indeed as I held out my hand to her. I calculated that she must be in her mid-thirties, as Fanny and Anna now were, but with her tiny frame and delicate looks she could have passed for twenty.

Cass came in then with the tea. Henry said they wouldn't

stay above half an hour as he had to get Eleanor settled in the room they were to have at the Great House. I watched him with a cold fascination as he fussed over his wife, pouring milk into her tea and sugaring it for her; sweeping the crumbs off her lap when she took a piece of gingerbread. Was this how a poisoner behaved? Was this how he had lured Jane into swallowing arsenic? Could he really be so utterly callous?

From the look of the gig outside, Cass's assessment of Henry's financial status was quite accurate. In their dress he and Eleanor looked exactly as one would expect a country parson and his wife to look: there was none of the style and dash of London tailoring about them. The inescapable conclusion was that he had not married for money but for love. And what a tender, selfless kind of love it seemed to be, for Henry had known the state of Eleanor's health when he wed her: Fanny's letter had made that quite plain.

As I watched him carry her back to the gig I felt a mounting sense of shame at the direction my thoughts had taken. I glanced at Jane's portrait on the wall. *Henry is no murderer, is he?* I asked the question with my eyes, not my tongue. For once, though, she was silent.

'Miss Sharp?'

I wheeled round, startled by the sound of Henry's voice.

'I had to speak to you.' He dropped his voice to a whisper. 'I owe you an apology. I should have written to you long ago.'

So taken aback was I that no words came in response. I stood by Jane's picture, as still and silent as the image in the frame.

'I beg your pardon, I must be brief. Eleanor is waiting in the gig and she must not get cold.' He glanced at the door, which he had left half open. 'I wronged you in my other life; the life I led before. And for that I am truly sorry. I take comfort from what Cass tells me: that you have raised yourself far above the station you occupied in my brother's house. But I ask your forgiveness, all the same.' He looked as if he was waiting for me to give an absolution. When none came he said: 'Like many people, I have searched for love in the wrong places. And God knows I've been punished for it. But out of despair has come the greatest joy: Eleanor is so much more than I deserve. She is the—'

'Henry!' Cass was calling from the kitchen. 'Are you still here?'

With a quick bow he rushed out, closing the door on a swarm of unanswered questions. Was that a confession? Was he actually admitting to an affair with Elizabeth? He said he had searched for love in the wrong places. What did that mean, exactly? The words carried a horrible resonance. Was I not guilty of a similar offence? *Searching does not mean finding.*

Henry and Eleanor swept past the window in a smudge of colours on their way to the Great House. The man who had begged my forgiveness was so very different from the Machiavellian character I had clashed with at the White Hart. I wondered if the loss of all that material wealth had brought on a Damascene experience. Perhaps his decision to enter the church had been more than just a last-ditch solution to penury. Certainly he seemed to have changed for the better. His unsolicited expression of regret softened my heart to the extent that I crossed him off the list of potential suspects.

Chapter Twenty-Nine

I was back in the kitchen, pulping quinces through a sieve, when a new possibility occurred to me. Cass had her hand in the jar of vanilla pods, which reminded me of the remedies I had seen on the shelves in the larder. Suddenly I was in London, at Henry's former residence in Hans Place; I was in his bedroom in the small hours, dozing fitfully by his sick bed, and opening my eyes to see Jane swallowing a draught of something I thought was intended for him. Jane's words came back to me with a horrible clarity. *It's Martha's tonic wine: I never travel without it these days.* How easy, I thought, for someone to slip into the larder where Martha stored her medicines and add poison to one of the bottles. Was that how Jane had died?'

'So this is where you've been hiding!'

I was so startled by this sudden intrusion that I almost dropped the sieve. There was a tall, willowy creature in a blue silk pelisse and ostrich-trimmed hat standing in the doorway. Her voice was the only thing that gave her away, for I don't think I would have recognised her otherwise. Before I could get up Fanny bounded across the room and took my face in both her hands, planting a kiss on my forehead. 'Uncle Henry said you were here,' she grinned. 'I've got so much to tell you!' Turning to Cass she said: 'Can I steal her for a half an hour?'

She took my arm as we walked through the village, chattering away at breakneck speed. She wanted to tell me all about the beautiful house she now inhabited; of its furniture and paintings; of its lakes and fountains; and of the army of servants she had at her command. I tried to concentrate on what she was describing but my brain was on fire with thoughts of Jane. We passed the blacksmith's and the post office and walked on until we reached a left fork called Mounter's Lane. Here the cottages gave way to hazel hedges dotted with purple-pink foxgloves and intense yellow clusters of St John's wort. These hedgerow herbs were the very thing Martha used in her remedies. Nodding in the breeze, they took on a new sinister aspect, like plotters whispering murder.

'Mersham Hatch is very like Godmersham, actually,' Fanny was saying, 'They knocked down the old house, which dated back to the fifteenth century. I'm rather glad – I hate old houses: they are so dark inside.' It struck me then that her voice sounded too bright and brittle. And she had not once mentioned her new husband. Suddenly she gripped my arm tight and doubled over. Staggering slightly, she launched herself towards the hazel hedge and retched violently.

'Fanny! Oh, Lord!' I cupped her forehead in my hand, trying to support her as her body heaved. When she had recovered a little I pulled out my handkerchief and wiped her chin, which was flecked with foaming spittle. She took one look at me and burst into tears, burying her head in my shawl. I managed to lead her to a nearby stile, where I sat her down and stroked her head until her sobs subsided. 'Can you tell me about it?' I said at length.

'I...think I'm...w...' she stammered, her teeth chattering.

'Are you with child?' I whispered.

She clenched her jaw, a look of terror in her eyes. 'I th…think so,' she nodded.

'Have your courses stopped?'

She nodded again.

'How long ago?'

'N…n…nine weeks.'

I pulled her to me, hugging her tight. No wonder she had behaved so strangely, I thought; she must have been desperate to unburden herself; desperate to confide the fact that her worst nightmare was upon her. 'It will be all right.' My words were more like a prayer than a reassurance. 'Lizzy has had four babies already, hasn't she? And she is just fine.'

'But Mama was fine after *ten* babies!' Fanny mumbled into my shawl. 'That didn't stop her from…' Her shoulders convulsed with more sobs. At a loss for anything helpful to say I stood there, just holding her, until she'd cried herself out. I have no idea how long we were there and it was a wonder no one came clambering over the stile in all the time she was upon it. Eventually her breathing slowed to something like normal and she looked up at me with swollen eyes.

'I'm sorry,' she murmured, blinking back the tears that were welling up again.

'You have nothing to apologise for,' I replied. 'It's no wonder you're afraid. Anyone who went through what you did would feel the same, I'm certain.'

'I was there when she died, you know. She was sitting at the table, just as she always did, laughing and talking. Then all of a sudden she fell sideways onto the floor. She was kicking out and clutching her stomach. Then her face went all…' she tailed off, pressing her lips together so hard the flesh turned white. She drew in her breath and said: 'Caky wouldn't have it, you know: she said it must have been the food. She played merry hell with the kitchen girls and the cook – called them every name under the sun. But as Papa said, it couldn't have been the food, could it? We'd all have been struck down if it was.'

I found it difficult to utter anything in reply, so struck was I by this. No wonder Sackree had worn mourning black all those years after Elizabeth's death; not only had she lost her darling, she blamed the death on the carelessness of others. Could she have been closer to the truth than she realised? But if Henry was not the culprit, who was? Had Elizabeth been murdered by some other member of the household for a reason I could never guess at? Or had the whole thing really been a tragic accident – the result of some random act of carelessness that had claimed her as its only victim?

'You say she ate all the same things as you did? There was nothing extra that she took? Some meat or fish dish that no one else was partial to?'

Fanny sniffed and shook her head. 'I suppose it's just one of those things that no one will ever be able to explain. Anna told me that almost exactly the same thing happened to her mother.'

'Anna?'

'Yes. She told me her mama collapsed after eating her dinner, just as mine did. The difference, of course, was that Anna's mother had not just been in childbed: Anna was two-and-a-half when it happened; she says it's her earliest memory – seeing her mama lying absolutely still on the floor of the dining room at Deane parsonage.'

'Poor Anna,' I said. 'I didn't realise.'

'It was very hard for her. She said Uncle James would never allow her to ask any questions about her mama. I think that was very mean of him, don't you? My father would never do such a thing to *his* children.'

'I suppose the difference is that Anna's father married again,' I replied. 'Perhaps it was a rule made by your Aunt Mary.' Highly likely, I thought, knowing what a jealous woman Mary Austen was.

'Probably,' Fanny nodded. 'I think I feel a little better now. Shall we walk back?' Leaning on me for support, she raised herself from the stile and took a few ginger steps along the lane.

'Are you sure you can manage?' I asked. 'You could always stay here while I go back for the donkey cart.'

'I'll be fine, thank-you. I don't feel nauseous any more; actually I feel quite hungry.'

We walked along in silence for a while. I was thinking about Anna's mother, wondering if her death was caused by eating food that had gone off. It seemed odd, though, that both she and Elizabeth had died while sharing a meal with others who were not similarly afflicted.

As we reached the fork in the road Fanny said: 'Aunt Mary was awful to Anna when she was a child, you know; when we were at Godmersham together we used to plot different ways of killing her.'

'I know,' I nodded. 'I heard you once.'

'Did you really? Goodness, how embarrassing!'

I almost told her what I'd overheard but thought better of it, remembering that what they'd actually been talking about was the possibility of Mary dying in childbirth.

'She came to Godmersham once,' Fanny went on. 'Aunt Mary, I mean. Anna and I were about fifteen at the time and the two of them had had the most almighty row in the carriage before they even arrived. Anna said she couldn't live with her any more and she was going to run away with the first man who smiled at her.'

I shook my head and said something about it being a miracle she'd ended up with a man as good as Ben Lefroy. But as I said it I was thinking about Mary: I had forgotten that she had been at Godmersham the summer before Elizabeth died.

'Do you know who it was?' Fanny was looking at me.

'Who what was?'

'The first man who smiled at her, of course! Weren't you listening to me?' She tilted her head at the sky.

'Yes, sorry,' I said. 'I *was* listening – I just got confused. Who was it?'

'It was Uncle Henry! I teased her unmercifully about it for the rest of the holiday.'

So Henry was there too. To my mind, that put a very different slant on the visit. Mary was bound to have noticed his closeness to Elizabeth. Knowing the bitter resentment she had displayed towards Eliza, how much more violently might she have reacted in this situation? If I was right about the long-standing affair between Mary and Henry she would have an obvious motive for murder. Could she have poisoned Elizabeth? Slipped arsenic into her food?

I quickly dismissed the idea as impossible, for Elizabeth had not died until almost eighteen months after that visit. But a new seed of suspicion began to grow as we walked back towards Chawton. As James Austen's wife, Mary was an obvious candidate for *his* murder, especially if she had been hoping to lure Henry into marriage. But what about Jane? What possible motive could Mary have harboured for wanting her dead?

That afternoon at Hans Place – the last time I had seen Jane alive – I had convinced myself that she knew about Henry and Mary. What if she had said something to one or both of them? Threatened to tell James, perhaps, if they didn't stop seeing each other? She had kept quiet about Henry's affair with Elizabeth, probably thinking, as I had done, that things had cooled off between them. But could she really have contained herself if she had discovered that Henry was cuckolding yet another brother?

I recalled the way she had placed a very thinly disguised Henry on the pages of *Mansfield Park*. What if she had threatened Mary with the same treatment? Told her that the next novel would contain a character so like her in every way that no one who knew her would fail to recognise her – a character who would commit adultery with her own husband's brother?

The more I thought about it, the more plausible it seemed. Before she had finished writing *Persuasion*, Jane had told me she already had an idea for her next novel. She said it was going to be called *The Brothers*. It had never struck me before, but now the choice of title seemed highly significant. It wasn't difficult to imagine Mary's mounting sense of dread each time she called at Chawton Cottage and saw Jane scribbling away in the parlour.

Of all the visitors to that house Mary was the most familiar with Martha's potions. She would certainly have watched her sister when she first began experimenting with herbs; she would probably know, too, whereabouts in Chawton Cottage the remedies were stored. She could easily have added arsenic to Jane's tonic wine and done the same thing to the medicine James was prescribed.

Such crimes would require ruthless determination and a complete lack of conscience. I recalled the image I had formed of the little girl, lying in bed with smallpox, overhearing the doctor say her prospects of marriage were ruined. Yes, I thought, determination she has in plenty. Her conscience or lack of it was something only she could answer for.

And what about Anne Mathew? Was that Jane's voice? The words drifted into my head and settled on top of the mounting pile of questions. James' first wife had died suddenly and unexpectedly at Deane parsonage – a place where Mary had once lived and where she was a frequent visitor. I recalled Martha saying that these visits were more for the sake of seeing her old home than out of a liking for its new mistress. Could Mary have begun her career as a poisoner as long ago as that? Could Anna's mother have been her first victim? I frowned at the rutted road. No, I thought, it doesn't work: she may have had easy access to Anne, Jane and James but what about Elizabeth?

'Oh, look! That's Anna isn't it?' Fanny's voice brought me back to reality with a jolt. We were nearly level with the cottage. I had been walking without any sense of where my body was going. She was pointing to a carriage that had drawn up outside the inn. Several people were getting out, although to my eyes they were nothing more than blurs of colour. She bounded across the road with a vigour that belied the sickness that had seized her not an hour since. Before I knew it they were coming towards me, arm in arm, caught up in a stream of chatter.

Anna looked remarkably well, I thought, for someone who had produced a baby every eighteen months for the past twelve years. She was undoubtedly the very best person to quell Fanny's fears on the subject. There was so much I wanted to ask Fanny; her mother's death was a crucial link in the chain of motive and opportunity that I was constructing. But how could I do it? How could I risk upsetting the fragile balance of her mind?

Chapter Thirty

'Where are they, then, those little Lefroys?' Fanny asked as we walked up the path to the cottage.

'I left them all behind,' Anna grinned. 'Now that Ben is Rector of Ashe we can afford a nursemaid.' Her eyes shone with excitement as she described the new gown she had bought for the wedding – and who could blame her? The days she had had to herself since her marriage must have been very few indeed.

'You won't mind having Jane's old bed, will you?' Cass asked as she took her valise.

'Of course not,' Anna replied. 'I don't believe in ghosts – and even if I did, I'm sure Aunt Jane would never harm me.'

I couldn't help wishing it was me who had been given Jane's old bed: what a bittersweet thing it would have been to draw those dimity curtains around me and remember the evenings and nights we had spent in that treasured space.

'I've had to put you and Miss Sharp in my old room,' Cass went on, 'because James-Edward is going in the spare room and Martha still needs hers – for tonight at least.' She gave a self-conscious smile, which Anna returned with a giggle.

'It's a strange sort of wedding, isn't it?' she said. 'Who would have thought Martha Lloyd would become a blushing bride at her age!'

'I suppose it is unusual,' Cass replied, 'but Martha is such a good woman: she deserves whatever happiness comes her way.'

It *was* hard to imagine Martha as a bride. I supposed that the arrangement between her and Frank Austen was essentially a practical one: he would get someone to care for his children while he was away at sea and she would have a home of her own to run as she chose.

I went back to helping Cass in the kitchen, leaving Fanny and Anna to themselves in the parlour. Later on, when Fanny had gone back to the Great House and Cass was putting the finishing touches to the pastries, Anna and I went upstairs to unpack.

'Fanny thinks she is with child,' she said, as she shook out the spotted satin gown she had carried with her all the way from Basingstoke.

'She told me,' I nodded. 'She's very afraid, I think.'

'The poor girl's spent the past eight years trying to prevent it. Goodness knows how she managed – I wish I knew her secret!' Anna gave me a wry smile. 'Anyway, I tried to put her mind at rest.'

'What did you say?'

'Well, Martha always gives me something for my confinements. It's a truly vile mixture of liquorice, figs and aniseed. It works pretty well if you can get it down. There's a posset she makes, too, which helps with the after-pains and increases the milk once the baby has come.'

'I should think Martha has people queuing up for those,' I said.

'All the married women in the village ask for them. And Aunt Cass always takes them with her when she goes to help anyone at a lying-in.'

I was arranging my nightdress on the pillow when she said this and I remember stopping dead, just staring at my own hands. This, I thought, could be the final link in the chain: Cass was with Elizabeth for the birth of that last child – and she would have taken Martha's medicines with her. Was *that* how Mary Austen had murdered her rival? Had she tampered with the bottles before Cass packed them up?

'Are you all right?' Anna was beside me, peering into my face.

'Oh, yes,' I gave her a bright smile. 'I was just thinking about Fanny's baby: wondering if it would be a boy or a girl.'

'A boy, I should think, knowing her,' Anna laughed. 'She always comes up trumps, doesn't she? Not like me, with six girls to find husbands for!'

'I'm glad you were able to talk to Fanny,' I said. 'You're just what she needs, you know.'

'Well, I feel sorry for her, actually: my stepmother's always holding her up as an example – telling me I could have married as well as she has if I'd only waited – but her husband's not exactly Mr Darcy, is he? I don't think she loves him; in fact, I don't think she even *likes* him very much.'

'I hope the baby will bring her some solace, in that case,' I replied. After a pause I said: 'I suppose your stepmother will be coming to the wedding?'

'I think she will be there, yes,' she said, 'although it's by no means certain. She lives in Newbury now, which is not vastly far from Winchester, but she uses the distance as an excuse not to visit Chawton very often these days. She hasn't been down here nearly as much as she used to when my father was alive. It's partly because of the business over Uncle Henry, I think.'

'Oh?' I bent over my valise and drew out my hairbrush and nightcap, trying to disguise my avid interest in what she might divulge.

'You know how much money he lost?'

'Your Aunt Jane did tell me,' I nodded.

'Well, shortly after my father died, the Crown sent my stepmother a demand for eight hundred pounds. He was one of the guarantors, you see, and as his widow, she was bound to pay.'

'Eight hundred pounds?' This was more than the value of both the houses Mrs Raike had left me.

'It's a lot of money, isn't it? Of course, when my father agreed to it he thought he'd be coming into a fortune anyway, and it wouldn't matter if the Crown ever came chasing him for it.'

'You mean the inheritance from the Leigh-Perrots?'

'Yes.' Anna grunted. 'Can you believe Aunt L. P. is still alive? She's eighty-three! Who would have thought she'd outlive Papa?'

Mary, probably, I thought grimly. What a shock it must have been, after losing Henry to another woman, to discover that she was going to be bled dry for his debts. 'What did your stepmother do?' I asked. 'Was she able to settle it?'

'She had to, in the end, although goodness knows how she raised the money. She tried asking Uncle Edward but he said he was having a hard time finding his own share of what was owed. Then she asked for a meeting with Uncle Henry to talk it all over. They were supposed to meet at a tearoom in Basingstoke but he didn't turn up. You can imagine how that went down.'

Only too well, I wanted to reply – but of course, I said nothing of the sort.

'I thought it served her right, actually. She was always needling Papa about how well Uncle Henry had done and what charming manners he had.' She made a face. 'Are all stepmothers as spiteful as her, do you think?' Anna was unaware of the resonance her words had for me. I murmured

304

something in reply, the substance of which I can't recall, for my mind was racing ahead again. How, I wanted to know, could the widow of a country parson find eight hundred pounds? Mary was known within the family for being money-minded, but from what Jane had told me, Henry's bankruptcy had hit them hard. James had lost several hundred pounds when the bank collapsed, so there couldn't have been much left when the Crown came knocking on Mary's door.

'Where did your stepmother go when she gave up the rectory?' I asked.

'She went to Bath at first,' Anna replied. 'She took Caroline with her, of course. James-Edward was at Oxford by then so he didn't go. After a few months she realised she couldn't afford to stay there. So she moved to a place called Daylesford in Gloucestershire to stay with a friend. In the end she found a house to rent in Newbury.'

Daylesford. The name sounded familiar, but it took me a while to remember why. For some reason it triggered an image of Mrs Raike's cousin, Miss Gowerton, eating lavender cake in the pastry shop in Bath. I frowned at my hairbrush as I laid it on the dressing table. 'What was the name of the friend in Gloucestershire?'

'Lord, I can't remember!' Anna said. 'Something beginning with an 'H', I think: Harris or Hargreaves or something. Why? Do you know her?'

'I might,' I said. 'Was it Hastings?'

I lay awake for hours that night, staring up at the tenting of what had once been Cassandra's bed, and listening to Anna's slow, rhythmic breathing coming from the place where Jane should have been. I raged inside at the thought of that sweet, bright life ebbing away as the poison worked its evil on her body. Every time I closed my eyes I saw Mary Austen, red-lipped and feline, as I had seen her in my dreams all those years before at the White Hart Inn. If she had come to the cottage that night I swear I would have killed her.

But you have no proof.

I heard Jane's voice as clearly as if she had been lying beside me. She was right, of course; I had not one shred of evidence to unmask Mary Austen as a poisoner. I turned onto my side, certain that sleep would never come to me in this fevered state. Through the wall I could hear Cass. Tucked up in her mother's old bed, she was snoring in just the same way. From the parlour down below Martha's voice drifted up to me. Like me, she was too worked up to think of sleep. She was chattering away about the wedding to James-Edward, who had arrived just as we were all going to bed. I could only catch parts of their conversation but I heard enough to learn that Mary had gone ahead to Winchester with Caroline, where she would be spending the night with a friend.

Another friend, I thought. Mary seemed very adept at finding people to help her out of tricky situations. I wondered what part Mrs Hastings had played in the resurrection of Mary's finances after the blow from the Crown. It must have been her, not her husband, who came to Mary's aid, for I had read the death notice for Warren Hastings in the obituary column of *The Times* the year after Jane's passing.

I cast my mind back to the last time I had seen them. Mary had been sitting next to me, at the ball in Bath, when Mr Hastings had come to ask me to dance. Yet he had not acknowledged her presence in any way. Were they strangers at that point, then? Had she got to know the Hastings later on? Warren Hastings had died the year before James Austen, so perhaps Mrs Hastings was in Bath at the same time as Mary, for the same reason. I tried to imagine the old dame with the snake eyes and the outrageous hats walking arm-in-arm around the Circus with her new friend. Why, I thought, would Mrs Hastings act in such a generous manner to someone she had only just met? Why would she offer a temporary home to a woman like Mary? A parson's widow who had neither warmth nor charm to recommend her?

I decided that they must have got together well before that, sometime after my visit to Bath. But then I thought of an obstacle to the friendship: Mary hated Eliza, whom Warren Hastings doted on. How could she possibly have borne his company? How could she have listened to him singing the praises of a woman she had banned from her own home?

Perhaps it was this very hatred, I thought, that had formed a bond between the two women. I recalled the look in those cold eyes when Mrs Hastings found out about my connection with Eliza. What was it Mrs Raike had said afterwards? I scoured my memory for the conversation we had had upon quitting the Pump Room. It was something about Warren Hastings' Will: some fear of his wife's that he would leave his estate to Eliza instead of her sons. I began to wonder if Mary Austen had played some part in preventing this, to the eternal gratitude of Mrs Hastings. But what could she possibly have done? How could she have come between Eliza and the Hastings fortune?

My thoughts returned to the ball in Bath; to the conversation I had had with Warren Hastings while we danced. He had been asking about Eliza. Gently probing me about what I had observed on my visit to London. And what was it he'd said later, when we were all searching for Mary? *You Austen men really should take better care of your wives...*

With a sudden, blinding clarity it dawned on me: Warren Hastings was one of the two main investors in Henry's bank – the one most likely to have caused the crash of the Austen business empire. What had prompted his decision to cut and run? I had always suspected Jane's portrayal of Henry in *Mansfield Park* had played a part. But such an act would require more evidence than a work of fiction. Could that evidence have been provided by Mary?

A ripple of laughter came up from the parlour, as if they had heard my thoughts and dismissed them as too foolish to contemplate. Why would Mary want to ruin Henry? Why would she do such a thing to the man she was in love with?

To bring him to his knees.

'Yes,' I whispered into the pillow, 'I can believe *that*.' I thought of Henry, riding back to Chawton with nothing but the clothes on his back, the Church the only option left to him. And Mary waiting in the wings; already slipping poison down her husband's throat. What a tempting prospect the living of Steventon would have been to a man in Henry's situation. And how easy for Mary to play the part of the poor widow-in-waiting as everyone watched James fading away.

What went wrong, I wondered? Had Henry always planned to marry Eleanor Jackson but kept it a secret until the living was secured? Had he simply humoured Mary to make sure she went quietly, knowing all along that he would never make her his wife? Or had he intended to marry her but discovered just in time her role in his downfall? Had someone warned him? And could that someone have been Jane?

Did Mary find out? Is that why she killed you? There was no answering whisper in my head from Jane. All I could hear was the gentle snoring of Cass through the wall.

Chapter Thirty-One

Sleep came somehow that night. My eyes were not closed for long, though, for the birds woke me a little before five in the morning. Anna was still asleep, lying on her back with her nightcap all askew, as if she had been pulling at it in her dreams. I didn't want to disturb her or anyone else in the house by going downstairs at such an early hour. On the night table was the poem of Jane's that I had copied out the previous afternoon. Comforted by the thought of having something of hers close to me, I reached for it and read it through:

When Winchester Races – a poem for St Swithin's Day
When Winchester races first took their beginning
It is said the good people forgot their old Saint
Not applying at all for the leave of Saint Swithin
And that William of Wykeham's approval was faint.

The races however were fixed and determined
The company came and the weather was charming
The Lords and the Ladies were satine'd and ermined
And nobody saw <u>any</u> future alarming.

But when the old Saint was informed of those doings
He made but one spring from his Shrine to the Roof
Of the Palace which now lies so sadly in <u>ruins</u>
And then he addressed them all standing aloof.
"Oh! Subjects rebellious! Oh Venta depraved
When once we are buried you think we <u>are</u> gone
But behold <u>me</u> immortal! By vice you're enslaved
You have sinned and must suffer, then farther he said

These races and revels and dissolute measures
With which you're debasing a neighbouring Plain
Let them stand – You shall meet with your curse in your pleasures
Set off for your course, I'll pursue with <u>my</u> rain.
Ye cannot but know my command o'er July
Henceforward I'll triumph in shewing my powers
Shift your race as you will it shall never be dry
The curse upon Venta is July in <u>showers</u>.

The strangeness of it struck me anew: not only the subject, but the fact that there was a rhyme that didn't work in the fourth verse – surely the word should have been 'dead' not 'gone'? And then there was the choice of words to be underlined: in some cases it was appropriate but in others not at all: why, for instance, had she chosen to emphasise the word 'ruins' in the third verse?

I sat staring at it for a while, then, on impulse, I reached for a pencil and paper. I jotted down all the underlined words, which were:

ANY; RUINS; ARE; ME; MY; SHOWERS.

Well, they don't make any sense, however you arrange them, I thought. I started playing about with the letters,

310

dividing the vowels from the consonants as I would for a game of anagrams. The first word that popped out was 'Mary'. Then I spotted 'Henry'. My heart began to beat a little faster. With the remaining letters I was able to make three other words. Rearranged, they made a sentence:

HENRY OUR NEMESIS WAS MARY

I whispered what I had written, my mouth so dry my tongue caught on my teeth. Had Jane *known* what Mary was doing to her? Impossible, surely? She would have made some attempt to save herself by telling Cass, not by sending some coded message to her brother. What was it Cass had said? The poem was dictated *two days* before she died: could it be that Mary had made some sort of confession, thinking Jane was too far gone to do anything about it?

I could just imagine the twisted satisfaction she might take in telling Jane what she had done to Henry and what she was about to do to her. If Jane knew she was beyond help at that stage the only thing to be gained by telling Cass was to make sure Mary hanged for it. Was Jane afraid of not being believed? Did she think her accusation would be put down to the effects of the laudanum she was taking?

If that was the case, I thought, any warning she wanted to give Henry would be dismissed in the same vein. Was the poem her only hope of getting the message to him? I stared at the words again. Then I heard a noise downstairs. The door of Cass's bedroom opened and closed. I waited a couple of minutes before slipping out of bed and pulling on my shawl.

Cass was in the kitchen. She was standing at the doorway with her back to me, waving at someone outside. I caught a brief glimpse of a man on horseback, the profile instantly recognisable.

'Henry is abroad early,' I said as she turned round.

'That wasn't Henry,' she laughed, 'it was James-Edward. He's going to Winchester to hire a carriage for Mary and Caroline.' She set the kettle on the range and took cups from the shelf above. 'He *is* the very image of his uncle. I can understand why you mistook him.'

I wondered fleetingly if Cass's mind had ever followed the pathways mine had. But no: Cass was the sort of creature who sought the light in people, not the darkness. If she sensed shadows, I thought, she would turn her back on them. 'Will they be coming to the wedding breakfast?' I asked.

'It's not possible,' she replied. 'They have the offer of a holiday in Lyme and must leave Winchester by noon.'

'Martha must be disappointed.'

'Yes, a little. But they'll join her in Portsmouth at the end of the week. Frank will have gone back to his ship by then.'

I watched her unlock the cupboard where the tea was kept. She placed the caddy on the dresser, next to the teapot then glanced over her shoulder at the kettle. Taking a deep breath I said: 'Anna told me that Mary and Henry have fallen out: I suppose that will make things quite difficult at the wedding.'

Cass clicked her tongue. 'Anna does tend to over-dramatise things. Did you know she writes? She has a children's story ready to be published.'

'I didn't know,' I replied. 'But I'm not surprised. I think that of all the nephews and nieces, Anna's character is closest to Jane's.' I paused for a moment. 'Jane didn't like Mary very much, did she?'

'Why do you say that?'

'Oh, it's just the impression Anna gives,' I said, my colour rising as I twisted the truth. 'She said Jane would have sided with Henry, as she did.'

'Well, they weren't the best of friends, that's true,' she nodded, 'but Mary was very good to her at the end. I think Jane saw a very different side to her in those last few weeks.'

More than you know, I thought. 'Was she there the whole time you and Jane were at Winchester?'

'Bar a few days in June when we thought Jane was getting better.' The kettle started to whistle and she went to fetch it. 'She would sit up all night with her sometimes so I could get some rest; she really was an angel.'

'I was reading the poem again this morning,' I said, 'the one Jane dictated to you. It's amazing to think she constructed all those verses in her head when she was so ill.'

'It *is* amazing, isn't it? I think it helped to distract her from...' Her voice died as she poured scalding water onto the tea leaves.

I nodded. 'I was curious about the words that were underlined: did she instruct you on that, too?'

'Oh, yes – she might have been ill but she was most particular. I just followed her instructions without paying much attention to the sense of it. Afterwards I did think it a little odd: I expect it was the laudanum – it must have fuddled her brain a little.'

'She must have wanted people to see the poem,' I said. 'Was it a sort of parting gift, do you think?'

'She did say she wanted the family to see it. They all did, of course, when they came for the funeral. But then I put it away. It hurt me to be reminded of those last days, I suppose. It was James-Edward who made me get it out – he's talking about collecting our memories of Jane for a book.'

I didn't tell her, of course, that I had already begun writing mine. I was thinking about Henry, wondering if he could have paid any real attention to the poem at a time when he was caught up with organising Jane's funeral. The message had probably never reached its intended target. The warning had gone unheeded but Henry had spurned Mary anyway. And she had got away with murder.

Chapter Thirty-Two

'Will you help me with my gown?' Anna's voice summoned me from upstairs, joined in quick succession by Martha who was begging for assistance from Cass.

I laced the back of Anna's spotted silk gown and stood back as she admired herself in the mirror. 'Could you pass me my brooch?' she asked. 'It's on the night table.'

I went to fetch it, biting my lip when I saw what it contained. 'Is that Jane's hair?' I passed her the silver disc with its mount of tiny plaits fashioned into the shape of a flower.

'It's my father's,' she replied. 'I have a ring for Aunt Jane, though I don't wear it very often.' She gave me a wry glance as she pinned the brooch to her bodice. 'I'm afraid of spoiling it with all the things I handle in a day.'

I nodded, stroking the ring on my own finger. *Stay with me, Jane,* I whispered to myself. *Come with me to Winchester, won't you?*

Cass, Anna and I travelled to the wedding together. Our carriage was lined up in the procession of vehicles provided by

314

the Great House, which consisted of a barouche for the bride, a curricle for the groom and best man, a chaise for the groom's children and a coach and six for Edward and his family. Henry's rather humble gig brought up the rear.

'Doesn't Martha look lovely?' Cass, whose only concession to the occasion was to swap her customary bombazine for black satin, gave me a tight-lipped smile. I wasn't sure if she was overcome with emotion at the sight of her friend in a bridal gown or just self-conscious about her teeth. 'She says she doesn't like dressing up, but that pearl grey silk really suits her.'

'And here comes Uncle Frank,' Anna grinned. '*He* looks rather splendid, doesn't he?'

'There's nothing quite like a man in uniform.' Cass's face turned wistful. I wondered how many years it was since she had gone to Portsmouth with her trousseau, only to find that her fiancé was dead. I felt I should say something; try to lift her spirits with some light-hearted banter about the day ahead. But my stomach was tied in knots at the prospect of seeing Mary Austen. I wasn't sure how I was going to control myself in the cathedral when I caught sight of her.

Thankfully, Anna filled in the silences with her chatter and after an hour or so we were on the outskirts of the city. We stepped out into dazzling sunshine. Cathedral Close was a hive of activity, a group of schoolboys marching in a crocodile across the green, and hawkers parading up and down, shouting their wares at every passer-by. Shading my eyes I searched for Mary's face in the throng. But there was no sign of her. Neither had she appeared by the time we all trooped into the porch.

It took a moment for my eyes to adjust to the shadowy world within. Here and there pools of jewelled light fell on the stones. I breathed in the ancient, unchanging scent of incense and candle wax and aged wood. My heart shifted against my ribs. *I'm here, Jane*, I said silently.

'We'll sit at the back, shall we?' Anna took my arm. 'Aunt Cass is going in the second pew with Uncle Edward and Uncle Henry.' As she spoke Henry walked past us, carrying the sweet-faced Eleanor, who was beautifully attired in a gown of fine apricot muslin trimmed with ivory rosebuds. *He has so much to answer for*, I thought, *so much to reveal.* But how could I interrogate him in these circumstances? And how would he react if, as I suspected, he was wholly ignorant of Mary's crimes? I had lost my dearest friend but he had lost a sister, a brother and a lover. A man of the cloth he may be, but he would have to exert superhuman self-control on discovering such a thing. And whatever he did would impact on Eleanor. How could I contemplate threatening the well-being of a woman who so needed and deserved his support?

'Come on.' Anna steered me towards the side chapel where the service was to be performed. To reach it we had to pass the very spot where Jane lay. 'Good morning, Aunt Jane – we've come to see Martha Lloyd marry Uncle Frank,' she whispered. 'But I suppose you know that already, don't you?' She kissed her gloved fingers and bobbed down to touch the stone. 'I know I said I don't believe in ghosts, but I bet she's looking down on us; she wouldn't have missed it for the world, would she?'

'She wouldn't.' I swallowed hard. It was almost unbearable to think of Mary walking past her grave, as she surely would any moment now. I glanced over my shoulder. Edward was coming through the door with Charlotte on one arm and Louisa on the other. No change there, then, I thought. Fanny was behind him, accompanied by a gaggle of young people who ranged in age from late teens to late twenties. Anna told me that some of these were Frank's children and some were Edward's but the only one I recognised was Brook-John, because, like James-Edward, he was the spitting image of Henry.

We took our places at the back of the chapel and watched the other guests arrange themselves according to their relationship to the bride or groom. I watched Edward give a little bow to Charlotte and Louisa before walking back down the aisle towards the porch. With Martha's father long since dead, he was to be the one to give her away.

'Where is your stepmother?' I asked Anna. 'Shouldn't she be at the front?'

'I don't know,' Anna hissed back. 'I think she must be late – I don't know why though: James-Edward is here and he was supposed to be travelling in the same carriage.' She pointed out her half-brother, who was standing behind the bridegroom and best man. There was a young woman standing next to him. 'That's his fiancée, Emma Smith. She's going with them to Lyme.'

At that moment the organ struck up a loud and throbbing chord, startling us into silence. Anna glanced over her shoulder. 'Here she comes!' I twisted my head round, expecting to see Martha coming down the aisle, but it was Mary. Caroline followed in her wake, both of them scurrying as fast as their gowns would permit. They dodged into the pew across from ours. I clenched my fingers round the prayer book I held and took a slow, hard breath. Mary was now standing just three feet away from me. Her face was obscured by a white gauze veil draped over the front of a blue satin bonnet. *No widow's weeds for you, then.* I dug my thumbnails into the cover of the prayer book. *How can you enter this place? How can you kneel and pray while she lies not fifty paces distant?*

I have a vague memory of Martha and Edward coming into my field of vision as a blur of blue and grey, but I have no lasting impression of the ceremony itself. My mind was seething with recriminations. I had a mighty urge to drag Mary from her seat with that veil pulled tight across her throat. I don't recall what hymns I mouthed or catechisms I mumbled as I struggled with this instinct; I can remember Anna remarking on the fact that Frank and Martha were kissing each other and the next thing I was aware of was Caroline squeezing out of the pew past her mother to get to Anna, who gave her a big hug. I saw Mary slip out of her place then. She was walking fast, out of the little chapel and back up the north aisle. I followed her.

She was heading straight for Jane's memorial stone and to my horror she walked not round it but right over it. I quickened my step. *She won't get away!* I whispered it aloud as I skirted the black marble tablet. Mary disappeared through the doors of the cathedral. I lifted my skirts and ran, almost knocking into a surpliced old gentleman carrying a pile of hymn books. He spluttered some admonishment but I didn't stop. A moment later I was outside, blinking as the sunshine stung my eyes. *Where is she?* With my hand pressed to my forehead I scanned the grassy expanse of Cathedral Close. A flash of blue satin disappeared behind the yew hedge.

'Mrs Austen!' I yelled it as loud as I could. A man selling wooden crosses looked askance as I ran past him. Mary looked back, startled. I don't think she knew who I was. 'Mrs Austen, wait, please!' I was panting as I drew level with her. 'Do you remember me? I am Miss Sharp: Jane's friend.' I spoke the words in a matter-of-fact tone, with no hint of the rage boiling inside me. Now I had her, I wanted to catch her by surprise.

'Miss Sharp?' She lifted the veil and tucked it over the brim of her bonnet 'Were you at the wedding? I didn't see you.'

'But I saw you.' I took a step closer. 'Why were you so late?'

'Oh…I…' She looked away and the sun caught the scars on her face. 'Why do you ask?' She turned back to me with a determined frown.

'Because I think you were wrestling with your conscience, madam,' I replied. 'You still have a vestige of it left, I assume? Tell me, why did you want to destroy Henry?'

She blinked once, twice. 'What on earth do you mean?'

'It was you, wasn't it, who turned Warren Hastings against him?'

'I don't know what you're talking about.'

'Oh, I think you do: I knew him, you see. Don't you remember the ball in Bath? You were sitting right beside me when he asked me to dance.' I watched the memory of it dawn in her eyes. Now for the gamble: 'I used to visit the gentleman and his wife at Daylesford. I was there the year Jane died. He told me all about the business with Henry.'

'You're mad,' she hissed. 'Henry always said you had an overactive imagination.'

'Jane warned him off you, you know: she got a message to him before she died. She knew, didn't she, because you told her when you thought she was too ill to do anything about it; you told her what you'd done to Henry *and* what you were doing to her.'

She stood motionless, the wind whipping loose strands of grey hair from under her bonnet. From the look on her face my lies had found their mark.

'You thought you'd silenced her didn't you? What did you do? Pretend you'd cooled things with Henry while you poisoned her? Waited for her to die so you could murder your husband and marry him? Well, she outwitted you, didn't she? She ruined all your plans!'

She opened her mouth but said nothing. I saw her teeth, small and sharp, just as they had been in my nightmare.

'You killed Elizabeth, too, didn't you? It took me a while to work that one out, but I know how you did it: Cass and Martha will kill you themselves when they find out how you used them.' I clenched my jaw, for my lips had begun to tremble. 'And what about Anna's mother? Was she your first? You've been doing this for years, haven't you? What a miracle for Henry and his wife that they don't need Martha's potions. Eleanor, I suppose, is beyond the help of anything medicine

319

could achieve: you'd have poisoned them too, wouldn't you, if you'd had the chance.'

She looked at me coldly. 'That's laughable. *You* are laughable.'

'Is that all you have to say?' I clasped my arms tight about my waist. 'Not a very spirited defence, if I may say so.'

'We all joked about you behind your back,' she said slowly. 'The way you looked at Jane; the way you followed her around. Cass only tolerates you for her sake, you know. You're unnatural; a freak.'

'Call me whatever you like.' My voice threatened to betray the pain her words had inflicted. 'You can't hurt me; and you can't stop me!'

Her lip curled as she looked me up and down. 'You wouldn't dare tell anyone what you've just said to me because it's all in your warped little mind! You have no proof do you, of what you're saying? So do what you want; no one will ever believe you!'

'All the proof *I* require is there in your eyes,' I growled back, 'But I won't rest until I *can* prove it, in a court of law. I don't care how long it takes. So think about that as you go about your daily business: there'll be nothing *natural* in the way you end your days, Mrs Austen: the hangman will see to that!'

My legs were shaking as I turned my back on her and strode across the grass. I felt weak and proud and stupid and a dozen other things besides. What was I thinking of, coming out with all that? How in God's name was I ever going to prove anything? The coded message from the poem was the strongest piece of evidence I possessed and what lawyer was going to take that seriously?

Ridiculous as it sounds, the overwhelming emotion as I stepped out of her sight into the shadows of the cathedral was a thrilling sense of vengeance: I might never have the evidence

I sought but at least I'd had the satisfaction of rattling her; of planting a creeping dread of what might lie ahead.

In the carriage back to Chawton I was barely able to string two words together. I told Anna and Cass I felt unwell and when we reached the village I asked to be put down at the cottage, saying I would follow them up to the Great House when I had rested a while. The truth was I couldn't bear to spend another minute in their company, not after what Mary had said.

It's not true, Jane whispered in my ear. *She only said it to hurt you.*

Rationalising it made no difference: I had to get away. I left a note on the kitchen table and boarded the next mail coach to London. I fixed my gaze on the parlour window as the horses pulled away, knowing in my heart that I would never see Chawton again.

Chapter Thirty-Three

I have kept up my correspondence with Cass and Anna, although the letters we exchange become fewer as the years go by. They no longer express the hope of a visit from me: I think that the excuses I have made about the school or the state of my health make them believe that I no longer wish to see them. It is not true, of course. But it could never be as it once was. All the pleasure would be soured by those wounding words of Mary Austen's.

Anna became a widow not long after Martha's wedding. With seven young children to care for, she was in a perilous position and I sent her money whenever I could.

Fanny stopped writing to me at about the same time. She was safely delivered of her child – a boy, as Anna had predicted – but she seemed to want to cast off her old life and connections with the onset of motherhood. Anna, who remains very angry with her, tells me that she thinks herself too fine for the rest of the family now and seeks to cover up her Austen connections. She becomes embarrassed, apparently, when people ask if she is indeed the niece of the famous author. It grieves me to hear it.

Cass continues to live at the cottage on her own and when she is not tending the garden she spends her time sewing for the poor, teaching the village children to read and entertaining her great-nephews and nieces – the sons and daughters of Edward's eldest son, who is now in permanent residence at the Great House. Edward himself continues to live at Godmersham with Charlotte and Louisa, the two women who have become indispensable to him.

James-Edward married the girl I saw in Winchester cathedral and three years ago, when Aunt Leigh-Perrot left this world at the grand old age of ninety-one, he inherited the Scarlets estate. Anna requires no more help from me now: her young half-brother has become her benefactor and protector. Her first children's story, *Little Bertram's Dream*, is to be published next year.

Cass makes occasional mention of Henry in her letters. 'He and Eleanor have retired to Tunbridge Wells,' she wrote to me this summer. 'Despite her frail constitution, she shows no sign of making him a widower for a second time. I wouldn't be at all surprised if she outlived him.'

And what of Mary? 'My stepmother continues as stout as ever,' Anna reported with thinly veiled sarcasm in her last letter. 'She is moving to another rented house in a hamlet called Speen near Newbury. Caroline is with her, of course. I think there is no prospect of my sister ever marrying now, as she is almost six-and-thirty. She reminds me in many ways of dear Aunt Jane. I never realised, when I was young, what life was like for her. Now I see, through Caroline's eyes, what it is to have the care of a parent when one might have hoped for children to nurture. Aunt Jane did at least have the solace of a sister to share that burden – and a burden it must indeed be in my stepmother's case.'

I have stored every scrap of intelligence I can gather about

Mary Austen in a special notebook reserved for the purpose. It has been very hard, knowing that she still lives a comfortable life while Jane lies in eternal slumber beneath the cold stones of Winchester cathedral. The certainty of her guilt is a heavy burden to carry. It has eaten away at me over the years. But I have never stopped searching for a way to prove my suspicions. What drives me on is my love for Jane and the thought of what she might have achieved had she lived to a ripe old age. The six novels might have become sixteen; the royal patronage she had begun to attract would have elevated her to the highest heights of literary fame – something she should have been able to enjoy to the full in her lifetime, but was granted a mere taste of.

It is almost unbearable that this crime should go unpunished and unnoticed. With every passing year the sense of despair deepens. Can I accept that it may never be resolved? Must I, like Jane and the others, take the hand that fate has dealt me? No, I cannot. I will not. I will go on searching for the proof to my dying breath.

Anne Sharp
December 1840

9ᵗʰ July 1843

Reading my own words again has shaken my resolve. When I brushed the dust off the binding I had all but convinced myself to parcel it up, climb into a carriage and deliver it in person to Dr Sillar. But those last few pages hold such bitter passion. I find that I am shocked by the intensity of my longing for vengeance. It eclipses everything: all the joy, the wonder and the tenderness of the years I had with Jane.

Looking up from my desk, I see her face before me. Sometimes it takes a while to hear what she has to say but this time the message is instant. She does not crow with triumph at the prospect of justice. No: she begs me to pause, to reckon what there is to be gained from chasing an old woman to the gallows.

'But Jane,' I whisper back, 'I was going to write to Anna: I was going to ask for a sample of her father's hair from the brooch she wears to give to Dr Sillar.'

'To what purpose?' she replies. 'Will it bring James back? And think what harm it might do: Anna could hardly hate Mary more than she does already, but what would become of Caroline if the case came to court? Would you set sister against sister?'

My eyes go to the ring on my finger; to the braided strands that are as familiar to me as my own face. So much of what I am is contained within it but for the better part of two decades I have felt nothing but a festering anger when I look upon it. I know that *I* have allowed this to happen: this tainting of the thing that was so dear to me. But if I was to abandon this relentless quest for justice could I forget? Could I look upon her hair and *not* feel that all-consuming rage?

❧

10ᵗʰ July 1843

Last night I dreamed I boarded a train that took me all the way from Liverpool to Newbury without stopping. When I alighted the whole station was thick with smoke and I blundered about with streaming eyes, searching for a way out. When at last I found the exit I spied a fine chestnut mare tethered to a post. I straddled the horse as a man would, the lower half of my gown disappearing as I did so. I remember the sight of my legs, clad in breeches of yellow buckskin, gripping the horse's belly as it galloped out of the town heading for open country.

We came to the hamlet of Speen, which was no more than a chapel and a few houses strung along the road like rosary beads. One of the houses looked familiar. It had a red door with a shiny lion's head knocker. Dismounting the horse I walked up and peered through one of the windows. There was Mary Austen, sewing a patchwork. She was bidding goodbye to Caroline, who said she was off to a fair with the servants. I hid behind a bush as they all departed, then slipped into the house by the back door.

'You!' Mary's cheeks blazed crimson against hair that was now snow white. 'How dare you come into my house!'

Putting my hand into the pocket of my breeches, I pulled out the lock of hair I had sent to Dr Sillar. It was black and brittle, as if it had been singed with hot irons. 'Look at this,' I said to her. 'It's the proof I told you I would find. Here! Taste it!' I stuffed the hair into her gaping mouth. Her face contorted and she slumped sideways like a puppet on slack strings. I clapped her on the back and she spat out the hair. Then I took her by the shoulders and tossed her about, demanding a confession. Her mouth began to move but no matter how violently I shook her, no words would come out.

I awoke with my hand across my face, Jane's ring pressed against my lips. The room was still in darkness save for a thin beam of daylight piercing the curtains. I stared at the pool of colour it cast on the ceiling. As I lay in that twilight state between waking and rising I saw myself with sudden clarity. The cause of the dream is, of course, blindingly obvious – but what drives this insatiable thirst for vengeance? Losing Jane so suddenly, not being able to say goodbye or even see her face in death: that has created an impotent fury within me. Someone must pay for this bitter loss, this theft of my heart. I see that my quest for justice is really a mask for something entirely selfish; it is not the crime of murder I wish Mary Austen to suffer for but the pain of my own unrequited love.

But I did love you. Was that Jane's voice or my own?

❦

12ᵗʰ July 1843

This morning a letter arrived from Dr Sillar. It is a polite reminder that I have not yet responded to what he communicated a week ago.

I am sure that Miss J.A. was very dear to you, he writes, *otherwise you would not be in possession of a token so intimate. I fear that my remarks about the strength of the evidence might tempt you to a course of action that would be most inadvisable. I urge you, dear madam, not to confront any person, if indeed a suspect has come to mind. In itself, the Marsh Test will not bring a guilty party to book. Evidence of both opportunity and intent would be required in a court of law, as I am sure you are aware, and to act in haste in such a matter may result in a lawsuit for slander. Given the lapse of time it could be a difficult case to prove without an admission of guilt on the part of the poisoner.*

Yes, of course. Even my sleeping self is aware of that insurmountable obstacle. What in this world would induce Mary Austen to confess? A gun held to the head of her son or daughter, perhaps? Nothing else comes to mind. Dr Sillar asks for a meeting to discuss the case but I am going to tell him that I have decided not to pursue it any further. What is done cannot be undone. I have tried to take a path the Bible tells us should only be taken by God Himself and it has led me to an utterly desolate place.

But I do not regret sending the hair to be tested, precious as it was. The secret it held has opened the wound in my soul and cleansed it so that it no longer festers. This evening I will ask Rebecca to light the fire in my study, even though the weather has been warm. The memoir can serve no further purpose, for I know now that I need no written record of what Jane meant to me: it is printed indelibly on my heart, wrapped in endpapers of crimson silk and bound in the softest hide.

Author's Note

Mary Austen suffered a stroke on 2nd August 1843 from which she never recovered consciousness. She died the following day. She is buried at Steventon, in James Austen's vault.

Anne Sharp died on 8th January 1853. Before her death she passed Jane's last letter to Dr Zechariah Sillar, physician to the Northern Hospital, Liverpool. He passed it down to his granddaughter and on 8th February 1954 it was auctioned at Sotheby's. The purchasers were Mr and Mrs Henry G. Burke of Baltimore. On Mrs Burke's death in 1975 it was bequeathed to the Pierpoint Morgan Library, New York.

On 3rd May 1948 a lock of Jane Austen's hair was auctioned at Sotheby's. It was bought by the same American couple who purchased Anne Sharp's letter. The following year the cottage at Chawton where Jane Austen spent the last eight years of her life was opened as a museum. Mrs Alberta Burke presented the lock of hair as a gift to be displayed alongside other artefacts collected by the Jane Austen Society. Before handing it over, however, her husband had the hair tested in a bid to discover the cause of death. It contained levels of arsenic far exceeding that observed in the body's natural state.

Lindsay Ashford, Chawton, 2011

Acknowledgements

While this is a work of fiction, it grew out of a fascination with the factual material painstakingly accumulated by Austen scholars in the two centuries since her death. Much has been written but two sources require special mention: Deirdre Le Faye's *A Chronology of Jane Austen and Her Family* (Cambridge University Press, 2006) was invaluable to me, as was Claire Tomalin's excellent biography, *Jane Austen, a Life* (Viking 1997). *The Mysterious Death of Miss Austen* is my interpretation of the facts, interwoven with some sequences that are purely imaginary. I urge those wishing to dissect the novel to consult these sources directly.

This book could not have been written without the wonderful research material housed in Chawton House Library – the 'Great House' once owned by Jane's brother, Edward Austen Knight. I am indebted to all the staff there for their help and encouragement – particularly Dr Gillian Dow, who cast a scholarly eye over the manuscript – and to Sandy Lerner, the American philanthropist who saved the house from ruin and restored it to its former glory. I have been lucky enough to spend the past three years living in part of the original medieval estate, thanks to Richard Knight, Jane Austen's five-times great nephew, who still owns the dovecote (now a cottage), referred to in the book. I would also like to thank Fiona Sunley, who, with her late husband John, invited me to spend a delightful day at Godmersham.

I am grateful to Tom Carpenter and Louise West of Jane Austen's House Museum for allowing me to examine records relating to the lock of hair donated by Mr and Mrs Henry G. Burke in the late 1940s. I am indebted to another American,

Elsa Solender, for recounting the conversation she had with Harry Burke before his death, about the testing of the hair for the presence of arsenic. Thanks also to Nancy Magnuson and her team at Goucher College, Baltimore, for searching the Burke archive on my behalf.

Michael Sanders, former consultant at St. Thomas' Hospital, London and a Chawton neighbour, took the trouble to investigate the prevailing medical theories about Jane Austen's death and passed on insights from leading members of the medical profession, including Sir Richard Thompson, President of the Royal College of Physicians.

Thank you to my editor, Caroline Oakley, for rejecting several drafts of this book and challenging me to write something better. I'm grateful to all the staff at Honno for their unstinting support and to my mentor and great friend Janet Thomas, whose encouragement has played a crucial part in my writing.

Finally, huge thanks to my partner Steve Lawrence, without whom I would never have discovered Chawton, and to my children, for the nights they've had to spend in a house they swear is haunted.

DEATH STUDIES

ISBN: 187020686X £6.99

A windswept seaside strip in West Wales – sleepy enough, until three bodies turn up within as many days. A shocking coincidence or a serial killer? Though she's on holiday Megan Rhys can't ignore the body in her backyard and with her journalist sister also on the case the closer they get to the heart of the matter the more their careers bring them into conflict.

THE KILLER INSIDE

ISBN: 9781870206921 £6.99

Megan Rhys is inside Balsall Gate jail when prisoner Carl Kelly dies, but is his death what it seems – another drug overdose the authorities would like cleaned up as quickly and quietly as possible? Pinning down the cause of death forces Megan closer to convicted killer Dominic Wilde than duty or professional pride warrants…

More great writing from Honno...

FLINT
by Margaret Redfern

ISBN: 1906784043 £6.99

Will and his brother Ned are commandeered into the army of ditch-diggers heading west towards Wales to prepare the foundations of Edward I's new castle. They are nervous and rightly so, because they have grown up under the tutelage of Ieuen ap y Gof, an exiled bard and Edward's sworn enemy...

'Its particular strength is the poetry of the language and the way it draws the reader into a stark, beautiful, dangerous mediaeval world, so rounded out and tactile that I believed I was there. It's a wonderful, miniature gem of a novel...a highly rewarding, skilled piece of writing. One for my keeper shelf' Historical Novel Society

HECTOR'S TALENT FOR MIRACLES

by Kitty Harri

ISBN: 978170206815 £6.99

The small Spanish town of Torre de Burros is known for its miracles, but Hector Martinez, his mother and grandmother live in the shadow of dark secrets. When Mair Watkins arrives all the way from Wales, on a mission to discover the truth about her Civil War volunteer grandfather, their meeting is explosive and their lives revealed as fragile constructions forged in the fire of a vicious conflict...

'Harri has an aptitude for creating devious plots and she doesn't flinch from revealing the inhumanity of war'
New Welsh Review

'An intelligent and sympathetic exploration of the lasting damage done to survivors of war'
Planet

ABOUT HONNO

Honno Welsh Women's Press was set up in 1986 by a group of women who felt strongly that women in Wales needed wider opportunities to see their writing in print and to become involved in the publishing process. Our aim is to develop the writing talents of women in Wales, give them new and exciting opportunities to see their work published and often to give them their first 'break' as a writer.

Honno is registered as a community co-operative. Any profit that Honno makes is invested in the publishing programme. Women from Wales and around the world have expressed their support for Honno. Each supporter has a vote at the Annual General Meeting.

To receive further information about forthcoming publications, or become a supporter, please write to Honno at the address below, or visit our website:

www.honno.co.uk

Honno
Unit 14, Creative Units
Aberystwyth Arts Centre
Penglais Campus
Aberystwyth
Ceredigion
SY23 3GL

All Honno titles can be ordered online at
www.honno.co.uk
or by sending a cheque to Honno.
Free p&p to all UK addresses.